Dau... Revenge

Thaddeus Nowak

www.thaddeusnowak.com

Published by Mountain Pass Publishing, LLC.

ISBN: 978-0-9852851-8-0

First Printing: February 2014

Set in Adobe Garamond Pro
Cover art Copyright © 2014 by Mallory Rock
Maps by Thaddeus Nowak

This is a work of fiction. All characters, names, places, and events are the work of the author's imagination. Any resemblance to events, locales, or persons living or dead is strictly coincidental.

Map of Cothel, Epish, Midland, Kynto, and Calis.

Map of Ipith, Tenip, Ulet, Selith, and Epish.

Acknowledgements

I would like to thank the many people who have helped make this work possible. My wife Sherri, my best friend Chad, my brother Joe and his wife Samantha, my other brothers Dave and Dan and their wives Jenni and Linda, and my parents. I would also like to thank my friends Priya S. and David J. as well as the others who have inspired and offered advice. Any errors left in the work are entirely mine.

Chapter 1

Stephenie stood motionless, her long, red hair blew about her head and carried aloft by the energy coursing through her body. Her eyes were shut to close out the noise and commotion, but it did no good; she could see far more without her eyes than with them. Ever since Kas had first led her to embrace the truth of what she was, her abilities to sense energy fields continued to grow and even solid walls of stone could not block her if she concentrated.

Today, however, she would rather turn off her abilities. The din of so much confused mental energy left her head throbbing and her heart uneasy. While she was now able to recognize the subtle waves and ripples in the energy fields that emanated from people's minds as thoughts and emotions, it was like trying to read mud to understand them. The patterns just made no sense to her. Gravitational fields were far easier to understand and control.

Focusing on her breathing, she narrowed her attention to the energy coursing through her own body, the air about her, and the wood of the floors and walls surrounding her. She could sense the density of the energy potentials, the wood having more density than the air, but much less than stone or even people. Her own body was different; while most of it carried potential energy, she could also act as a void to quickly pull energy into herself. As with heat, which was just another form of energy, the energy always moved from areas of higher potential to those of lower potential until there was no longer a difference between the two. She knew it was this ability to both draw and expel energy that allowed her to perform magic, *or witchcraft, as too many people would call it.*

Mentally looking away from herself, she noted a patch of sunlight coming through the open doorway into the dark hall behind the stage. She sensed the currents of power moving about, swirling and mixing with the cooler air hidden in the shadows, pursuing the innate goal of equalizing the differences. In that shaft of light, the dust danced about the currents of the air, sparkling with elevated potential, just waiting for its minute energy to be released. Kas had told her it was this movement of energy that allowed anything to happen at all.

She watched some of that energy, in the form of heat, flow into Henton. While out of the direct light, he was standing close to it. Carefully positioned beside the stage door, he was watching and waiting, but just out of sight of the crowd that had gathered. His mind was focused and quiet as always. He was a cornerstone on which Stephenie could rely.

Opening her eyes, she nodded her head as the twenty-eight-year-old soldier gave her a quick smile. Strong and fit, he had more endurance than most people she knew, but he was not overly muscled. He was more like her, nimble and quick.

"That is why we are here! That is why we need your support! That is what we will do for you!"

Stephenie directed her mental focus through the wooden wall that formed the back of the stage. She had not been paying close enough attention to Will and the speech he was giving. She appraised the scene with her mind as Will moved about on the other side of the wall with vigorous purpose. Before him were at least two hundred people, most of whom were packed into the small area in front of the stage. As the High Priest of Catheri, he had called this gathering.

The emotions of the crowd were high, that much Stephenie could sense. Always trying to be vigilant, she looked for anger, or hate, or rage, as these stronger emotions tended to be more perceptible, but, if there were any people with those emotions, she could not pick them out of the crowd.

"And now, what many of you have been waiting for," Will's voice carried strongly even through the wooden wall. "I want to introduce her Royal Highness, the Prophet of Catheri, Defeater of the Senzar, and Protector of Cothel, Princess Stephenie!"

Henton motioned her forward. She gave him a forced smile as she passed, still not happy with all the titles her brother added to her name.

She could feel Douglas guarding the doorway on the right hand side of the stage and sensed his own heightened irritation. Douglas was usually verbally quiet around others, but his mind had never been as focused as Henton's. She did not want to be without any of the three, but would have preferred that both Henton and Douglas had avoided the open-air playhouse. The risk to them would be too great if something did happen.

Putting her friends aside in her thoughts, she walked onto the stage. The bright afternoon light was somewhat blinding to her eyes; however, she could clearly sense everyone and everything in the full playhouse if she concentrated. Most of the people were crammed into the small area at the foot of the stage. Those without a front row position sat in the lofts set into in the outer walls. A quick glance told her even those sections were filled.

It was disconcerting to be standing before so many people who wanted to hear what she had to say. Ever since her secret was discovered, she expected any crowds that gathered because of her would be actively trying to burn her, not listen to her. Being declared cleansed of Elrin's evil had been something she had never really expected and the idea that people would actually embrace her had not sunk in completely.

She looked over the crowd as her eyes adjusted to the daylight. Ignoring her awareness of the energy, she actively watched the people. Many of those gathered appeared to be of the middle class, with tailored clothing that was still vibrant in color. The expressions on their faces were hopeful, yet there was also a hushed eagerness. While the purpose of the gathering had been to see her, many here were waiting to call out demands. At the moment, she suspected they were still too frightened to actually vocalize anything.

"Good afternoon," Stephenie said and then repeated it using her powers as Kas often did, amplifying the sound of her voice. "I am Princess Stephenie and I am glad to be here today to speak with you.

High Priest William, whom I have known for quite a while now, has been asking me to attend a gathering for several weeks. I can only offer an apology and the excuse of being busy working on projects for my King."

Stephenie could feel the tension still in the crowd. This was the first time she had publicly addressed anyone as 'The Prophet of Catheri' and despite Will's constant assurances, no one truly knew how anyone was going to react. She glanced over at her friend, both shorter and less muscled than Henton, but definitely fit and handsome. He was dressed in a fine white tunic; the only marking was that of a large claw-like hand woven of the deepest black threads. The emblem was a disturbingly accurate representation of the mark Kas had left on her left breast when he tried to freeze her heart.

Will gave her his sly smile, which she knew could charm most people, especially young woman. She returned the smile, though they both knew she wanted to be elsewhere.

Looking back to the audience, she continued, "I wanted to thank everyone for coming today and all the support you have given William, my brother, and myself. To mark my first appearance, William has saved an announcement for me." She paused a moment, still watching the hesitant crowd. "I can tell you that we have finalized the purchase of land and buildings to make a new temple complex dedicated to Catheri. I can say that through monies I have secured from His Majesty, my own travels, and your donations, you will have a place to meet regularly in the northeastern part of the city near Fuminari Square." A small rumbling of cheers moved through the crowd, but it was definitely more reserved than when it had just been Will on the stage. "Additionally, there will be rooms to house other offices and facilities, including rooms for teaching new disciples. It will likely be next summer before it is complete, but as each building is ready, we will open it."

Stephenie mulled over the trepidation she could feel, hoping it was from the fact that she was a Royal Princess. However, in the back of her mind, she expected most of it was undoubtedly from the fact that until a few months ago, everyone considered her to be a witch and possessed by the demon god, Elrin. There were still many people who were not certain the claims of the late High Priest of Felis were true.

"I want to thank all of you for your support. As a nation, we routed the Senzar invaders and survived an attempted coup by the Burdger family. We have survived difficult times and now we have much to look forward to." She looked around the crowd, wanting to see the hopeful faces of those that had risked much to lend her their support. "The future is always a challenge and I know there are questions about me. However, I promise you that I have always worked to do what is best for Cothel and her people. I have always done what I could to help those whom I could help."

"Then purify me!" came a strongly accented cry. "Cleanse me of Elrin's tainted evil!"

Stephenie did not have to search the crowd long to find the speaker. Despite the tightly packed area at the front of the stage, those standing around a young woman pressed backwards. Meeting the woman's brown eyes, Stephenie felt a slight chill move through the crowd.

"I can't live as I am. Purify me or kill me."

Stephenie motioned for the young woman to approach the stage. "What is your name?" she asked, trying to place the speaker's heavy accent.

"Earisa," the woman said as she climbed onto the four-foot high stage. "I came from Demuth for you to remove Elrin's taint," she added as she regained her feet and stood proudly.

Stephenie glanced at Will, but he remained where he was near the side of the stage. While his face was calm, she could feel a sudden spike of panic from him. *Damn it, I knew something bad would happen.* Turning back to the girl, who was now standing before her, she lowered her voice and hoped her face did not show her own fears, "Earisa, this is a dangerous thing to do. You should not do something like this in such a public forum. You should have come in private."

"I cannot go on living like this," the brown-eyed girl said softly, then raised her voice. "I would rather burn than continue to live and spread evil. I will not hide the truth from these people. If you are a Prophet of Catheri, cleanse me in fire!"

Stephenie looked out to the crowd. They were silent, waiting to see how Stephenie was going to respond and while they had accepted her as cleansed of evil, she was not certain how the crowd would react to this girl. There was a good chance someone, even one of her strongest supporters, would hunt down the girl and burn her if Stephenie did not offer a solution. The problem was she had no way to 'cure' anyone. She, herself, was the same as she had ever been. While she had been surrounded in flame, her survival was not due to any divine influence, but the fact that her body simply reacted in a way to handle the enormous amount of energy she had drawn through it.

Will moved forward. "Do not think to dictate to the gods what manner you will be judged!" He looked at the girl, who had turned slightly toward him. "Catheri removed herself from the world a hundred years ago because of the sins of man and man has learned nothing since then! However, the world is changing and we are facing demons that we cannot fight alone. It would be unfair to allow the innocent to suffer because of the sins of others, so Catheri has returned. But, since nothing has been learned from her absence, she will not persist in following the old ways. For her help, she is demanding change! She is bringing a new order. If you are to be cleansed, it will be in a manner of her choosing, not yours!"

Stephenie's hands relaxed from the fists she had formed. *Will had taken to heart my concerns.* However, unease still filled her and she could sense the crowd was growing hostile. Looking back to the young woman, Stephenie's eyes lost focus for a moment as she subconsciously reached out to look for signs of active threats before they occurred. Her eyes narrowed as she observed threads of energy radiating out from the girl, touching Will, herself, and even reaching into the crowd. However, instead of coming from the girl's mind, these threads were emanating from a concentrated area on her chest. *Holy symbol,* she growled to herself.

Noticing even more subtle threads of power moving through the crowd, Stephenie identified four other people using augmentation devices. Her hands clenched again. *They are making everyone edgy,* she realized. Slamming raw energy through herself, Stephenie created a more powerful energy field of her own, modulating its pattern to interfere with the priestess and her friends. The change in the mood of the crowd was sudden and palpable. So much so, that not only the priestess, but also most of the crowd had an intake of breath.

Stepping forward, Stephenie's hands grabbed the woman's shirt, easily breaching the subconscious field of protection the woman's body naturally raised, for even though she was a priestess, the woman was as much a witch as Stephenie or anyone else with power. Tearing as much with her fingers as her mind, Stephenie ripped the shirt from the woman, revealing a holy symbol of Ari. With an easy yank, she snapped the cord the medallion was hanging from and stepped back from the woman, her source of power augmentation in Stephenie's hand.

A gravity wave was forming from one of the men in the crowd and Stephenie drew off the energy before the field was complete. "I wouldn't if I were you," she said over her shoulder, her voice carrying through the stunned crowd. "I know where the four of you are standing and can take you down as easily as a mountain." She hoped the reference to what she had done in the Grey Mountains would keep these priests of Ari in check. She did not want to engage them in battle when surrounded by so many people; *the innocent would get hurt.*

Stephenie shook her head at the panicked woman, who was covering her bare breasts with her hands, but had not removed her eyes from her holy symbol dangling from Stephenie's raised fist. "How dare you come to this gathering and pretend to be a witch while using your powers to manipulate the thoughts of all those present. What is your purpose? Why would you do this?"

The woman stood straighter and took a moment before meeting Stephenie's eyes. "We do not believe you are cleansed! We would prove you a lie! I would die to prove it!"

The crowd, no longer influenced by the artificial chilling of their mood, was growing hot with anger at the priestess. Stephenie shook her head. "So you," she emphasized, "would come here and lie to everyone and use your powers against these people. The High Priest of Felis declared me cleansed; you have no authority or justification to be here. Be gone from my sight! I want you and your four friends to leave here at once!"

The woman swallowed, but remained standing, looking desperately at her holy symbol in Stephenie's hand. Anger building in her, Stephenie tossed the cold piece of metal to the edge of the stage, never changing her focus from the girl's face.

The girl rushed to it and retrieved her precious source of additional power. One of her companions quickly helped her down while Stephenie watched with both her eyes and her senses. The five of them had ceased to use their powers, but she would be ready if that changed. Noting the hostility of the crowd, Stephenie softened her expression and raised her voice. "Let these people go. While they are deceitful and rude, I am not here to promote violence. They are no longer welcome, but if they do nothing else, then we can let the issue rest."

A man further back and to the left hand side of the stage raised his voice. "Your Highness, what of myself? I am a priest of Dalmic, am I required to leave? I only came to hear what you have to say and make my own judgments about you."

Stephenie met the balding man's eyes. "No," she said, forcing herself to relax further. "You were not using your powers against those here. As long as you remain respectful, I welcome your presence."

The man nodded and many of the people around him visibly sighed.

Stephenie waited until the five priests of Ari had exited the front doors of the playhouse. "I am sorry for the disturbance." She moved a couple steps to the right, meeting the eyes of those staring up at her. "I welcome questions and doubts of who I am and what I represent. I just ask that you are open about it. I've never held someone's concerns against them." She looked across the crowd, hoping there would not be any further disruptions.

"When will Catheri bring more priests to us?" an older man standing near the front of the stage asked.

"That is a good question," Will said, coming forward. "Princess Stephenie is her chosen prophet and together we have already started adding laymen who wish to serve into the fold. As I said just a bit ago, Catheri is choosing her priests differently than the other gods." Will held up a polished rock from his chest. The reddish stone glinted in the sun. "Her Highness brought down a mountain on the Senzar to route them. Catheri is coming back through the bones of the world. The very rocks exude her power."

Stephenie watched as Will continued to move about, drawing in the audience. What he was preaching annoyed her, and although she agreed it was necessary if they were to slowly change things, she had flatly refused to make the claims he was making.

"Prophet, will you heal my daughter? We have no money to pay the priests."

A young woman just below her drew Stephenie's attention. Behind the twenty-year-old woman was a man cradling a child of five or six in his arms. The entire crowd looked up at her expectantly.

"Ma'am," Will said, dropping into a squat at the edge of the stage. "I'm afraid Her Highness is not available for such requests."

Stephenie stepped forward and put her hand on Will's shoulder. She had told Will more than once that she would not be a healer, but the sudden crushing of the woman's spirit was easily seen and felt. "What is your name?"

"Emil, Your Highness."

"What High Priest William is trying to say is that I'm not very good at healing others. My experience has been in defending Cothel and so, unfortunately, my skill with healing is limited. Is she close to death?"

The frightened young woman shook her head. "No, Your Highness. She has a growth on her back and cannot feel her legs or walk."

Stephenie nodded her head and looked at the girl who was staring back at her with a look that indicated she knew she had to be quiet, but had no idea why Stephenie would be considered so important. Stephenie gave the girl a smile and then turned back to the mother and the man holding the girl. "I could probably heal her, but I worry I would cause her great pain in the process. And worse, I probably would not do the greatest job at the healing." The woman's eyes grew moist as she nodded her head. "However, Will and I have friends with the priests of Felis and we will make sure your daughter gets the healing she needs."

Tears fell from the young woman's eyes, but these were tears of joy and not the fear of disappointment that had been threatening just a moment ago. "Bless you, Your Highness. I've been so worried. My husband is dead in the war and Yuvin, his friend, has spent all his earnings taking care of us. I did not want to see my daughter waste away."

Stephenie gave the girl a smile and then motioned for Douglas to join her from where he was standing on the far right side of the stage. When he was close enough, she asked, "Can you arrange for a second carriage to take them with us to the castle."

Douglas nodded his head and although Stephenie could see he was reluctant to leave his post in protecting her, he dropped nimbly from the stage to help lead the three of them to the side where they could walk up a set of steps. Stephenie watched the crowd graciously part for them and could feel an overall sense of approval from those gathered.

Will quickly turned back to his audience. Obviously sensing this was a high point in the meeting, he raised one hand toward Stephenie. "This is Her Highness, Princess Stephenie, Prophet of Catheri, and Defender of Cothel. I am glad to have been able to introduce her to all of you and we will definitely have her back for other gatherings. While she has to return to Antar Castle shortly, I will continue to meet with you and discuss Catheri's teachings."

Stephenie bowed her head to the crowd, who tried to curtsy and bow in the packed area. The crowd cheered as she followed the man with the child through the right hand stage door. She glanced back at Will and was rewarded with a smile. For a moment, she felt that perhaps Will's insistence in claiming she was Catheri's prophet was the best course to help the people.

Stephenie smiled at Henton and Douglas as they stared at her from the other side of the carriage. It had taken Douglas a while to hunt down and pay for a second carriage. The backdoor of the old playhouse opened onto a very narrow lane. Her own carriage had been waiting on a busy side street that ran next the playhouse. That street was also quite narrow and carriages were forbidden to use it. Her's being a royal carriage garnered an exception, but Douglas had to go all the way to the main street that ran in front of the playhouse before finding any carriages present. However, many of those were already hired and it took some searching to find one to convey Emil, her daughter, and Yuvin all the way to the castle.

"Why are you doing this?" Douglas demanded, "You don't believe anything Will is saying."

"Douglas," Henton growled, "watch your tongue, one of the guards might overhear you."

Stephenie opened herself and could feel her brother's guards riding in the driver's seat and hanging onto the back of the enclosed carriage he had lent her for this trip. With the thick padding and upholstery, as well as the noise from the city, she felt relatively safe, but this type of conversation was indeed better left for when they were in her rooms of the old tower.

Despite Henton's verbal warning, Douglas continued, "If you want to remain true to yourself, you can't start letting others dictate who you are."

Stephenie leaned forward, but still had to stretch to be able to pat Douglas on his knee. "Because it's the only thing I can see that will help rebuild the country." She sat up, "And rebuilding and protecting the country is who I am. Will's claims started when we were back in the Greys and because of them, the High Priest was able to declare for me."

"I know all that. I want to know why you stopped standing your ground. You can rebuild the country without all this. We brought back more money than had even been in Cothel's treasury. You said that yourself."

Stephenie sighed. "Because I can help more people through the lie than I can with the truth. I don't want to see people like me burn because people don't understand the truth." She looked out the window, uncertain if Will even believed the truth, what he said to everyone, or something different yet. "And the lie has grown too large to stop." Turning back to the two of them, she continued, "Let's talk about something more pleasant; my brother's birthday is coming up in several weeks and neither of you have stated officially you are going."

Douglas frowned, but relented in his attack on her. "Well, Sir Henton here might fit in and Will's a High Priest, but someone like me don't need to attend the King and his friends."

Henton glared at Douglas for a moment before turning back to Stephenie. "I really don't feel comfortable in that crowd myself. You don't need protection there. Plus, I doubt the King would want us there."

Stephenie flattened the skirt of her dress. "I don't need protection at all. You are my friends. My only friends." She sighed. "It is not my kind of gathering either, and I don't care about protocol and what the other nobles will think. They might even expect me to bring all of you anyway."

Douglas shook his head. "No Steph, I'm not going. I'll stand my ground, even if you won't."

Henton leaned forward so he could look Douglas in the face. "For calling me Sir, you are hereby ordered to attend."

Stephenie grinned. She knew Henton had not wanted to be made a knight, but her brother had insisted. Henton had even been given a small land grant southwest of Antar. However, when she had requested that Douglas and Will be knighted as well, her brother had refused. He insisted only Henton had gone so much further above and beyond. She suspected there were other factors at play, but did not have the heart to try and force Joshua to provide her his reasons.

"And just who will be buying me new clothes?" Douglas kept looking back and forth between Stephenie and Henton. "I've got better things to do with my money than pay for some overpriced garb."

"I'll buy it," Stephenie said as a grin spread across her face. "And I'll take care of the arrangements for what the tailor will make."

Douglas quickly shook his head and raised his right hand. "Oh no, I'm not going dressed as a flower or some pompous fool. I'll buy my own clothes and you'll have to deal with what I get."

She smiled, sensing Douglas was more griping to gripe than to give her trouble. "Thank you, both of you. Having you there does mean a lot to me."

Chapter 2

Once they were through the gatehouse, which was a monstrous structure protecting two sets of large double doors and portcullises, they disembarked the carriages. After accepting several more expressions of gratitude, Stephenie and Henton returned to what had been designated as 'her' part of the castle while Douglas escorted Yuvin, Emil, and her daughter to the temple of Felis on the east side of the complex.

Stephenie's domain had increased since her return and now included all of the old seven-story-high tower, which stood between the gatehouse and the temple. It also now officially included the old great hall that was attached to the tower, a building she had always assumed to be hers. And because they were housed beneath those two, she claimed the storage rooms that were accessed through her tower. They housed entrances into tunnels that needed to be secret and secure, therefore her brother had agreed.

These oldest parts of the castle complex were made from grey stone and boasted many architectural details, overhangs, and subtle lines. However, they were drafty and the style was no longer in fashion with the designs of the last couple hundred years, and so, few people objected to her claims.

Her brother lived in the large square keep that dominated the southern part of the castle grounds. The tan keep, with its sharp lines, large blocks, and square corners, stood like a four-story-tall box of stone. Most of the other parts of the complex had been built or rebuilt in the last few hundred years and all of it was dull in

Stephenie's mind. However, she had to grant the new buildings the benefit of very thick walls, *most of which were filled with hidden passages.*

On approaching her long and dimly lit great hall, she sensed several men inside. She recognized the feel of their minds as she followed Henton through the open doors at the top of the steep steps. The men inside turned and glanced at Henton, but when they saw her, she felt a sharp flash of fear in the workers.

"Your Highness," one of them said quickly to cover the involuntary flinch he had on seeing her. All those on the ground bowed deeply; those up in the rafters grew very quiet.

Forcing herself to ignore their reaction, she smiled at the men. "How are you doing today, Fradin?" She did not bother to glance up at the three other men who were thirty feet over their heads. These men were a birthday gift from her brother, or at least their work was. Her one wish had been to have the rotting roof repaired and while her eighteenth birthday had been several weeks earlier, she was glad to see the repairs finally starting.

"It is slow work, but we will keep as much of the detail as we can."

She smiled at him, despite the slight taste of his fear in the air. She knew that Fradin also liked the historic beauty of the building, even if so many others continued to want it updated. "Keep yourself well; I will not disturb things by hovering." Acknowledging their bows at her departure, she walked the length of the great hall, passing the old and worn tables on her way to the door leading to her tower.

Her tower was the largest in the complex; standing fifty feet in diameter and seven stories high, it was truly an imposing structure. However, many years earlier, the outer curtain walls had moved beyond the original castle design and her tower no longer offered a strategic advantage over the shorter and stouter towers built into the wall. Therefore, it had been mostly abandoned, along with the old great hall, until Stephenie chose to call it home when she was old enough.

She strode confidently through the door, headed left, and up the wide staircase that curved up the outer wall. The wide stairs allowed easy access for large supplies, including her bed, to the first five floors. Access to the sixth and seventh floors, as well as the roof, was through a set of steep and narrow spiral staircases leading up from the fifth floor.

Glad to be away from the unease of the workers, she climbed the stairs quickly, her magic automatically reducing the physical strain on her body that Henton had to endure in order to keep pace. At the second floor, he stopped in front of the door leading to an old storage room that had been converted into a bedroom for him, Douglas, and Will.

"You're not coming up?" she asked from half a dozen steps higher, not caring that a little pain leaked into her voice.

"I figured you'd want to spend time with Kas."

She reached out with her senses and could just feel Kas' muted presence in her room. "I'll have time to spend with him later. I want to at least eat dinner with you and Douglas. Unless you'd rather do something else."

He smiled at her as he shook his head. "You're almost as bad as your brother; you know we've got nothing else to do. But, since you're a lot better to spend time with, I'll come up with you."

She brightened and as she turned back to the stairs, she remarked just loud enough for him to hear, "You should like me better than Josh, you spent weeks pretending to be my husband, not his."

As she approached the fourth floor, she reached out with her powers and lifted the heavy bar that locked the door from the inside of her room. She knew she probably did not need to lock the door anymore. Now that she had returned, almost no one willingly entered the tower, leaving her and her men to be the ones to maintain her bedroom. There seemed to be an underlying fear in the castle that she had cast spells of protection that might kill an intruder.

Initially, she had laughed when she first heard that rumor, but as the days passed, the truth of the unspoken isolation weighed heavily on her. The very belief that she had enchanted her rooms showed how little people really understood magic. While it would theoretically be possible for her to create a permanent effect, she lacked the skill to form the proper lattice and structures in an object that would be required to maintain any magical fields, let alone to embed sufficient intelligence to allow it to make any decisions.

Kas continued to tell her to ignore those who did not understand. He did not want her happiness contingent on others, but she still missed the carefree days of being Joshua's youngest sister who enjoyed the privilege of playing with swords and fighting with the soldiers. To have those friends, who respected her for her abilities, now work so hard to avoid her, left an ache in her heart.

She walked through the doorway into her bedroom. The first half of the room held her large bed, which was standing against the wooden wall that divided the floor. There was a desk and a chair against the right hand wall, and now a small table with four additional chairs next to one of the fireplaces on the left. The backroom, which was the other half of the floor, was her storage room and was still mostly empty. Her prized possessions, which had been weapons, armor, books, and equipment, had been removed by her mother when she had been imprisoned in the tower. She replaced a few things, but lacked the desire to substitute new things into that part of her life that could never again be as it was.

She ignored the contents of the room and crossed quickly over to her desk where Kas sat reading a book. When he did not look up, she poked a finger into his mostly translucent forehead to get his attention. However, he continued to sit unmoving and focused on the page of the book.

She waved her hand in front of his face, but having died more than one thousand years earlier, he technically had no physical form or eyes. He read by sensing the energy reflected from the page through the entirety of his energy field and her hand waving would not block his perception.

"Kas," she groaned, leaning over her desk and putting her face in front of the blue-green form that he luminesced to resemble his appearance in life. "I want to tell you what happened today."

He looked up slowly as he appeared to exhale, making a conscious effort to pretend he had a physical form. Changing his luminescence, his form became more opaque, though not any more accurate in its coloration. "I have been quite aware of your presence for some time. If you will note, this book is written in a rather obscure language that requires a significant level of concentration for me to translate in my head."

"Yes, yes," she said as she quickly slid an old letter into the book and closed the cover. "Some annoying priest tried to pretend to be a witch in an effort to discredit me. She wanted me to cure her or burn her right there on the spot. How are we ever going to overcome people's distrust and hate?"

Kas softened his expression. "It is still early in your attempt. While I would have been more than satisfied to have you burn someone who perpetuates the use of those augmentation devices, I expect they wanted to test how you would treat witches, which William has been weak on when pressed by inquiring minds."

Stephenie narrowed her eyes, "I had not realized you were paying that much attention to Will."

Kas shrugged. "I endeavor to hear things so that I might be of use, though my grasp of Cothish is not always complete." He leaned back in the chair as he generated a gravity field that caused the chair to move as if he had mass. "Those that believe you secretly support this Elrin—which your mindless ancestors created in their imagination— are looking to see if you support Elrin's demons, as they would call them, or if you will support one of their other imaginary gods." He rolled his eyes. "The very notion that anyone using an augmentation device is getting their power from a god is absurd." Kas pursed his lips at Stephenie's expression. "I know, you have heard my complaints too many times, but my people died trying to stop people from using those traps. To accept bleeding another creature to death simply because it comes from another world shows how depraved people are. You want to know why this imaginary god, Catheri, left your world, well it was because the being that the ticks were draining of life finally died and—"

"Kas, please," Stephenie said to stop his passionate argument. She wanted to boast about arranging healing for the girl, but that would only anger Kas in the trading of one life for another. "I just wanted you to sympathize with me."

Kas relaxed his shoulders and gave her a smile. "I would agree that this person was incredibly rude and should be punished."

Stephenie shook her head, "I finally figured out what I've been seeing from the priests. I don't always see them doing it, but I've seen these tendrils of energy flowing around, sometimes touching people. I had thought they were just feelers, where the priests were trying to sense the world around them. But that's not what I saw today. I saw these priests actually manipulating people's minds or at least manipulating their emotions."

"What?" Henton asked, finally injecting himself into their conversation. "I wasn't sure what was going on today, I felt a little out of sorts, but I could tell the crowd had been impacted by something."

Stephenie turned to where Henton was sitting. "These people were much more obvious about it. Most of the priests I've seen do it before were more subtle, so I never realized what they were doing."

Kas nodded his head and floated into the air in a way no one with a physical body could. "It is something to expect. It is one factor that always put those with power at odds with those who lacked the ability to perform magic. When there is an organized body in control of anything, be it a household or a country, they tend to push their agenda and work to convince everyone else that their ideas are the best ones. For those without magic, they have to use words, behaviors, and physical coercion. For those who can use magic, it is much more effective to use subtle mental reinforcement, than to rely on smiles, thank-yous, and sound, rational arguments."

Henton leaned forward. "So, you are saying people with power are putting thoughts into our heads?"

Kas shrugged. "In a crowd of people, generating a basic emotional energy would be more effective than specific thoughts. Generate a sense of pleasure and security while talking about their god. Then, generate fear and uncertainty and talk about witches. Do that for years and years and you reinforce the agenda you want to the point you do not need to use the mental reinforcement." He locked eyes with Henton. "However, even generating the mental energy is not a certainty. A passionate speech will move those who would already tend to agree and anger those who do not. Using subtle magic might just cause confusion or even an angry response in someone significantly opposed to what the mage was attempting. In those cases, a more forceful invasion of thought and emotion would be needed. But even then, someone more thoughtful or reserved would be impacted less than a person who is used to being a follower."

Stephenie nodded her head. "And, Henton, your head is pretty disciplined. I'd imagine the impact on you is limited."

Henton looked at Stephenie. "That still does not make me feel better. People should be free to decide for themselves what they want to believe."

Kas scoffed. "They should learn to perceive reality and not impose what they want reality to be. To choose a reality is absurd."

"Hey, old guy, you know what I mean."

Kas smiled at Henton. "I do, but that does not mean I have to respect inaccuracy in your statements."

Stephenie walked around the desk and headed over to the door. "Okay, boys, enough. I think Douglas is coming up with our food."

Douglas had brought up several platters of food, mostly sliced meat, bread, and some bowls of lukewarm vegetable soup. There were a few sweetmeats as well, but Stephenie was not in the mood for the candied fruit.

"And I went out of my way to get it," Douglas said with a smile as he picked up several pieces while Stephenie picked up some slices of venison. "I guess we could play some cards while we eat."

Stephenie narrowed her eyes. "You never play cards with the guys."

"I don't find gambling to be entertaining, but since you're forcing me to go to the party, I might as well use your money to buy clothes I don't want to buy."

Stephenie stuck out her tongue, but walked over to the table and put her plate down next to the deck of cards Douglas had brought with the food.

"No cheating, mind you," Douglas said as he placed some beef strips on a chunk of bread.

"Douglas," Henton said, still gathering his own food as Kas returned to his book, "Considering neither I nor Steph tend to gamble ourselves, you either have some hidden talent or are simply hoping we are worse than you."

Douglas shrugged and sat down. "You'll just have to see."

"Kas, you going to join us?" Henton asked.

Stephenie held her breath waiting for his reply. She could tell Henton had been working hard to include Kas in more of the things they did, but Kas would refuse as many times as accept.

Kas frowned and then closed the cover of the book. "There is little of use within those pages," he said in the Old Tongue, which only Stephenie and Henton could understand. "It continues to be as I expected, information on living transformations was not widely shared. The search for how to rebuild a body for me is not going to be easy, Stephenie, but there are more books still to review."

Stephenie pulled out the fourth chair next to the curved outer wall and sat down so she was facing Kas on the other side of the room. She tried not to look at him expectantly, but she could hardly contain her emotional desire that he would join them. To Kas, that would be even more obvious than any visual display.

"I will join," Kas said slowly in Cothish, which he was still normally reluctant to use. "On condition we play a game I know."

Douglas moved the deck of cards to the empty seat they left for Kas and bit into his food. "Just no cheating, either you or Steph," he mumbled.

Kas quickly explained the rules of a card game he played when he was still alive as he removed several cards from the deck to make the game work. After three hands, and the pile of coins growing in front of Kas, it quickly became obvious that he had started to make up rules during the game.

"Let's play something where the rules are not changing," Douglas said, taking the deck into his hands to shuffle it. Kas simply grinned as he generated small gravity fields to stack the coins he had amassed into a series of neat piles.

After several more hands, which Douglas was actually winning, Henton interrupted the quiet. "Do you need to use the chamber pot, Steph?" She looked up to meet his eyes with a questioning glance. "You have an expression that speaks of discomfort."

She relaxed and set her cards down on the table. "I've gotten so used to sensing things, I am having to work real hard to not pick up any surface emotions from any of you, plus, I had not ever thought about this until Douglas demanded that I not cheat—which I think he might be doing," she added, looking and leaning in his direction.

"But I wanted to see how easy it would be and so I tried to sense my cards before picking them up, and if I let myself, I can detect the different energy potentials in the inks." She shook her head while staring at the table. "I'm now having to work very hard not to be aware of what you have in your hands."

Henton laughed and leaned back, tossing his cards down. "Well I won't win with that hand anyway."

Stephenie looked up. "Douglas has three knights, a river, and four soldiers of various rank. It does beat your hand."

Kas leaned forward. "Stephenie, I am forever amazed. I would never have been able to sense anything like that when I was living. As I am, it is possible for me to spread myself out and see the whole table, even while projecting the appearance of sitting, but that would allow me to see only the exposed cards."

Douglas pulled the pile of coins toward him. "Well, I guess that ends the card games with Steph and Kas."

"I really tried not to notice," she said almost as a moan. "Everything I used to enjoy is getting ruined because of my powers. It's like trying not to listen when you have ears. You can't help it."

Douglas stopped counting his coins. "I didn't mean to upset you, Steph. We can keep playing if you want."

She forced a smile. "No, it's not that, it's just...." She looked at Kas who mentally acknowledged her unvocalized request and simply dropped through the floor. "Someone's coming up the stairs."

"Who?" Henton asked.

She shook her head, signaling Henton to wait. A moment later, she felt Kas reach out to her mentally.

It is one of the gate guards and he appears to be carrying a letter.

"A man with a letter," she said for the benefit of Henton and Douglas.

Shortly after she spoke, Kas returned, but remained invisible at her side. A few moments later, there was a knock on the door, which Henton was already in position to open. "Can I help you?"

The young man bowed his head. "My Lord, a man came to the gate with a message for Her Highness. He said it was urgent and that she should get it at all cost." The guard held the folded letter out and

Henton took it before handing it to Stephenie, who had approached the door as they were speaking.

My mother? She observed to Kas as she took note of the seal. Pulling away the wax, she unfolded the letter and started to read. After only the first line she turned back to the guard. "Who dropped this off?! Where is he?!"

The guard stepped back, his limbs trembling. "Ma'am," he stuttered, "I don't know. The letter was given to me by the Sergeant to bring to you."

"What is it Steph?" Henton asked, stepping closer, but avoided looking at the contents of the letter.

"When was it dropped off?"

"Less than a quarter turn ago. I do know the man left immediately."

Stephenie paused and then nodded her head. "Thank you. Please send the Sergeant and whoever took the letter to my great hall and have them wait for me. I want to know more about this person."

"Do you want me to raise the alarm?"

"No. Tell them I want to know about the man, but that is all. Nothing else needs to be done."

The soldier bowed quickly, turned, and then rushed down the stairs as fast as he could. Stephenie had already turned back to the letter.

"Do you want me to go looking for the man?" Kas asked. He appeared very translucently beside her; his legs not completely formed.

She shook her head as she hastened to read, her hair rising about her head as energy leaked from her body. "Bitch," she swore. Frustration boiling over, she could no longer hold all the energy she had drawn and she flung an angry hand toward the fireplace on the outer wall of her room. Dry wood burst into flames and exploded, sending charred fragments of burning debris across her floor.

"Steph!"

She took a deep breath and looked at Henton who was obviously angry and frightened. "They took Will," she retorted to his visual reprimand.

"What?"

"The letter is from my mother," she demanded, "or people who have her seal." Her hands shook with rage. "They want me to surrender myself or they will cut him up and send him back in pieces until there is nothing left."

"How? We left him at the playhouse with his guards. When did they take him?"

Stephenie shook her head. "He always meets with some followers and investors. I should not have left him alone." She looked about the room, and then with a magically enhanced pull, ripped the dress she was wearing from her body as she moved toward her backroom where she kept her clothing and weapons.

"We'll get him back," Henton swore. "Douglas, run over to the keep and let his Majes—"

"No!" Stephenie yelled from other room. "They said for me to come alone. If they see a force coming, they'll kill Will. You have to stay here and Josh can't be told; he'll try to stop me."

"Steph, it is going to be a trap. You can't be serious."

She emerged from her backroom, boots, weapons, and the letter in one hand and a shirt in the other. She had her breaches on and a roughly wrapped binding around her chest. "I'm not going to have one of you die because of me. Not if there is something I can do about it."

"They are going to do everything they can to get advantage over you. They know what you can do."

Stephenie dropped the boots and weapons on the bed so she could pull the shirt over her head. "They may have an idea, but they've not seen me mad yet, and they will regret ever thinking to harm one of you."

"Steph—"

"And," she emphasized, interrupting Henton, "they don't know about Kas. Together, we can make sure it's not a trap I can't get out of. Getting myself killed won't help Will, I know that. But they want me alive. My mother still wants to cut out my heart and eat it, so they can't kill me. That gives me two advantages."

"Steph, this is ridiculous. You know I can't let you go; your brother will put my head on the gatehouse as a warning."

She paused a moment and met Henton's eyes. He was more than a head taller than she was, so she had to crane her neck. She hated to see the fear in his eyes, *but I don't have a choice.* "You can't stop me. Explain it to him." She paused, "Besides, it's likely they don't have Will with them. I want you to get some people, and some of Lady Rebecca's holy warriors, and go back to the playhouse and start looking for him. See if you can track him that way. I'll work back from the other end."

"Stephenie," Kas said aloud, "I can make a quick check of the playhouse, just to make sure he is not there. Perhaps they did not actually take him."

Stephenie nodded her head. "It's possible, but you'll have to do it on the way."

Henton reached for the letter still in her hand. "Where are you supposed to meet them?"

Stephenie held the letter a moment, then released it as a section of the paper blackened and started to smoke. "You can give the letter to Josh, but I won't have him sending people on his own."

"Damn it, Steph, where are you going? How am I to help you if you need help?!"

Stephenie could truly feel Henton's frustration and the weakening of his normal reserve broke her. "Several miles north of Antar. There is a crossroads leading to Merton and the town of Stillcreak. Please, do not tell Josh, he'll send people after me and that could cause them to kill Will if they do have him." She met his eyes, "I promise I will be careful."

Turning away before she lost any more of her nerve, she sat on the bed and quickly pulled on her boots. "I'll have Kas with me. He'll scout it out and if it looks hopeless, then I'll fall back. They just didn't give us time to think about it. I'll barely have time to ride there as it is."

Henton nodded his head at Stephenie and then turned to Kas. "Make sure she stays safe. She's...important to a lot of people."

Kas nodded his head, but spoke in the Old Tongue. "I remind her quite regularly that she will not become a ghost if she dies. So if she wants to stay around me, she will need to remain alive."

"Enough, I don't plan to get myself killed. Just wait until I am away before going to Josh." Strapping on the sword and long dagger that had been a birthday gift from her four men, she headed out of her room and down the stairs.

Henton paced about the room, constantly checking the window facing the stables and the gatehouse. He wanted to shake her, tie her up, and lock her in her rooms, protecting her from those that wanted to hurt her. However, his first real conversation with her had been in this very room when he was her captor. He would never try to hold her against her will ever again; even if there was the slimmest chance it would be possible.

"She's making her way to the gatehouse," Douglas said to break the silence. It was the first thing he had said since she had left the room.

Henton knew how much Douglas cared for Stephenie and so no words were needed between them. Without further delay, Henton led Douglas down the stairs, descending two steps at a time. They rushed out of the great hall, crossed the yard, and were knocking on the large double doors of the square keep just after Stephenie cleared the second set of doors of the gatehouse.

"We need to see the King immediately," he demanded of the soldiers who were standing guard.

"Sir Henton, His Majesty has no appointments for today."

"Damn it, it has to do with his sister, Princess Stephenie, so I suggest you let us in and inform him we need to see him urgently."

The guard nodded his head and signaled for one of the three others with him to inform a superior. After what felt like half a turn of the glass, a finely dressed man arrived. "His Majesty will see you, Sir Henton. Please leave your weapons here with your companion and follow me."

Henton almost growled, he had helped to save His Majesty and was not a threat, but he could not afford further delays. Barely containing his frustration with the situation, he quickly shed his weapons, handing everything he had to Douglas. Without a word, he turned back to the middle-aged man who had come to collect him and raised his eyebrows, fearful that speaking would release an insult.

The man nodded his head, turned sharply on his right heel, and led Henton into the castle. Henton tried very hard not to imagine breaking the man's neck as they ascended the grand staircase to the second floor. On the way to the third floor, the man had grown winded and started to slow. *Stephenie is getting further away with every step, move your ass!*

Possibly driven by his mental command, but more likely by Henton's poorly veiled irritation, the man picked up the pace and hastened their journey to the King's chambers. After passing two more sets of guards and several anterooms, he was finally introduced into a small office with a large desk and richly embroidered tapestries.

"Your Majesty," Henton said, bowing politely, despite his irritation. Angering the King would not help him and he already knew Joshua would be furious that Stephenie went off on her own.

Joshua brushed back his brown hair. It appeared to lack the use of a comb and although he sat behind his large desk, Henton could tell he had dressed quickly in what clothing had been available. "What is it? I was told this was very urgent and about Steph."

Henton nodded his head. "Yes, Your Majesty." Henton, having only glanced at the letter enough to know that it was written in Kyntian, a language he could not read, stepped forward and handed it to Joshua. "A man came to the gate and insisted that this be given to Stephenie with all haste. She said Will has been taken and the threat was that if she did not go to meet with them, Will would be cut up and sent to her in pieces."

"What?" Joshua demanded, yanking the letter from Henton's hand and quickly scanning it. He looked up when he was halfway done, having reached the part that Stephenie burned away. "Where is my sister?" The threat obvious in his voice.

"Your Majesty, she has gone to meet with these people in an effort to rescue Will."

Joshua jumped to his feet, but he was only a couple inches taller the Stephenie, so he still had to look up to meet Henton's eyes. "You let her go? Your job is to protect her and make sure she stays in line. Are you incompetent?"

Henton waited. The veins on his King's neck were pulsing and he knew that if Stephenie lived, she would protect him from Joshua without hesitation. However, if she died, it would not likely be long before he found his own life ended. "Stephenie has a mind of her own and while I can offer advice and council, even plead with her, there is not a person alive that can control her. Nor would I want there to be."

Joshua straightened from where he had leaned over the desk. "Who burned off the location of where she is to meet them?"

"That was her. She took Kas and promised that he would scout and confirm that she would be able to get out of whatever trap they have devised. But she does not want anyone to follow her."

Joshua looked into Henton's eyes. "And you do not know where she is to meet them?"

Henton, having spent years on a ship full of sailors and gamblers, met Joshua's eyes and shook his head. "I have no idea where they are." He took a deep breath, "If you think I am the least bit happy about this, you are mistaken. I am here because I am hoping that perhaps Will might still be in the city. Perhaps we can rescue him. With your permission, I would like to have...."

The door in the back of the room opened, interrupting Henton. A young woman, just a handful of years older than Stephenie, entered the room. Her brown hair pulled back into a long ponytail. She wore steel-grey robes and the holy symbol of Felis rested on her chest.

Henton bowed to her. "Your Excellency."

"I heard shouting and felt raised emotions. What is going on with Stephenie?"

"Rebecca," Joshua said, shaking his head, "she's run off like a stupid little child. Someone with my mother's seal has sent her a letter saying that they've taken William and will kill him unless she comes to them."

"What?"

"Your Majesty, Your Excellency, may I continue. I am in haste."

Both Lady Rebecca and Joshua turned back to Henton.

"Stephenie has gone to confront those that claimed to take Will. She has Kas with her. However, she wants me to take some soldiers and, if possible, some holy warriors, so that I can go into the city and look for Will. We want to start at the playhouse where we last saw him. It's possible that he may still be in the city and someone may have seen something."

Lady Rebecca, High Priest of Felis, turned to Joshua. "It would be very bad if the High Priest of Catheri was taken and killed right out from under us."

Joshua shook his head. "Why did she ever make that fool the High Priest? She should have taken on the role herself. A High Priest without the powers of the god? That is...that is just stupid. He would have been able to defend himself. He's only a soldier, not a leader."

Henton was often frustrated with Will and his willingness to bend rules and push boundaries, but to hear Joshua insult a man he mentored in the marines was almost too much. Knowing Joshua was already angry enough and this was not a time to pick a fight, Henton held his tongue, as he would not have if it had been Stephenie. *Of course, she'd never behave like that.*

Rebecca moderated her tone, but there was power in her voice. "Josh, I happened to approve of Stephenie's choice. But regardless, at this point, we need to try to recover him. If you allow the church of Catheri to fall, then you risk the people's support for Stephenie as well. This is still a point of contention in the kingdom." Lady Rebecca turned to Henton, "We can send some people after Stephenie and some with you."

"The stubborn girl ran off without telling anyone where she was going."

Henton kept his face emotionless under Joshua's glare. While the king might suspect he had lied, he had no proof. However, Rebecca had the power to enter his mind and find out if she chose to do so.

Rebecca spoke first, "Then we'll send people with Henton. The only trouble is we don't have that many here in the castle at the moment."

Joshua shook his head. "Send a squad of soldiers and only one holy warrior with Henton. I'll send others out to find which direction she went and then pursue her. I'll not let my mother's men have off with her."

Henton cleared his throat, "Your Majesty, she did not want people pursuing her. She feared they would harm Will if they saw a force coming."

Joshua turned back to Henton, his eyes narrowed, "He's simply a soldier who was supposed to be protecting her, as you were. His role is to die in that effort if needed and I'll gladly trade him for her. The stupid girl will get herself killed." He turned back to Rebecca. "One holy warrior for Henton, have the rest that are available gather in the court yard. They should ride north to the bridge over the Uthen River. If she crossed there, someone will have spotted her and we can narrow the search for her." He turned back to Henton. "Get out of my sight."

Henton bowed and quickly retreated from the King's chamber. He started walking back to the stairs and stopped when Lady Rebecca called to him from behind.

"Henton, go to the stables and tell them to get some horses ready. You'll want to get there before Josh sends orders for the horses to be used to go after Steph."

"Yes, Ma'am."

"I'll have someone come to you with some soldiers."

"Thank you."

Lady Rebecca put her hand on Henton's shoulder and squeezed it. "Josh is angry and he can overreact. He'll come to his senses once he has a chance to think about it."

"Ma'am, if I may speak freely?" Henton waited until Rebecca nodded her head. "Stephenie will risk herself for Will. If His Majesty does something that gets Will killed, she's likely to react far more harshly than His Majesty. It's not a threat; she loves her brother, but she is passionate when it comes to protecting the people she cares about."

Rebecca nodded her head. "Understood. Get some horses and be ready to leave. I'll send Lady Sara and some soldiers to you. I am a High Priest, so I have the power to make some decisions myself, and I will bring Josh around."

Chapter 3

"Sir Henton," yelled a soldier running from the gatehouse.

Henton turned his head briefly to take note of the youthful guard, but continued to mount the horse a stable hand held for him. The sun was already in the last quarter of the sky and finding Will after it turned dark would be that much harder; he did not have time for more delays.

"Sir Henton," the boy panted, obviously in need of conditioning. "There's man...at gate...says he saw...His Excellency taken."

Henton dismissed the thought of asking the soldier for more details; the boy needed to spend time running back and forth from the castle to the city until he could do it without passing out. Kicking the horse forward, Henton managed to stay on, but his legs and hands were flailing about in a most undignified manner; he knew he needed his own training.

Lady Sara gracefully passed him on the way to the gatehouse, and using her horse to help guide Henton's, they both arrived still mounted. Behind the two of them, Douglas and two other soldiers followed more slowly. The rest of the soldiers were still saddling horses.

At the gatehouse, Henton slid from the saddle, feeling too uncomfortable in the unfamiliar setting. One of the dozen guards standing under the raised portcullis took the reins from Henton as another led him over to a thin man in his early thirties. Henton recognized the man's tanned face and rough-cut hair from the playhouse.

"Sir," the man said, bowing at the waist. "Forgive me, My Lord, I do not know your name."

"You can call me Henton, but don't delay; I was told you saw Will taken."

The man righted himself and nodded his head. "Yes, My Lord. I was cleaning and repairing some canvas near the back of the stage. I heard a commotion and steel ringing against armor. Uncertain, I looked around the corner and His Excellency was grabbed by a group of men. The High Priest's soldiers looked to have been overwhelmed. I could swear I saw a holy symbol around the neck of at least one of the men who took His Excellency." The man cleared his throat. "I panicked and ran back to the stage, but no one followed. When I heard the back door bang, I poked my head around the corner again and they were gone and so was His Excellency."

"How many men?"

The man shook his head as he ran his hands through his hair. "I was scared. Maybe a dozen. Counting them was not in my thoughts and it was dark behind the stage. It took me a moment to even build the courage to check when I heard them leave. But, when I walked past His Excellency's men, I knew them to be dead. However, I wasn't that long," he quickly added, "because I knew His Excellency was in danger. But when I went out the back door, they were gone into the wind. I ran down to Fairnessway, the street that runs beside the playhouse, but there was no sign of them." The man looked between Henton and Lady Sara. "I ran straight here after that. I wanted to warn the Prophet."

Henton's mind was racing and all he wanted to do was get to the playhouse as quickly as possible. On his way back to his horse, he asked over his shoulder. "What's your name?"

"Arn, My Lord."

Putting his foot into the stirrup, Henton pulled himself up and onto the saddle. "Arn, thank you for the report. Please allow these men to take you to report to His Majesty. He'll want to hear what you saw as well." Looking at the guard that had escorted Arn to Henton, he added, "And make sure you get Arn something to eat."

Seeing the other fifteen soldiers following from the stables, Henton kicked his horse, which lurched into motion. He pulled on the reins, slowing and directing the horse out of the gatehouse and toward the city of Antar.

Lady Sara quickly caught up and shook her head. "Don't kick; just squeeze his sides gently with your legs to get him to move. And steady your hands. You'll have him hating you if you keep jerking on his mouth like that."

Henton nodded his head, but as he bounced along at a fast trot, he just could not seem to put the pieces together and Lady Sara continued to frown. He turned his head slightly, "I've never ridden a horse faster than a walk and that was a long time ago. I'm a bloody sailor."

"Lean back and resist with your seat to slow him. You'll fall off and so will Douglas if you try to keep this pace."

Henton did not want to slow down, but he was feeling quite loose in the saddle and falling to the ground would not help them get to Will. Trying to do what the holy warrior said, he gradually managed to slow the large bay enough so he could concentrate on more than just staying on the horse.

"What are you thinking?" Lady Sara asked as they approached the southern edge of the city.

"If what Arn said is true, then they sent the message to Stephenie well before they had actually taken Will. It took me at least half a turn of the glass to keep His Majesty from hanging me for letting Steph leave on her own and more time to gather the soldiers. If they had grabbed Will before sending the note, Arn should have arrived first or at least, about the same time."

"What do you think it means?" Douglas asked from behind them.

Henton glanced at Douglas, "I'm hoping it means they've divided their forces, but I fear it means Will's dead and the others have gone off to tighten the trap around Stephenie.

The sun had already reached the horizon and was setting fast by the time Henton and the others reached the old playhouse in the southeast part of the city. The distance from the castle was not all that great, but Henton could already feel the forming of blisters on his legs where the stirrups had pinched him against the saddle flap.

Dismounting in front of the playhouse, he quickly led Douglas, Lady Sara, and a handful of soldiers to the closed front doors. "Douglas, head down the side road and see if anyone still around might have seen anything unusual. Don't mention to anyone who was taken. Take six men with you."

Douglas silently broke off, pointing to the trailing six men to follow him. Henton knew Douglas could handle the task with less instruction, but he wanted the other soldiers to hear his orders. Focusing on his own task, he stepped forward and gave the playhouse doors a hard shove. The blow popped the old lock out of the wooden doors and Henton moved quickly through the short tunnel under the upper seats and into the open area in front of the stage. "Do you sense anyone?" he asked of Lady Sara as he kept to the right hand wall in case there was anyone in the seats above them.

The priestess paused and held her holy symbol for a moment before shaking her head. "I can't feel anyone nearby except for us."

Henton nodded his head and moved forward, cutting across the open area despite the uneasiness it caused him. "Let me know if that changes," he said over his shoulder, hoping the others would keep up.

At the stage, he easily launched himself up and onto the four-foot high platform. Nimbly rolling back to his feet, he moved to the back wall and slid closer to the door. Despite Lady Sara's assurance, he could not bring himself to charge through the opening into the dark rooms behind the stage.

Peaking around the corner, he let his eyes adjust to the darkness. Looking on the positive side of the fading light, he was not sun blind and so he did not have to wait long. Checking for any obvious traps that might have been left, he carefully moved through the opening and into the backroom. His hard-soled boots, deftly used on the wooden floor, hardly made a sound as he walked.

Frowning as the others followed with less grace and more noise, he noted the iron smell of spilled blood. Giving up on stealth, he quickened his pace. Moving beyond the passage directly behind the stage, he descended a series of wobbly steps to the larger storeroom that held the rear door of the playhouse. Lady Sara's sudden intake of breath told him she had noticed the bodies lying about the room.

Still being careful to watch for any traps those who took Will might have left, he moved among the carnage. Henton recognized all of Will's guards and noted three other men among the dead. Most of Will's men were soldiers who had been in the Greys when Stephenie had brought down the mountain peak. All of them had been released from service to the King and had embraced Will's message.

"I count eight of them," Sara said.

Henton noticed the shudder run through her body and reminded himself that she was young. *Too young to even have fought much in the war.* Standing straighter, he looked toward the soldiers that Lady Rebecca had sent with him. "Three of you check the rest of the playhouse to see if there are any others. Be careful, just in case they left traps." He turned to Sara, "We'll assume that Arn's story is correct and they took Will from here." Without waiting for a response, he headed to the back door and carefully pushed it open. Behind him, he noted a change in illumination as one of the soldiers lit an oil lamp to aid in their search.

Henton stepped out into the very narrow alley that ran behind the playhouse. A couple people could walk abreast or one-person ride a horse down the street, assuming the rider would duck to avoid the signs and overhangs. Squatting down, he examined the ground. At one time, the alley had been nicely cobbled, but years of dirt and neglect had taken its toll and only a few cobbles were visible through the sediment. Looking to his right, the alley opened into the busier side street that even at this time of day had a fair amount of foot traffic.

To his left, the narrow alley continued for as far as he could see. At its high point, the buildings here had been shops and high quality flats. However, time had taken its toll on more than the cobbles. From where Henton squatted, he could see many of the buildings boarded up and abandoned. This part of town had still not recovered from when all the people left Antar in fear of the war. The low cost nature of renting the almost abandoned playhouse was one of the reasons Will had been using it.

Looking down at the ground again he exhaled; there was not a lot of traffic down the alley, but enough that no clear tracks could be discerned. *Perhaps if I had learned to be a land tracker.* Standing, he moved to the far side of the alley as Douglas entered from the side street. Douglas shook his head 'no' as he approached. Henton nodded and motioned the others to follow him deeper into the alley.

"You think they went this way?" Lady Sara asked at just above a whisper.

Henton held back an irritated retort; he was not used to explaining himself in the middle of a conflict. Making allowances for her youth and knowing he needed her help, he quietly responded to her. "Someone would have noticed them if they went the other way. And there are a lot of abandoned buildings here. Since Arn didn't see them running away, I'm guessing they are hold up close by. Keep your senses open and let me know if you feel them."

Sara cleared her throat. "There are limits to what I can sense." Acknowledging Henton's look, she nodded her head. "I will do what I can."

"We're looking for Will and perhaps a dozen men, maybe less since at least three of them fell in the playhouse. Steph's mentioned before that soldiers feel different to her than average people; harder, more reserved."

"If I sense them, I will let you know. But my range is limited, and there will be others about."

"Not many, most of these buildings are abandoned." Henton said no more as he continued to move carefully down the street. With Douglass and Sara, there were seventeen people following him. Even if that made it better odds, the trouble would be getting Will out of danger while the soldiers engaged each other. *And hoping Sara can handle any holy warriors they might have.*

After another hundred paces, he stopped. "Anything?"

Lady Sara frowned. "There are a number of people in that building just ahead of us. I can't tell much. The buildings we've passed have been empty or just had a couple people in them." She looked up at him with her brown eyes, "How did you know to stop here?"

Henton leaned away from the building they were standing against and looked up at the one he suspected. "First, if Arn followed with any reasonable speed, they would not have been able to get far or he'd have seen them. Second, this building up ahead is boarded up, but the boards over the windows have larger gaps and those gaps were recently exposed. Probably to watch for trouble or shoot through."

Stepping back so he was again crouched against the building, he looked down the line of soldiers. The war had taken most of the older soldiers, as well as a large number of the younger ones. He was dealing with a couple of seasoned men, and the rest were fresh recruits who just came of age over the summer.

Turning back to Sara, he finished his explanation. "If the gaps had just been sun faded, I wouldn't have noticed it in the failing light, but there was an old whitewash done on the building at one point and the boards that were moved exposed the bright color under them."

Douglas crowded closer, pushing Sara into Henton. "What's the plan? We can't charge in the front and there are no back doors. I know from walking the area with Will, this is a long row of buildings wall to wall, back to back."

Henton glanced behind himself and down the alley. Fortunately, there were no side branches to worry about watchers and the lane was just too narrow for things to be left out to hide behind. "Anyone inside this building?" he asked Sara, indicating the one they were standing against."

She closed her eyes and concentrated, then after a moment, shook her head 'no'.

"Is Will upstairs or down? How many men are guarding him?"

Sara shook her head, annoyance clear in her eyes. "I can't tell. There are a number, but I can't sense where they are exactly."

"Can you at least tell if they are on the first or second floor?"

"First floor." She paused a moment. "Her Highness can sense what you're asking?"

Henton ignored the question. "Douglas, get into this building quietly and take the soldiers with you." Henton nodded to the soldier just behind Douglas, "private, what's your name?"

"Sam, Sir."

Henton bit back the comment that he was not a 'Sir', Joshua had changed that by making him a knight. "The shirt under your armor, it doesn't look the proper color."

The private swallowed. "No, Sir. I ruined my uniform and had to borrow this from my brother. I—"

"You're not in trouble. I want you to strip out of your armor so you don't have any colors on. I'd ask Douglas to do it, but I expect they would recognize him or me on sight."

"What do you want me to do?"

"I'm expecting they didn't lease the building, so I want you to go up there, knock on the door and demand that they pay you some money or you'll threaten to turn them into the owners of the building and the city guard."

"Sir?"

"I want you to be a distraction while I take position in the building. Make sure you stay far enough out in the street that they can't grab you and drag you in." Turning to Douglas, he continued. "Have someone watching from the door here, if there is trouble, have someone with a crossbow shoot them so Sam can get away."

"What are you going to do?"

"I'm going in through the second floor and will come down from the inside. This building," he indicated the one beside them with his head, "is a single story and I saw a shuttered window on the side of their building. Once I'm in, cause the distraction, then give me another count of one hundred and come back to the front door and charge in. Creep low under the windows and they might not see you."

"How are you going to get up there without them noticing?" Sara asked, a bit of concern in her voice.

"You're a holy warrior, right? I want you to fly me up there."

"What?" She shook her head. "We crush people, fling them from walls, and knock them to the ground. I've heard that Her Highness can fly you, but—"

"Then fling me up onto the roof and I'll manage from there. You just have to push from the ground against the bottom of my feet."

Sara took a deep breath and nodded her head. "I will try."

"Sarge?" Douglas asked, reverting to his old title. "What if they have a holy warrior of their own?"

Henton nodded his head. "For our sake, I'm hoping they sent them all to capture Steph, but Sara, you will need to be ready to fight their mag..." he was about to use Stephenie's term of 'magic', "fight their power."

The soldier behind Sam peeked his head around, "door's open, Sir."

Henton nodded as the line of soldiers filed into the abandoned building. "Get changed, Sam." He turned back to Sara, "Just think of it as a pass or fail exam. You fail, several of us are likely to die."

She glared at him for a moment and then nodded her head. "I'll try, but this will likely hurt." She stepped back and leaned out to get a view of the window. With her head, she motioned for Henton to step into the middle of the alley. Grabbing her holy symbol with both hands, she closed her eyes and started to mumble some words that Henton could not quite hear. The last thing Henton noticed before his legs buckled under him was Sam handing off his armor to Douglas.

Grunting under the pain of what felt like landing from a three-story jump, Henton flailed his arms about as he rose well above the height of the two-story roof. His stomach dropped and he expected he was going to feel a lot of pain as he started to drop the thirty feet toward the tiled roof. Having fallen from halfway up a mast before, he resisted the urge to tense his body, but was not prepared for a second wave, of what Stephenie called gravitational energy, to hit him, launching him upward again. He knew his ankle was twisted from that impact and his seat bone radiated pain.

However, this time his flight was much less energetic and he was close to the two-story building. Reaching out desperately, he caught the edge of the roof as a third wave of energy collided with his legs, sending more pain through his ankle, but it slowed him enough that he was able to gracefully swing his feet into the windowsill.

Letting out the breath he had been holding, he let his nerves settle a bit before moving his hands one at a time from the edge of the roof to the top of the window that was centered in the wall. He refused to look down as he scooted to the right so he could pull open the shutter. An old latch resisted for a moment, but the weathered wood gave way and the shutter opened.

Henton looked at the opening and was thankful that the window was just an opening behind the shutter. Perhaps at one time mica panes or even glass might have been used, but the building had been stripped of most of its valuable parts long ago.

Carefully moving in through the opening, he took a moment to glance back at the street below and gave the frightened Lady Sara a smile. Despite the fact that the ride had been painful and somewhat terrifying, she had managed to get him into the window and that was what counted. *She's not Steph, but it's good to have magic on our side.*

Taking a quick look around the room, he suspected the small space had been a bedroom. Currently, dust covered the wooden floor, which showed the passing of recent feet, but nothing else remained in the room.

Not moving for fear of the floor creaking, Henton craned his head to look through the single door on the other side of the room. Beyond the partially ajar door was a dimly lit hall. He could see a couple more doors down the hall. One was off its hinges and leaning against a wall. There was also what appeared to be a staircase going down toward the back of the building. Fortunately, no one seemed to be present.

He took a tentative step forward and winced as he put weight on his ankle. The floor groaned ever so slightly. Very slowly, he shifted his weight forward, but did not take another step. Holding position, he drew out his sword and a throwing knife he carried ever since a Mytian pirate incident during his second month at sea.

After what felt like a whole turn of the glass, Henton heard pounding on the front door of the building as well as footsteps and voices downstairs. Moving as gracefully as he could, he crossed the narrow room and slipped into the hallway. Downstairs, he could hear Sam raising his voice and generating a commotion. However even with the cover, by the time he reached the stairs, he was certain there would be half a dozen men waiting for him because of the noise he had caused. Peaking around the corner, he was relieved there was no one present. The stairs, he noted, made a right turn at the back wall and continued to the first floor.

Out front, Sam's demands might have been answered, because the commotion had stopped and there was no sound of violence. Henton considered taking the first step down the stairs, but held back. While old floors always creaked and groaned under one's feet, old stairs tended to scream at being used and if Douglas stuck to the plan, it would be a hundred count before he could expect reinforcements.

After reaching a count of eighty, Henton rolled his shoulders and prepared himself for conflict. After counting another thirty-five, he heard pounding on the door again and the people below saying something angrily in Kyntian. Knowing he would still need to find Will, Henton moved quickly down the stairs and paused only briefly before rounding the corner at the back wall.

He emerged from the stairwell in a dimly lit kitchen that was illuminated by an oil lamp sitting on a worktable. He immediately noticed Will gagged and bound to a chair on the far side of the room. To Henton's immediate right, two men stood listening against a door leading to the front part of the building. One had already turned at the sound of Henton descending the stairs. That black hair man cried out an alarm as Henton threw his knife.

The knife struck the man in the shoulder, but that man was already rushing toward Henton. The second man reacted a little slower, but headed for Will.

Cursing, Henton switched his sword to his right hand and deflected the black haired man's knife thrust in the process. The second man was drawing a short blade as he closed on Will.

Limited by the close confines of the small kitchen, Henton pushed forward into the black haired man, punching him in the face with the crossbar of his sword while grabbing his throwing knife from the man's shoulder with his left hand. The move staggered the man back, but not before he sliced through the leather of Henton's gambeson.

"He die!" the second man said with broken speech, pointing his blade at Will while looking at Henton.

Henton kicked out the knee of the black haired man to buy more time and moved toward Will and the second man. *Steph, we need you here,* he swore while wishing for once that he had magic of his own.

Will caught his eye and then flung back his bruised and battered head, causing his chair to tip backward, buying his upper body some distance from the blade.

The Kyntian man cursed, considered trying to stab the falling Will, but turned to engage Henton, who had closed the distance. The Kyntian deflected Henton's thrust with a short blade and tried to grapple with Henton's left hand to tie up his throwing knife.

Not bothering to curse the fact he brought the wrong sword for this close quarter combat, Henton dropped the blade, grabbed the man's left forearm, fell backwards to the floor, and using his good foot, launched the startled man over him and into the black haired man who had regained his feet.

Scrambling to turn himself around, Henton gained his feet before the others, who were struggling to untangle themselves. Not hesitating, Henton kicked the second man in the face, stopping his struggles and leaving him on top of the black haired man. The sounds of conflict came loudly from the front part of the building, but the two men he had disabled were blocking the door.

Turning, Henton quickly went to Will, and using his knife, cut away the rope tying his arms and legs to the chair. With his right hand, covered red in his own blood that was running down his arm, Henton pulled Will to his feet and then helped him remain there. After a moment, Will removed the gag from his mouth, while Henton turned back to the two men. The black haired man was working his way to his feet when the door flew open to allow Douglas and Lady Sara entry.

The black haired man dropped the knife he was holding, raised one hand, and used the other to put pressure on the shoulder wound Henton had given him. "I surrender," he said with a heavy accent.

"You good, Sarge?"

Henton nodded his head. "How's it out there?"

"Two dead on our side, plus a few injuries. We've got people taking care of them. What about you and Will?"

Will nodded his head, but was barely holding his feet. He inclined his head to the black haired man, "That bastard did the worst to me."

Douglas stepped closer to the man who had backed into the wall.

"Demand prisoner of war."

Douglas moved quickly, striking the man in the gut with a fist and then bringing his knee up into the man's face. The black hair man slipped to the floor and Douglas dropped a knee into his back so he could tie the man's hands.

"You are bleeding," Lady Sara said to Henton.

"See to Will first. I've just got one cut and it's not too bad yet." Henton moved over to the man he had kicked in the face while he pulled a bandage from a pocket in the gambeson. A quick check told him the man was dead, likely a broken neck. Henton frowned. He had let his anger at the man get to him. That kick to the face was not something he was proud of doing.

"Let me tie that off, Sarge," Douglas said, coming over after having secured the black haired man. "He might think he's going to get an easy death as an enemy soldier, but I think the King will show him otherwise."

Henton walked over to the black haired man, who had rolled onto his side. "Who and how many were sent to capture Stephenie?"

The man sneered. "I do the work of gods. I say nothing to help you save the witch."

Henton stood up; afraid he would kill the man if he tried to talk with him more. "How's Will?" he asked Lady Sara instead.

The holy warrior looked up and turned toward Henton. "He's got lots of cuts and bruises; some are deep. It will take time."

Henton nodded, "See to it." Two of the soldiers had come into the kitchen and started to drag the dead man out of the small room, to them he said, "Send three people to find some reinforcements. I want this place secure until Will can be moved. Plus, I want to see what we can do to help Steph."

"Sarge, we don't know where she is, remember."

"The King thinks she's north of Antar, that's good enough for me." He limped over to Douglas, "But my ankle's twisted and there's no way I can ride there." He closed his eyes and balled up his fists. "I just hope she can manage for a time on her own." He turned to look at the black haired man. "If they do manage to capture her, Josh will get the details of their travel plans from these men. Lady Rebecca will rip it from them if need be." *Of course, we'll need her and a lot more holy warriors to go after Steph if they've sent someone who can actually take her.*

Henton was cursing the King, albeit silently, when additional soldiers finally arrived. There were two more priests and a handful of men to start questioning and preparing the prisoners to be removed to the castle. The holy warriors he had hoped for had already been sent north and he would not be included in the effort to help Stephenie.

The two priests helped Lady Sara treat the wounded, which included himself, and while his arm was no longer bleeding, his ankle was still sore and the three with magic were exhausted by the time they were done with the immediate healing. *One forgets just how powerful Steph is, though I don't want her healing me.*

"Sarge," Will said from where he was sitting in a more comfortable chair in the front room of the building, "you can head out to find her if you want. Douglas and I can handle things here."

Henton wanted to agree, but too much time had passed and truthfully, these men were his responsibility. *And mostly, without magic, I would be more of a distraction to Stephenie than any help.* The best he could do would be to try to track the people, if they did actually take her, and for that, he would need to wait for the morning light. Since Kas had not come for him, perhaps Stephenie was safe. To Will, he shook his head, "I won't do any good against what she faces."

Chapter 4

The sun was dropping below the horizon as Stephenie turned her horse further north onto the road heading to the village of Merton. The wooden sign pointing the way at the crossroad was old and faded, but even in the twilight, she had no trouble reading the carved words.

Before her, fields spread in all directions, with short fieldstone walls dividing the land between the families that performed the work. In the distance, she could see clumps of trees that had sprung up in the hollows and near the creeks and streams that ran across the countryside. It had been many generations since this land was fully wooded.

She reached out with her senses, but there was no one currently in range to feel or, hopefully, notice her passage. The hay that had been in the nearby fields had already been cut and gathered, and she expected the farmers would be tending other crops as the hay started to turn dormant for the year.

Fighting the urge to gallop down the road and confront those who would dare to take Will from her, she forced herself to keep a slow pace. The rational part of her mind knew she needed to know what she would be facing. If the situation was hopeless, she would have to turn away and try a different approach and that thought scared her more than what she might face. Her arms trembled with relief when she finally sensed Kas' return. *Have you found them? Was Will there?*

Kas drifted closer before responding. *There is a carriage sitting at the crossroad just down this lane. There is an open space, and I hesitated to get too close in case anyone might be able to sense me. Ten men are gathered along the wall, all dressed as your stupid 'Holy Warriors'.*

Stephenie could feel Kas' disdain for those who would use the augmentation devices. *You see Will?* She interrupted before he could lose focus and delved into his normal complaints.

No. There is a vague possibility he could be in the carriage. I have a reasonable certainty that at least one person is contained within its walls, but I remained too far away to know anything about the occupant. Kas gave the mental appearance of clearing his throat. *There are other watchers of which you should be aware. I found three men perched in trees. They are too far away for anyone to sense from the crossroad, but they appear to have spyglasses, bows, and signal horns. You have already passed two additional ones, both of which were hiding behind walls well off the road.*

Stephenie frowned. *I'd guess they are watching to make sure I approach by myself, but there may be other people even further out who are holding Will. If I don't cooperate, they signal the others to harm him.* She clenched her fingers around the reins; she had grown close enough to see the series of lamps that were illuminating the meeting point. "If they've harmed Will, they'll wish for death."

I do not know that this is the best course. They are many to your one and all appear to be empowered. Getting yourself captured or killed will not help William.

Stephenie shook her head. *They don't know about you, so it is two against their many.* She stared for a moment at her targets. *When I get closer, start taking out the watchers as quietly as you can. I don't want to risk them going for Will or calling in more reinforcements. Then come back and help me if I need it. They want me alive, so for a little while I have the advantage. If they don't know the watchers are down, they'll hopefully wait a while before getting serious, so I'll try to stall them.*

Sensing Kas' reluctant acceptance, she urged her horse forward with a gentle squeeze. As the chestnut moved into a faster trot, Kas drifted to her left and was quickly out of her range. She hated to be away from him, but it was the only way they could cover everyone.

Still fighting to keep her pace slow enough to allow Kas enough time to do what he needed, she managed to close on the group of men with an air of confidence that she did not entirely feel. If it had much of an effect on them, she did not know. The emotions of these men were as muted as any priest or holy warrior she ever faced. Her only clue to their state of mind was a slight fidgeting from a couple of the younger men standing at the edge of what was a reverse wedge formation. The others stood as statues, with the two significantly older men at the apex watching her approach with frozen expressions of contempt.

Beyond the line of holy warriors, who were all armed with crossbows, sat the expensive carriage hitched with four horses and appeared ready for departure, though no one was in the driver's seat. A dozen more horses were tied in a line even further down the fieldstone wall. Aside from the muted presence of the person in the carriage, whom Stephenie suspected was a man; there was no one else within her range to sense.

"Your mother wasn't sure you would come," the center man said in accented Cothish, his Kyntian background heavy in his consonants. "It is good that you decided to take us seriously."

Stephenie brought her horse to a halt. "Taking my friend captive was a mistake," the snarl she felt not quite hidden from her voice. "If he's been harmed, you will see just how angry I can become."

The man chuckled. "Witch, you are out manned and out classed. You cannot hope to defeat all of us."

Stephenie reined in the power that was coursing through her, filling the air, and making it harder to sense what these men might be doing. Forcing herself to be calm, she continued, "You must be under the impression I will hesitate in killing any of you. I know my mother wants me alive, which puts you at a disadvantage. Now, if any of you want to see the morning light, you will tell me where Will is being held, release him, and leave Cothel, never to return."

The old man standing at the center of the line shook his head. "Drink this and then we will discuss your friend." He held out a wooden tankard he had been holding in his left hand. "It won't kill you; just make your trip to your mother more pleasant."

Her horse moved slightly under her, fidgeting after the long ride as well as sensing her agitation. "I have no intention of simply allowing you to take me to my mother so she can cut my heart out to eat it. I am offering you one last chance, tell me what you have done with Will and I'll let you walk away with your lives."

The older man smiled with confidence that Stephenie hoped was false. "You harm us and your heathen friend will die. Come the morning, if we have not sent word that we have you properly calmed and under control, they will start cutting him up piece by piece to make sure he gets a full understanding of what it means to promote Elrin's evil."

Stephenie dismounted and nudged the horse away from her, not wanting it to come to harm. When the horse had moved off a few feet, she squared her shoulders and drew the sword and dagger she was wearing. She knew Kas could move quickly and hoped he had already taken out at least a couple of the watchers. "I have no reason to trust you. I highly doubt you would free Will regardless of what I do. There's a good chance you've already killed him. So, I see no reason to let any of you live."

Movement in the carriage drew her attention and she was forced to change her focus as a man stepped out. She was instantly aware he was a mage and was not pretending to be a holy warrior or priest. Invisible energy threads sprung from his mind, spreading over the whole area. By contrast, the other ten standing before her had only a few threads due to their limited ability with magic, relying instead on their holy symbols to augment their powers.

Sensing one of the ten start to move in her direction, she prepared herself for impending conflict. She was not sure how much longer Kas would take, but her willingness to remain on the defensive until he came to her aid was crumbling. She knew her mother wanted her alive, but the fact that she had sent someone so obviously not a priest was unexpected. She almost closed her eyes to avoid the visual distractions to the energy moving around her. Reaching out with her own threads, she tried to anticipate their next move.

"It seems our friend interests you."

She heard the old man's voice, but the sound felt distant. A vague haze seemed to fill her mind and her sense of the energy threads around her suddenly faded.

You are no match for me.

Stephenie felt the richly toned voice in her head at the same time she felt a sudden detachment fill her, as if she was briefly in multiple places at the same time. The sensation of being split across multiple locations was gone before she realized what it had been. However, the mental detachment remained. She was aware of herself, but it was as if she was deeply drunk or suffering from a severe lack of sleep. She was unable to make her body respond as she wanted it to and panic began to overwhelm her thoughts.

You're too late. I have you now little girl.

A sense of contempt and superiority filled her, but it did not originate from within herself. Fighting not to lose all control of her mind, she struggled to move her arms.

You are mine. At least your mind is. These foolish idiots will take you to your mother and she'll do some very unpleasant things to you I am sure. However, before you die at her hand, I have been given leave to take everything of value from your pretty little head. Perhaps I may even take some physical enjoyment from you. Perhaps you'll enjoy it as well; I know your body will.

Stephenie felt his desires and pushed against them, knowing they were not her own.

Don't worry, these fools think you are evil and would never consider laying with you. But before I am done with you, you'll willingly give yourself to me in every way possible.

She pushed against his presence, trying to drive his voice from her mind, but it was like holding back the sea; he simply washed around her, overwhelming her efforts. *Get out of my head you bastard!*

Stephenie knew he was laughing at her. *You cannot escape.* He loosened his grip on her just enough for her to realize she had dropped her weapons and was now holding out her hand for the mug. *You will drink the poison and then we will take a long ride in the carriage where I will explore your body as well as your mind.* The man raised his eyebrows. *Interesting, you are hoping for your dead friend to save you. I have never encountered a ghost before, but thank you for showing me how to kill one.*

Stephenie wanted to cry, to scream, to tear this man's head from his shoulders. She had underestimated her mother and it would cost her everything. Powerless, she reached out to the man. *Please, leave my friends alone! Don't hurt them! I'll do what you want!*

That you will, Stephenie. That you will. You defeated us in the Grey Mountains and we will learn how that happened. The man paused. *Interesting, what is this city you are trying to protect? A library? That could raise my standings...where is it?*

Get out! Get out! She screamed until he allowed her to sense Kas' approach. Realizing that she could not fight him, she turned inward, not wanting to witness him killing the man she loved. Retreating away from him, she tried to hide her memories and feelings, but too late she realized that hiding herself deeper in her own mind simply allowed the man free access to more of her memories since she could not take them with her.

Mentally sobbing, she felt numb and powerless. Her confidence had cost her everything.

There, there, little Stephenie. You cannot hide from me. He poked at her, trying to draw her back. *I want you to experience this. I want you to know loss. You killed a woman close to me, so now I will kill someone you care about and do things to you that will make you yearn for what your ignorant mother will do.*

Stephenie tried to take a breath, but her body was not her own. Turning her mind back to face the man, she sensed a deep growl coming up from within herself. Rage filled her until she was not aware of anything but the man who had invaded her thoughts, raping her mind and intending to do the same to her body. A primal need screamed at her, overwhelming her thoughts until she had no conscious ones left. Nothing would ever be allowed to dominate her; that was counter to the natural order.

Kas was rushing back to Stephenie. He had no eyes, ears, or anything physical to sense the world around him. However, he had long ago learned to understand the ripples in the energy currents as they interacted with the energy fields that comprised his being. He sensed Stephenie was motionless, her weapons discarded on the ground as the cursed holy warriors approached. More frightening was the change in her mental presence, as if her mind was no longer functional.

He had killed the watchers he had found by drawing as much energy from their bodies as he could, effectively freezing their hearts solid. He would do the same to those who were now harming the only living person he truly cared for. Unlike the watchers, these men had magic to draw upon. However, he was confident he would survive anything their limited abilities could call forth.

He slowed slightly as the eleventh man turned his mental attention on him. Stephenie was not dead yet, Kas knew that. However, this man, who was not using an augmentation device, had sensed him and was trying to draw off his energy, in what Kas knew was an effort to destroy him.

Drawing energy from his surroundings, Kas, tried to back away while holding cohesion with the energy that comprised what was left of his being. His efforts stopped as a deep growl filled the air and vibrated the very ground. It was a growl of an angry beast and for a moment, Kas felt the tremors move through the fabric of the energy that permeated the physical world. A moment later, he was blinded by a surge of power and a sense of primal rage.

When the flash subsided, he sensed Stephenie springing forward and twisting in the air with the grace of a cat. Two of the closer holy warriors crumpled to the ground as fist sized holes exploded through their chests.

Crossbow bolts flew at Stephenie, but slipped past her fluid motion and flew out of the sphere of light the lamps provided. Lightning crackled from one of the holy warriors, flowed over Stephenie's body, and then angled off into two other holy warriors, leaving them dead. The lightning behaved as if she was somehow at one with the electricity and an old friend to honor and respect.

Not slowing her movement, Stephenie danced around a man that was drawing his sword, her red hair blowing free as she spun. Moving faster than the man could turn his head; she rammed her fingers through the man's armor and plunged her hand wrist deep into his back.

Continuing her spin, she flung the screaming man into the disintegrating line of holy warriors. A moment later, lightning ripped through the line of men, charring flesh and melting armor. The rumble of thunder that followed, which shook the ground, was still less intense than Stephenie's initial growl.

Three of the holy warriors were running, trying to escape into the growing night. Before Kas could even move to engage them, he sensed a draw of gravity. It was so strong that it pulled on the subatomic particles that comprised part of his being. As suddenly as it had formed, the gravity was gone, leaving three flattened corpses.

Casting about, Kas noted the only man left standing was the one who was not using an augmentation device and who had initially sensed and attacked him. Stephenie strolled over and stood directly in front of the well-dressed man. She paused a moment, in which the man flinched and struggled, but was not able to move. Without warning, her right hand plunged into his chest. Her left hand followed and then she pulled her hands apart, tearing open his chest.

Kas sensed this man's screams as the vibrations in the air that they were. The agony was very short lived, as Stephenie tore out his lungs and organs, discarding them to either side as the man crumpled to the ground.

She remained standing over him until his mind finally died. Then slowly, she turned and faced Kas. Based on the wavelengths of the light reflecting off her face, he could sense her blue eyes focused on him despite the fact he had not chosen to burn energy in an effort to generate an illumination her eyes could see. *Stephenie*, he said, directing his thoughts to her. If he had a body, he knew a chill would have filled his spine. While her body stood before him, her presence was so muted he would not have been able to recognize her in a crowd.

She simply stared at him as if he was a complete stranger. Power and energy crackled in the air, invisible to living eyes, but obvious to Kas.

"Stephenie," he said, using his powers to not only vibrate the air into sound, but to bring forth illumination which she would be able to see. "It is me, Kas." His form swallowed, as she made no reaction. "Please, Stephenie, come back to me." He said, slowly backing away. He did not so much fear his own death. He had lived too long by his own reckoning and often thought about ending the torment he felt in the half existence he had. However, he did not want Stephenie to destroy him and then later, if she returned to her senses, realize what she had done. He knew that would destroy her and he loved her too much to allow her to suffer that guilt.

His movement provoked a response from her. Kas sensed a surge of energy coming into her, and then it faded away into the ground. She blinked once and then as a person wakes from a dream, she slowly turned her head to see the devastation left in her wake. She examined it as a person seeing it for the first time, but already knowing exactly what was there.

"Kas," she said softly, her mind still muted, but more recognizable.

Stephenie he said mentally, almost weeping with relief.

She flinched and shook her head, managing to keep him completely out of her thoughts. "No. Stay out of my head for now. I don't want to hurt you."

"What happened?"

She looked around again as she used her powers to fling blood and gore from her skin, though it was soaked into her clothing. Bending down, she picked up her weapons, sheathing them as she walked over to her horse. Kas' form frowned; despite the carnage, screaming, and energy charged air, all of the horses had remained calm and were still standing quietly. Kas wished he was as sensitive as Stephenie to the energy currents and threads, for he was certain she was somehow emitting a calming influence on them.

"I know where they have Will. Hopefully he's still alive. Their plan was to start cutting off pieces in the morning if I had not shown up." With a quick hop, she flew herself into the saddle and immediately squeezed the chestnut into a canter.

Kas paused long enough to notice the horses tied to the wall and hitched to the carriage grow agitated as Stephenie rode south toward Antar. Suppressing his illumination, he quickly followed.

Chapter 5

Stephenie sighed with relief when Kas came back and told her Henton had already secured Will and that they were safe. *I don't know what I would do if something had happened to Will because of me. My mother has to be dealt with.*

Stephenie, how are you fairing?

She slowed her horse to a fast walk as they moved onto a more crowded street. Kas had asked or hinted at wanting to know what had happened too many times to count. She had only just let him back into her head in the most limited sense so that they could communicate without words; the idea of anything more terrified her.

"Stephenie, please."

She flinched at the pain in Kas' voice. For him to generate an audible sound in the middle of the city, albeit, well after dark, weakened her.

Kas, I don't know what happened. Gernvir had beaten me. He had won. He was going to destroy you and make me watch. He had taken over my mind and I couldn't do anything to stop him. She looked in his direction, though he was not visible. She could not bring herself to admit just how violated she felt; the man had delved into her most personal thoughts and read them with impunity. *Then suddenly...I don't know...I snapped...or something did. I really wasn't in control. It was like a dream. I just knew I would not be controlled and I...I...the only thought in my head was to destroy. I almost killed you. I could have killed anyone who was close at that point and wouldn't have stopped.*

She felt him try to touch her mind gently, to try and reassure her, but she resisted allowing Kas any further into her head. She had the power to kill in an instant and that thought left her trembling.

Stephenie, you stopped when you realized it was me. Additionally, you kept all the horses from panicking. There was still something of your kind heart in you. Lashing out at those trying to harm you is not something to be ashamed of.

Seeing the castle in the distance, she picked up speed again, pushing the tired chestnut into a fast trot and gave the horse a pat on the neck in appreciation of the effort. She had tried, but was unsuccessful in relieving her anxiousness to get to Henton, Douglas, and Will.

As she approached the gatehouse, the guards called on her to stop and dismount. A group of soldiers came out with their crossbows level until they recognized her. "Your Highness," the sergeant said, bowing deeply. "His Majesty instructed that you are to go to him immediately."

Stephenie felt her back straighten. "My horse needs attention... and I need to check on Will," she added.

"Your Highness, I have been told High Priest William is recovering in the temple of Felis." The sergeant's cheek quivered slightly. "His Majesty was very clear; you are to see him immediately."

Sparked as much by the unnecessary fear these men had of her as her own desire to avoid the confrontation with Joshua, she started to walk forward, leading her horse. "Once I have taken care of this horse, I will go see my brother." To Kas she added, *please find Henton and let him know I am back and make sure Will is okay.* The soldiers parted for her and while the sergeant seemed to want to protest further, he quietly instructed someone to inform Joshua she was back.

Stephenie entered her brother's study and dropped into the chair in front of his desk without a word. It was past the middle of the night and she was physically tired as well as drained from the emotional toll of the evening.

"Is that how you greet your king?"

Stephenie looked up to meet Joshua's eyes; her own were already narrowed. "If it escaped your notice, I've had a rough evening. I'm still covered in blood and could use a chance to refresh myself. However, your gate guards demanded I come see you straight away, so here I am."

"I've got holy warriors running all over the countryside looking for you. Now I've got more men out looking for them to tell them to come back here." He shook his head. "How dare you risk yourself for William? He's your bloody bodyguard! It's his job to die for you, not the other way around! I've told you before about getting attached to these people. Obviously, you can't be trusted to be rational. I'm having them all replaced immediately!"

Stephenie sat up in her chair. Cold anger filled her limbs. "You will do no such thing."

Joshua leaned back and shook his head. "You've changed, Steph. And not for the better."

Stephenie bit her lip, trying to hold back her anger, but finally gave in. "I've changed?" She shook her head. "I've not changed. I'm the same as I ever was."

"Disobeying my orders? Talking back? Being thoughtless and senseless?"

"I've never obeyed orders, yours or fathers. You just never gave me any before and you didn't give me any tonight. I acted as I knew I needed to act." Her jaw tightened, "Perhaps, when we were younger, I was afraid to speak up; afraid someone would find out what I was and burn me. Now I'm no longer afraid my secret will get out. So perhaps I will speak my mind more, but what I say now is always what I thought before."

Joshua paused a moment. "You are the last family I have. I will not have you risking your life for a common soldier."

Stephenie rose to her feet. "There are four people that when I walk into a room do not flinch when they suddenly realize I am there. I can sense the fear people have of me and that is something that has changed." She shook her head, "I will not allow anything to happen to the four people who are actually happy to see me. They are my friends and not your soldiers. They've all been released from your service."

"I am afraid for you, not of you," he said slowly.

Stephenie wanted to shake her head, she had sensed his fear before and it was there now. However, she remained still, trying to hold back the tears forming in her eyes. Never before had she admitted to anyone just how isolated she felt. Growing up, she could truly confide in no one, now that she had people she trusted with all aspects of her life, she was not going to lose them. More calmly she continued, "Know this, Josh, I will do anything and everything for those I care about. I will risk my life every damn time, and if you try to stop me, you will regret it."

Joshua leaned back in his chair.

Stephenie shook her head and then continued. "I don't want your crown or any other one. I will never be a queen, and that doesn't bother me. It actually makes me happy to know that, because I know I would be a terrible queen. I don't have what it takes to rule." She kept his gaze, "I will always support you and do what I can to protect Cothel and her people. However, I will not now, nor will I ever, take orders from you, or anyone else. I will not be told what to do and how to do it." She forced her expression to soften again. "I love you, Josh. I always have and to know what you and father risked all those years to protect me is beyond words for me to describe. But I just cannot be owned."

Joshua shook his head and looked about the room. "I don't know what to say or how to react."

Stephenie nodded her head. "You should be aware that I am leaving."

"What? Because of this? No. We need you here."

"I know where Islet is."

Joshua's jaw dropped, "How?"

Stephenie sat back down, sensing Joshua had calmed down and she no longer had the strength to be angry. "One of the men mother sent to abduct me was a Senzar warlock." She bit her lip at the use of the term she despised. *We are all mages; we should not have to hide.* "He had been with Islet, questioning her about me, hoping to find a weakness to exploit. She's being held in a small town on the Endless Sea. There is a castle there and a small Senzar force. I'm going to go get her and bring her home."

Joshua was leaning forward over his desk. "How many people are there? You talked me into releasing the men you took to Kynto with you; I can order them back or replace them with others...."

Stephenie noted how fast Joshua's mood had changed, his anger at her gone with the idea of bringing Islet home. She had always felt his mood could change too quickly, but now with the pressure of the crown upon him, he could become even more volatile at times. Focusing on the issue at hand, she shook her head. "No, this has to be a small group. I'll take Kas, Henton, and Douglas, if they choose to come. Will needs to stay here, he's the High Priest of Catheri and he has to continue in that role. However, I want Lady Rebecca to assign some holy warriors to help protect him until we find some people Catheri can turn into priests." She hated to perpetuate the lies with Joshua, but he truly and deeply believed in Felis and the evil of Elrin.

"I don't like this. I don't want to risk you for the hope of bringing back Islet."

"Josh. I killed ten holy warriors and a Senzar warlock tonight. Kas took out at least five other soldiers. I think I can protect myself." Though the words came out of her mouth, she felt a chill roll down her spine. She knew she had been beaten, not physically, but mentally and she was afraid of how she survived. "I just need four horses. I've got plenty of funds left over."

Joshua nodded his head. "When will you leave?"

Stephenie had been dreading that question. "Tomorrow if I could, but most likely it will be a few days. I probably need to make another public appearance to make sure people don't start thinking someone killed me."

"Before my birthday? Before the wedding? I suppose I could put it off, until you get back, but—"

"No, you need an heir now more than ever. Marry Rebecca. She's not a bad match; her family has money and influence in the southwest. Plus, you like each other and she has a fair amount of power to protect the both of you. Mother will likely send others and they might strike at you to get to me."

"I'll send Uncle a letter explaining that if something like this happens again, there will be consequences. Perhaps he can put her in-line."

"I'd like to stay longer, but I can't wait for the wedding, it's going to take a long time to get to where I need to go. Moving it up would be too disruptive. I'll make sure everyone knows I support the match and quietly disappear. I'll hint that perhaps I am going to visit mother. That might cause her to keep her wolves close instead of sending them after you or Will."

"Where is Islet being held?"

"I don't know for sure, I just have a name, Vinerxan and I think it is in Ulet."

"Ulet? But they stayed out of the war. You said there is a Senzar force in a castle."

Stephenie shrugged. "I don't have answers right now, but perhaps I will when I bring Islet back. I'll give you everything I learn before I leave."

"Unlike the letter you burned this evening?"

She rose to her feet, not wanting to rehash the discussion. "I need to get some rest; I'll talk with you in the morning."

Stephenie woke late in the morning. Her sleep had been troubled. The fact everyone felt she would attack them if they did anything to displease her would not leave her. She had never believed herself to be the monster that they feared. However, that Senzar mage had revealed something very violent deep in her subconscious. *What if something else sparked that rage and savagery? What if I hurt someone I love?* She forced herself from her bed and quickly dressed. She was not in the mood to let herself think about it anymore; she had done that through the night and it had only made things worse.

She moved down the stairs and greeted Henton and Kas as they came out of his room on the second floor of the tower. "Where's Will?" she asked.

"Will stayed in the priest's domicile. They wanted to monitor him overnight," Henton offered verbally as Kas conveyed the same thing to her mentally.

"How are the two of you?" she asked, sensing a little hesitation in Henton's movements.

"My left ankle still hurts a bit, but it's not bad."

What about you Stephenie? Kas asked over Henton. *How are you doing today?*

Better, I just need time, she thought back to Kas before replying to Henton. "Then take it easy, I'll go check on Will." Before either could protest or offer to come with her, she continued down the stairs and out into her great hall. Sensing that neither of them were following her, she allowed herself to relax slightly as she went outside and walked around the side of her tower and the barracks to what had at one time been the outer wall of the castle. The large and imposing temple of Felis was before her. Only earlier this year, she had been fearful of the building and those inside, certain that someone would look at her and know she was tainted with evil. Of course, learning the truth about herself had removed the self-loathing, but few people shared or believed the truth. Now she simply relied upon the proclamation of the late high priest, and the support of the new one, *for what it's worth.*

The air inside the stone temple was cool, but pleasant. She passed through the main temple and into the domiciles on the western side of the building. Most of the rooms were empty, either due to the time of day or the fact that Felis' ranks of priests and holy warriors were still limited as a result of the war with the Senzar.

Reaching out with her senses she easily found Will. Her familiarity with her friends had extended her range of sensitivity to them. She quickly navigated the halls, homing in on his location. Reaching the door, she knew Will was not alone and so she knocked. Based on the movements of those inside, she suspected the priest—*priestess*, she amended, had already warned Will of her approach.

"Steph," Will said as she cracked open the door; a blanket wrapped around his shoulders.

Stephenie immediately understood what had taken place at some earlier point in the morning; the odor of the activity was just discernible to her. "I'm sorry Will, I didn't mean to interrupt." She started to turn away, but he slipped out into the hall.

"Hey, no interruption. Sara was just making sure my injuries were all healed up."

Stephenie pushed down the irritation she was feeling. *He's not mine, I should be happy he's had a chance to enjoy himself.* She took a deep breath, but the feelings of possessiveness had not left her completely. *He's not mine!* She repeated, knowing that she did not even desire him in that sense.

"Will, you are free to enjoy the company of anyone you want, you don't have to make excuses." She knew her tone was a little bitter, despite trying to sound calm and at ease. "I just came by to make sure you were well." This time her voice was a little softer with less hint of betrayal. "I also wanted to let you know that I need to leave for a while."

Will stood a little straighter. "We're just getting things going. How long will we be gone? It could set things back a bit." He glanced over her shoulder, "I suppose I could have—"

Stephenie shook her head. "No. I will be leaving, probably for several months. You'll need to stay and keep working on what you're doing."

Stephenie looked beyond Will at the young woman who was standing in the doorway. She was dressed in a robe and her hair quickly brushed to take care of the wildest parts. Catching Stephenie's eye, she curtsied, "Your Highness."

"Steph, I think you talked briefly with Lady Sara last night."

She glanced at Will, who had stepped to the side, and then back to the priestess. Stephenie nodded her head but could not think of something polite to say to the woman who had shared Will's bed. *He's not mine!*

"Ma'am, may I make a request of you?"

Stephenie nodded her head, "Yes, what is it?"

The woman swallowed and shifted slightly. "I would like to become a priestess of Catheri."

Stephenie felt the strength drain from her limbs. "Lady Sara, you'll need to take that up with your superiors. I am not sure they would approve."

Sara stepped forward quickly and continued before Will could interject. "I understand what it means. I...I ended up learning things

I had not intended. Will was hurt severely and needed deep healing and then afterward, when we...well, I had not intended to learn those things, but...."

Stephenie glanced once more to Will, whose face was expressionless, but she could sense his tension clearly. Turning back to the priestess, she quickly noted there was no one close enough to overhear, but she felt too exposed to discuss this in Felis' temple. "Both of you get dressed and come to my rooms."

Before Will and Sara reached Stephenie's tower, she had filled in Kas and Henton about what had been said and neither of them were happy.

"Is it that easy to read someone's mind?" Henton asked in the Old Tongue.

Kas nodded his head. "It can be. It all depends upon the people involved. Some people are able to isolate their thoughts more. Generally, a more disciplined person is harder to read, but there are layers. There are thought projections, surface thoughts, deeper thoughts, and then there are memories and layers of memories." Kas took a seat in Stephenie's desk chair. "There are always risks when going too deep. One's own mind cannot easily distinguish its thoughts from that of another person. Deep mental links can result in a confused jumble of memories where it takes work to sort out what belongs to each person." He picked up a feather pen and flicked the end. "If the person trying to read the other one's mind can cause the person being read to bring something into their active thoughts, then it is easier to get to." He turned back to Henton, "like putting the goods out on a counter to be observed will potentially trigger memories of those goods"

Henton shook his head. "I've always known that in the process of healing, the priests sometimes learn things...and that priests can force their way into people's minds if they need to."

"Sex is an even better way to break down the mental barriers."

Stephenie shook her head. "We'll just have to hope that the others who know so much about us, including about you, Kas, don't start hanging out with mages." She rose to her feet as Kas disappeared from sight. "They are coming up the stairs."

Stephenie had left the door open and it was not long before Will and Lady Sara knocked on the open door. "Can we come in?"

Stephenie nodded to Will and then waited until they were both in the room. "So, Sara, you want to be a priestess of Catheri?"

Lady Sara curtsied and then looked up. Stephenie could feel her fear and even a little from Will. "Yes, Ma'am. I did not intend to learn what I did from William, but once I did, I realized immediately that I wanted to help your cause. I know what you've shared with Will is true."

Stephenie narrowed her eyes, but other than a sense of fear, she could get nothing from the Priestess. Taking a gamble, she continued, "You knew you were a witch before you became a priestess."

Sara bowed her head. "Yes, Ma'am. At the time, I feared what was happening, so I applied to be a priestess when I was thirteen. I remember being relieved to discover that perhaps I was not a witch and was happy to be one of Felis' chosen. But I have always had some doubts and when I discovered what Will had seen and what you had explained to them, I knew it was the truth." Sara swallowed, "I will even submit myself to have you read my mind to know the truth of it."

Stephenie felt her shoulders tense. She dared not risk connecting with someone else's mind. She would not risk her friends and not risk someone probing her own thoughts. Shaking her head, Stephenie stepped closer to the pair, both of whom were older than her by a couple of years. She looked into Sara's blue eyes, hoping to know how she should respond. After some consideration, she said, "I do not try to keep things secret to give myself power or advantage. I keep things secret so that in time we can change people's opinions and let them realize people with powers are not innately evil. The country has suffered enough and while I do not seek to be in a position of leadership, too many would assume I do, and they would try to overthrow my brother."

Stephenie looked to Henton, but he was even more reserved than normal. Turning back to the two of them, she continued, "Will needs additional people to help support him, so I have no objection.

However, it is not me you need to ask. You need to talk with your High Priest and see what Rebecca has to say. Also, you would need to learn to use your innate powers and not the augmentation device."

"Of course, Your Highness." Sara hesitated, but then gave in to her curiosity, "Are you implying that Lady Rebecca knows the truth as well?"

Stephenie pursed her lips. She did not want to reveal too much, but she had no idea how much information Will had unwittingly disclosed. Lying with regard to something that, if not already known, but would eventually become obvious, would not garner any trust. "She is aware, but that is all. You are not to discuss this with anyone else. Not without talking to myself, Will, or Henton."

Sara bowed her head. "Of course, Ma'am."

Stephenie nodded her head and moved closer to Henton. "Then please go see your High Priest. Will, I need to speak with you further."

Sara curtsied again and then quickly left. Once Stephenie knew Sara was out of range, she turned back to Will. "I guess this answers the question of what you actually believe."

"Hey, I never said I didn't believe what you were saying. You just assumed the worst of me."

Henton shook his head. "Which is exactly what you intended. Get the smug look off your face and answer us this, you going to stay true to that girl?"

Will's surprised expression did not fool Stephenie. "Henton's right, her body language says she's attached herself to you. You hurt her and you might cause her to reveal all the secrets she's learned."

"Hey, I just met her last night and you can hardly say I was in any shape to make good decisions. They had knocked me senseless and given me who knows what. I—"

"Will," Henton growled, "I don't care what led up to it, but you'll have to take care with how you treat her. We know nothing about her and she now knows some of our deepest secrets. If it gets out that you've been lying to everyone, it won't only be our necks, but your neck as well."

Will straightened. "Don't lash me to the keel, Sarge. I realize what's at stake and the only time I've pissed off a girl is when I had to ship out the next day. So, give me some credit, I'll handle it. Okay?"

Stephenie held up her hand. "Yes, Will, I think you can handle it. It was just a surprise to find out how easy it was for the truth to get out. We just want to be careful. And we won't be here to help you if things get bad. So I worry."

Will softened his expression, instantly changing his demeanor to a kind and sensitive one. "Yes, tell me more about what's going on to cause you to leave suddenly. We've just started building Catheri's church and the timing is terrible."

"The men who tried to capture me were primarily priests loyal to my mother. However, she included a Senzar mage in their number. In exchange for his help, he would get to read my mind and learn how it was that I was able to defeat them and bring down that mountain peak. I got lucky and was able to escape their trap, but in the process, I learned that the Senzar mage had been to the place where they are keeping Islet."

"Your next older sister," Henton commented.

"Yes, she's the Queen of Ipith."

"Only the kingdom's fallen, I've heard." Will added just a trace of condolence to his tone. "The Senzar set up a bunch of puppets to run the country for them when things started to get rough."

Stephenie nodded her head. "Well, they are holding her, and a number of other key prisoners, in a small port town that has a keep."

"How many guards and how many Senzar?" Henton asked from where he stood, but Stephenie only shrugged.

"I couldn't tell. I just got bits and pieces of his memory when we fought. I have a name, Vinerxan, which I think is in the country of Ulet."

"Never heard of Ulet," Will quipped. "You sure the information is accurate? What if it's just a ploy to get you out of the country?"

Kas appeared next to Stephenie. "When a mind is read quickly, thoughts...are often incomplete," he said with a little hesitation in Cothish.

Stephenie smiled at him, *you're getting better*. To the others, she said, "It's a huge peninsula, about twice the size of Ipith and it juts out into the Endless Sea. It's pretty much directly west of Midland and Epish. I think we are looking at six or seven hundred miles from here to there." Will raised his eyebrows, but Henton kept himself perfectly still, which Stephenie had learned was a sign of his uneasiness. "I know, the year is getting late and we'll be deep in snow before we get there. Plus the maps I was able to quickly glance through showed no direct route and mountains along the more southerly route."

Will spoke up, perhaps due to a subtle cue from Henton. "And Epish has had a lot of trouble since the war; infighting in the royal family because half of them wanted to negotiate with the Senzar and those closer to Midland and us wanted to fight."

"It'll just be Kas, Henton, Douglas, and myself going. Hopefully, we'll look intimidating enough to be left alone, but not too threatening to draw attention. I'll get some horses from my brother for this trip."

"Douglas and I don't ride," Henton said too quickly.

Stephenie's grin deepened, "you will before we get there."

Chapter 6

Although Stephenie wanted to leave as quickly as possible, she could not rush off as she had done on her last two trips. Too many people were aware that Will had been taken prisoner and used as a hostage against her. To help reassure people that nothing serious had happened to either of them, they scheduled numerous public appearances over the next several days. By the end of the first day, Stephenie was almost ready to slip away into the night anyway.

The public appearances where tiring and all the emotional feedback she picked up from the crowds left her with throbbing headaches. However, that was nothing compared to the frustration she was feeling with her brother. This time, he was insisting on scheduling and planning her trip for her, all with the pretense of wanting to make sure she would be safe. Her last trip north to Kynto had been so quick he did not have the chance to interfere.

Wanting some time alone, she left Kas in her room, sneaked past Henton and Douglas, who were in their room, and headed to the stables. She had no intention of going for a ride, that would cause too much trouble, but one of her favorite places had always been the stables. When the war had been raging, there were scarcely any horses present in the castle. Now that things were mostly settled in Cothel, the stalls were filled once again.

As she approached, she made note of the fact that there were several people present, but avoided them and headed toward the stall of the chestnut she had ridden to face her mother's holy warriors. She stopped a couple dozen feet from the stall when she realized the gelding was not there. Opening herself, she cast about for the horse. Sensing him in the cross ties at the end of the barn; she headed quickly in that direction. When she was close enough to see him, a growl escaped her lips; *someone's going to ride him!*

The soldier who was standing next to the chestnut jumped and then quickly bowed when he realized who she was. "Your Highness."

Seeing his hands tremble, Stephenie paused. Knowing how she must appear, she forced down the incredible sense of possessiveness that filled her. *What is wrong with me?* She felt one of the stable boys move further into the tack room behind her, obviously hoping to avoid her notice.

Knowing the impulse of ownership was wrong, she forced kindness to her face. "I'm sorry; I didn't mean to startle you. I...I was planning on grooming that horse."

The soldier responded quickly, "Of course, Ma'am, I had not realized you were going to ride. Please, allow me to finish getting Argat ready for you."

Stephenie reached out and put her hand on the man's arm. "I wasn't planning on riding, just grooming him. He took care of me the other night and I wanted to return the favor.

The soldier seemed to ease as he connected her meaning. "Of course, Ma'am. I can ready another horse. That is not a problem."

"Thank you," she said, knowing any offer to help him would simply make him more uncomfortable. "Again, I didn't mean to startle you. I was just worried something had happened to him." She turned to the horse and his big brown eyes. He was watching her with both ears forward. "Argat, was that his name?"

"Yes, Ma'am. He's a bit wild sometimes. A bit too smart for our good, if you know what I mean."

She smiled, already having moved closer to rub Argat's neck. "That I do. Thank you again..."

"Corporal Tilling," he finished.

"Thank you, Corporal Tilling."

She allowed the Corporal to bow away and go off in search of another horse. She continued to rub Argat's neck with her hand for a moment while meeting his inquisitive eyes with her own. She pulled a treat out of her pouch and slipped it into his ready mouth. The sense of possessiveness had diminished, but was not completely gone. She wanted to call the Corporal back and have him take Argat to prove she could be trusted and reasonable. However, she could not actually bring herself to vocalize the request. *There's something wrong with me,* she admitted again.

Swallowing down her discomfort, she went to the tack room and gathered brushes and a hoof pick. She ignored the stable boy who had moved to a smaller back room. *I'll work this out,* she told herself, hoping that the act of grooming Argat would help clear her head.

The next two days passed quickly, though not any more pleasantly. The mornings and afternoons were filled with public appearances and many questions. She and Will avoided the specifics of what happened, saying only it had been a failed attempt at revenge by her mother.

In the evenings, Douglas and Henton quietly gathered perishable supplies, but most of the things they needed for the trip Stephenie had procured shortly after they had returned from Kynto with the gold they had stolen back from her uncle. She had armor and clothing for everyone, all without colors or insignia. The last time they left with minimal protection to avoid any ties back to the Marn family or Cothel. Hating the risk they had taken, she had prepared for any future travels, making sure that they would always be better equipped.

For her, the evenings continued to bring meetings with her brother and Lady Rebecca. Joshua continued to push his plans for her trip, which involved heading west across Cothel, Selith, and then to use a northern trade route across Tenip. He wanted her to finish the trip using a ship to reach the port of Vinerxan in Ulet. While the route might be easier and avoided the mountain range that divided Tenip from Ulet, Stephenie silently made her own plans for the journey, which would take her further north, avoiding the countries of Selith and Tenip altogether.

After her taxing meetings, regardless of the time, she went to the stables to groom Argat. It allowed her to relax and put aside the frustration of the day, even though she knew it was reinforcing her sense of ownership over the horse. It had become a forgone conclusion she would take Argat on their journey; there was no point in trying to avoid that decision. She told herself it was okay because she had not had a fit of possessiveness with anything else lately.

"And you like me, don't you, Argat?"

The gelding twitched his ears, but his head dipped a little lower as she continued to brush his neck. She could see his eyes starting to sag and knew he was ready to snooze, but she did not really want to put him back in his stall. However, she knew her time was up when she felt the approach of Lady Rebecca and another person, *Lady Sara*, she thought with a grimace. The smell of her on Will came back, threatening to spark a reaction. Keeping herself in check, Stephenie glanced to Argat and silently asked, *What do they want?*

The gelding did not bother to reply.

"Your Highness," Lady Rebecca said with a bow of her head.

Stephenie knew that one day Rebecca would technically outrank her, *but that day has not yet come.* "Your Excellency, what may I do for the two of you?"

Rebecca shook her brown hair from her face. "If you recall, for the last few months we were supposed to work on theological issues together. Neither of us has had much time to do so. Now that you are leaving—"

"Tomorrow," Stephenie interrupted with a little too much pleasure. "I'm leaving first thing tomorrow."

"Which is why we should at least discuss some minimal tasks." Rebecca glanced at Sara, "And since Lady Sara will be joining Will as a priestess of Catheri, I thought it prudent that she should receive some guidance as well."

Stephenie knew Rebecca was right, but she still did not feel up to the task. With a sigh, she nodded her head. "I'll put Argat away and we can go into the storage rooms under my keep. They'll be private enough."

A short while later, Stephenie led Rebecca and Sara down the spiral stairs of her tower and into the first level of underground storerooms. Anything of value had long been removed, leaving only the aged cedar flooring that was raised a hands width over the stone below it. Kas had conveyed the fact that Henton and Douglas were finishing the packing when she had entered the tower. Then he retreated back to her rooms to avoid the potential for Lady Sara to sense him. As of yet, they were not certain if she had gained information about Kas from Will. It was assumed she would eventually learn of the ghost, but they had no intention of hurrying the knowledge if she did not already know.

Standing in the middle of one of the dimly lit rooms, Stephenie turned to face the two holy warriors. Lady Sara's presence still irritated her, but she did like the idea of Will having magic at his disposal. She only hoped the convert could be trusted.

"Please forgive me, Your Highness, but did I do something to anger you?"

Stephenie looked at the timid expression on Sara's face and forced herself to soften her own expression. "No. And call me Stephenie."

The priestess's subtle stiffening said she disagreed. "I just get the feeling you are angry with me."

Stephenie's shoulders sunk; she would need to win the woman's trust, as much as Will, if she was to ensure secrecy. "It's nothing you did. At least not intentionally." She knew where most of her frustration was coming from: Joshua. However, she also knew that was not entirely true, because she was still having trouble pushing down all the jealousy she felt. "Look, we didn't get off on the right foot. But it's not you and I really appreciate everything you did for Will and Henton and the others." Taking a deep breath, she continued. "Let's discuss some quick basics, and then I need to finish packing."

Using her powers, she turned up the wick on the lamp that was on the other side of the room. "First, remove those augmentation devices. You won't learn anything if you insist upon using them. A long time ago, everyone knew they were a crutch for the lazy. The selective killing of anyone with hints of significant power has weakened the countries around Tet and is one of the reason the Senzar were able to so easily march through our lands."

"But Your...Stephenie," Lady Sara corrected, "if we lack any real power, taking away the holy symbol will make us weaker."

Stephenie reached out with her powers and pushed the medallions further from where Rebecca and Sara had placed them on the wooden floor. She applied the force on the chains their medallions were hung from; using magic against the devices themselves caused them to react very negatively. After she was certain the two priestesses could not use the devices, she opened herself further and examined the fields the two woman were generating. Rebecca was absorbing more energy than Sara, pulling it into her body, though the flow was not that great. She suspected both of them were more than a little intimidated and fearful without their 'holy symbol' to rely upon and that could be a factor.

"I won't hurt you, but you will need to learn to use your own innate abilities. There is energy all around us, inside of us, and within every object. To use the power, you can draw it into your body and generate a field driving the power through you that influences the world or you can learn to draw small amounts of energy through your body and generate separate fields that in turn influence the energy in the environment to do what you want." She pursed her lips and was glad Kas was not present to call her out as a hypocrite on what she was teaching. "I will tell you that someone skilled enough to do the second can easily defeat someone who relies solely on the first option." She stepped backward slightly, feeling more than hearing the movement of the boards under her feet. "However, learning to use subtle manipulation of the energy is hard to do. It takes years of practice and study. Therefore, you will more than likely start by pulling all the energy through your body. It is easier to learn to do. Just be aware that drawing energy through your body puts a toll on yourself. Pulling or absorbing too much energy could injure you, kill you, or even worse, burn out the parts of your mind that allow you to control the energy, thereby leaving you without any ability at all."

Rebecca nodded her head. "And you have learned the subtle control?"

Stephenie shook her head, deciding not to lie. "When I have time to approach a problem, I try to draw as little energy through myself as possible. But, too often, I rely upon my body's ability to handle the raw power." She shifted closer to them. "I am not a good example. From what I can tell, I can handle far more energy than most and that gives me an advantage, but until I get better, I am always at risk of someone more skilled being able to overcome me." She would not mention just how many times that had already occurred. Kas reminded her enough and she doubted even he realized just how beaten she had been in some of those events. "So, the important item to remember is that even if you lack a tolerance for drawing large amounts of energy through your body, if you learn to be more efficient, you can do as much or more than someone who is lazy."

"And when will you show us how to do something?" Rebecca asked, subtly chastising Stephenie for avoiding her over the last couple of months.

Moving to the floor, Stephenie sat cross-legged before them and indicated they should sit as well. She was not sure how best to teach them to use their own magic; she saw the actual fields and could sense things that Kas had never expected her to be able to. In fact, her learning was primarily from watching the effects from what others did and simply worked to reproduce them. The mental state simply came naturally to her. *It will be like teaching a blind person to read a language I don't know*, she mused while at the same time, reassuring herself that it was possible, because others had learned to use magic before her.

When they were seated, Stephenie continued. "First, close your eyes and calm your minds. You should already be able to sense that I am here in the room. Most mages can sense movement or living beings near them. However, I now want you to try to feel the energy around us. Try to find a source of power." Borrowing from the technique Kas had initially tried to show her, she created two separate fields in the stone floor on either side of herself. In one, she drained away the energy, blocking the natural flow and forming an area of low energy potential. In the other, she pushed in more energy, holding it in place with her will. Mentally, she could see the differences clearly. Physically, she could sense a cold chill forming above the area of low potential and the warmth from the high potential. "Now, can you feel where the best source of power is in the room?" She watched both of them hesitating and resolved that this would be a very late night.

Despite being up into the early morning, Stephenie was awake before the sun brightened the top of her tower. She spent a little more time gathering her gear and when she felt she had let the others sleep enough, she went down and woke Henton, Douglas, and Will. Including Kas, the five of them went to the stables carrying their gear. With a grunt born more from lack of sleep than effort, she dumped her gear near the stable doors, startling one of the older stable hands.

"Your Highness," the man said, bowing deeply when he realized it was her. "How can I serve you?"

Stephenie ignored the frightened twitch of his shoulder. "I'm going to take Argat and three other horses...calm horses," she amended, "on a long trip."

"Yes, Ma'am," he said, "I can get the chestnut and three others."

Stephenie, already moving toward Argat's stall, shook her head. "Thank you, but I'll get Argat myself. If you would be kind enough to help Henton and Douglas find some mounts, I would appreciate it. The third horse, we'll want saddled, but that one will need to carry some extra supplies and grain."

The stable hand bowed again and led Henton, Douglas, and Will in the other direction down the aisle while Stephenie and the invisible Kas approached Argat's stall. "Hey Big Guy," she said as the horse eyed her hands for treats. "You ready to go on a long journey?"

Argat looked at her with his large brown eyes, but then nosed his way toward her pouches only to have her push him away. To which, he simply dropped his head further and raised his eyebrows as if he had lost a favorite toy.

"That's not an answer."

Perhaps, in his own way it is. A trip, not so much to be desired, but carrots or treats would be most welcome.

Stephenie mentally acknowledged Kas as she patted Argat's neck and opened the lower door of his stall. He inhaled, blowing himself up and expanding his chest and barrel before snorting once into her shirt, after which, he resumed his hunt for treats. Not to be deterred, Stephenie slid on his halter and led him out of his stall. "Don't worry; I'll give you plenty of treats along the way."

As she gathered a saddle and pad, she noted the older stable hand and two of the younger boys had managed to quickly get Henton and Douglas a pair of horses, both of which the stable boys were saddling. Stephenie would have preferred Henton and Douglas do that themselves, *but they will have plenty of time to establish relationships with their new horses*, she thought with a grin.

As she gathered a bridle and saddlebags for Argat, Stephenie sensed her brother, Rebecca, and a number of soldiers approaching the stables. Joshua swept into the main isle immediately behind a pair of leading guards. "Steph, you still here?"

Trying not to get annoyed with answering questions that were obvious, she emerged from the cross ties. "Of course, but we'll be on the road shortly." She watched him nod his head stiffly. None of the meetings over the last few days had removed the undercurrent of frustration they both felt with each other. "We'll be fine," she said to fill the silence, "and it's best that people know I am leaving town for a while. Perhaps mother will leave everyone in Antar alone while I am gone."

"Yes, I know. I just worry about you." He reached out and pulled her close so he could hug her. After a moment, Stephenie stepped back.

"Thank you. I'll miss you as well, but we'll be back."

Joshua reached backward toward one of his guards, who promptly handed over a messenger's satchel. "I have a series of letters for you to deliver on your trip. If you can deliver to Baron Turning first, then the others, that would be great."

Stephenie nodded her head. While this was mostly a cover story he had insisted upon with the intention that someone would leak the news, they had both agreed that visiting Arnold Turning on her way was prudent. To pass through his lands without visiting such a strong supporter would be considered an insult and that would not be acceptable. However, after that visit, she would continue northwest and head out of Cothel instead of following Joshua's proposed route west into Selith. Whatever Joshua had given her, she would arrange for Arnold to deliver as needed.

Rebecca smiled at her. "And before you ask, I will make sure Will is kept safe and gets the support he needs."

Will grinned, "Thank you, Your Excellence."

Rebecca grinned back, "You are most welcome, Your Excellence."

Stephenie rolled her eyes and then regretted it immediately; Joshua's scowl could become trouble for Will. While she felt the exchange was silly, her brother obviously saw it as more evidence of her 'poor choice' in a High Priest. She could only hope Rebecca would continue to protect Will. "Well," she said, slipping the satchel over her shoulder before turning back to Rebecca and Joshua. "I wish the two of you the best for the wedding. I would have stayed, but for the urgent matter that I need to see to before winter sets in."

"Of course. We wish you the best for your journey."

After another quick embrace, Joshua and his escorts departed with Rebecca, leaving the five of them standing with the four horses. The stable boys had silently finished their tasks and left during the exchange.

"Everything okay between the two of you?" Henton asked quietly.

She looked into his concerned eyes and tilted her head as she looked down to kick away a bit of manure laying in the aisle. "He's a good man, but the crown weighs heavy on him." She met Henton's eyes again, "I hope he'll get back to his old self before long." She turned back to Will, not wanting to voice any more acknowledgment of the changes she was seeing in her brother. "I want you to keep out of Josh's way. He's not one to have a sense of humor regarding you."

"Of course, Your Highness, I will endeavor to become the model High Priest and win so much of the love of the people that he would have no choice but to embrace me as honorary brother."

Stephenie shook her head, but could not help smiling. Stepping forward, she embraced Will and gave him a strong enough squeeze that he grunted. "I will miss you. Be good to Sara and let Rebecca help you."

"I will, Mother." Will turned to Henton. "Well, Sir Henton, you watch after Stephenie and Douglas and Kas. I expect to see the lot of you on your return."

Henton clenched his jaw. "Enough with the Sir crap." Sighing, he added, "Keep yourself safe."

Stephenie turned back to her chestnut horse, not wanting to draw out the goodbye any further. "Ready to go, Big Guy?" The horse nosed her for treats again and she tussled his forelock before slipping him a clump of grain held together by a light coating of honey. "Enjoy that, that's the only one of those I have."

After helping Douglas and Henton into their saddles, she tied a long lead from the fourth horse to her saddle and easily mounted Argat. "Take care, Will," she said with a bow of her head before she led everyone from the stables, across the yard to the gatehouse, and out of the castle.

Once they were halfway between the castle and the city of Antar, Stephenie pushed Argat into a fast trot and rose with his motion. It had been many years since she had taken anything more than short rides. The last long trip on horse had been a training exercise with Joshua. She had been fourteen years old at the time. They had traveled for three days into the low lands west of Antar, camped out in war tents, and fired trebuchets at a ruined castle. It had been one of the happiest times Stephenie could remember. Now she was again riding out on horse, but instead of being at the head of an army, she was leading three of her closest friends into unknown danger.

"Steph, slow down!"

Ignoring Henton's tone, she continued to enjoy her ride a little longer, then, having a bit of mercy on her friends, she stopped posting, leaned back, and eased Argat into a walk. She glanced back to see Henton and Douglas nearly bouncing out of their saddles and grinned. "We've got our work cut out for us."

Once Henton was close enough, he glared at her, "I told you, I'm a sailor and don't have use for a horse." Her grin deepened his glare and provoked a continuation of an argument he had not fully dropped, "The horses will just slow us down."

Stephenie patted Argat's neck and smiled, feeling better than she had in days. "I'll teach you to ride as we go. We might get a slow start, but once you have the hang of it, you'll enjoy it."

Chapter 7

By late afternoon, Stephenie was certain she would have been sore if it had not been for her body's subconscious rebuilding and repairing of her muscles. The horses, also not used to working for the whole day, kept looking at her with their large questioning eyes, begging to be allowed to munch on the ragged grasses along the road.

Knowing Henton and Douglas would be suffering from even the slow ride, in the early evening she turned off the main road that mirrored the Uthen River and led them to a small town where they could stop for the night. They found a family who would allow them to sleep in the barn and managed to spend the cold night under the cover of a roof.

The next morning, they left early. Stephenie's offer to heal their legs silenced the protest from Henton and Douglas with regard to their discomfort. They both understood how painful her healing was and neither of them had been willing to undergo the procedure just to cure soreness.

During the day, they kept to the road and Stephenie allowed for an easy pace as she instructed the two sailors in the basics of riding. She wanted them to love it as much as she did, but in order for that to happen, they could not be in constant pain. Showing some mercy on them and the horses, she stopped more frequently than they did on the first day. However, to keep a reasonable pace, she pushed them on until later in the evening, where they again stayed in a small town off the road.

By the fourth day of travel, even her exuberance for riding was beginning to fade some. When they reached the city of Venla in the late morning, Stephenie agreed to stop and allow everyone a chance to rest.

Venla was situated along the Uthen River, and many smaller barges would stop there to transfer goods for later transport further downriver to Antar. Stephenie's memories of Venla were mixed. It had been where Elard Burdger had seen her and in an attempt to secure the throne for his family, he sent men to kill her and those who had been with her at the time. However, it was also the location where Douglas had first started to talk more openly with her. She grinned at her lanky protector, wondering if he recalled their discussion about woman acting as soldiers. She hoped his opinion had changed based on her example, but it was hard to tell.

"Any suggestions of where to stay?" Henton asked, drawing back her attention. "We made a hasty retreat from here the last time."

Stephenie shook her head. On official visits she knew her brother or father had stayed in the stone manor house belonging to the Lord Mayor; that was something she wanted to avoid. Getting more of a concept from Kas than actual words, she sensed him hurry further into the built up section of the town. "Kas will find us a place."

Venla was not large, though several hundred people did make the city a permanent home. By the time they had traveled a third of the way along the main street, Kas had returned and directed them to an inn that also had stalls to stable their horses. The building was in decent shape, but the facade had suffered some neglect in recent years. The interior was clean, but not warm, so after the horses were tended to, the four of them went about town replenishing their supplies. When the sun started to fade into the last quarter of the day, they went into a small public house on the other side of the old cobblestone street from their inn.

"We're not really making any better time than if we were walking," Henton remarked as they waited for the barmaid to bring the food they had ordered.

"We will, once the two of you are used to riding. But it will be even more important when the number of people in our group grows." Her memories of Islet were conflicted; while Islet had not normally been mean when on her own, too often she sided with Regina and her mother. "Your aversion to riding will pale in comparison to the next person's ability to hike any distance at all, let alone hike with gear."

Stephenie glanced in the direction of the barmaid, who was returning with three bowls of stew balanced on one arm and three mugs of warmed cider in her other hand. She noted the barmaid had tidied her hair and reddened her cheeks.

"Here you go, my valiant soldiers," she said, gracefully sliding Henton's bowl of stew from where it sat on her arm to stop directly in front of him. She placed Douglas' in front of him and halfheartedly slid Stephenie's across the table. "Is there anything else I can provide?"

Stephenie's eyes narrowed. The woman's intentions might be visually subtle, but her mental state was broadcasting a strong desire. Struggling to push down her irritation, Stephenie started to quickly eat the stew. The first bites were pleasantly hot and she almost forgot the barmaid until the woman slid her hand over Henton's arm as she turned away from their table.

Douglas chucked, "Sir Henton has himself an admirer."

"Enough, Douglas," he said in a low growl. Turning back to Stephenie, he changed the subject. "We'll have to watch our finances. The stabling of the horses and the extra supplies are definitely going to add up."

"I've got about three times as much on me as I gave each of you. We'll be okay." She set her spoon down and took a deep breath to clear her head. Picking up her mug, she sipped the warm liquid; there was just enough spice to offset the alcohol. Feeling better, she went back to eating and even felt herself relax again as Kas whispered silent, and somewhat disparaging, comments to her about a couple sitting on the other side of the room.

"Would you like some more stew," the barmaid asked Henton as she approached from the other side of the room. "Or I can probably get you some pie if you want?" She knelt down next to Henton so that she would have to look up at him. "Are the three of you going to be in town long?"

"I could use some more stew...and some pie," Douglas offered.

The woman nodded her head, but did not take her smiling eyes from Henton. "What about you? Some pie."

Stephenie's fists tightened around the mug as she stared at the blond woman. She allowed the heat of energy, or perhaps anger, to flow through her body. When the woman shivered and turned her head, she screamed and fell backwards.

"Witch! Witch!"

Stephenie glanced to her hands and saw the layer of frost that covered the mug and the table all around her. Immediately stopping the draw of energy, she set the frozen mug down and pushed heat back into the environment. She realized Kas had been trying to get her attention for some time, but she had inadvertently blocked him in her rage.

Around her the public house was in commotion, with the half dozen patrons clamoring out of their chairs. Henton was already on his feet, one hand on his sword.

"Stop," Stephenie said, then raised her voice above the squeak that had initially come from her throat. "Please stop shouting 'witch'. I am not a witch; I am Her Highness, Princess Stephenie." Slowly standing, she pulled the cowl from her head and tugged loose the leather thong that she had used to tie back her hair.

The barmaid, still on the floor, had backed herself against a bench a dozen feet away. While she had stopped her screaming, Stephenie could sense she had not lost any of the fear she was emitting. Stephenie met her eyes and then bowed her head to the barmaid. "I did not mean to startle you. I...I was cooling the cider and overdid it," she offered as the only thing that came to her mind.

A well-dressed man in the back of the room stepped cautiously forward, "You'll forgive us if we call for a holy warrior to confirm this claim."

Stephenie nodded her head. "Please, do so if you want." She sighed and sat back down, trying to hide the trembling in her hands. *How could I allow myself to lose control?* She asked herself, still keeping Kas from her thoughts for fear of what he might learn from her terrified mind. Glancing to Henton, she indicated he should also return to his seat. Grudgingly, he did, but only after rotating the chair so he could keep his eyes on the pub's patrons who were all staring with varying degrees of concern.

It was not long before a series of soldiers charged in through the front door, four of the six held their crossbows leveled and readied. The older man in the back exchanged a few words with the sergeant, but no one said anything to Stephenie. She knew there was a holy warrior coming and had no desire to hurt anyone in Cothel. More importantly, for now she did not consider Henton or Douglas to be in danger. While a typical witch would not be able to stop a crossbow at close range, from her own practicing, Stephenie knew she would be able to protect her friends. *And, at the very worst, I'll pull off my shirt and show Kas' handprint.*

Stephenie, what happened? Why are you shutting me out?

She sighed and dropped her defenses some, knowing that Kas had to broadcast his message with a lot of power for her to have heard. If he kept that up, others might be able to sense the mental communication. *Kas, I don't know, but I need to concentrate on what's happening. We'll talk as soon as this is done, I promise.*

Stephenie felt the holy warrior coming before he swept in through the front door with two other men trailing behind him. He was taller than Henton and had broad shoulders that amplified his presence. His finely woven tunic bared a large emblem of a soldier working a field. It was an unofficial symbol and one that had been more strongly adopted by those that had supported Duke Burdger over her family.

The holy warrior quickly took in the scene, ordered the men to stow their weapons, and then bowed, if not as deeply as others might. "Your Highness," he said, his tone entirely neutral. "We have never met formally, but I have seen paintings of you as well as witnessed you from afar when I have been to Antar. I am Sir Esin, Lord Mayor of Venla"

The other people in the room, including the soldiers, quickly bowed or curtsied. Stephenie sensed the fear in the room had changed ever so slightly; now they feared the wrath of a noble instead of the powers of a witch.

Slowly standing, Stephenie bowed her head in return. "Sir Esin, I apologize for the disturbance. I...over-chilled my drink and frightened the barmaid."

"Ma'am, there is nothing to apologize for. If I had word of your coming, we could have arranged for a party to meet you." He glanced at Henton and Douglas and then to where Kas was hovering. "Is the rest of your party elsewhere?"

Stephenie shook her head, sensing Kas disappear through the wall behind them. "No. I am traveling with a small party for speed. We didn't send word ahead because we planned to just be here for the night and leave with first light. We didn't want to trouble anyone."

"Your Highness, it would be my pleasure to host you, even if only for the night."

Stephenie nodded her head, knowing she would not be able to refuse the offer. "Of course, Sir Esin, we would be honored." Stephenie could not help but notice the trembling barmaid and the tears leaking from her eyes; the fear radiating from her was palpable.

With Stephenie's attention on her, she stepped forward. "Please, Ma'am, please forgive me. I...I didn't—"

"It is fine," Stephenie said, still struggling with a sense of possessiveness she was feeling over Henton. "You did nothing wrong. I didn't mean to frighten you. I simply over chilled my beverage." The barmaid bowed and said nothing more; though it was obvious she did not believe Stephenie.

Sir Esin looked around the room and finally said, "Your Highness, if you will follow me, I will give you my room for the night. Do your men need help gathering your supplies?"

Stephenie looked to Henton, who gave her a quick glance that she interpreted as 'splitting up is not wise.' Turning back to the holy warrior, she responded, "Our things are across the street, we can gather them on the way."

Sir Esin's manor house, which belonged to the duchy for the use of the Lord Mayor, was of a modest size. It was of stone construction and three stories high, but it was taller than it was wide because it was nestled among many other buildings. Without private stables, they chose to leave their horses at the inn.

The manor's entry hall was nicely furnished and comfortably warm. Sir Esin had obviously put his mark on the house, including many large tapestries featuring the soldier farmer. "After the war ended, I was displaced," he said as he led them into the middle of the room. "There were so few holy warriors left in the north that anyone willing was given the opportunity to relocate. Because of the vacancy here, and the kindness of my patrons, I was assigned to be Lord Mayor." Sir Esin smiled, but it did not feel genuine to Stephenie. "Are you in need of refreshments? I do not know what happened in the public house, but it did not appear you had finished your meal."

"It was nothing really. The people there gave no offense," she added, fearing the barmaid might be made to suffer for a perceived injury to herself. "We did have some dinner, so do not trouble yourself on our behalf."

"Nonsense, I have not really eaten yet myself. Adding another setting...or three," he probed, "to the table is not a trouble. And if you like, I can report on the state of Venla for you."

Stephenie nodded her assent, knowing that despite her desire to simply hide away, refusing would reflect badly on her and her brother. "Thank you, that is most gracious."

"Good." He nodded to the butler, who had been standing against the back wall. The old man quietly exited through an interior door. "I am sorry there was so much commotion over your presence. As I am sure you already know, there has been an increase in witch and warlock events. The word we hear from the barge traffic is the war has emboldened many more to embrace Elrin. With fewer priests and holy warriors around, they are able to cast their spells over the good citizens and take control of many of the smaller towns and villages. We believe their hope is to entrench themselves before order is fully restored."

Stephenie felt her frustration building; she had not heard any such reports and immediately wondered if Joshua and Rebecca were aware and had kept it from her or if they had yet to hear this rumor. "How widespread is the problem, do you believe?"

He spoke as he walked toward a humble set of stairs along the right hand wall. "While they prepare some extra settings, let me show you to the rooms." He started up the stairs and turned around to walk up backwards so he could resume the discussion, "The trouble with the witches appears to be mostly to the northwest, where the Senzar were active. If I may offer my opinion?" To which Stephenie nodded and he continued, "I feel the Senzar likely cast spells on many of the good citizens, bewitching them into embracing Elrin. I fear that many of these people have been infected with the demon god's evil and that it will be hard to effectively cleanse the population. It may take generations to root out all the evil."

At the top of the stairs, Sir Esin looked up and down the hall. "Your Highness, you have a choice. As I am unmarried, you may take my room or you may have those intended for the Lord Mayor's wife."

Stephenie could sense nothing from the holy warrior, as with Henton, Sir Esin's mind was very reserved, but she knew he was likely a strong believer. "I do not wish to disturb you more than we have, so I will take the wife's room if it is unoccupied."

Sir Esin smiled. "You have chosen the better of the rooms. If you would like, I can have a female servant come and attend to you."

Stephenie shook her head. She had a vague sense Kas was hovering outside the front of the building. "No, I have been traveling like a soldier for some time now, I will be fine. Though if we can take some time to freshen up before dinner, we would appreciate it."

"Of course. I will send someone to fetch you when the food is ready." He looked to Henton, "There are servant rooms on the third floor that you can use. I will show you."

Stephenie nodded her thanks and entered the bedroom as Henton and Douglas were led up the stairs at the end of the hall. The room's interior was dark, but Stephenie could see well enough. Alone, she felt the frustration of the evening descend upon her. *How could I have lost control like that?* Feeling her eyes starting to tear, she shut them and sat down on the bed. She could just barely feel Kas through the wall, but hesitated to call him inside the room. Eventually, she felt Sir Esin heading back down the stairs to the first floor. Shortly after that, Henton and Douglas quickly came down to her.

"Steph, you here?" Henton asked, coming into the room.

"Yes," she choked out, ashamed for what happened.

He came over to the bed as Douglas entered the room with a lamp. "Steph, what happened? Are you okay? Is there something wrong?"

She looked up and saw the concern in Henton's and Douglas' eyes. She felt Kas come through the wall and acknowledged him, silently asking for his forgiveness. Looking in the direction of the three of them, she shook her head. "I...I don't know what came over me."

"The expression on your face said you'd rip that girl's flesh from her bones," Douglas said as he stepped back to close the door and set the lamp down on the dressing table. "Then the cold...there was ice all over you."

Stephenie felt her hands tremble and put them in her lap. "I don't know what is wrong with me." She looked up to meet their eyes again. "When I went to confront the priests that took Will, there was a Senzar mage." Henton and Douglas nodded, having already heard her general account of the events. Deciding to admit what she had not told them before, she continued, "The mage had me beaten. Not physically, but mentally. He got into my head and...and he...I'm not sure what happened, but he pushed me until I lost control." She looked down at her hands. "I ripped open that man's chest with my hands. It was me, but it wasn't. I killed all of them, I remember doing it, but I had no control over myself." She could not hold back her tears. "I'm scared. So very scared."

Henton and Douglas moved closer and knelt in front of her. "Steph, it's not your fault," Henton said, his hand on hers.

She shook her head. "But tonight...I shouldn't have lost control."

"Well, she was being a bit disrespectful in her behavior," Douglas offered.

"It is no excuse and she hardly did anything others haven't done in the past." She closed her eyes and exhaled. "I just need a little time to rest."

Henton and Douglas rose. "We are just up the stairs in the first room."

She nodded her head. "I felt where you had gone." To Kas she added silently, *please stay.*

"We'll be waiting. If you want, we can go down and tell Sir Esin you decided to simply rest for the evening."

She shook her head. "No, we need to learn more about this uptake in witch and warlock 'events' as he called them." They nodded their heads and left the room, leaving her with the lamp.

"Kas," she said softly in Dalish, "I don't know what's happening to me, but this wasn't the first time. I'm scared I'm going to hurt someone."

"Tell me what is going on," he responded softly in Dalish as he luminesced into an opaque form.

Stephenie noted the concern in his slightly brown shaded eyes. "It was a horribly powerful sense of possessiveness I felt tonight. But, it first happened when I went to check on Will and found he had slept with Lady Sara." She swallowed, not liking the trace of venom she still heard in her voice. "I didn't like the idea that he had slept with her. And Henton tonight, with that woman flirting with him. I could have killed her."

Kas sat down on the bed next to Stephenie. "This is an odd confession to make. In my day, a woman would never claim such feelings over other men. At least not to the one she professes to love."

"Kas," she pleaded. "I don't have feelings for Will or Henton or any of the others like that. They are my friends and I love them as friends. I don't want to bring them to my bed." She put her head in her hands, "But...I don't know why, but, I just...had this overwhelming sense of ownership over them." She lifted her head and looked at Kas. "You're the one I care about and I never want to feel that I own anyone."

"I was not accusing you of desiring their physical comforts. I was simply observing the oddity of this conversation." He put his hand on hers; though his touch carried no warmth, he generated a field to apply pressure. "I cannot say exactly what has triggered these reactions in you, but perhaps you sense change in your relationships and this frightens you. Your relationship with your brother has changed and now Will has another person in his life that is likely to consume time he might have dedicated to you."

"But I don't want him dedicating his time to me exclusively."

Kas nodded his head. "I know you have felt more isolated since our return. You have not said anything specifically to me, but I notice that sometimes you flinch when others jump at noticing your presence."

She did not bother to stop the tears. "Everyone fears me, even Josh. You, Henton, Douglas, and Will are the only ones that don't and I'm not certain Will wasn't frightened of me finding out about Sara."

"Perhaps that triggered a response in you. Picking up on other people's emotions. Perhaps you are even..."

"Even?"

"Perhaps even are a little frustrated. I have no body to share with you, but the others do."

"Kas, not this again." She rose to her feet and crossed the room. "Why is it always about the physical relationship with you men?"

Kas rose as well, "Stephenie, I am only trying to offer suggestions. I do not know the reasons why you are reacting as you are."

"Could the Senzar mage have done something to me?"

Kas nodded his head slowly. "It is possible, but there is not much to be done about it. Trying to adjust people's thoughts is dangerous and often unsuccessful, at least in attempts to undo things that are done to someone else." He moved closer. "If something was done, they would simply be memories or thought patterns in your brain. How would a person tell one memory from another to know what did not belong? If there was indeed something done, unless you recognize it as something you don't like about yourself and decided," he emphasized, "to willfully behave differently, there is little that I can do." He rested a hand on her shoulder. "It is like a bad habit, with enough determination, you can make it go away. But it would be something you have to consciously do."

She bit her lip and slowly met his eyes. "Kas, I don't think he planted any memories or anything like that. I think he awoke some instinctual monster in me. It's like grabbing something hot, you drop it even before you realize it was hot. I'm reacting without thinking about it."

Kas nodded his head. "There is no monster lurking inside of you that is any different than anyone else. The man violated you on the most personal of levels. It is not unreasonable for you to react more strongly and quickly. But, even an instinctual response can be overridden with enough focus and determination."

She exhaled. She felt drained, but her tears were dried up and she actually felt slightly better for the discussion. Though, she still did not want to face Henton or anyone else at the moment. Her loss of control was inexcusable, *but still, I am not a child to hide in my room.* "Thank you, Kas."

"You do know that just because this is something you have to get through in your own time, it does not mean we will not be here to support you. For instance, I should start showing you how to block entry into your mind without shutting out everything around you."

"Thank you," she said and then looked away, "I feel very vulnerable when I shut out everything. I can't see the energy as clearly."

He lifted her chin, "and I do know how you feel about me. I am glad you felt comfortable enough with me to bring this up."

She gave him a weak smile. "I love you. Who else would I talk to?"

Chapter 8

Stephenie awoke with the sun, and she only spoke briefly with Sir Esin before leaving his manor house. The rumors they had discussed over dinner the night before lacked any real specifics, but she did not want to dismiss them out of hand. He had claimed to have sent word on to Antar already and so she decided not to try and send a message herself. It would show a lack of trust and if he had lied, any messenger she used from Venla would likely be intercepted. When she had the chance, she would send a letter from a different location and hope that it would get through.

As they rode out of the town, it was obvious that word had spread about her presence. Although there were only a few people outside in the crisp morning air, all of the ones who had been unable to avoid them bowed deeply. Many of them, she could tell from their stilted movements, were not happy to see her, but a few radiated a sense of approval, and a couple openly praised her for saving Cothel. One person even asked for a blessing from Catheri, for which Stephenie obliged, if only from the guilt of the prior night.

Once they were on the road, the miles quickly passed under their horse's hooves, and even though she was not in much mood for conversation, she found the sun set quickly enough. That night, wanting to avoid notice, they found an abandoned farmstead and took shelter in the decaying buildings.

They continued to follow the road toward Uthen for another two days before turning southwest onto the road heading toward East Fork. Joshua originally intended for her to travel through East Fork, which had been the seat of the Burdger Duchy, but she did not want to travel that far south nor to go through a city that might still be hostile to her. Instead, as they reached the southern tip of the Uthen Mountain Range, they turned west off the main road and traveled the back roads through the rough terrain. On horse, the deep ruts and fallen branches were mostly annoying, but not as troublesome as it would be if they were pulling a wagon. Each night they found willing families to stay with, none of which appeared to recognize Stephenie as anything more than a common soldier traveling west with her friends.

Two days after they rounded the tip of the Uthen Range, the cold weather broke, warming slightly, but it left them with a light drizzle. Stephenie had been comfortable, but that was due to her subconscious drawing of energy into her body to generate warmth and form a gravitational shield to block the water from actually hitting her. Initially, she had not even realized she had been doing it until Henton had asked how she was remaining dry. After that, she consciously avoided blocking the drizzle. The further they were from Antar, the smaller the chance anyone would take her word as being the Prophet of Catheri. She knew she needed to be more careful and avoid accusations of witchcraft.

"Steph, slow up," Henton said from where he was riding beside her. While still not quite enjoying being on a horse, he was at least getting comfortable with his skill at remaining mounted.

She followed his gaze to an area just outside the edge of the small town into which they were riding. Kas immediately moved forward to investigate the movement that had drawn Henton's attention. Stephenie squinted, but the distance was too far to make out exactly what was there.

Carrion eaters, Kas sent to her. *Looks like perhaps seven bodies. Some have been here longer than others, but they all look to have been partially burned at some point.*

Stephenie felt energy start to leak out of her body and slowly brought her anger under control. "Witch burnings," she said aloud while replying the same to Kas.

As they neared the site of the bodies, the birds squawked angrily before flying off at the threat of larger predators. The smell was strong, even with the light rain and wind dispersing the odor. Stephenie had never witnessed an actual execution before, as the youngest princess it was always something considered too grisly for her. While she was thankfully spared having to witness one growing up, she knew with incredible detail just how they 'purify' someone of Elrin's evil. It had always been a fate she had feared: being dragged through the streets, beaten and hit until there was little strength left in the body, then, before they burned you, they would cut two lines on opposite diagonals across your face, just under your eyes so the blood would not blind you. They tied you to a pole, and then would dump thick lamp oil over you. The oil stung in the deep cuts on your face to keep you conscious until the flame and smoke took your life. Large pyres of dry wood were seldom used to burn someone. Even though they allowed the person to live longer while burning, it usually took too much effort to arrange. Once dead, the bodies were normally buried and forgotten. However, if a warning to others was to be sent, the bodies would be placed just outside the town for everyone to see.

"We should be careful here Steph, perhaps go on to the next town."

She turned to Douglas and then looked up into the sky. "It's already late, the horses are tired and low on grain, and the clouds indicate the rain will get worse overnight."

Henton nodded his head. "And there are no other towns close, but Steph, you don't want to get into the middle of this. We've got a long way to go before we get to your sister."

Stephenie nodded her head, but did not look at either of them. *Don't you give me trouble too, Kas. I can feel you want to say something.*

On the contrary, my Love, I would rather you found the murderers and killed them.

She looked away from the bodies and urged Argat forward. *Unfortunately, that is likely the whole town, and I won't kill that many.*

The town was nestled into a hillside with many ancient trees sheltering the stone and wooden buildings. There were scattered clearings covered with the remains of fall vegetable gardens. Situated on a more heavily traveled road heading north along the western side of the Uthen Mountain range, there was a large building bearing the shingle of an inn and public house. Stephenie also noted a large stable just a few hundred yards further down the muddy road.

"Do you want to check on rooms or stabling first?" Henton asked as they came to a stop in front of the inn.

Stephenie reached out and found there were a dozen people inside the lower area of the building, in what she presumed was the public house section. There were three people on the upper floor. Gauging the size of the building, she inclined her head toward the stables. "I imagine there will be plenty of room at the inn. Let's take care of the horses and then get a room."

After Henton negotiated a rate for the four horses and the purchase of extra supplies, they went back to the large inn, carrying their personal gear on their shoulders. Inside the wooden building, a large portion of the first floor was dedicated to a series of tables and benches, with one corner containing more durable dry goods and salted meats.

The mood of those inside was quite muted; what conversation that did exist, was hushed and reserved. Most of the people present appeared to be local, with the exception of a group of older men in the corner.

Taking a table next to the open hearth, Henton arranged for dinner and two rooms for the night as Stephenie and Douglas spread their things out to dry. Before long, their food and drink arrived, carried by a woman who was at least two years younger than Stephenie.

"If you don't mind me asking," Stephenie said to the girl. "What happened that there would be so many witch burnings in a town this size?"

The brown haired girl paled. "Ma'am, I'd rather not discuss it. A new priest came through town and purged Elrin's evil is all I'll say." With that, she started to walk away, but Stephenie caught her arm.

"Is this priest still here in town?"

The girl pulled her hand loose. "No, Ma'am, he's not." Free, the girl made a hasty retreat out of the common area and into what Stephenie assumed was the kitchen.

"Steph, you need to focus on your sister," Henton whispered between bites.

She nodded her head. "We'll push through to Berylam tomorrow. I want to see Baron Turning."

Berylam, based on legend, was named for a lady who forced her husband to build his keep along a twisting river so that she would be able to look out her bedroom window to see a series of three waterfalls cascading down a cliff face. Stephenie was not sure if there was any truth to the legend, but the small city was not situated in a place that was of much strategic value. The land was rough, which made rapidly traveling to quickly respond to threats difficult. In addition, to see the falls, the castle and city were down slope, which ceded the best defensive position to aggressors. However, with little of value to protect, that weakness had never been exploited.

Baron Arnold Turning's family had lived in the small keep for the last two hundred years, making just enough money from trappers that they were able to purchase other supplies and pay their taxes to the crown. There was an active population in the area, and the walled town protected anywhere from five hundred to one thousand people, depending on the time of the year.

When Stephenie first saw the city's walls and the keep situated near its eastern edge, she knew she would have loved to call this remote city home. The city walls and keep were more than four hundred years old and built with the architectural details not seen in more recent construction. Gargoyles and stone dragons adorned the towers and friezes stood above each door and archway in the many interior walls throughout the city.

Most of the city was constructed from stone. The streets were paved with gutters and channels to direct away the heavy rains and snow melt. Large trees, twisted from the relentless wind, were scattered about the city, offering a few remnants of color where some stubborn leaves had hung on when all their relatives had long since blown away.

The people, while bundled in furs and heavy wool, had no trouble meeting each other's eyes as they passed. They were inquisitive, yet polite enough not to interfere. When they finally reached the hexagonal keep's front door, Stephenie could see the mist blowing off the water from the falls several hundred yards away. The dampness in the air could be felt on her face and seen forming on the leather of her saddle and tack.

Dismounting, she patted Argat's neck. He of course turned his head around in the hope of a treat, which Stephenie slipped into his mouth as she approached the guards who were moving to meet them.

"Good evening," she said when they were within a dozen feet. "Can you please inform Baron Turning that he has visitors from Antar bearing messages?"

The two closest men looked to each other, while the one behind them bowed deeply. "Of course, Your Highness."

Stephenie searched her memory, but could not place the man's name, despite her remembering him from the Baron's personal guard when the Baron was last in Antar.

"Simons, Your Highness."

She smiled at him, "Yes, that's right. Is there a place we can take the horses?"

"Please follow me inside and out of the cold. We'll have your things brought in and the horses cared for." He moved up a couple steps and turned back to her. "If I may, young Lady Isabel was looking forward to seeing you in two months in Antar. She will be quite pleased by this surprise."

Stephenie smiled again, grabbed the messenger's bag from the saddle, and followed the older soldier up the stairs and into the keep with Henton, Douglas, and Kas just behind her.

The inside of the keep did not disappoint her in the least. There were plenty of signs of wear due to its age, but that just enhanced its character and beauty. Pulled away from admiring the construction, she turned to watch as Baron Turning descended the narrow steps into the entrance hall with his fourteen-year-old daughter in tow. "Your Highness, I wish I had known you were coming. I would have arranged for a feast and a ball to be thrown for your arrival. It is a great privilege and honor to have you here." When he reached the bottom of the stairs, he bowed deeply while his timid daughter curtsied just behind him.

"Baron, I am glad to be here. But, I cannot stay long and so a feast is not necessary. If you've got room for us and our horses, plus a warm meal, that will be plenty."

"Of course, Your Highness, you shall have my rooms."

"Call me Steph, everyone else does."

"Of course, Steph." He looked about the entrance hall and then signaled a young man to come over. The boy of no more than fifteen bowed, but Stephenie could feel his unease. "Varn, please go have the cooks prepare a meal, nothing too fancy, but we'll have everyone join us in the dining hall." Arnold turned back to Stephenie. "I have a cousin, Lord Mesir, staying here with me, so I'm not talking a large affair, you, your men, Mesir, Isabel, and myself."

"I don't want to put you to any trouble."

Baron Turning waved his hand to dismiss her hesitation. "Nonsense. We seldom have guests and it will do us good to actually eat together from time to time. I scarcely remember what Mesir even looks like, and he's been here for weeks."

Stephenie smiled at the Baron; he was happy that she was here, despite a slight unease. "Then I would be most grateful. May we freshen up before sitting to eat?"

"Of course, where are my manners? Let me show you to my rooms. There are plenty of spare rooms for your men and myself. And if you want a tour of the keep, I can do that at the same time." He grinned. "It's not that large of a keep, you'll see pretty much all of it on the way to the rooms."

The dining hall was on the second floor and quite small in comparison to the halls in the square keep of Antar Castle. Despite the legend and amount of practical usefulness, Berylam Keep's design was intended to control the rural lands around it, not to entertain a multitude of guests. Still, Stephenie found the small room full of character and charm. She took the time to admire what appeared to be some winged fairies carved into the worn stone mantel of the large fireplace. Stoked to provide warmth for the whole room, she found herself pushing energy from her body to keep herself cool.

Once she was done with admiring the room, Stephenie accepted the position of honor at the end of the table, which was next to the fireplace. Henton and Douglas sat on her left with Baron Arnold at the far end, but that was only five chairs away. His older cousin, whose dark hair was dosed with a heavy sprinkling of grey, sat opposite the young Isabel. Stephenie smiled at the shy girl who could have easily been a timid doe trying to avoid the hunter's sight.

"So, my cousin tells me you are pretty decent with a sword, Your Highness," the older man added the last as an afterthought.

Stephenie smiled, Mesir's slight wobble in his movements spoke of the drink he had likely already consumed before being called to dinner. "I do not like to brag, but I do fancy myself competent."

"You are being modest, My Lady, I have seen you on the practice field, you are quite brave and no one could face you when you used two blades."

Douglas frowned as a young serving boy poured wine into his glass. "You should see her facing a real enemy. On the way to rescue His Majesty, we crossed south over the Uthen at Venla, that night Stephenie rushed forward and cut down a handful of soldiers who were sent to kill us. She's a bloodied warrior better than many seasoned soldiers."

Stephenie glanced at Douglas who lowered his eyes. She could easily feel his own sense of protectiveness for her, but the intensity had silenced everyone else, including the three servants. "I've seen more than I like to remember on most days, but let's talk about more pleasant things. Isabel, I apologize for not knowing your birthday before this, but I heard that you just turned fifteen."

The girl blushed. "Indeed, Your Highness."

"Call me Steph."

"Yes, Ma'am...Steph." She glanced to her father and then back to Stephenie. "Father held a grand ball and there were many people who came to celebrate with me."

I want to grab her by the shoulders and make her sit up proud, she thought to Kas, then spoke aloud to everyone else. "I tended to avoid the balls when I could, but my father held several each year. When I turned fifteen it was a grand affair as well." Stephenie smirked, "I remember several suitors trying to woo my affections. To no avail," she added looking at the meat pies that were piled on the center of the table.

"Did you have a young man you fancied?" the young girl asked.

Stephenie met Isabel's blue eyes. "No, not really. I thought most of them to be silly and too puffed up, like a stallion thinking he was going to gather a mare for his herd."

"And now, as the Prophet of Catheri, my father says most men are afraid of you."

"Isabel, I didn't say they feared her," turning to Stephenie, he continued, "I think I said you might be intimidating to an average man. It was not a slight against you, Your Highness. I have the utmost respect for you."

Stephenie shook her head. "Please, Arnold, be at ease. It's not much of a secret. I do frighten people, men and women alike." She turned back to Isabel, "but truly, I don't want people to be scared of me. If anything, I try to be more forgiving than most. I'll not take offense to anything you might say, so long as you don't go after my friends."

Isabel's shoulders eased and she nodded her head. "Your...Steph, I know when we saw you right after the High Priest declared you to be cleansed, I said I wanted to be a priestess of Catheri." After a moment, she continued, "Would you be angry if I changed my mind?"

Stephenie hated the fact that so many people had bought into the idea that there was a god called Catheri or even one called Felis. However, her strongest supporters were generally those who had become the strongest believers in Catheri. "Of course not, Isabel, you can do whatever you like. You have my support to be what you want." She smiled at the girl, "I'll even put in a good word with your father."

Isabel beamed, "I was so worried you might think I would be dishonoring you."

"Nonsense. What do you want to do?"

Isabel blushed again. "I am going to marry and have sons for my father. There was a young man, Camris, the son of a Lord who has lands near the Epish border. At the ball he asked for my hand."

Stephenie bit back the comment that she could be far more than simply a broodmare used to produce children. While the thought of being tied down to a man and trapped by a hoard of children made her nauseous, she did not want to judge Isabel with her own views. "If you like him, then I am happy for you."

Isabel looked slightly askance and continued with a little more caution. "My father's title will eventually pass to me because your great grandfather declared the title will stay in our family, even through the female line, as long as my husband will adopt my name. It is my duty to ensure the people of my father's barony are cared for and have a clear line of succession."

Stephenie nodded her head despite the rebellion in her heart. "Most definitely. My brother will marry soon, to secure my own family's line as well." She did not admit aloud that if the line of succession relied on her, the crown would fall to a different family. *I'm proud of myself, Kas. I guess through age comes wisdom.*

Kas' mental snort was loud in her head. *Age does not provide wisdom. I have seen many people grow old and learn nothing. Wisdom comes from experience.*

Stephenie grinned despite herself. *I stand corrected.* Sensing his hesitation, she added, *what?*

Well, technically you are seated.

"Will you come to my wedding?"

Baron Arnold quickly clarified, "It will of course be after His Majesty's. We would never think to usurp his day."

"If I can, I will definitely do so. However, I am truly sorry to say this, but in all likelihood, I probably will not be able to. I have some business to attend to and I will not even be present for Josh's wedding. I wish I could, but what I am doing cannot wait."

"Traipsing across the country again?" Mesir asked, setting down his empty glass. "You should have been a man."

Douglas' knife, stacked with meat, slowed on the way to his mouth, but Arnold beat him in responding. "Cousin, you dare insult Her Highness in my house and at my table?"

Mesir, not quite picking up on the anger in Arnold's voice shook his head. "No, Cousin, I merely stated fact. If she was a man, no one would comment on her travels or her playing with weapons. As a woman, she is looked down upon. It's a scandal to travel unmarried and unescorted with a couple of men across the country."

Stephenie raised her hand to stop Arnold. "Peace, I said I won't take offense and I don't. There is truth in what Mesir has said, but I don't allow those who would comment to bother me. I am not seeking to attract a man to marry." *Save for you Kas.* "Since there are tasks that I am best suited to handle, I simply do those."

"But if you were a man—"

"I am not a man and have no desire to be one. If men and women want to despise me, let them, they can't do anything about it. I'm not seeking their approval."

"There are many who do look up to you," Arnold injected, "I for one and Isabel as well."

"Yes, Ma'am. I admire you."

Stephenie smiled at them. "I appreciate it." She glanced toward Henton and Douglas, but did not react to the grins they were trying to conceal by continuing to eat.

You would make a rather silly looking man, Kas added.

And you would be an ugly woman.

"Baron," Henton said, taking advantage of the pause in the conversation, "I had never been in this part of the country, but I must say the falls do look magnificent."

The Baron smiled, relief spreading across his brow. "Let me tell you about Lady Berylam."

The conversation carried on through the rest of the meal and well into the night. Isabel eventually excused herself when they decided to retire to the drawing room, where Mesir, who had finished a bottle of wine with dinner, slipped into a heavy sleep just after taking a seat in an oversized chair.

"Please forgive my cousin...he's a good man, but things have not gone the best for him."

Stephenie smiled as she leaned back in her own oversized chair. The stuffing was incredibly soft and the crackling of the fire a relaxing distraction. "He does seem to be good at heart and I never stop someone from speaking their mind."

But you do not always listen, Kas said, settling down to hover invisibly beside her.

"I appreciate the leniency with him."

"Baron," Henton said, leaning forward in his chair. "On our way here, we came across a town where at least seven people had recently been executed as witches. Can you tell us anything about that?"

Stephenie wanted to hug Henton. Will had always seemed to drive the topics of conversation for Henton, effectively acting as a mouthpiece and allowing Henton to appear independent of the conversation. Now Henton seemed to be doing the same for her.

"Yes, Sir Henton, I am aware of some troubling reports." Arnold emptied the rest of his drink and set the glass aside. Without any servants he would have to refill it on his own. "I am not certain when it really started, but we have been hearing of an increase in witch burnings. I've actually sent a letter to His Majesty and Her Excellency to inquire about the events."

Henton prompted the Baron, "I find it hard to believe there is suddenly such an increase of witches in these small towns and villages."

"So did I. In fact, I sent a trusted adviser to investigate. He was accused of being a warlock and burned. I found out about that after Mitchel did not return and I had to send someone else, more discreetly." Arnold shook his head. "I know Mitchel was not a warlock. He never could have been. But the message to me was clear, stay out of it." His shoulders slumped. "When I first heard the reports, I thought the Senzar might have come in and started to corrupt people, turn them to Elrin's evil. But now I do not trust these priests that are burning everyone." He looked up to meet Stephenie's eyes, as though Henton had not been the one to ask the question. "What I understand, in some of the towns, the local priests have died mysteriously, some of them, after defending people who were accused. There are new priests, not staying in the towns, but moving from place to place in an effort to eradicate Elrin's demons. The word is they are working their way east. Of course, word is also spreading quickly that many of those who are witches and warlocks are heading west to lands the Senzar still control."

"Have you done any further investigation?" Stephenie asked; the hair on her neck erect.

Arnold shook his head. "No, Ma'am. I have not wanted to risk any more of my men. When I first saw you, I had thought that perhaps you were here to find the source of all the burnings, but my letter had not been gone long enough for you to have been dispatched."

"No, we had no idea of these events when I left." She sighed, feeling the conflict growing in her. The very fact that Kas had not interjected told her what he wanted, but was too hesitant to ask. "I am actually heading north, though my brother had intended for me to make a circuit around the country."

"I heard word that your mother had attempted to harm you. The report arrived not long before you. Are you planning to deal with her?"

Stephenie inhaled, but said nothing. After a moment, she continued, "We are not at liberty to say. However, we'll be missing the wedding. Would it be possible for you to take some additional gifts with you? We left several with Will, but I thought another small token from Berylam..."

"Of course, I think I know the very thing. We have some stunning rocks that have been cut and polished that would be quite appropriate coming from you."

Stephenie smiled, thankful that Arnold would not press her further on their destination. She did not know where her mother was and so could not even make a reliable hint as to a false destination. "That would be most appreciated."

Chapter 9

Although Stephenie would have preferred to leave with the sunrise, she could not ignore her family's or her personal obligation to the Baron. After a heavy and filling breakfast, she listened to Arnold provide her with a brief overview of his barony, both hearing of his successes and troubles. She quickly realized Arnold was hoping she would be able to provide some advice or mediate between him and her brother regarding a probable shortfall with tax revenue. The mundane nature of the subtly hinted request took her by surprise. All her life she had been shielded from those types of discussions. She had never before been sought out as a person who held significant influence in the country.

After recovering from the shock, she forced herself to accept that even those she thought of as devoted to her would try to use her influence when possible. Penning a quick missive to her brother regarding her appraisal of the barony, she sealed it and gave it to Arnold to take back to Antar with the gift he would present on her behalf. *A gift I just bought with that letter.*

Once they were finally outside the city gates, she allowed herself to relax her shoulders. The movement of Argat under her was calming and he flicked his ears back in perhaps a response to her thinking of him. She patted his neck in appreciation just in case.

"I wouldn't have thought Arnold would have done that to you," Douglas remarked quietly, "used you just like any other noble."

Stephenie shrugged, determined not to let it affect her. "He's doing what he has to do to survive." She nodded her head to a small group of people in the distance who were headed into Berylam and knew Arnold would at least use what she gave him to help them. She dared not consider what others might do.

"Steph, not to question your sense of direction, but don't we want the west road back toward Warton so we can turn north on the good road there?"

"Sorry, Henton, but it won't take us that much more time to ride north through the smaller towns and villages."

Henton rode closer. "Steph, you don't want to get involved. I know we asked Arnold about recent activity, but I had hoped—it appears in vain—that it was to avoid trouble."

Stephenie smiled at Henton, who was dressed quite finely in his recently cleaned leather gambeson. "If they are doing this because of me, I plan to stop it. But, I have a feeling there is something more to it. There are just too many all at once."

It was late in the evening when they rode into the small village of Gravel Ridge, which was the second community they had come across. The town of Ridson, which they had passed through around midday, had not seen any unexpected visitors in recent weeks and no witches had been found for at least three years.

Gravel Ridge had only a handful of buildings clustered together as most of the town's population was scattered in the narrow valleys between the mountain ridges. However, their appearance along the road did not go unnoticed and by the time they reached the center of the village, several people had gathered to watch them approach.

"Good evening, Ma'am," Henton said to an older woman who had an air of authority. "Is there a place we can stay for the night? A barn will do if that is all to be had."

The woman squared her shoulders and gave each of them a calculating appraisal before speaking. "We are not without protection. Many of our young men fought in the war and still possess the swords they earned."

Henton nodded his head in understanding, "Ma'am—"

"Good lady," Stephenie said as she dismounted. "We mean you no harm. We rode out of Berylam this morning and will happily pay for any food and lodging you might have available." She pulled out a small coin purse and dumped out five square coins. While generous for a location such as this far off village, it was not extravagant.

The old woman walked over, her movement slightly stiff, but not decrepit. She took the coins without examining them and then motioned with her head toward a house near the edge of the village. "You can stay in my barn. I'll give you a share of my dinner and your horses can have a meal of hay, but not oats."

Stephenie glanced at Henton, but his face was expressionless as normal. Douglas dismounted behind him, stretching his tired legs in the process. Without further comment, she started leading Argat after the woman.

Stephenie, I have found some burned bodies and fresh graves.

Kas' mental voice woke her senses to the faint stench of recent death in the air. "Ma'am," Stephenie called out to the woman who was already a couple dozen paces ahead of them, "do you have a priest in town?"

The woman stopped walking. It took her a moment to turn around to face Stephenie. "We did. Millor was old, but not as old as I. He died in his sleep ten days ago. Why do you ask?"

She could feel the tension in the air, from the old woman as well as the handful of younger men and woman who were still gathered around them. "We are checking in with local priests as a favor to Baron Arnold."

"You are the Baron's men?"

"We are not on retainer, but as we are carrying other messages north, he asked if we could check on the state of things."

The woman considered Stephenie again, then closed the distance before speaking. "We are good people here. Do not let recent events reflect poorly on us. Two of Felis' holy warriors came through and cleansed any evil from our village. I am sure Millor's age might have prevented him from seeing any signs."

"Signs?"

The woman's eyes narrowed. "We do not harbor witches and warlocks here. Those who turned to Elrin must have done so recently. There was a man who had come though a few months back. He had a bad air of him and I am sure it was his doing."

"How many?"

"The two holy warriors found three, but there were two others who had run off after the first day, before the three were found guilty." The woman shook her head. "Sal, a young man apprenticed to the black smith, who also turned out to be a warlock, and Betra, an old woman living alone near the mountains for years. She was always bringing food to anyone who was sick or injured. The two of them disappeared the night after the holy warriors preached a day long sermon on the evils of Elrin and what they would do to any found guilty of witchcraft. The next day, they used a holy artifact to test each person to see who had ties to Elrin. That is when the blacksmith and two others were found guilty."

"When was this?"

"The burnings were yesterday morning. The two holy warriors left after that for Eugin, a town to the north. They said they were on a mission to rid Cothel of any of Elrin's evil."

Stephenie glanced at Henton, whose upper lip moved ever so slightly in what she knew was an exhausted plea to avoid trouble. Turning back to the woman, she asked, "and how far is Eugin and what are the roads like?"

"Half a day's walk on decent roads. We have a wagon that travels between us."

Turning back to Henton and Douglas she raised her eyebrows and was rewarded with a sigh and Henton shaking his head. "It will be dark soon," Henton said of the obvious. "We'll need light and the horses are going to be very tired."

"Thank you," she said to Henton and Douglas, "I know you are both exhausted." Turning back to the old woman, she asked, "Ma'am, instead of food and lodging, can you sell us some lamps and oil?"

"You are going to travel to Eugin tonight?"

"You said they left yesterday morning, so these two priests would have arrived yesterday evening. If they do the same as they did here, they would have preached today and tomorrow they will look for witches and then leave. If we want to get there before they leave, we have to travel through the night."

The woman glanced to the other villagers and then nodded her head. "For an additional silver crown, we can give you two lamps and oil."

Already planning how she would approach the holy warriors, she nodded her head and allowed Henton to pay the requested amount. After a short while, two lamps on poles were provided along with a small cask of oil. Taking one lamp herself to avoid forcing both Henton and Douglas to carry them, they mounted their tired horses and headed down the road.

Henton's voice woke Stephenie and she quickly rubbed the sleep from her eyes. She would have liked to sleep longer, but it was already light outside and it seemed as if the stable boy had discovered them.

"Of course we will pay for staying," Henton was explaining calmly, though the lack of sleep in his voice was evident to Stephenie. "As I said, we did not want to wake everyone when we arrived so late."

"I'll still need to report this to my mistress, she won't like it, but she's heading to the gathering and I'm supposed to be there as soon as I feed the horse...I wasn't expecting there'd be five."

Stephenie moved to the open stall door, still pulling a few loose bits of straw from her shirt. "Where's the gathering?"

The boy stepped back, slightly surprised by Stephenie's appearance. "Everyone is supposed to meet under the large apple tree at the end of the park."

I will go check what is happening.

Douglas came up behind her with her armor and swords, "Then let's get going."

"The park is just down the main street and off to the right."

Stephenie tossed the boy a coin as she took her armor from Douglas. "Stay here and if you don't mind, take care of our horses as well." She slipped on the armor and buckled it up as she led them away from the stables. By the time they were halfway to the park, Kas had returned and reported that two men were already lining up people who had gathered.

"All of you stay behind me; we don't know what we are facing yet."

When Stephenie approached the growing mass of people, she saw two dark haired men dressed in all the regalia of a Holy Warrior of Felis: red shirts, dark pants and boots, and chainmail over padded armor. However, it felt wrong. Having grown sensitive to the fields that augmentation devices generate, Stephenie could immediately tell the holy symbols of Felis that were proudly displayed upon their chests were cold pieces of metal and nothing more. That these men had power she could not doubt; it was radiating from them and the strange metal object in the closer one's hands. However, priests they were not.

"Felis has declared you clean," they said to the young woman, still trembling slightly before them. Stephenie narrowed her eyes. She could sense the ever so tiny threads of energy coming from the girl and wondered if the woman might not even realize she had the potential to use magic. However, the fearful nature she exuded indicated she was likely aware.

The men shuffled over to the next person in line, an older man with thinning, but long hair. The imposters narrowed their eyes. Stephenie sensed the quick release of energy as the closer man created gravitational threads that lifted the older man's hair, flinging it up as if a strong breeze had caught it. Gasps of surprise rang out from those gathered.

"It seems someone has turned toward Elrin. Did you sell your soul for something useful?"

"No! I've not—"

"No! You sold it for something worthless!"

"I am not one of Elrin's!"

"Take him."

Stephenie had enough and raised her voice. "Stop! That man is not a warlock and you know it."

Everyone turned in her direction. The man with the metal device turned and narrowed his eyes. He still held the object, which bulged in the middle and had two slender arms that extended out into his hands. The man raised his voice, "How dare you challenge the word of a holy warrior?"

Stephenie pushed her shoulders back and stepped closer, leaving Henton and Douglas another step behind her. "You two are the warlocks. You used your powers to fling the man's hair in the air."

"Heathen!" the second man shouted. "She's a witch as well!"

Stephenie shook her head. "I am——" She did not have a chance to finish her statement as a rapid series of gravitational pulses came at her from various angles. She deflected all but one, which ripped a small hole through her left arm. She forwent her own attack, instead shielding Henton and Douglas from a similar assault that would easily kill them.

Kas rushed forth, but the first man formed an energy shield of his own that shimmered in the morning light. Rebuffed, Kas moved back, uncertain, but still looking for an avenue of attack.

Sensing her feet ignite with pain, Stephenie drew off the flood of energy one of the men had dumped into the ground under her. Still concentrating on the shield around Henton and Douglas, she grunted as another round of attacks struck her. Several connected with her flesh, but her instinctive responses blocked the blows from doing significant damage.

They're too fast, she thought more to herself than Kas; she could not risk them gaining access to her mind. Knowing they were outpacing her speed, she resorted to one thing that had always worked for her; she dropped a massive gravity well centered under the closer man and unloaded as much energy into that field as she could while still maintaining her scattered defenses.

The closer man grunted under the sudden pull and resisted for half a heartbeat as his partner stepped up his attack on Stephenie. However, the closer man could not compensate for the strength of Stephenie's field and collapsed into a heap of broken bones. Several people toppled forward before Stephenie could stop the field. While the town's people were not crushed, they landed on a messy pile of blood and gore.

The second man dropped a stone that was in his hands and started to run away at a speed that would challenge a horse at full gallop. Stephenie moved forward to pursue while reaching out with her powers to try and stop the man. However, before she could fully form the gravity field, she sensed something wrong with the stone that had been dropped and was now under her feet.

"Bac—" she started to cry as an intense wave of mental energy exploded outward from the stone, slamming into her and overwhelming her senses as if a thousand people were shouting different things at the top of their lungs directly into her ears. Pain ran through every nerve of her being, but she knew there was more coming. Even as blinded as she had become, raw energy was following the first wave, bursting forth in all directions and it was moments away. The amount of power was immense. It would easily kill her and everyone within a hundred paces.

Instinct took over and she gorged herself on the energy, pulling it into herself faster and with more fury than she had ever before done. Throwing her arms into the air, she did not pause in unloading the energy. Unlike when she had used a similar technique to heal herself from the damage she sustained in the Grey Mountains, she could not hold this much energy in her for any length of time.

The initial surge of pain dropped away, but her head still throbbed as energy continued to run through her. She hoped desperately that no one was immediately around her because she suspected there was a large plume of flames shooting into the air. Burning from the inside, she stood there for what felt like days, but she knew could only be a few moments in time.

As suddenly as the energy had erupted, it was gone and she immediately felt cold and empty. She had closed her eyes at some point and now opened them. The world felt like a vague concept, no longer real, just a memory of a dream. While she could see and hear, her mind's senses were numbed beyond anything she had ever experienced. She had less sensitivity to the people and fields around her than she had before she learned of her powers.

Looking in the direction of the second man, she caught his eyes as he crouched upon a rooftop a hundred yards away. He immediately turned and launched himself the rest of the way over the building and out of her sight.

Are you whole? She heard Kas calling out to her, obviously in the equivalent of a mental shout, but it sounded like he was a mile away.

"I am okay," she said aloud, unable to respond mentally. "Follow him and stop him if you can," she added in Dalish, to make sure only Kas would understand.

Feeling weak, she sunk into Henton's arms as he wrapped a cloak around her shoulders and bare chest. No longer covered in flames and energy, she shivered from the cool morning air.

"You okay?" he asked from behind her. Douglas had moved in front of her, his sword drawn.

"Your Highness," several people stammered in something between a question and awe. Stephenie was unable to mentally feel anyone's presence.

"Thank you," she whispered to Henton, who continued to hold her upright. "My head is killing me and I don't want to do that again."

"It's the prophet, she's come!"

"She was covered in flames, just like they said."

"I saw Catheri's mark."

Stephenie tried to put aside the comments that were building around her. She wanted nothing more than to sink to the ground and close her eyes. However, even more people were gathering, drawn in by the column of fire and energy she had directed into the air.

"Did Catheri send you here?" a woman asked.

Her legs trembling slightly, she continued to rely on Henton to remain vertical, even if it would not be quite as impressive of an image. She could see scorch marks around the ground and even her pants were burned and singed, though they were still held up by her sword belt. Her leather armor was burned away to a few charred fragments on the ground. Her shirt was mostly gone. All that remained were a couple of smoldering pieces hanging down over her belt. Only Henton's cloak was providing some amount of modesty.

There were now at least thirty people gathered, and she could see more coming. She reached out her hand and put it on Douglas' sword arm, causing him to lower the blade. While she could not sense anything at the moment, none of the people gathered appeared hostile toward her.

"Good people of Eugin," she forced herself to say, despite the growing desire to sleep. "I am Her Royal Highness, Princess

Stephenie. Those men who were here were not Holy Warriors of Felis or any other god." She swallowed, now feeling incredibly dizzy. "Do not believe any accusations they have made."

She felt Henton tighten his grip around her and then sweep her legs out from under her. It took a moment for her to realize he had lifted her into his arms. "She'll be okay," she heard him say. "She just needs to rest after what she did to save everyone." She had the sensation of movement, but her eyes were now closed and she was not sure if it was real. All she knew was it was good not to have to stand.

Henton tried to flex the fingers of his left hand, but whatever had erupted from the dropped stone had reached out and struck his hand. He could hold Stephenie; her he would not drop, but he had no feeling below his elbow except for pain. Several people around them were crying and one was sobbing, but most people were staring at him and Stephenie.

Henton nodded his head to Douglas, who sheathed his sword and bent down to check one of the several people who had been struck by the bright flashes that had arched past Stephenie in the initial moments before she had sucked the energy through her and directed it into the sky.

"Is your priest around," he asked of the stunned crowed.

One man shook his head and then several blurted out in unison that the priest had died nearly ten days earlier. "Those men claimed a minion of Elrin living in our town must have done it," the first man added.

Feeling his own strength waning, he glanced to Douglas who shook his head to say the man still on the ground was dead. "Her Highness will recover. The act of diverting the...," he almost said 'magic', "witchcraft those two used has worn her out. We'll head back to the stables where we have our horses."

"Please, take her into my home. I own the stables." An older lady stepped forward as the crowd parted.

Henton nodded his head and quickly headed back in the direction they had come and followed the woman into the single story building next to the stables. The interior decor was plain, but the main room was warm from a wood burning stove against the center wall. Led through a side door, Henton was shown the bed, where he gently placed Stephenie.

"Thank you, Ma'am," he said, hiding his left hand behind his back. "I appreciate the use of your bed."

"Please, call me Elim. My husband died two years ago, so it is just me and Jarel, the stable boy. We can stay elsewhere while Her Highness, The Prophet, recovers."

Henton nodded his head. "Thank you again." He turned to Douglas who was still in the doorway. "Gather anything they dropped, but be careful. Don't touch anything directly. Bring it back here, but leave it outside the house. We don't want someone triggering it again and we don't want it too close if it should go off on its own."

Douglas turned to go, but was stopped by Elim. "I have a basket you can use."

When they left, Henton shut the door and walked back over to Stephenie. She was breathing slowly, as if she was in a deep sleep. He pulled back his cloak and quickly examined her arms and upper body. She smelled heavily of smoke, but her skin and hair was unmarked, save for the blackened handprint covering her left breast and heart. He had examined the claw like mark that Kas had left many times when he was caring for her in the Grey Mountains. The deep black of the mark appeared unchanged.

"You keep your personal connection to Kas," he said softly, knowing the mark had darkened to pure black after the events in the mountains. He draped his cloak over her chest and arms, hiding her small breasts from his sight. He had heard her remark a few times that she would not mind larger ones; however, he saw nothing wrong with her body. "They are large enough," he mumbled aloud.

Moving to her lower body, he pulled back her charred pants to look through the holes that had burned through the cloth. Frowning, he pulled out his knife and struggled to cut away the material with only one hand. Once the pants were cut away, he found red welts and blisters up and down her legs. She had flatly refused all claims that she was impervious to fire. On the way to Kynto, he learned that when she had used large amounts of energy to heal herself, her body was only protected in the places where she extruded the energy. Today, she had only pushed the energy out of her upper body, instead of igniting her whole self. The flashes of lightning that had struck her legs had left their marks, but the damage was more limited than what he had expected.

Rising from the side of the bed, he went into the main room looking for Elim, but found no one in sight. Grabbing a metal pot, he poured in water from a pitcher and set the pot on the wood stove to heat while he returned to Stephenie to check for more injuries. Finding only the burns, he grabbed the warm water and with a clean shirt from Elim's dresser he started to clear away the pieces of burnt clothing fused to her legs.

He could see the warm water disturbed her sleep, but she did not wake. Once he tended her lower body as best as he could, he took the rest of the pitcher of water and cut small strips of cloth. Soaking them in the cool water, he placed them over her burns, and then covered her with the quilt from Elim's bed.

Douglas returned shortly after Henton had finished tending Stephenie. By this time, the pain had receded in his left hand leaving a tingling sensation that was almost worse than the throbbing. He could move the fingers somewhat, but doing so felt like he was moving someone else's hand.

"You okay, Sarge?"

Henton nodded his head. "It's only my left hand. I'll still be able to swing a sword."

"How's Steph?"

"She'll be fine." He did not want to voice his own fears in case that could cause them to come true. "Did you get the things they dropped? That rock and that metal thing the first one was using?"

Douglas shuddered slightly as he sat down across from Henton. "It was a bloody mess. I still have a hard time looking at a pile of shattered bones and shredded flesh after she crushes them like that. To have to pick through it..." He took a deep breath. "At least I didn't get pulled down onto the mess. One girl has blood and brains and perhaps a bit of liver matted into her hair."

Henton silently agreed with Douglas. It was unsettling to see how little is left of a person when they have been crushed in the same manner as a bug he might step on. He was a dealer in death, any soldier was, but that did not mean he enjoyed or liked killing. In fact, the majority of his time was spent making sure his men would not be the ones to die. The actual killing had been fairly rare.

"But, I've got the things in the basket. I hid them out front, behind the grasses that are next to the clump of trees. The metal object is bent, but looks whole. The rock is cracked and melted. I didn't bother with the small bits, including the money, which is flattened and bent into a small blob of metal." Douglas looked around, "Kas here?"

Henton shook his head. "I don't know exactly what she told him, but my guess is he went after the one that fled. She seemed okay at the time; otherwise I think he would have stayed." Despite his apprehension about the ghost, he voiced his fear, "I hope Kas doesn't get hurt chasing the mage."

Douglas said nothing and then eventually changed the subject. "There are a number of people gathering out front to wait and pray for her. There are also a number of people who had been lined up that were injured to some degree. They are waiting in the stables to be healed."

Henton sighed; he knew how much she hated trying to heal others. "Well, they'll have to wait."

Douglas stood up. "There's a window in the bedroom, I didn't see any other door earlier."

Henton nodded his head, "I've got the shutter closed, but I should get back in there and keep watch."

Douglas walked toward the kitchen area, "I'll borrow some of Elim's food and make us something to eat. Then you can get some rest while I keep watch. Your hand hurts and that will take its toll on you."

Henton nodded his head in agreement; Douglas was continuing to show leadership. *Soon, I'll be following him.*

Chapter 10

Henton rolled his shoulders as he paced in the nearly faded light coming in from the shuttered window. Kas had come back briefly in the morning and when he saw Stephenie's condition, took off angrily. Kas had said enough that Henton knew the Senzar mage had traveled only a short distance from the town and appeared to be waiting. Knowing that neither he nor Douglas would be able to fight the mage's powers, he hoped Stephenie would recover before the man decided to come back and see what her condition was.

The reality of facing a skilled mage, not just a typical witch or warlock, put Henton's mind toward poison. If the mage could be injured with a strong enough dose, then there was a possibility of equalizing a fight. However, none of them had any poison with them and the risks were always there that one could accidentally poison themselves. He was reluctant, but considering their current situation, he intended to bring up the discussion. *Assuming we live to have the conversation.*

He glanced over to Douglas who was quietly watching from the chair he had placed in the corner of the room. While it would protect him against being seen by a normal person looking through the slats in the shutters, it would not hide him from someone with magic.

Douglas returned Henton's glance, then resumed focusing on watching the window and the door. It was already growing dark outside and while the lamp sitting on the floor in the far corner of the room provided enough light to avoid tripping over things, it was turned down low enough to prevent them being night blind.

Henton forced himself not to check Stephenie again and turned his gaze at the basket of remnants he had decided to bring into the house. With the number of people outside, he had become more afraid someone would be overcome with curiosity and disturb what might still be very dangerous. Cautiously peaking over the top of the basket, he noted the bent and twisted piece of metal the first man had been holding as well as the melted and cracked rock the second had dropped. "I wish I knew what these things did. Perhaps we could use them against that mage."

"Do not worry about the Senzar, I have killed him."

Henton jumped back despite himself. "Kas," he growled. "How long have you been here?"

Kas' form appeared as a very faint blue-green outline of a person, but there was no real distinction to his features. "I have been here only a short period of time, but long enough to know that what you have gathered is worthless in any fight." Kas spoke slowly in his accented form of the Old Tongue, which Henton sometimes had trouble following.

Still feeling less than whole because of his left hand, Henton sat down on the bed next to Stephenie, but for Douglas' sake, he responded in Cothish, hoping Kas would follow suit. "It was definitely more than nothing. It killed one person and would have killed a lot more if Stephenie hadn't drawn the energy through herself."

Kas' form solidified to be somewhat less transparent, but his features were still vague. "The Senzar warlock chose to sleep for a short period," he said in the Old Tongue. "I took advantage of that and froze his brain. He is dead. What he unleashed on you was what I would call a battery. Or at least, a form of one that had been modified into a bomb."

"I don't understand," Henton replied, giving in and switching to the Old Tongue. He sensed Kas was not going to cooperate and making the ghost angry would not help. "I don't know what those words mean."

"The terms are irrelevant for you because they no longer exist in your primitive world." Kas huffed and then his shoulders slumped. "A battery is simply a device to store energy for later use. Almost all things that have permanent magic will have at least a small reserve of power they store. This one had a large reserve stored in it." Kas held out his hands. "Then consider the energy is in two forms, each wanting to interact with the other, but divided by a wall between them. When the wall was destroyed, the two polarities of energy interacted violently. Somehow they added a delay mechanism, which turned it into a somewhat useful explosive."

"Are there more of these batteries about?" Stephenie mumbled from where she was laying.

Henton spun around and carefully placed his hands on her shoulders, which slowly drew open her eyes. "How are you?" He watched her look into his eyes for several moments, and then she blinked and tried to sit upright. Keeping the blankets over her shoulders, Henton helped her scoot back against the wall behind the bed.

"My head hurts still. It was like my skull was split in half when it went off. I couldn't sense anything at the time and now things are still a bit hazy." She looked to Kas, "what did it do to me?"

Kas drifted closer. "I am sorry, Stephenie, I cannot say exactly what forces were released. These devices were not often used in my time. They were usually too unstable and could go off unexpectedly." He sat beside her, "However, I believe that the initial pulse that exploded from the device carried a strong level of energy frequencies that mimic mental activity. Either a side effect from the battery's intelligence dying or something done intentionally to disable the target so the subsequent explosion of energy would kill." He sat down on the foot of the bed. "Though, most people would not have survived the second blast at such a close range even if they were not disabled from the first."

Henton watched the interaction between them and noted the continuation of a trend he had observed for some time: the lack of mental communication between them. He was fairly certain Stephenie was the one holding back, but not certain as to why.

"But I don't understand what they were trying to do," she said, drawing Henton's attention back to the conversation. "The first girl we saw them check, she's got powers and they declared her clean. The second one, they simply invented the accusation and would've burned him if I hadn't gotten involved. And these Senzar, they were definitely trying to kill me. I could sense it in the nature of their very first attacks. I thought the Senzar wanted me alive."

Henton opened his mouth to reply, but Kas responded first. "Darling, I know everyone from Cothel is in complete agreement at all times, that is why you never fight each other over anything, but—"

"Shut up, Kas," she said, but there was no irritation in her voice. "I get it; different groups might want different things." She sighed, "It was almost like they were trying to..." she looked over at Henton, "They are trying to drive off anyone with powers. Kill the real priests and frighten everyone who might suspect they could be next."

Henton nodded his head. "If what you said is true...if they knew the girl has powers and purposely skipped her, then perhaps they are trying to divide us."

"And she knows she has powers. I could see her trembling ever so slightly. She might not use them, but she knows there is something different about her." She glanced down at his left hand. "Are you hurt?"

"Just a bit. I'll heal. I just wish the tingling would go away." He smiled at her, "You saved a couple dozen people. There are a few who were hurt and one died, but if you had not done what you did, everyone would have died."

"What is it?" she asked, her scrutiny increased.

Henton cleared his throat, "Their priest was killed about ten days ago, so they are looking to you for healing."

She groaned. "I hate getting into other people's heads."

Henton said nothing; he hated people getting into his head, so he could sympathize.

"I'll go get you something to eat," Douglas said after her stomach rumbled.

Henton watched her smile as Douglas patted her hand as he walked passed. "Thank you." Turning to Henton and Kas, she added, "And if you could all give me a little privacy, I want to use the chamber pot and put on some clothes."

Henton pushed himself to his feet. Now that he knew Stephenie was awake, he felt the toll of the emotions he had kept in check all day. He steadied himself, working to keep up the mask he had built in his years at sea.

"Henton, wait a bit, I'll take care of your hand."

He turned back around to face her as Douglas closed the bedroom door behind himself. The slight dimming of the illumination in the room told him that Kas had disappeared from sight, but perhaps had not left. He looked down and met Stephenie's blue eyes and noted the pain and weariness that was behind them, but also the kindness and caring she always held for her friends.

"Thank you for catching me. I left myself exposed again."

He smiled at her as he sat down. "I was glad to be there. You can always count on us. We'll be there when you need us."

She took his hand in her own, just barely keeping the blanket up at her shoulders. He watched her as she stared at his hand, but said nothing. He knew she would need to reach out and touch his mind in order to heal him and he never liked the feeling.

"I over estimated my abilities again. Only this time, I almost got you and Douglas killed as well."

"You handled it well enough," he said, leaving his hand in her care. "We've had a number of close calls, but you've always been a match for what we've faced. Even when I doubted you early on."

"When I went to confront the men who had taken Will." She looked up to meet his eyes. "The Senzar warlock who was with them...Gernvir was his name. I don't think I ever mentioned that to you before." She bit her lower lip, "Henton, he beat me. He had control of my body and..." She swallowed. "He let me know just what he had planned to do to me...I couldn't stop him and he was going to make me watch him kill Kas. He wanted to enjoy my suffering."

He saw the pleading in her eyes; the fear under her confident exterior. "Steph, we would have come for you if he had taken you away."

"Henton, that's not what I fear the most. What scared me was what happened inside me. Something in my head just snapped. I lost control. I was aware of what was happening, but as if it was a dream. It was an emotional response. Something in me reacted violently to the idea of being dominated. I slaughtered everyone in sight without remorse and almost didn't come back to myself. Somehow Kas managed to bring me out of it. What if it happens again?"

He wanted to pull her close and comfort her, but then he would not want to let her go. Unfortunately, he knew she viewed him as only an older brother; one she was very close to, but a brother nonetheless. "And the event in Venla felt the same to you?" She nodded her head. "Steph, I'll risk it. Don't worry about us deserting you."

The fear did not leave her eyes, "but I almost wasn't able to protect you today...at least I think it was today...those mages were just so fast. Too fast for me. I only stopped their attack by drawing more power than they could."

He took her hands in his. "Steph, you've only been learning to use your powers for the last half year. I'd imagine they've been using their powers for years. You've come so far in such a short time. You can count on Douglas and Kas and me to always be there. We'll have to work on how we can be more of an asset to you and not a distraction, but we'll be there." She finally sighed and appeared to relax. He hoped she believed him, but suspected she was still hesitant.

"Thank you."

He watched her look back down at his hand and took it into hers again. A moment later, he felt her touch his thoughts and then felt warmth and a sharp pain move through his body. Slowly the pain receded and the tingling in his hand was gone. Flexing his fingers, his hand felt strong and whole. "Thank you," he said to her. "As good as it ever was."

"Sorry about pushing too much energy at first. It's really hard for me to regulate it. I guess I'll get some practice on all the injured people."

"You still look tired. Let Douglas get you some food and deal with them in the morning. Everyone out there will survive until then." He rose to his feet, seeing the thanks in her eyes. "Just let Douglas know when you are ready for some food."

Stephenie was wide-awake well before the morning light started to brighten the bedroom. She had talked with Kas for a while, rehashing the events of the prior day and even her conversation with Henton. She had not intended on opening up so much to Henton, but the fact that she had barely protected him or Douglas had scared her. She would have died several times over if they had not been there and could no longer imagine being alone again. She had grown up always knowing she would never be able to trust anyone, now that she had found people who believed in her, she could not bear the thought of being without them.

When morning finally did come, she pulled on her boots, which were only slightly damaged and in good enough condition to wear, and then headed out of the bedroom. Douglas already had some eggs and oatmeal cooking. After a quick meal, she headed out of the house to greet the people she had sensed were waiting for her.

"Good morning," she said to the solemn crowd, all of whom bowed or curtsied with an obvious lack of practice. She smiled to reassure them. "I wanted to thank Elim for allowing me the use of her home. We will do our best to repay your kindness." She glanced around at a group of people who were emanating varying degrees of distress. "I am not a great healer, but I will do my best to help anyone who needs healing." She paused a moment. "Yes, you have questions?"

An older man spoke up, "Your Highness, they claimed to be priests of Felis. Why would they accuse innocent people of being in league with Elrin?"

Stephenie noted the man appeared familiar, perhaps a brother or close relative of the man who had been accused just before she intervened. Though it made her sick, she decided to stick to the story she had worked out with Kas, much of which was likely true. "They were Senzar warlocks and not priests. They were wanting to eliminate the next generation of priests. We lost many people in the war and the gods want to refill their ranks. They were trying to target people who may be the next group chosen by the gods."

"But that happens only with the young."

Stephenie shook her head. "Things are changing. Catheri, and even Felis, are not holding to the old rules. Our lives are being turned over by invaders from distant lands and we need to be able to defend ourselves today, not a decade from now." She moved closer to the gathered people. "Please, spread the word, before you accuse someone of being a witch or warlock, take those people to Antar to have a priest verify the suspicion. It may be that they are being chosen to come into the fold. If you burn them, you could be burning your next priest." She could feel the uncertainty of the crowd. What she was asking was more than they had done before; the effort to take someone to Antar was a large undertaking. "If you cannot take them yourselves, take them to the Baron and have him bring them to Antar. It is important not to condemn someone before you are certain."

"But, Your Highness," said a middle-aged woman, "if they are possessed by Elrin, we could be in grave danger."

"It may be a slight risk. However, we know the Senzar were targeting innocent people to remove them as a potential threat. Would you rather take a slight risk or end up with no priests at all to defend you against the Senzar."

"I thought they were driven away by you...Your Highness."

Stephenie nodded her head to a young man, "I killed thousands of them by bringing down a mountain peak. But, that did not drive them completely from the lands around Tet. They control much of the land on the Endless Sea. And now, it seems, they are starting to probe our weaknesses." She turned away from the man who had just spoken. "I will evaluate those who need healing and may recommend some people make the journey to Antar. I'll provide a letter of introduction for either the High Priest of Felis or Catheri. Simply go to the person you would feel more comfortable talking with." She glanced at Henton, whom she knew wanted to get back on the road; it was a desire she shared. "I will barrow Elim's home a little longer and heal those I can."

They left Ecais just after midday and stopped where Kas had left the body of the other mage. Being cautious to avoid triggering any magical bombs, they searched his possessions and found a fair number of coins from various lands, many of the coins no one recognized. However, nothing currently on the man appeared to possess any of the structures necessary to make it a magical device.

The only item of interest was a small, leather bound, journal. The writing was not familiar to any of them, but Stephenie did recognize what appeared to be a series of lists with a varying number of marks beside each one. She suspected they were city and country names, but the characters on the page eluded her understanding.

Without anything giving them a particular direction, she led them northwest in the hopes the road they were following would lead to the north bound road into Epish. When evening came, they decided to camp along the narrow road they had been using. Having seen no other travelers the whole day and with Stephenie having burned up all the coin she had been carrying in the fire that consumed her clothing, they chose not to push on to the next town.

The following day they reached the north road between Warton and Mulid. Unfortunately, the road was in no better shape than the smaller and less traveled ones. Instead of having to go over fallen branches and limbs, they had to deal with deeper ruts and holes as well as navigate around the occasional wagon carrying supplies for the upcoming winter.

Three more days of riding led them into Mulid, the first major city in Epish. The walled city was at the foothills of the Gawain Mountain Range, which was named for an early explorer who had charted many of the routes through the numerous small peaks. The people of Epish were friendly enough. However, while they avoided the ravages of the war, there were mixed feelings over the Senzar invasion by different factions in the country.

With no westerly road out of Mulid, the four of them continued north after spending a day purchasing supplies. Two more long days of traveling, with the snow-covered mountains on their right, led them to the massive city of Iron Heart. The city's air was as smoggy and filled with the acrid stench of rotten eggs as Wyntac had been. However, the amount and quality of the steel produced here could not compete with Wyntac; the Kyntian foundries were simply more sophisticated and efficient.

"You're not planning to have us buy a bunch of steel stock here are you?" Douglas joked as he walked with Stephenie along the deep river that fed barges into the heart of Epish.

She smiled at him, remembering how he tried to avoid her eyes as she stripped out of the bloody dress when they were running from Wyntac with the stolen gold. She knew him to be somewhat shy when it came to women, but she had vowed not to interfere. *I am not a matchmaker*, she repeated to herself. "We are low on money, but if you want me to look into it, we can. I just don't remember either you or Henton being that good at driving a wagon."

He shook his head, "We were as good as you were."

Seeing the shop she had been looking for just ahead of them, she crossed the road and walked up the couple of stairs to knock on the door of a bookseller. It was the third one they had stopped at so far. After a short delay, a young woman with long red hair opened the door. Overall, the girl was about the same height as Stephenie, but was bigger boned and had a rounder face that lacked the distinctive cheekbones that Stephenie bore from her Kyntian heritage.

"Good day," Stephenie said in Pandar, "I would like to speak with someone regarding some markings I found."

The young woman nodded and stood aside so they could enter. The inside of the building was slightly musty and dimly lit. Bookshelves covered the walls of the narrow shop; some of them were even full. In the back of the long room was a desk covered in papers and books. An old man sat writing in the light of the lamp next to him.

"My father can assist you," the young woman said smoothly, obviously quite fluent in the trade tongue. Leading them to the desk, the old man looked up, his thinning red hair falling in front of his eyes.

"What is it I can do for you?" he asked as his ink stained fingers pushed back the loose hair.

Eying the chair in front of the desk, Stephenie sat down while Douglas stood behind her. "Good Sir, I have stumbled across some markings that I hope you can help me with."

The man frowned. "I am quite busy copying this document." He moved his hands to indicate a delicate piece of parchment placed carefully on his desk. "My time will cost you."

Stephenie nodded her head; she hated having limited funds, but understood the man needed to make a living. "Let me show you some of the markings and then you let me know what it will cost." She pulled a folded piece of paper from a pouch she borrowed from Henton. It had been a blank page from the journal onto which she had replicated parts of the journal as well as a similar set of markings they had found on some of the coins that had been in a highly decorated pouch carried by the second mage.

The old man behind the desk took the page from Stephenie and unfolded it. After a moment he looked up, his expression schooled, but his emotions having gone from annoyance to excitement. "Young lady, please tell me where you came across this page."

It was Stephenie's turn to smile; she had scarcely had any hope this man would be able to help her. With his interest piqued, she hoped they might be able to barter knowledge for knowledge. "How much will your time cost me?"

The man sat straighter and then glanced down at the page once again, eventually, he looked up to meet Stephenie's eyes. "What you have here is likely random markings, but there are those who believe in an ancient society." He bit his lip, "Perhaps we can simply exchange information?"

Stephenie nodded her head and leaned forward. "I copied some of the markings from a journal. The ones at the bottom came from a set of coins."

"Do you have the journal?" the man asked, his focus on the paper.

"I might," Stephenie said, not ready to produce it unless she was confident she would get useful information.

"Jes, go to my room and bring down the red book. You know where I keep it," he added, still not removing his eyes from Stephenie's page. "Have you shown this to anyone else?"

"A bookbinder and another bookseller near the castle. They had some guesses, but none of them appeared to know anything about the language." Stephenie had been fairly certain that none of them had lied based upon their emotional response.

The man leaned forward, placing the paper on the table so Stephenie could see it as he pointed to characters on the page. "The marks here at the bottom. They are a combination of a number and a special accent." He isolated a section of the complex marking with the tip of a piece of bone used for binding books. "This set of three lines, connected with the large dot and the triangle, you see that in these other two characters, yes?" He pointed to two of the other characters she had drawn near the top of the page.

Stephenie looked closer, but remembered the similarity when she had copied them. "Yes, you said that is an accent?"

"I do not know a name for this language, but there are a few of us who look for anything we can find." He lifted his head toward her, "We hope to prove the existence of a secret society. Most scholars believe we are deluded, but there is enough evidence to say otherwise. Only no one believes we have not forged our evidence."

"What does the accent mean?"

"The other part of this character at the bottom of the page is a number; I believe it is the number seven. The accent makes it special, but I do not know why. The mark at the top of the page I believe is a name because of the squarish block here, but it also has the accent at the end. The second one at the top of the page, it may be a place or a time. We have not fully puzzled out the language, but we have deciphered some key symbols." He stretched his shoulders. "This symbol I know means dead. This other one, it means either the color blue, mountain, or journey. It depends on the context."

Stephenie looked at the two symbols he was talking about; they were the ones after the list of items, the first one was on most of the items and the second one on more than half of the entries that had the first mark. *Each town, priest killed, mages driven onto their journey west?* She felt it was likely.

Stephenie looked up as the young woman returned and handed her father a small leather journal stained red with dye. The man quickly opened the book and scanned through a couple of pages. "Yes, that is the number seven and this other mark you have on here means tree."

Stephenie looked at what he was indicating on the page and remembered just randomly picking a symbol from a page full of text.

"May I see the journal?"

Stephenie pursed her lips. He had more than fulfilled his end of the agreement, but she was feeling a strong sense of possessiveness over the volume. Breathing deeply, she pushed down the feelings that were building in her. *I will do it, if for no other reason than to prove that I can.*

"I will not harm it. And your man would be more than a challenge for me."

Stephenie glanced at Douglas who was standing slightly behind her and then turned back to the old man. She was carrying a sword on her hip just as Douglas, but gender stereotypes were more engrained in older people. *The insult will not break me.* "Okay, I will let you see it." She reached back and took the book from Douglas' hand and then placed it on the desk. The man eagerly picked up the journal and opened it to carefully leaf through the pages.

"Only a small portion has been written in. It looks like there are a couple of languages written in here." He paused in the section where Stephenie believed was the list of towns. "I am not certain what these are, but it looks like names." He looked up from the pages. "This was recently written. There is a date here. It is not based on our calendars, but on the positions of the two moons. How much do you want for this?"

Stephenie shook her head. "It is not for sale, but I have an idea." She forced herself to breathe deeply. "I will leave it with you tonight, you may make a copy of it, but in the morning I will be back for it and I want your red book." She held up her hand, "I am certain you have a copy of that somewhere, if it is something that important to you, you won't just have the one."

The man took a moment to purse his own lips. "My red journal contains a wealth of information and I doubt you would be able to read the cross-reference language—"

"That will be my problem if I cannot." Sensing his hesitation, she pulled out the small pouch the Senzar mage had carried. Slipping one of the coins into her palm, she placed it on the desk. "And, I will give you that coin."

The man picked up the coin. "The mark on this side, it is your seven. The other side, it is a name."

"Do you know what name?" she asked.

The man shook his head. "I would say no one knows the sounds for this language, but this journal and this marker would indicate otherwise. The coin would likely be a token from a lord or person of power and would not have a specific value, but would represent a favor or a promise of a reward."

"Interesting," Stephenie said, taking back the coin and looking at it closer before again meeting his eyes, "Do we have a deal?"

Henton walked through the market with a burlap bag over his shoulder. He had picked up most of the things they would need for the next leg of their journey, which he calculated as being about two thirds complete, though they were more than halfway through the money he and Douglas carried.

He avoided glancing around, but moved with a methodical purpose in the hopes to keep anyone from marking him as a target. Kas was supposed to be watching and following him to provide assistance in case something happened. If the ghost was with him, Henton had no way of knowing;   but he was beginning to trust Kas more than he ever thought he would. Aside from his occasionally abrasive nature, Henton felt Kas did care for Stephenie and he might even like Douglas and himself. He was less certain about Kas' thoughts on Will, but Will had pushed Stephenie to embrace the idea of Catheri, which Kas definitely disagreed with.

Henton slid through a group of people and stopped in front of a stall selling sweet rolls. Waves of heat distorted the air above the enticing food and while he could resist the impulse of the treat, the man he had been following had stopped to partake of the hot food.

"Pardon me," Henton said in Pandar after he lightly bumped the man's side. The large and hairy man glanced at Henton and simply nodded his head, turning his attention back to the hot roll. "One please," Henton said to the woman running the stall. To the man he added, "I couldn't help but notice the anchor. Where'd you earn yours?"

The man turned to face Henton, the tattoo of a ship's anchor now clearly visible on his cheek. While Henton was not positive of the meaning, he knew that many sailors on the Endless Sea took on the mark of an anchor.

Henton returned the man's gaze confidently. Although they were about the same height, the man was definitely wider and had thicker arms. Henton could tell the man was sizing him up and trying to consider how to respond. *A bit of a slow thinker, perhaps.* "I asked because Iron Heart isn't a port city and was wondering if I might find work on Oakval." Henton slid up the sleeve of his left arm, proudly showing his own set of tattoos: a fully deployed sail with a trident added to the flapping canvas on his tenth year of service.

The man's expression softened as he nodded his head. "There's no work to be found in Iron Heart for a sailor. I've quit the sea. I know nothing of Oakval."

Henton, having already gathered that from a conversation he had overhead, feigned surprise. "Really, I was hoping the waters on the Endless Sea would be better to me than what Tet offered."

The man shook his head. "I sailed for Tenip for five years. When the Senzar came through, they sank most of our ships and threatened our king with what they did in Ipith. The heathen Elrin worshipers took the west. Anyone with sense is heading east."

Henton nodded his head, considering what the man said. "East is not an option for me and I fear the north is too cold," he shivered, partially for effect and partially because he was truly cold. "Ulet stayed out of the war and I heard they have a fair navy." Henton hoped that was true, he knew very little about the country, but he took the risk that a country which was little more than a long narrow peninsula into the sea would indeed have a strong navy.

The man sneered, which was not completely unexpected, he was from the country just to the south of Ulet. "They raid others and impress them to work on their ships. More thieves than sailors." He shook his head, "but you don't want to go there. The king of Ulet is harboring the Senzar under everyone's nose. I jumped ship in a small little port town that is mostly used for smuggling. The Senzar are running the place, offering sanctuary to any witches and warlocks who managed to avoid the righteous fires of the gods."

Henton raised his eyebrows. "I'd not heard that. Perhaps north it will be."

The man nodded his head. "You want to sail, go north, Kynto or Delwin are good countries. Stay out of Ulet and Vinerxan. It's a cesspool of evil and the locals have embraced it."

Henton thanked the man, took his sweet roll, and headed back to the inn. *At least I know we are going to the correct place.*

Chapter 11

The next morning, on their way out of Iron Heart, they stopped at the bookseller's shop and knocked on the door. The morning was cold and few people were on the streets.

"You sure they won't have run off with the book," Henton asked, still unhappy with the situation.

Stephenie ignored the even less pleasant comment from Kas and stepped back from the door. Under her breath, she whispered, "I had felt both were home before I knocked. I never got the sense I could not trust them."

When the door opened, the young Jes nodded her head to the two of them, Kas had already drifted through the wall invisibly and Douglas remained in the street with the four horses. "Good morning. My father is still dressing, but please come in."

Stephenie entered, passing the girl, who was still in her own dressing gown. "Did your father find anything interesting?"

The girl nodded, closing the door behind Henton. "He did, please come back to his desk. Would any of you like something to drink?"

Stephenie nodded her head as she followed the young woman. The girl's father emerged, his thinning red hair in as much disarray as his clothing. He held up both journals as they approached his desk.

"Quite fascinating. Very intriguing."

"What did you find," Stephenie asked, taking the seat in front of the desk before it was offered.

The man held out both books to her as he sat down in his chair. She took a quick glance through the pages to ensure everything was still there. The red journal, she noted quickly, appeared to be written in a form of the Old Tongue.

"The journal you have was indeed in two languages. The predominate one I believe is called Kantipic Script. It is a language that we have seen show up with the Senzar. Quite likely one of them had the journal with him. The other language is, of course, the ancient one that most people deny even exists. What is intriguing is that it appears the person writing the journal was trying to improve their understanding or use of that language." He indicated she should open the journal and had her flip to the second page. "You will note the three lines, the circle, and the triangle are part of that symbol there. The sentence basically translates to 'I am the seventeenth'. But we do not know of what."

Stephenie frowned. "He was mixing the languages as he wrote?"

"Well, in the context, I would say he was using it more as a title than truly mixing words in a single sentence, but the journal is a mixing of the languages." He nodded to the red journal. "That is written in the language of the court and the priests. It was a priest who first put me on this quest to find more about this secret society. You will probably not want to show it to too many people." The man looked carefully at Stephenie. "How did you know it was a man who had written the journal?"

"We found it on his body."

"I see."

Stephenie nodded her head. "You may, but you also may not. Is there anything else I should know about the journal?"

The man nodded his head. "The list at the back, which had the symbol for dead and the symbol that I would assume now to mean journey. I believe the characters that make up the listed items are more phonetic than literal. As if the man may have been using the characters from the dead language to represent sounds in another language. If you know what the list represents, perhaps we can start to put sound to the language."

Stephenie nodded her head. "You've been quite helpful, so I'll give you this, but I suggest you are careful with what you do with the knowledge." When the man nodded eagerly, she continued, "Try looking for the names of towns and villages in western Cothel."

The man's face froze in sudden understanding. "There is mention of ships and travels. I did not have time to translate much of either the Kantipic or the other language, but some words I recognized on sight. Also be wary, the men responsible for this book I believe are warlocks, though you may already be aware."

"It was a dead Senzar warlock the book was taken from." She stood up, placed the promised marker on the desk, and bowed her head to the man as she led the others from the shop before any more questions could be asked.

"Is it wise to have shared so much?" Henton asked quietly as they descended the steps toward the horses. "I think he might have guessed who you are."

"He knew more than he shared and it would not have taken him long to come to that conclusion. Perhaps on our return trip we can come back this way and check on what more he learns while we are gone."

They left Iron Heart immediately after finishing with the bookseller and headed northwest. The snow covered road stayed in the foothills of the mountains for more than a day before opening up to the cold winds rushing south off the sea, or at least an inlet wide enough that they could not see the land on the other side. Due to the weather, it took them six days to reach Oakval and then another ten to reach West Port, which was the last city in Epish before they would cross the border into Ulet. The journey was hard and Stephenie had little time to examine the books, but the small bits she was able to translate were inconsequential details of travel.

In West Port, she hoped to find a little rest before moving on, but the city was expensive and they needed to save funds for the return trip. Therefore, instead of rest, they headed directly into the city to buy supplies.

"I've talked to a number of people along the way," Henton said, "And it's not been easy to do without drawing suspicion. In every city, there are rumors all over the place that Ulet, and even sometimes specifically, Vinerxan, is a hive of witchery and evil. But the consensus is the only safe route there is to follow the road north to Gren Haven, then go south to Tusr and take a boat to Vinerxan."

Stephenie shook her head. "I heard many of those conversations and there were a few that talked of the paths through the mountains. Vinerxan may not have any coastal roads open this time of year, but we can't break into the keep, rescue Islet, then head to the docks and wait for a ship to take us away. We need to know if the mountain road is passable and what to expect so we don't get lost escaping."

"Damn it, I hate it when you are right. But the mountain passes are going to be worse than what we've experienced so far. We'll need the horses to carry more food, since we won't be able to count on being able to resupply as often. Probably we'll end up leading them more than riding."

Stephenie nodded her head and patted Argat's neck. "And if I had not burnt up most of our money, we'd have enough to buy a couple of mules to carry extra feed."

"That was not what I was implying."

She smiled at Henton. "I was more griping at myself than saying that was your complaint. But it is still true." She looked between her men, "We'll find a way."

It ended up taking two days to resupply and wait for a break in the weather before they were able to leave West Port. Stephenie spent the time practicing mental exercises with Kas and discovering just how little use the red book would be in translating the journal.

When they finally left West Port and crossed into Ulet, they declared themselves travelers going to Gren Haven to collect an inheritance from Douglas' fictional uncle who had moved there ten years ago. After paying a small toll for their horses, they followed the road long enough to be out of sight of the small town and headed southwest across the windswept and snow covered fields.

Stephenie crafted a gravitational lens, as Kas called it, to deflect the worst of the biting wind that was blowing from the north. It gave relief to the horses as well as Henton and Douglas, but the effort to maintain the field during the entire day was leaving Stephenie exhausted. It also brought a little blood to Stephenie's nose and throat, something that had not happened to her in a long time. She covered the effects of drawing too much energy through herself with the scarf wrapped around her face. However, she was not happy experiencing what people often referred to as Elrin poisoning, the imaginary side effect of using power meant for his demons, the elves.

After three miserable days of traveling, the winds and snow let up and they were able to spot the rising of smoke in the distance. Taking the chance on a bit of shelter, they approached the small community and were thankful to spend the night in a barn. In the morning, after they gave the horses some extra attention in the comfort of shelter, they left their leery hosts with money for supplies and continued southwest toward the mountain range just visible in the distance.

At the foothills of the mountains, it took two days and three false starts before they found what appeared to be the actual pass through the range. Stephenie continued to block the wind and even started to push small amounts of energy into everyone's bodies to counter the biting cold. The effort further eased the toll on the horses as well as Henton and Douglas, but it left her even more worn out and mentally exhausted. Heating their moving bodies required a higher level of concentration that left her with a headache and a bad temper.

Once they were deep into the pass, they found a road that appeared to receive at least occasional maintenance. In most places it was wide enough and clear enough for the horses to walk three abreast. While it would not be suitable for wagons with the drifting snow, they did encounter a trapper heading to the northeast pulling a line of three mules loaded down with a number of dead animals. While they shared no common language, it appeared the man was likely heading toward a sheltered side valley with his catch.

Another three days into the mountains, they came across a small settlement in a long valley between the ranges. For the first time in days, they slept under a solid roof and ate fresh stew. The lodging, as well as additional supplies, were at a premium. Stephenie was certain that was due to the fact they were not part of the normal group of mountain dwellers, but they willingly paid the price and continued on the next morning. The estimate they received was that Vinerxan was another ten days through the steeper climbs and difficult passes that lay to the southwest.

On the eighth day out of the long valley, the snow had turned to rain and Stephenie worked even harder to try and keep everyone as dry as possible. As the light was fading, they dismounted in front of a two-story building just off what had become a muddy road. Stephenie believed the sign over the door meant the building was an inn. However, she was still struggling with the Uletian characters; too many of the symbols looked the same to her.

There was a set of large barn doors leading into the ground level and a narrow set of stairs leading up to a small landing and door on the second story. "I'll run up and see if they have room for the night," Stephenie said as she headed toward the stairs with Argat honoring the ground tie where Stephenie had dropped the reins.

Warmth washed over Stephenie as the door opened just as she reached the landing. A dark haired woman in her mid-thirties stood in the doorway. Stephenie cocked her head at the woman's question, not understanding what had been asked. "You speak Pandar?" the woman asked before Stephenie could.

"Yes, please forgive me if I misread your sign, but do you have room for us and our horses?"

The woman nodded her head without even looking down at Henton and Douglas standing in the cold rain at the foot of the stairs. "Have your men bring them in and use any stall available. I've got a room or two you can use."

Having heard the comment, Henton headed directly for the barn door while Stephenie followed the woman into the building. The first room they entered was cozy, with a fireplace in the middle of the interior wall. Several chairs and small tables were scattered about and one lamp illuminated an area where Stephenie assumed the woman had been sitting.

"You're not a witch or warlocks, are you?"

Stephenie could see the stiffness in the woman's movement, but with her exhausted mind, she hesitated to open herself up to any emotions. "No. Why do you ask?"

The woman's shoulders eased and her hands slowed their fidgeting. "I've had a few stay here on their way to Vinerxan. Mostly they are okay, but many of the people round here are still god fearing and don't really like having Elrin worshipers under their roof. Not that we have much choice. With the Senzar in these parts training all of them to fight and no one in Gren Haven willing to step in and do anything, well...we don't make any trouble."

Stephenie nodded. The road they were on only went to Vinerxan, so she could not pretend to be going elsewhere. "We're to meet some friends who are coming by ship into Vinerxan."

The woman's brows rose. "Really? There are better ports to sail into, especially this time of year. Why are they going there?" The woman frowned. "I suppose they might be pirates or those not quite pirates. There is fair enough trade from trappers and the like who live further up in the mountains and don't want to pay their taxes." She grinned. "Can't say I don't make a little money from time to time from that lot myself." She shook her head and turned toward one of the three doors along the inner wall. "Not my business. You three be wanting food tonight and in the morning?"

"We would greatly appreciate it."

"What coin do you carry?"

"Mostly Epish and a little from Kynto."

"Either coin will work. I'll want half a crown for you and your horses."

Stephenie pulled out her coin pouch and counted out the required amount as she heard the creaking of the outside stairs through the walls of the house. Instinctively opening herself up, she felt Douglas on the stairs with Henton and Kas still tending the horses below.

"There are a couple rooms through the far door. I'll bring some food out to you in a little bit." Slipping the coins into her apron, the woman left through the door on the right.

Eventually Henton and Kas joined her and Douglas in the outer room. The food that Alianor provided was warm and hearty, if not a little bland. She joined them after they were all served and asked general questions about the road and any other travelers they might have seen, 'in case she should expect any other visitors.'

"The road was pretty lonely," Stephenie said between spoonfuls of the stew. "We've never been to Vinerxan. What can we expect? Any places we should stay or avoid?"

Alianor smiled. "It's a bit far for me to travel on my own. My son will go there from time to time and do some trading, which is where he is tonight. I was there a few times when I was younger. It's got a decent port, but then almost any spot along our shores makes a good harbor. There are several hundred people in the city, so it is a good size. The keep is the real gem. It overlooks the sea and it has high curtain walls around a large bailey. When I was just a girl, the bailey was full of gardens and paths for the lord and lady of the castle to stroll about. My son tells me those were all ripped out to make room for practice fields to train the witches and warlocks."

"Ma'am," Henton said when Alianor paused to take breath. "Your King is not concerned about the Senzar?"

Alianor's shrug hinted there was a deeper story, but she did not elaborate beyond a couple of sentences. "Nothing official has been said, save that Lord Favian was granted these lands. We make no trouble and the Senzar leave us be and pay a decent coin for what they need."

After dinner, the four of them retired to the series of nested rooms behind the door on the left side of the wall. With no one else staying, Alianor indicated they could use any or all of the three rooms. Stephenie decided the first room would be best, since it was closest to the exit if they should need it. It also put them further away from Alianor, who's set of rooms went back and then behind the kitchen.

"How do you want to handle Vinerxan?" Douglas asked from where he was laying out his wet clothes next to the backside of the fireplace, another reason Stephenie chose the first room.

"Well, if the road is as wet and muddy as it was today, we'll be getting there late." Henton said, he had knocked most of the mud from his boots, but they were still dirty from leading the horses over the slick terrain. "If Kas can scout out the keep and find Islet quickly enough, perhaps we can do this with only staying a day or so in town."

Stephenie shook her head. "If there are only a few hundred people, while that is a decent town, it will be obvious if we ride in, wait a day, and then disappear overnight with one of their royal captives. I'd rather wait outside of town, even sleep in the snow if we have to, and never take rooms in the city." She could see the groan building in Douglas, who was enjoying the cover of warm shelter. "Look, we're heading down slope and the weather might be better once we get to the shore. There are not that many routes overland, so if they don't know who helped Islet escape, they might think it was someone using a ship."

Henton nodded his head, "You are right, a cautious approach is the best one."

Kas shook his mostly opaque head. "We will not know until I scout the castle."

The morning was cold and while nothing was falling from the sky, the ground had frozen. Even the extra handful of grain Stephenie gave Argat simply resulted in a quizzical flick of an ear when the chestnut took a look at the road. She patted his warm neck and agreed it would be much nicer to stay in bed a while longer. However, more sleep would not rescue her sister, so they embraced the cold and led the four horses over the frozen mud.

By late afternoon, they came out of the high mountain valley they were traveling through and were able to get their first glimpse of the Endless Sea through a break in the trees. The sky was grey, as it had been for days, but the winds were mercifully light and the dark waters that stretched out to the horizon held only a few whitecapped swells.

Below them, the road descended through more forest covered slopes. Subtle gaps in the trees hinted at the switchbacks they would be using to get to the city sitting along the shore. Smoke rose from the numerous distant buildings. There was even a hint of movement in the city, but they were still too far to see the details.

Energized to get to a place where they could camp, Stephenie led them down switchbacks carved into the mountainside. Just before evening they reached the wide tree covered valley that lay between the mountains and Vinerxan. Breaking away from the road, Kas quickly located another small valley to the north that offered some shelter and protection from the weather. Once they were settled, he left for the city to find Islet and help plan a safe route through the castle.

"What's your sister like?" Henton asked as Stephenie rubbed down Argat and cleaned off the mud that had even found its way to the top of his hindquarters.

"She's about my height. She's got brown hair and eyes, which was just a bit darker than my other sisters. She's a year and a half older. Islet used to be kind enough, when she wasn't around Regina," Stephenie added. "I remember her trying to mediate an argument between me and my mother once." Stephenie chuckled as she wiped dirt from her face. "Islet didn't try that again. Mother was not kind to her for her interference." She met Henton's eyes. "I can't say I've seen her recently. Shortly after her fourteenth birthday, she was married to King Fraden Green of Ipith, who was almost fourteen years older than her."

Douglas raised his eyebrows and shook his head. "I'm glad my parents were too poor to worry about arranging marriages for me or my brothers. Though I had an older sister who was married off before she died of sickness."

Stephenie continued to watch Douglas, surprised by his sudden revelation, but he had already turned back to picking the fourth horse's hooves. "Well, she was married in Ipith, but only my father and mother went to the wedding with her. Kara was already married and in Esland and Regina in Durland. Josh had to stay behind in case something happened and mother didn't want me to go." Putting aside the brush, Stephenie came up under Argat's neck to pick his feet and was rewarded with a nose against her rear. "Regina, the pain in my ass, came back several times to visit my mother. Kara came back a couple times, but Islet was queen and so she could not travel."

"Then let's hope for a good reunion," Henton said, drawing Argat's attention from Stephenie's clothing by giving him a handful of grain.

Kas returned in the early morning before the easterly sun was high enough to shine into their secluded valley. Henton had already crawled out of the small tent the three of them were sharing and had fed the horses. "What's the verdict?" he asked the mostly transparent Kas.

"The situation is not promising."

Stephenie, who had not slept well, crawled out from under the heavy canvas flap and deftly avoided the worst of the mud that had risen to the surface from their wandering about the camp. "Were you able to find Islet?"

Kas shook his head and waited until Douglas joined them. "I was not able to get close to the keep. They have many magic users along the walls at night, patrolling and keeping watch. I tried to slip past them, but several of them reacted to my presence. I am not sure if they realized what they sensed or not, but I did not want to risk raising an alarm."

"So we don't know if she's still here," Douglas remarked, since Kas had spoken in Cothish.

"We do not." Kas turned back to Stephenie. "I counted at least thirty people on the walls through the whole night. There was one change of the watch which appeared to be even more disciplined than anything I saw at Antar castle. It was quiet and orderly. The only interesting aspect was that the makeup of the people appeared to vary greatly. While I was not that close, I did notice ages ranging from young to old and both male and female guards."

"Alianor said witches and warlocks were coming through to be trained. Could there be that many in Vinerxan?"

"The whole of the bailey was filled with the type of items I observed in the practice fields around Antar Castle." He frowned. "If last night was indicative of their normal procedure, you will not be able to sneak into the castle."

"Damn," Stephenie swore. "How many were Senzar?" she asked, turning her head up to look at Kas.

He shrugged and then moved into a sitting position on a rock that was in the middle of their camp. "I stayed back to avoid detection, so I was only able to observe things from afar. However, if I was to put forth an educated guess, it would be that most of them are your witches and warlocks that are going to Vinerxan to be trained. I did not see any threat from the city that would require such a heavy guard. In fact, I observed several people come and go between the city and the castle during the course of the night. Most of them were in the early part of the evening when there were still many sailors and others about the city."

"How's the harbor?" Henton asked. "Full of ice or is it clear? How many ships?"

"The harbor was clear of ice and probably a dozen ships of various sizes. I have to apologize; I did not pay much attention to that aspect of the town."

"It sounds like the city might be busier than we would expect. A fair amount of traffic from the sea."

"There is also a road going north along the shore. I imagine it connects Vinerxan to the rest of the country. It is more exposed with fewer trees and a deeper covering of snow."

"So, Steph, what do we do now?" Henton asked, "We can't hope to fight that many magic users. Douglas and I might be able to offer support or perhaps if we get some poison we might be able to surprise one or two, but..."

Stephenie shook her head. "We didn't ride across two and a half countries to simply give up. I'm not going to abandon my sister when she could be just a few miles away, locked in a dungeon, desperate for someone to do something to save her. She's been a captive for more than a year now."

"I'm not saying give up, but we need to come up with some kind of plan that doesn't involve fighting. The four of us just won't be a match for that size of a force."

Stephenie rose to her feet, her mind whirling with different options. One kept rising to the surface of her thoughts, *but the risk...* Sighing, she finally stopped her pacing in front of Argat and looked into his large brown eyes. His nose dropped to the hand she had raised to pat his forehead. Tussling his nose, she slid her hand up his face and rubbed the long hair of his white blaze. "What do you think? Is there any other option?" Argat pushed against her chest with his nose and then went back to searching her hands for food. "You need to learn some manners. I know Henton fed you already."

Turning away from the horse, she met three pairs of eyes that were watching her as intently as Argat had searched for a treat. "I'll go to the castle and offer to join them."

"What?" Henton and Douglas said in union. Kas simply watched her in silence and she knew he suspected what her decision would be.

"The Senzar are driving witches and warlocks from Cothel and if the rumors we heard in Epish are true, the priests of Mise and Vatar are pursuing rumors of magic with more zeal than before. And as you pointed out, Henton, we heard the rumors of Vinerxan all the way back in Iron Heart. They'll accept me as just another witch coming to join their ranks. They'll trust me because of the whole idea that the enemy of my enemy is a friend."

"Steph, neither Douglas nor I have magic. Do you think they want common soldiers as well?"

Stephenie turned toward Kas who shrugged. "I can watch again, but I do not want to get too close."

"No, it would look odd for all three of us to join them and I can't risk them using any of you to control me. We don't know exactly what we can expect. I'll leave Argat with you and head into Vinerxan on foot and go directly to the castle. If the three of you come in later in the day that should hopefully be enough of a gap between us."

"Steph, we can't split the group; it's too dangerous."

"Henton, it doesn't sound like we can sneak into the castle, so someone has to be let in and then break Islet out from the inside."

"Stephenie," Kas said, fully opaque and having a slightly brown tint to his eyes. "I will not be able to protect you or watch for trouble. You would be entirely on your own. Unprotected."

"Kas," Stephenie said, moving to stand directly in front of him. "I know, but I should be safe. I won't do anything until I can talk to you. You said people were coming and going, I should hopefully be able to go into town and talk with you."

"Stephenie, the risk—"

"Kas, we came all this way. I can't simply turn around and go back home. Islet is sitting there waiting for someone to help her. I can't abandon her any more than I could Josh."

Henton stepped closer, drawing Stephenie's attention. "It could be days before they would let you out. New recruits in Cothel are often kept under close watch for a while. In part to make sure they don't suddenly have a change of heart, as well as to prevent them from running off with supplies."

"I know. And it may take me a little time to be able to get access to the dungeon. Since we can't sneak in and escape in a single night, this could take longer."

"Which means you'll be in more risk of eventual discovery," Douglas said, joining Henton and Kas in directly facing her. "What if they read your mind to find out the truth of what you claim?"

Kas spoke up before Stephenie. "It is unlikely. It is a risk for any person to enter the mind of another. The initial linking could go either way and the person trying to invade the other may find their own mind is open to their victim. Linking minds is only generally done by those who have great trust in the other." He turned back to Stephenie. "However, I do not like this idea. You have learned to shield your thoughts much better than you could before we started this journey, but you are not always perfect in this."

She smiled up at him. "That, my love, is because I don't like keeping you out. However, I will be much more cautious with the Senzar."

"And if you get into trouble?" Henton demanded, his anxiety unusually obvious to Stephenie's senses.

"I'll make a commotion that Kas will be able to sense." She stood a little taller. "Look, I know this is a risk and I am putting all of you in danger, which is what I worry about the most. But unless any of you have a better suggestion, I don't see any other option." She waited for anyone to speak.

After several moments of awkward silence, Henton spoke. "What do you expect us to do while you are in the castle?"

She paused a moment to consider the options. "Find a place to stay near the edge of the town. Someplace with a stable. Even with what I burned up, we still have a fair amount of coin. Keep to the story of waiting for friends coming in on a ship. Just be ready to go when I let you know the time is right. Most likely, I'll have to get Islet out on my own."

She watched as Henton looked to Kas and Douglas. The three of them shared some silent looks and then Henton spoke. "I think I can say we don't like this, but I don't think there are any better options at hand."

"Thank you."

"Don't be too happy about this. We want you to get out and update Kas as soon as you can do so safely. We don't want you to suddenly have 'an opportunity' and try to break Islet out without talking to us first. We need you to take it slow and make sure you don't get caught. We've already seen the Senzar have weapons that none of us expected. There is even more reason to assume they could have things we don't know about in the castle. And if there is no clear way to rescue Islet without getting yourself killed or caught, you may have to leave her. None of us will be able to break you out if things go wrong. You will truly be on your own."

Stephenie took a deep breath, finally feeling the depth of what she was planning. Eventually, she nodded her head. "I understand and I will be very careful and I will make sure I get out and keep you all updated."

Henton puffed himself up, but softened his expression slightly. "Then go, but know that we won't be happy until you leave that castle for good."

She reached out and wrapped her arms around Henton, squeezing him until he grunted under her strength. Releasing him, she embraced Douglas, giving him a quick peck on the cheek before letting go. To Kas, she opened her mind as she reached out her hand to his cheek. *I love you and I will come back to you. Have faith in me.*

Of course, Stephenie. However, that does not mean I do not worry and fear for your safety. Go, be safe, and come back to us.

She smiled at Kas, and then quickly gathered her pack and the reduced set of gear she would take. With a final hug to each of them, physical or mental as appropriate, she quickly departed and disappeared from their sight.

Chapter 12

Stephenie forced herself not to look back. What she was planning was both thrilling and terrifying all at the same time. She had been alone mentally for most of her life, but aside from her exploring of the secret passages through and under Antar castle, she had seldom been physically alone. The majority of her life, there were always guards and people to protect her.

When she had escaped her mother, getting lost in the ancient passages of Arkani was not something she had been able to enjoy. She was injured and fully expected to die. Once she had met Kas, she formed something of a support group that looked after and took care of her. This would be the first full expedition she would be able to do entirely on her own and she was looking forward to being able to prove to herself that she was capable. Her excitement was tempered only by fear of failure and what that would mean to everyone else.

Her anticipation sped her pace and she was out of the trees and crossing a snow covered field before she knew it. The city of Vinerxan sprawled across the rolling valley that was before her and stretched toward the shore. Now out of the protection of the trees, she could feel the bite of the wind blowing off the Endless Sea. The salt laden smell carried more strongly in the wind.

The buildings that she could see so far were made of stone with wooden crossbeams for support. In Antar, many of the buildings were waddle and daub with thatch roves. Here, each building had a slate roof with a steep pitch to quickly shed any snow or ice.

In the distance, she could see the bulk of the keep. It was sitting on a section of high ground along the rocky shore. The dark stone appeared weathered, even at the near mile distance she stood from the outer walls. It had a definite box appearance, built for strength and durability instead of beauty.

When she passed through the city, she observed that while many people took note of her, no one greeted her or paid her any overt attention. It was a city used to strangers and willing to ignore what most places around the Sea of Tet would riot over.

As she approached the outer walls of the keep, she could see sections of recent repair, where stones devoid of moss and lichen stood out from the rest of the aged blocks. She kept her mind withdrawn as much as possible, but she could still feel the mass of men and woman hidden from sight on the other side of the walls. The sounds of conflict and training rang out with grunts, shouts, and the thuds of wooden practice swords hitting metal and flesh. In addition to the sounds of traditional combat, she could feel the turmoil in the energy fields as it was drawn and pulled and manipulated just out of her physical sight. It was a cacophony of disjointed sensations.

Blocking out the chaos, she slowed her pace as she neared the open gates. Five men stood at a relaxed, but attentive guard. They called out to her in what she assumed was Uletian. She shook her head and responded in Kyntian, "I speak Kyntian and Pandar."

One of the men scowled slightly, but responded in an accented version of the trade tongue. "Pandar will work for most. We don't see many new faces from Kynto. What is it you want?"

Stephenie nodded her head and continued in Pandar, hoping her accent sounded more Kyntian than Cothish. "I understand the Senzar are accepting recruits."

"We don't need any more hired swords. You a witch?"

Stephenie could feel all five of them drawing energy from the environment, though it did not seem like a focused intent as it was a very slow draw. More importantly, she sensed no fields being directed at her. "I am a witch."

"Care to prove it?"

She looked around and noticed a small rock on the ground next to her feet. Deciding to keep the extent of her skills secret, she stared at the rock for a bit with her hand outstretched. Not wanting to seem too weak, she pulled the rock quickly to her hand and then, turning her hand over, held out the rock for the others to see.

"Wait here, we'll get someone."

Stephenie waited patiently as the first man walked into the castle complex. One of the other four men smiled at her and took a step forward. "You come from Kynto?" he asked and she nodded her head in confirmation. "I had a sailing friend who was from there. When the Senzar came and spread the word they would accept those of us cursed with Elrin's taint, I left my ship the first chance I got and joined. Now I no longer fear being drowned at sea."

Stephenie nodded her head. The man was in his early twenties and sprouting a beard just starting to turn scraggly, but his hair was still trimmed. His darkened skin stood in contrast to the light tan leather of his coat. "My name is Steph," she said, never having liked Henton's alias of Beth.

"I am Carac. Don't let them scare you off. It's not really that bad once you learn some basic spells and combat skills. I'm sure you'll pick things up quickly enough," he added a bit more quietly, probably having sensed the approach of a tall woman wearing only a thin tunic of green and silver.

The woman's black hair was tied back tightly, giving her face a severe appearance. Stephenie kept her senses reined in, but she did not need them to know this woman was used to being obeyed because of her rank. She had the air of her older sister Regina, even though the woman was a head taller than Regina and as thin as a pole.

"I understand you wish to join the Senzar forces here in Vinerxan." The woman's voice startled Stephenie, breaking her image of Regina. Instead of being harsh and gravelly, it held a subtle kindness that was incongruent with Stephenie's expectations.

"Yes, Ma'am, I would like to join you. I understand you are offering training and through your influence, protection from persecution."

The woman nodded her head and beckoned Stephenie through the open gate. "We are, but I am not a Senzar. I am merely one of the first to join Lord Favian here. What is your name?"

"I am Steph of Wyntac. I come from Kynto."

"You may call me Captain or Captain Nerida. If you prove to have skills we need, we will consider taking you in for training. You will of course be expected to join our war against those that oppress and murder us. We are training soldiers, not collecting strays." The Captain's eyes fell over her body, judging and evaluating. "Is that sword merely for show or do you actually know how to use it?"

"Captain, I have had a couple occasions to use it."

"And what witchcraft can you do?" The tall woman asked as they walked across the open bailey. To their left, many groups of people were practicing various forms of combat, some obviously magical in nature.

"I can move things...if they are not too large."

"What about fire? Can you use that as a weapon?"

Stephenie's stomach cramped ever so slightly. The screams of the woman she had killed all those months ago in the tavern came back to her. *I had not intended to burn her*, she told herself, knowing that burning was not a pleasant way to die. "Not intentionally," she said aloud, uncertain if the tall woman would be able to detect lies or even exaggerations.

"Anything else you can do? Do you read minds?"

Stephenie shook her head. "I have trouble reading people. I can sense when someone is coming up on me and get a general idea of their mood."

"Anyone can do that," the woman said with the subtle hints of acid in her voice that Stephenie had initially expected.

"I can put out fire and make things cold," Stephenie said, knowing that Kas considered extracting energy from a specific location to be more challenging than simply dumping energy into an object or area to make it hotter.

The woman nodded her head, reassessing Stephenie. "If you are accepted, you will not worship Elrin in any fashion. Once you have served the Senzar for a period of time and contributed to our cause of ridding the land of the gods that persecute us, the Senzar will have their god cleanse you of any of Elrin's evil and withdraw the demon that threatens to eventually eat your soul." The woman stopped and stared into Stephenie's eyes. "Do I have your word? We have borne the curse of Elrin's evil, but with the Senzar's help, we will eventually be free. Which is what the gods of these lands should have done instead of simply trying to burn us. They will learn the folly of their mistake and regret ever trying to kill me."

Stephenie quickly digested the various bits of information, creating a larger understanding of what was driving this woman. She paused long enough to wonder if the Senzar actually believed in Elrin and were offering some unknown treatment, *perhaps to destroy a person's ability to perform magic.* Realizing she had stood silently for long enough, Stephenie spoke. "I have never worshiped Elrin. I did not choose to bring this curse upon myself."

Hearing the answer she wanted to hear, Captain Nerida nodded her head. "Good. I will show you where you will bunk and introduce you to Sergeant Simon. He will teach you some spells to protect you from Elrin's evil. You cannot use Elrin's magic without some protection; it is not designed for humans, but for his demons." The Captain waited for Stephenie to nod her head before turning on her heals and heading toward a pair of long stone buildings along the outer wall. On the way, the Captain waved over a man standing among a group of people.

The man, dressed in heavy leather armor, fur boots, and a fur cap, came quickly. He greeted her in a language Stephenie did not understand. After a short conversation, Captain Nerida walked away, leaving Stephenie with the sharp-eyed man.

"I am Sergeant Simon," he said slowly in Kyntian. "I understand you came from Kynto."

Stephenie nodded as she smiled; the man's wide grin was infectious. "Yes, my name is Steph. You don't look or sound like you are from Kynto."

The man laughed as he turned and held his hand out to indicate they should move toward the nearer building. "No, I'm a long way from Kynto. But you remind me of a young girl I used to know who came from Kynto. She wasn't in Ulet by choice, but she managed to escape those who had her and she made something of a life for herself in Zan Haven." He stopped in front of the heavy wooden door. "This is the woman's barracks," he said, opening the door and leading her inside.

The barracks had a strong odor of women and sweat, but it did not seem to bother Simon. He walked into the dimly lit room, which was long and narrow with two rows of cots and a chest at the foot of each one. About halfway down the long building, he stopped in front of a neatly made cot. "This will be where you will sleep. You can put your things in the trunk, including the sword." He glanced up and down the long room, but they were the only ones present. "The men and woman sleep separately...a woman with child makes a poor soldier," he added, leaning closer to Stephenie as he said it, but then grew serious and stepped back. "That is not a problem for you, now or in the future, is it?"

"No. That will not be a problem at all."

Simon frowned, but then smiled. "So much the pity, but if you change your mind, as combat often does to people, we have healers that can mix up a drink to make sure it won't be an issue."

She grinned, despite herself. She was sure Simon's charm could easily rival Will's if he wanted to. "Do I get any pay?" she asked, setting her things into the trunk. She put in the sword, but left her smaller blades where they were.

"You know much about the military?"

She shrugged. "A bit."

"Well, if you show promise, we'll make you a private. But until you are assigned to a company and sent off to where the company is, your pay is the training, food, and shelter we give you. You do good work and your pay will eventually be based on that."

"So we won't stay here? You'll ship us off somewhere else?"

"That a problem for you? You got people waiting for you?"

"No," she said, hoping he could not detect lies. "Just curious as to when and where I'll be and for how long."

Simon relaxed a little. "Well, those details will depend on who needs people and when you are ready." He smiled again, "Now, some basics you need to know. I am sure the Captain told you not to worship Elrin. If you do, give him up. All of us here have. If you don't, you might get put on a fire here just as easily as in Kynto.

However, they will cleanse you and break any ties with Elrin, once you've proven yourself." He started heading for the door now that Stephenie's belongings were in the chest. "In a month or so, the next ship will arrive and take anyone ready to somewhere in the south. That's where the bulk of the forces are needed. You'll get paid while you work and after a few years, or sooner if you show a lot of promise, they'll break Elrin's hold on you. Until then, they don't want to give you everything you want and have you run off on them."

Stephenie nodded her head as they exited the building.

"So, let's get you started with training. You'll need to build some strength and we'll teach you how to really use a sword and cast spells."

After spending the afternoon running around the inside of the curtain wall, up and down the stairs leading to the top of the wall, and carrying large sacks of grain to test her physical fitness, she was feeling quite tired. Wanting to avoid standing out too greatly, she was careful to keep her magic use in check, even in the subtle ways that most people would never notice. The trouble was, she had no way to judge the multitude of people who had watched her throughout the day and what they may or may not be able to sense and that worried her.

Sensing fields and other people using energy had become second nature to her; something she had to consciously turn off if she did not want to be aware of it. However, the subtler aspects of what she could see clearly, not even Kas could sense. Kas told her she was not the only one who was able to sense the tiny fields, so each time she slipped and drew in some energy to relieve the soreness of her muscles, she hoped that with the countless mages in the castle, all drawing energy, generating fields, and subconsciously probing the world, no one would notice her activity amongst the tangled web of energy currents in the air.

During the more grueling aspects of the physical activity, she allowed herself to wonder if the chaos about her was how it felt to live in Arkani when Kas was still alive. Never before had she experienced that level of concurrent usage of power and it left her feeling like a country girl on her first trip to a big city.

She had initially smiled and nodded her head to those observing her, but the stoic appraisals offered her little feedback. Knowing she was a cadet at her first review, something she had not experienced in many years, she worked on keeping her focus and performing the tasks set for her.

"All right, you can put the sack back in the shed," Sergeant Simon told her.

Using her left shoulder to wipe the sweat from her brow, she adjusted the sack on her right shoulder before returning it to the storage shed attached to the men's barracks. She estimated there was enough oats in the stone building to provide a morning meal to one hundred people for more than a month.

"Okay, I think they've seen enough of what you can do. I have to say that you held up better than I had expected. In a day or so, we'll put you into one of the three shifts, but for this evening, I'll pull someone out of training to show you around."

"Thank you, Sarge."

He grinned at her as they walked over to a group of people Stephenie could tell were working on creating fire. "Isa," Simon said as he approached a tall, dark haired man who had been giving orders to the others. He had a brief conversation in a language Stephenie did not understand, and then a woman about Stephenie's age stepped forward. "Jerylin, this is Steph, our newest trainee. If you'll show her around, I would appreciate it."

"Yes, Sarge," she said, with what Stephenie interpreted as a bit of relief in her voice. "What have you seen so far?" she asked Stephenie as they followed Sergeant Simon away from the training field.

"Lots of stairs up and down the wall," she said softly, seeing Jerylin's smile, she hoped that meant the woman had a sense of humor.

"Don't worry, they'll expect that you keep fit, but after the first day, it gets better." Jerylin winked at Stephenie and led her in a different direction than Simon. "Let's start with the mess hall, I doubt they've fed you today and I won't say no to another meal myself."

Stephenie's stomach growled on cue as they crossed to the opposite side of the castle where the smell of cooking had been drifting outward all afternoon.

"They serve six meals a day, two for each shift. We're between meals at the moment, but we should still be able to get something to eat. It's your first day, so they won't turn us away."

"That's good. I'm a bit hungry."

Jerylin looked her over as they walked. She was half a head taller and Stephenie found herself looking up at her freckled face. "So where are you from?"

"I'm from Kynto. Made the trip from Wyntac."

Jerylin nodded her head. "My parents were from Calis, but I won't hold your Kyntian blood against you. Our countries have gotten on okay for a while now."

Stephenie forced a laugh. "Don't worry. I'm not really tied to Kynto. It's not like they want me there."

"That my friend, I do understand," Jerylin said as they walked into the long mess hall. The interior was filled with tightly packed tables and benches, all of which were empty. "Let's go press the cooks for something to eat."

The kitchens were massive, challenging even the size of the ones in Antar Castle. More than a dozen people were busy cooking or preparing meals. There were large pots of stew boiling, bread baking, fish being cleaned, and even three lambs roasting in one of the four large fireplaces that would allow Henton to stand fully upright. After Jerylin explained that it was Stephenie's first day, they were provided food and sent on their way.

"Are any of the cooks witches or warlocks?" Stephenie asked as she picked at the breast of some bird that had been nicely roasted.

"Nah, plenty of the castle staff are just regular people. Quite a few were part of the castle before Lord Favian came. Those that couldn't handle living with us 'evil ones' were driven away. Some people tried to fight I've been told, but most people in Vinerxan are profiting from the Senzar being here, so they don't mind."

"I wasn't sure what I would find when I first decided to come here. To be honest, it wasn't this."

Jerylin smiled. "The Senzar got a bad reputation when they first came to these lands. They had some leaders who thought they could just walk through the countries without resistance. Unfortunately, it didn't go that well and then, just before they got what they were after, some demon turned on them and brought a mountain down on them." Jerylin shook her head. "I understand the reaction Cothel and the other countries had. But really, the priests were behind most of it, calling us evil and driving everyone to fight the Senzar. And some of the Senzar probably did deserve to die, but now that I've been here for a month and have learned so much, I'd never betray the Senzar. They want to cure me of Elrin's evil without killing me; make me a tubitan, which is their word for witch or warlock without Elrin's evil."

Stephenie recognized the Denarian influence of the word, but was not familiar with its meaning. Wanting to keep Jerylin talking, she added something she could say honestly, "I'm just glad they don't want to burn me for being what I am."

"And with all the gods stepping up their war on us, more and more people will join the Senzar. It's only a matter of time." Finishing her meal, Jerylin tossed the bones into a nearby barrel. "Come on, I want to show you the baths."

By the time Stephenie turned in for the night, she had been introduced to so many people that she had forgotten almost all of their names. The people who had come to train were from numerous countries to the north and south, several even from Cothel, though none of them seemed to recognize her. That was a benefit of not having been paraded around the country in fancy coaches to attend different balls and functions. Instead, she had grown up mostly out of sight from all but the soldiers.

In addition to meeting people, she had learned through various complaints that there were three shifts in the keep. Once her initial training and evaluation was done, she would be placed into the rotation. One morning shift on the walls, then one in the dungeon, followed by a set of evening shifts, and then a set of night shifts. The guard duty was always followed by one to three full days of training. That allowed those in charge to mix up the people to prevent any one group from being together through too many rotations. Additionally, even on the days she had to serve on a guard shift, she would be expected to spend the equivalent of another shift, either in the morning, or evening, or split between both, in training.

"It leaves you constantly tired, but by the time they are ready to ship you out to the company you'll end up with, you'll know what you're doing."

"Any down time to explore Vinerxan?" Stephenie asked.

One girl with shortly cropped hair laughed. "No. Not any real need to and we don't have any money to do anything there anyway. The regulars that don't ship out get to have fun, but getting a fixed position here is hard."

Stephenie nodded her head and tried to project a positive attitude, but it was difficult. She needed to make sure Kas, Henton, and Douglas knew she was safe so they would not do anything stupid, such as try to reach her. And she had promised them she would take no action before consulting them. To make matters worse, while she was ecstatic that she would get a chance to explore the dungeon as part of her duty, the fact that those who would be on shift would be different each time, meant it would be heard to observe consistent patterns in any short time frame.

"But don't worry, in a month or two, three at the most, they'll be ready to send you south to a place where you can be of use to the Senzar."

"Yeah, if you've got any skills at all, you'll be out of here in two months," said a brunette from a couple cots away. "Only the really weak ones end up staying for three months and most of them get kicked out before then. If you can't cut it, we don't need you on the front lines with us." There were several grunts of agreement from others nearby.

"Just don't piss off the Captain," said the woman with the cropped hair. "She'll drive you off or worse."

"That's always good advice," Stephenie said. "Captains like to be obeyed."

"As do the Captain's favorites," Jerylin said quietly. "Well, you'll have a full day tomorrow and I'm on an early guard shift, so I'm going to get some rack time." Jerylin excused herself and headed to the far end of the barracks, where she quickly stripped down and climbed into her cot.

After a short time, the rest of the women also headed off to their cots, which were only about one third occupied. Stephenie understood that the third shift was finishing their training for the day and would soon relieve the second shift. Not wanting to stand out, she pulled off her boots and slid under the blankets of her cot. It was not the most comfortable bed she had slept in, but she was truly exhausted, so it did not take long for her to fall asleep.

Chapter 13

Henton, Douglas, and Kas waited until the evening sun was casting its warm glow across the sky and then started their journey toward Vinerxan. The distance was not far, but the lack of activity during the day had put a chill into their bones and when they emerged from the trees, the strong wind off the sea stung their faces and cut right through their coats and wool pants.

There is an inn not far. It appears they also have room for horses on the ground level. I must confess, we never kept our animals beneath us in my time.

Having grown somewhat used to Kas reaching out to his mind, Henton was able to keep his face free of surprise. Unlike Stephenie, he could only communicate back to Kas by relaxing his mind and letting the ghost read his surface thoughts. He still had to repeat thoughts from time to time, but he was seeing the appeal Stephenie found in this manner of communicating. *We don't tend to do it in Cothel, but I have seen it in many places I've sailed. It helps to keep one warm in the winter, as the body heat of the animals rise.*

And the smell. I am glad I lack that capacity.

Henton could tell that was the end of the conversation, but he wondered just how Kas knew how bad it could smell if the animal pens were not kept clean. *Perhaps he can sense the odor somehow.*

"There should be an inn just ahead," he told Douglas in Pandar. While they would not be able to hide the obvious fact that they were from Cothel from anyone familiar with the country, they did not want to advertise unnecessarily. Douglas nodded his head, which was angled away from Henton and the wind.

When they got to the three story building, which was in a line of other buildings, all sharing common walls, Henton allowed Douglas to go up and arrange for a room and stalls for the horses. He held the leads of all four horses and tried to stomp the feeling back into his feet while he waited. Eventually, Douglas and a young man opened the large door leading to the stalls and helped him lead the animals out of the wind.

"I've booked room for at least a week, then we can extend it if we need to."

Henton nodded as he led Argat into a stall; the chestnut continued to look around, as if he was searching for Stephenie. "Don't worry, Big Guy, I know you miss her, but you'll see her soon enough." The horse looked him in the eyes and flicked his ears before nosing around Henton's hands for some treats or grain. "You telling me if I feed you enough, you'll like me as much as her?" Henton shook his head. "After we pick your feet and rub you down."

Once the horses were cared for, they went up the inner stairs to the second floor and a sizable common room. A fire was burning in each of two fireplaces on opposite sides of the room. There were a couple of small tables and several chairs. Two oil lamps provided light to navigate the room, but lacked enough brilliance to read.

"Welcome," said a dark skinned woman with long black hair neatly pulled back into a ponytail. Her clothing was well cut and vividly dyed, which Henton noticed even in the dim light. "I am Arabella. You've met Henry. He's a bit shy, so won't say much."

"Good evening Ma'am," Henton replied in Pandar. "I am called Henton and you've already met Douglas."

"Yes," she said, indicating they should sit in a group of chairs next to the fireplace. "Please warm yourselves. It is a cold day to travel."

"Thank you," Henton said, leaving the better seats for Arabella and Douglas. "I am glad to be indoors."

"Your friend mentioned that you were uncertain how long you needed the rooms. If someone should inquire about space for next week...it's not so much the rooms, but the stalls..."

Douglas spoke up, "I mentioned we were waiting for a friend to arrive on a ship, but we were not certain of the actual date, just a general idea of when he might show."

Henton rubbed his hands together, enjoying the warmth from the fire. "Douglas is right; we don't know when to expect Fish. If his ship was delayed due to weather, it could be a couple of weeks." The woman's pondering was growing into a frown, so Henton decided to offer her an option. "How about this, mid-week, if we think we need another week, we'll pay you for the next week. If we leave early, keep the extra, if not, when we get to half a week of board left, we'll pay for another full week again, unless we have more specific dates."

The woman smiled. "That is fair. I like the fact that you are waiting for someone on a ship and not someone in the castle. Mind you, we get along well enough with Lord Favian, but most people find disappointment when they learn the people they are waiting for will be shipped off to the south and they can't join them. At least not on one of His Lordships' vessels."

Long used to remaining stoic regardless of what life brought, Henton merely nodded an understanding. "Our friend's traded some labor for passage on ship. We're planning to head to his family's home in Epish. His father's dying and he's hoping to get back into the old man's good graces. Perhaps he'll get a piece of land."

The woman's eyebrows rose, but she said nothing. She looked at the two of them for a while, then stood up and pulled a pair of keys from her pouch. "Your room has a red lamb painted on it. It's up the stairs through that doorway. I ask that if you come and go late at night, you lock the outside door and remain quiet. The kitchen is for me and those who work for me, you'll have to eat your own food or dine at a public house. I don't like cooking, so I won't do it for others. If you need something, I have a young couple on this floor who tend the rooms, you can ask them or if you see me, ask me."

Henton took the keys and put one in his pouch and gave the other to Douglas. "Thank you, Ma'am. We're generally quiet people, so hopefully we won't be a bother."

Arabella smiled. "Very good. There are other guests that stay here as well, don't be surprised if you meet them from time to time. Now, if you will excuse me, I will get back to my own dinner."

When Arabella had walked through one of the doors on the back wall, Henton sat back down. "Now we sit and wait."

"Or we find a pub and get some food ourselves," Douglas said, getting to his feet.

The next morning, Stephenie was roused early from her cot by Sergeant Simon, who was waking several people from the warmth of their blankets. "Get a move on it. You all need to dress and eat before the glass turns. If you're not on the field before it does, you'll regret it."

Used to early mornings after long days, Stephenie pushed herself from the cot, pulled on her boots, and slid into her coat. As she was walking out the door directly behind the Sergeant, she heard a couple grunted complaints cut off by the door closing behind her. Hungry, she headed for the mess hall, grabbed a quick breakfast, and was out on the practice field where Sergeant Simon was waiting even before some of the others had left the barracks.

"You are an early riser?" he said, his breath hanging as a white cloud between them.

"One can't sleep through the morning when you're traveling," she replied.

He pulled a small stone out of a pocket in his coat. "Do you have a focus?"

Uncertain of what he was referring to, she slowly shook her head. "What's a focus?"

He grinned, with his smile widening slightly on his left check. "Here, take this." He held out the dark stone, which appeared to have flecks of mica throughout its polished surface. "A focus is something that will help channel and amplify your spells. It will also help filter out Elrin's evil, making it safer for you and keeping Elrin's demons from eating away your soul."

Stephenie's first impulse was to laugh, but this was actually not the most absurd statement she had heard regarding magic. Most beliefs tended to have some hints of logic, but many of them had great gaps in reason when examined in detail. Hearing the tones of seriousness in his voice, despite the flirting twinkle in his eyes, she restrained herself. "So, how do you use it?"

"When you cast your spells, have it on your body and concentrate on directing your spell through the rock. Once you get good at it, you won't need to have it in your hand, just somewhere on your person. This is just a basic focus. You can get more effective ones later. Right now, this will be yours, so make sure you don't lose it."

Stephenie held the smooth stone in her hand. It felt like a simple rock to her fingers as well as her mind. She could see the potential energy within the stone, just as she would expect to see in any similar rock, but nothing more. Testing the stone, she pulled energy from it, but it felt and responded normally.

"Don't worry about learning new spells. We'll start with some simple things later today and then move on to more complex craft as you advance. This morning, we'll teach you how to properly use a sword. You can only cast so many spells before Elrin's evil takes its toll on you. The poison builds in you and wears you down even with the focus. Until it clears, you may have to rely on your sword arm to keep you safe."

Stephenie looked at the stack of wooden practice swords at the end of the training field. It had been too many months since she had been able to train with someone. However, like her magic, she would have to limit the skill she displayed.

"Sarge," called out a young girl that Simon had awoken with Stephenie. She flipped her reddish blond hair over her shoulder in a move Stephenie had often seen courtiers do in an attempt to influence the men around them. "I'm on-time."

"That you are, Ryia."

Stephenie guessed the girl was a couple of years younger than herself. She was definitely half a head shorter.

"We didn't talk last night. I was a bit tired. My name is Ryia."

Stephenie nodded her head to the girl. "My name is Steph."

"Sarge, will you put in a good word for me this next round? I've been working real hard and doing extra sets of stairs and Jerylin and I have been training with the single swords as well as long daggers."

Simon smiled, but Stephenie could tell it was forced. "I've noticed the work you've put in, but it's not just work with swords that count.

The Captain can only send on people who demonstrate real skill and power with their spells."

Ryia nodded her head. "I know and I've improved there as well. This is my last shot, if they don't put me on the next boat, I don't have a home to go to."

Stephenie heard a snort of dissension; she did not have to look up to know it was from one of the men she had seen watching her evaluation the prior day. She could feel his sense of superiority, even with her filtering out as much mental sensitivity as she could.

"Anyone who's been here as long as you won't get a ship. Give it up now and save the rest of us the trouble of dealing with you."

Stephenie glanced once at Simon, expecting him to respond, but he was conveniently busy looking at the other three woman who were supposed to be training with them. The man who had berated Ryia put himself directly in front of Stephenie. She watched as his eyes examined her body, finally to settle on her face.

"My name's Isa."

Stephenie continued to try and place his accent, but had no idea where he was from. "Steph," she replied curtly.

"Well, you watch me carefully and I'll show you some useful tricks."

Simon interrupted any response she was about to blurt out and started pairing off partners, including two other men who joined the three woman. Everyone picked up a single-handed sword and for the first round, Stephenie faced a woman whom she had not been introduced to. The woman's opening attack was fast, but her body betrayed her intent, allowing Stephenie more than enough time to block her strikes. After more than a dozen swings and blocks between them, Simon started offering advice to both Stephenie and the other woman. The advice was fair, but Stephenie was capable of doing far more; only she did not want to demonstrate how skilled she really was.

After some time, they shifted partners and even before Stephenie could engage the brown-haired man before her, she heard a cry of pain from Ryia, who was facing Isa. The tall, dark haired man had knocked the sword out of Ryia's hand and still delivered three hard blows that brought Ryia to the ground.

"That is how you take someone down," he said as he turned away from the injured girl.

Distracted, Stephenie barely dodged the attack from her opponent. The twenty-something year old she faced was far more skilled than the first woman. In addition, she sensed his use of magic to enhance his speed and the force of his attacks. She was not sure if his use of magic was instinctual or deliberate, but she only managed to avoid a broken arm by absorbing some of the energy from the strike that slammed into her upper left arm.

His follow up attack knocked her left leg out from under her and she hit the cold ground because she avoided using her powers to keep her balance. The man moved in, already swinging, but Stephenie, who managed to keep her right foot under her, lunged forward, just under his swing, and rammed her head into his groin. The impact sent the man backward and onto the ground. He cursed and groaned from the pain, but appeared relatively uninjured.

Turning away, she went over to Ryia, who was still on the ground. The girl had not shed any tears, but Stephenie could see the pain in her eyes. The odd angle of her wrist told Stephenie it was bad. "Are you okay?"

Ryia swallowed and with an effort nodded her head. "I think he broke it again."

Stephenie bit her lip but said nothing as Sergeant Simon came over. He knelt down and looked at her arm, causing Ryia to wince as he touched it. "We'll have to send you to the healers in a bit. But, we need to finish the rounds."

Stephenie noticed that he had glanced behind Ryia at the people who were watching them from across the field. Many of them were in unusual clothing, with slightly clashing color choices and dramatic folds of cloth that were cut at a diagonal across their chests. She knew a few of them had watched her the prior day and suspected they were Senzar mages.

Simon stood up and motioned for Stephenie to get back into position. "That was a good lesson for everyone. Sword combat can involve much more than just the sword. Heads, fists, feet; don't expect your opponents to play fairly. When your life is on the line, you'll learn to fight with whatever you have." Simon shifted Isa in front of Stephenie as everyone else changed partners, leaving Ryia and the first woman Stephenie had faced standing by to watch.

Isa took a quick swing at Stephenie as she was saluting him to signal the start of their match. She leaned back, slightly augmenting her balance to avoid the blow and keep her feet. Isa smiled at her. "You know, most woman shouldn't be out here playing with swords. They are best put to use keeping my bed warm."

Stephenie did not bother to reply; instead she tested his quickness with a jab that she made obvious by leading with her shoulder. He blocked it easily and tried to take advantage of her swing, but she had hoped he would do that and had already shifted further to the right instead of coming back left. As a result, she caught him with a glancing blow off his lower leg. Stephenie let a grin come to her face at seeing anger rise to his. In the back of her mind, she knew she wanted to minimize the skill she demonstrated, but it was getting harder with the conceit in front of her. She could feel the beast rumbling up inside her.

Isa feinted in, drawing a defensive block from her, but then muscled through her block with a sudden burst of magic. Trying to avoid using her powers, she allowed him to push her back a couple steps. As she disengaged, he purposefully caught her left breast with the tip of his blade. The scrape hurt, even through the padding of her binding and heavy shirt.

"I guess you must not have many assets to work with, perhaps you need to spend time cooking to warm my stomach and grow your chest." He came at her again, this time she blocked the attack and launched one of her own, but was unable to connect with his arm. "Nothing to say?" he asked just as he swung hard at her face with an augmented blow. As she ducked to avoid the wooden blade, dust leapt from the ground and pelted her face. Instinct drew energy to block any of it from hitting her eyes.

Not disabled, but still in a compromised position, she sensed him swinging again, this time aiming for her back. Unwilling to take the blow, she used her powers to get her sword around and block the strike that could have done significant damage. Taking advantage of his surprise, she slammed her heel onto the top of his foot. His hand whipped back to strike and she continued her movement, bringing the pommel of her wooden sword squarely into his fingers, smashing them against the handle of his sword. As the blade fell from his hand, she drove her sword hand up into his face, connecting her fist and the crossguard of the sword with his chin.

She straightened as he fell onto his back, blood dripping from his fingers and cheek. She waited a moment, reaching out with her senses to make sure he would not attack her. "I tend to talk with my blade and not my mouth."

"Wow," said the first man she had hit in the groin, "I'll not underestimate you next time." He held out his hand to her, "very good show of it." She nodded her head and shook his hand.

"Where'd you learn those moves?" Simon asked, ignoring the hateful looks Isa was giving all of them from where he was, still on the ground.

"I grew up on the streets," Stephenie said. "Some men thought to have me warm their beds. I found if I had a stick available, I could dissuade them of that notion."

Simon chuckled. "Indeed. We may have to graduate you to something more than sticks. That is, if you've managed to use steel in the same fashion."

Stephenie continued to hope no one could sense her lies. "Rarely had the need to use actual steel much. That tends to be more permanent of a solution."

Isa sneered. "This is war, you better learn to like killing."

Stephenie ignored him and walked over to Ryia. "You need help getting to the healers?"

Ryia closed her eyes, her face was pale, but she shook her head. "No. I just hate the healers." She glared at Isa, "Why'd you have to break it again? We're just supposed to be practicing."

"You're too weak to be of any use. Go be something useless like a healer or even better, leave. You've missed two boats already; they won't be putting you on the next one either." He spit out some blood from his mouth, but his face and hands were no longer bleeding. "Next time Steph, I won't be so easy on you."

Simon cleared his throat. "Let's have some order here. Ryia, go get your arm looked at. Everyone else, work on your drills. I'll start teaching Steph some spells."

*   *   *   *   *

Stephenie worked with Simon off to the side of the field while her group was joined by dozens of others who all started work on their sword drills. For her, Simon demonstrated many spells, each with specific gestures and sayings. By the end of the afternoon, she was giggling and laughing with Simon at her frequent mispronunciations.

The idea that she needed to say something, toss sand in the air, or move her hands in a specific way was completely absurd to her. However, she noticed Simon had his own trouble performing magic if her comical attempts at repeating his commands caused him to laugh so much that he could not accurately execute the ritual himself. Kas had speculated that these might have been early teaching tools that got out of hand, where people lost the understanding that magic was purely mental and were now fixated on the physical.

Without one of the others actively trying to hurt her, she was able to display far less skill with magic than she had with the practice sword. Half the time, her need to repeat inhuman sounds that did not appear to have logic or order kept her distracted enough that it was fairly easy to not 'cast the spell'.

By evening, she had demonstrated the ability to knock over objects that were not too heavy. She showed that she could pull light objects to her hand, but kept from showing any real control. There seemed to be a different set of words for every action and she was told that there were more sophisticated spells that could do more complex things.

Throughout the day, she kept wondering how the priests were taught to use their augmentation devices. She had not observed many of them in action when she was younger, having wanted to avoid being discovered as a witch, but she remembered many of them mumbling things under their breath or doing subtle hand gestures. If they were as limited as these warlocks, it was not surprising how the Senzar beat them so easily. The Senzar appeared to have some understanding of magic, as Stephenie had never seen them 'cast a spell'.

"Do you always have to say the spells aloud?" she asked as they were picking up the bucket of stones she had been knocking over.

Simon shook his head, "No, once you get good enough, you'll be able to cast spells without having to say the words that loudly." He grinned at her, "It'd be too easy for your enemy to know what you are doing if you always shouted it." Offering his hand to carry the bucket, he continued, "For now though, keep saying it aloud so we can help you correct any mistakes."

"Sure, that makes sense."

"Put those other practice swords away and then get yourself some food. Tomorrow will be another busy day of the same. Then the next day I'll wake you early for a shift on the wall."

Chapter 14

Henton sighed again. He knew Douglas was getting annoyed with him, but he would not feel at ease until Stephenie was out of the damned castle and somewhere he could at least offer to help her. *Even if my help is getting more and more pointless.*

He set the mug down on the counter and made the decision not to order any more ale. He was not impaired...yet, but it would only take one or two more for him to be a risk to the others. Even before he had made sergeant, he had never allowed himself to drink so much that he would be at a disadvantage should trouble arise. The other sailors and soldiers had been merciless with their taunts, but Henton was never one to give in to that kind of pressure. However, the frustration in feeling helpless in their current situation was tempting his resolve to remain sober.

"This food is costing us a lot, if our friend's ship doesn't show up soon, we'll have to look at perhaps changing to a cheaper inn. We've been sitting and waiting for three days now."

Henton glanced over at Douglas, who was eating a bowl of some fish stew. Although he had spent years at sea, Henton still preferred the taste of beef or venison to most fish. "We've got enough money for now. It's a good inn. The location is pleasant. Perhaps we can find cheaper food." He was not going to say aloud that when it came time to make a quick exit from the city, they needed to be as close to the edge as they could get. It might cost them double what he would like to pay, but it was a question of minimizing risk.

"I'm just thinking about the trip home and how much that will cost."

"Then get a job while we wait," Henton growled. He glanced down at the bar, "Sorry, I'm just frustrated."

"Actually, I was hoping you'd say that. Even if it won't be for long, it'd be better than sittin' around all day."

Henton pursed his lips. They all were rather odd retainers, often spending their own money to help achieve Stephenie's goals and now here Douglas was looking to take on more work so he could make some additional money to help fund their task. He knew what drove him to the extremes in protecting her, but he wondered at the others. *And really, it's a fool's dream,* he admitted, though he knew he would not change. "If you want to do it, I won't stop you."

Douglas pushed aside his empty mug and stood up. "I'll check by the docks and see what I might be able to find. Surprisingly, there are quite a few ships that come through this secluded port."

Henton nodded his head, wishing he could distract himself from his worries that easily. "Be safe." He watched Douglas smile as he quickly left the public house. He trusted Douglas' judgment, but he would still worry. That was his job, or at least it had been, when he still thought of himself as a sergeant. Giving in to hunger, he ordered a bowl of the stew and a mug of water.

Where was Douglas going? Henton heard faintly in his head, *I saw him going to the docks.* Kas sometimes had a hard time breaking through, but he was getting more effective and that bothered Henton. The idea that someone could easily steal his thoughts was not pleasant. It was one of the things that the priests always said of witches as a means to keep people from trusting them. Of course, he knew the priests could steal thoughts as well, so on hindsight, it seemed a double standard.

To get a job, Henton thought back to Kas, remembering the question. *How is Stephenie?*

She seems safe, but I have not been able to talk with her. Today, she is guarding the wall.

Henton frowned. *If she was on the wall, why not talk to her like this. I know you can do it from a distance.*

My dear Henton, while I can sense what she is doing from a distance, mental communication has a more limited range. And, most importantly, it is not private. The stronger the field I generate to 'talk', as you might describe it, the more readily others would be able to pick it up. If I grew close enough to avoid a strong field, the numerous others on the wall, and in the practice area behind the wall, would sense me. Even if they did not understand what it was they felt, it would create suspicion and if there are any descendants of the old Denarians present, they may know me for what I am.

Henton got a sense of Kas' condescension, but he also felt Kas' complete frustration with the situation. *And here you are close enough to avoid someone listening to our conversation?*

Henton felt Kas hesitate. *I am practically on top of you, so the chance someone will overhear us is limited.* He gave a mental sigh. *I just needed someone to talk with. I am at a loss of what to do.*

Henton grinned. *And getting a job won't help you.* He bit his lip, knowing that half the problem was Kas had nothing to do but float around and watch Stephenie all day. Watching and obsessing over someone always just out of his reach. *We need to explore alternate routes out of town. The path up and through the mountains is limited in options once we are on it. Anyone following us will know which way we have gone. Perhaps, if there is a good opportunity, such as at night when she's sleeping, you can look for safe places. I'd do it, but I can't cover the ground as fast.* He felt Kas give another mental sigh and knew the ghost would do the scouting and that would give him something productive to do.

Stephenie had felt the faint echo of Kas leave the area. She doubted anyone near her had noticed him at all. She was so familiar with his presence that her sensitivity to him had pretty much doubled since she had first encountered him and the other ghosts in Arkani. She had wished he had been close enough that she could have at least whispered an 'I love you' to him, but she understood why he had not and even wondered if he suspected she might slip.

"Don't worry, it's a bit boring, but at least tomorrow you won't be outside in the cold."

Stephenie looked over at the young man who was standing his watch close to her. She guessed he was a year older than her, maybe two, but he was smaller and thinner than she was and in his oversized clothing, far from the image of a soldier. He had mentioned living on the streets from the age of six and she had decided that was likely a factor in his size. She stifled a yawn as she started to speak, "It's not that bad. I've had to sit still for half a day before, while trying to avoid being found." It was an exaggeration, but she felt justified by all the time she had hid in the walls and spied on her mother, too afraid to move and make a sound. "I'm just surprised there are so many of us on the walls."

Larence laughed, "They have to do something with us. There are almost two hundred of us here and the practice area is not that large. Put all the extra people on guard here or in the dungeon and that keeps us out of trouble and their hair."

Stephenie raised her eyebrows. She had not had a chance to do a full count, but based on the female barracks, she had guessed at a total of just over one hundred people in training. Making a quick adjustment for a guess at the number of men to woman and she could see how two hundred might be possible. "What's it like on duty in the dungeon? Anything interesting to look at there, or just walls and cells?"

Larence laughed again, an honest laugh that echoed the twinkle of amusement in his brown eyes. "Mostly walls and cells. There are a number of highborn prisoners. It's good to see them reduced to living in squalor and muck. The privileged always had it easy while the rest of us ate dirt and food they wouldn't share until it was rancid and covered in bugs."

Stephenie had heard those types of complaints before and knew that some places were worse than others. She had always believed her father had been generous and shared the wealth he had accumulated with those who needed it, but even in Cothel, his influence only went so far with the lower nobles, who had more interaction with the common man.

"Personally, I don't like it when they are torturing someone. That's normally one advantage of rotating into the night shift." He glanced over his shoulder, "Of course I am just as dedicated as the next to taking on the enemy and showing no mercy, but they keep cutting on a few of them down there, only to heal them and do it again the next day." Larence looked down, but was seeing only memories. "The screams and moans…"

Stephenie nodded her head in agreement. "That would unnerve me as well."

Larence rubbed his nose; his expression now quite sober. "Hearing it again and again is what gets under your skin. Don't know why this one guy won't talk. I'd never last that long." He glanced past her and inclined his head toward the stairs on the inside of the wall. "Looks like our relief is here. Now for a quick break and then on to the practice field. Guard duty is not a rest day."

"You're the new girl," a tall woman said as Stephenie approached the practice field alone, Larence had already broken off to join up with a group who was supposed to be learning advanced flame control. "I'm Elvira," despite speaking in Pandar, the darkly tanned woman's voice had a musical quality Stephenie had never heard before.

"My name's Steph," she replied while sizing up the woman's solid build and guessed she had spent a fair amount of time learning to use a sword. Her face carried a sense of resolve, as she stood without reaction in the cold wind that blew her shortly cropped hair freely about her head.

"I'm supposed to work with you on improving your spells to disable someone." She indicated a bucket, sitting on a wooden block twenty feet away near the outer curtain wall. "Do you have your focus?"

Stephenie could tell that was one of those questions only a complete fool would get wrong. She pulled the stone she had been given from her pouch to show the woman.

"Good. Once you can show me you can knock out a target, we'll show you how to block a force attack."

Stephenie nodded her head. Behind her, she felt a dozen others lining up in pairs. Out of the corner of her eye, she noticed Ryia heading to a spot against the curtain wall next to her bucket. After a little shuffling, Isa had come up across from the girl, whose face dropped as she noticed her opponent. Despite Stephenie's desire to block out mental energy, Isa's sense of smugness leaked into her head.

"A bucket is a formidable opponent. Just two weeks ago, Ryia had been demoted to facing one again as well."

"Isa, watch yourself," Elvira said. "While you might be gifted in spell work, I heard that Steph bested you two days ago with the sword."

"It was a stick, not steel, and you can be certain it won't happen again."

Stephenie could feel his cold anger with the curling of his lip. He looked away from her and back to Ryia, whose expression of dismay had not improved.

"Right, Steph, ignore that twat." She turned her back on Isa. "Do you know the spell called gurtwik?"

"I don't think it was one of the ones Sarge showed me yesterday or the day before."

"Use your focus." Elvira pulled a piece of quartz from her pouch and held it firmly in her hand. I will show you the spell and you will need to repeat my words and gestures. While doing that, you will need to concentrate on what the spell needs to do. In this case, it will be to push the bucket straight up."

Stephenie looked toward the wall. She could hear the others muttering the pointless phrases behind her and could hear the grunts of impact from the gravitational fields she sensed filling the air.

"Don't worry your pretty face. The bucket can't hurt you."

"Isa, leave Steph alone."

He turned back to face Ryia and Stephenie focused her attention on the field he created. Though he mumbled some words and flicked his wrist, she could tell no power moved through the rock in his hand. The gravity field he created sprung into existence and smashed into Ryia. The weak field she had formed to deflect the blow crumbled under his much stronger force, which continued on, striking her in the chest and sending her back into the curtain wall with a sharp cry of pain.

"If you can get back to your feet, we can see if you can brush my hair," he taunted. Several of the men and a woman in line with him giggled and congratulated him on the taunt.

"Steph, focus on the bucket. Try to lift it. We'll teach you how to block later. Right now you need to focus on simple spells that don't draw Elrin's evil into you."

Stephenie tried to focus, but her anger built as Isa continued his taunts at Ryia, which were obviously thinly veiled jabs at her. She barely heard the words Elvira repeated for the spell she was supposed to cast, though the flick of the wrist seemed easy enough to duplicate. *Kas, you would find these people so backwards*, she thought to herself to try and keep Isa's behavior from bothering her.

Noticing no one along either side of the line actually drew any power through their stones, Stephenie did the best she could to imitate Elvira's instructions, pointless as they were, while she crafted a weak gravity field that lifted the bucket a couple of inches before dropping it back onto the log.

"Such a powerful force," Isa commented, "you'd be a good match for Ryia." He mumbled his spell as he spoke to her, knocking the girl's legs out from under her and causing her to hit the ground with a grunt. "Get up you Epish cur!"

Elvira turned her back to Isa again. "That was well done, Steph. You need to hold the third syllable longer though, that will get you more power. Try to lift it higher."

Stephenie looked toward Ryia, who was crying out in pain as Isa hit her with a multitude of blows. Stephenie saw the blood splatter off the young girl's face and a solid blow flung her back into the curtain wall again. With each hit, she could sense Isa's fields getting strong. "Stop it!" She cried as she shielded Ryia with her own fields.

Isa glanced her way, but kept up his assault on Ryia, whom she could feel radiating pain. No longer hesitating, Stephenie smashed the field Isa was using to protect himself. The strength of her attack knocked him into the next two people, sending all of them to the ground. "Stop attacking her. Can't you see you're going to kill her?!"

Belatedly, Stephenie realized she had failed to cast a spell when she had attacked. Her protecting Ryia would likely be unnoticed, but her attack on him would not. When Isa tried to retaliate from where he was on the ground, Stephenie mumbled the words for gurtwik and waved her hand in the air. His attack she blocked without effort as she flung Isa's stone from his hand and high into the air. In the process, she hoped she broke a finger or two.

Sensing a field coming at her from her left, instinctively she reached out with her senses and was just able to stop herself from retaliating as she realized the attack was coming from Captain Nerida. Subconsciously knowing the field was strong, but not likely to kill her; she took a calculated risk and allowed a significant amount of the force to hit her. She found herself flying through the air toward the curtain wall. Her sense of preservation overrode conscious thought and she stopped herself just before slamming into the stone. She hoped the Captain had not noticed.

Grunting and offering a stagger from the impact that would have been, Stephenie turned toward the Captain who was already within fifteen paces. Anger radiated from the tall woman and Stephenie's stomach tightened. She expected she'd be able to fly herself over the curtain wall and out of harm's way, but if she retreated, she'd lose any chance of rescuing Islet.

"You dare to attack Isa from behind!"

Stephenie stood straighter, quickly deciding how to respond. "Ma'am," she said, bowing her head and trying to be as differential as possible. "Ryia was severely hurt and he was continuing to attack. I had to stop him or she'd be dead." Belatedly, Stephenie opened her senses enough to check to make sure the girl was still alive.

The captain glanced at the bloody mess that was Ryia's body, but showed no compassion. "The girl is weak and she was given the option to leave. She knew the cost of staying. You have no business interfering with the training."

"Training? How is allowing Isa to kill Ryia training?" Stephenie could not keep the disdain from her voice. Isa was now standing a few feet behind the Captain, a sick expression of satisfaction on his face. Further behind them, some of the Senzar had drawn closer to watch the confrontation. Feeling exposed and vulnerable, Stephenie was glad the wall was behind her, though she sensed two people above her and to the right.

"I am the Captain here. I am in charge of the training. You will not question me." Nerida flicked her hand and Stephenie blocked what would have been a lashing across her face without even thinking. "How dare you challenge me?!"

Tears welled up in her eyes as she was realizing her chances to free Islet were likely lost, but she decided she would at least save Ryia, a girl for whom she knew she was starting to feel possessive. "What kind of a Captain stands by to let those under her be murdered when they should be protected?"

"We are at war! We must be tough and not afraid to kill. Accidents happen in training and that is accepted. I will not have cowards under my command. Someone too weak to kill will get others killed. By killing the weak and injured, we learn how to kill the enemy." A grin grew on the Captain's face. "She's been to the healers more times than the rest of the squad combined. If you want me to make you a good soldier, prove yourself and kill her now."

"Killing is not what makes a person a good or effective soldier. Teaching people to be cruel and sadistic simply creates monsters. Monsters that can't be trusted on the battlefield." Stephenie could feel the energy flowing up from the ground and coursing through her body. Her mind was alive with the multiple fields around her. She knew the Captain's defenses were strongest directly between them, but the woman had crafted no protection under her feet. ·

"Then you are useless and pointless. Isa, finish her."

"Just because I won't murder someone doesn't mean I won't do what is necessary." Stephenie's fingers itched as the energy practically dripped from her body. She wanted the Captain or Isa to attack. "I will not let Isa or anyone else hurt Ryia," she growled.

Captain Nerida's eyes narrowed, but she seemed to sense the threat behind Stephenie's cold expression. "Get out. Get out of the castle now! You are a worthless chit. A coward. Get out or your head will decorate the walls."

"Wait," said a middle-aged woman whose plump figure moved gracefully forward. Her dress and thick accent marked her as a Senzar. "If the girl wants to be a healer, I will take her."

Nerida turned; hate and contempt laced her voice. "Madam Farfelee, this is not your concern. I'm in charge of the training of the soldiers! Go back to the sick and useless."

The five-foot tall woman did not look impressed. "Nerida, you may have been honored with privilege and earned a commanding position training the witches and warlocks of your lands, but I am equally empowered to train healers and if I say she will stay, she will stay, there is nothing you can do about that."

Stephenie hesitated for a moment, not wanting to risk the possible reversal of her fortunes. However, she could not leave Ryia to be Isa's and Captain Nerida's victim. "I will gladly become a healer. But, Ryia...."

The older woman nodded her head. "Then bring the girl, she needs healing anyway. We will decide what to do with her later."

Stephenie released some of the energy she had been holding. Subconsciously, she noted holding it no longer burned her insides as much as it used to. Quickly moving to Ryia's side, she picked up the unconscious girl, augmenting her strength with her magic. Madam Farfelee motioned Stephenie to follow. Glancing more with her mind than her eyes, Stephenie watched the contempt and astonishment of the crowd that had gathered. While she limited the mental energy she allowed into her mind, she couldn't help but feel the rage from Isa and Nerida.

Stephenie followed Farfelee to the keep itself. The large square block of stone was imposing with a long and steep set of stairs leading up to a huge set of double doors. Arrow loops and gutters for pouring oil loomed overhead to deter any foolish enough to attack. Ryia stirred, but did not wake as Stephenie carried her into a dark entrance hall. Tapestries, marble statues, and paintings were obscured by the lack of light, but Stephenie had a sense that they all spoke of great wealth.

Off the entrance hall, Madam Farfelee led her through a side door and down a narrow hall to a series of rooms with beds. "Place the girl on that bed."

Stephenie could hear the heavy accent of the Denarian tongue in Farfelee's voice. She gently placed the girl on the bed and then stood up to look at her body. There was blood on her chest and a deep cut somewhere on the girl's head.

"Do you know how to heal?" Farfelee asked.

Stephenie shook her head. "I can heal myself, but I am not good at healing others. I've killed one person trying," she said, thinking of Oliver, "and when I can actually heal, the people are normally in a lot of pain from what I do."

"Then stand aside and I will help the girl." Farfelee moved forward, quickly glanced over the injuries and then grabbed Ryia's arm.

Stephenie could sense energy flowing from Farfelee into Ryia and even see some color return to the girl's face. A few moments later, she heard Farfelee mumbling some incoherent words, as if she belatedly remembered she was casting a spell. Uncertain how much the Senzar mage would be able to sense of Stephenie's powers; she blocked the mental energy around her and tried to pay attention to the healing.

After a moment, Farfelee released Ryia's arm and turned to Stephenie. "She will recover in time. She has shown only minimal ability in combat. I do not expect that she will make a powerful healer. Many of you that come from around your Sea of Tet simply lack the capacity for truly powerful witchcraft." Farfelee moved toward the door, leading Stephenie back into the narrow hall. "You have made some very powerful enemies today. I do not personally have anything to fear. I came with Lord Favian from the old country, but you will need to be careful that an accident does not befall you. The Captain has trained some very competent soldiers and has the favor of our Lord."

Stephenie shook her head. "An army isn't a group of killers driven by fear and the pleasure of killing. Its strength comes from discipline and respect for its leadership. She's training murderers who take pleasure in the suffering of others. The force will be ineffectual at best."

Farfelee looked deep into Stephenie's eyes. "You seem to think you have an understanding of warfare."

"I know people who were soldiers."

"Fighting with spells and witchcraft is different than with swords and spears. However, I do not disagree with your assessment."

Farfelee took a deep breath. "The first rule of healing I will teach you is that while those who have the skill can do all of their work with a spell, it is usually much more effective if you augment the process with herbs and minerals. We will mix up a drink for Ryia that will speed the healing without taxing ourselves."

Chapter 15

L ate in the evening, Stephenie had gone back to get Ryia's and her belongings from their chests. Those in the barracks gave her cold stares and so she kept her eyes forward and ignored them. She hoped some of them did not actually despise her and were simply doing as they were expected, but without lowering her defenses, she would not know.

When she opened her chest, she smelled the damage before she saw the urine and feces that covered her belongings. Her sword, the gift she had received from her men, was twisted and bent in half. Cold rage filled her and she felt the violation deep within her core. Struggling against the possessive feelings she had toward the equipment, she forced herself to remain motionless, if she did otherwise, she might kill someone. Focusing on her memory of Islet, she calmed herself. *I will not let it beat me*, she finally swore to herself, pushing down the possessiveness.

As the rational part of her mind won out, she closed the lid and left the trunk as it was. On the way out of the barracks, she paused in front of Ryia's chest, the odor and a smirk from someone a few bunks away told her not to bother. Keeping her face expressionless, she continued out of the barracks and returned to the keep and her assigned room. By the time she reached her room, which was a small chamber without windows or a fireplace, her rage had turned into a low smolder.

The room held a single armoire and two sets of bunk beds. Ryia was already laying on the bottom of the beds that sat against the left hand wall. An old man was sitting on the lower bed on the right side of the room. He glanced at her and said something in a language she did not understand. Madam Farfelee mentioned he did not speak the trade tongue, just an odd dialect from a northeastern country Stephenie had not heard of.

She nodded to the wrinkled and frail man before she glanced at Ryia, who seemed to be asleep and unmolested. Madam Farfelee warned her that the old man had never touched any of his roommates, but he tended to fondle himself, often in full view of others. It was not something she wanted to see and if there had been another room available that would hold both her and Ryia, she would have gladly taken it.

Satisfied that nothing untoward had happened, she climbed into her bunk above Ryia and closed her eyes. A slow stream of tears started to slide down her face. In protecting Ryia, she had placed herself at risk and while she had been lucky enough not to have been kicked out of the castle, she was no longer in a position to easily find her sister. *Kas, I really wish I could talk to you.*

"Why?" Ryia's voice carried through the room.

Stephenie wiped her eyes and leaned over the edge of her bed so that she could see Ryia looking back up at her.

"I wanted to be a soldier, not a damn healer. I wanted to be a hero, not someone stuck in the back, fixing those that do the great deeds." She looked away, rolling onto her side, putting her back to Stephenie. "I'd rather be dead than useless."

I threw away my one chance on you! Ungrateful— Stephenie calmed herself, hoping no one close had heard her thoughts. She rolled onto her back and looked up at the ceiling and tried to calm herself. *I am at least now inside the keep. There is that.*

Morning came early, but not as early as the last two days. Madam Farfelee sent someone to summon both her and Ryia to a long storeroom in the first level under the keep. The room had originally held food and supplies for the defenders, but now it had long tables and many shelves with ceramic jars. The discordant odors that came from the room gave Stephenie an instant headache, but Madam

Farfelee was waiting at the far end. A series of oil lamps hanging above the tables provided more illumination here than in any other part of the keep she had seen.

"This afternoon, we will work on using...spells, to heal each other. However, this morning you will learn the properties of many of the plants and minerals in the area." She indicated a shelf beside her and just above her head. "We also have a small collection of items from where you will likely be sent to support those in combat. You will learn the look and use of those plants as well."

Stephenie nodded her head and stepped forward. Ryia was more reluctant, but came in silently. She had said nothing to anyone since the night before.

"If the two of you plan to be gloomy and unpleasant, I will show you two just how hard healing can be."

"Sorry, Ma'am," Stephenie said. "I know it is not easy work."

"And when you add in the fact that you think healing is beneath you, I expect your attitudes will be insufferable." Madam Farfelee squared her hips. "If you fail to demonstrate a willingness to be here, I will have you removed from the castle."

Stephenie bowed her head. "Of course, Ma'am. I promise to give it all my effort."

"And you, girl?"

Ryia shrugged. "I have nowhere else to go. I've just never been good at making potions."

Farfelee shook her head. "These are not potions. They are things your wise women knew hundreds of years ago and you would know them today if your people didn't burn them." She looked each of them in the eye, "You have been warned. Do not give me cause to dismiss you." She turned away from them, "Now, come over here, I will show you what you need to learn."

The morning was challenging for Stephenie, but it was obvious Ryia found the memorization of minerals and dried herbs to be nearly impossible. Stephenie kept fearing Madam Farfelee would tire of Ryia's lack of effort and banish her. However, the older healer simply continued to drill the two of them.

By late in the afternoon, she had put away all the components and instructed Stephenie and Ryia to take seats in the back of the room. With a dagger in hand, she asked them to extend their arms.

"Why," Ryia demanded, her tone having grown more insolent as the day had wore on.

"Because, I need to assess your abilities. We will start with Stephenie trying to heal a small cut on your arm." Farfelee did not give Ryia a chance to argue, with speed that belied her apparent age, the middle-aged healer slashed a cut across the top of Ryia's hand.

The girl flinched back, pulling her bleeding hand to her chest. "What in Elrin's name?"

"Silence girl." Farfelee turned to Stephenie. "Now, take her hand in yours. I will have you chant a spell of healing to relax your mind. Then reach out of yourself and touch Ryia's mind. Her cut will be painful, so it should be easy to find in her mind. Then you will need to chant another spell while concentrating on closing the wound." Farfelee took one-step back. "Get out your focus and repeat after me."

Stephenie took out her useless stone and started repeating the nonsensical words that Farfelee spoke. She felt no different repeating the words. Ryia's mind she could feel easily, even before she started 'casting the spell'. The girl was not disciplined, but she had a genuine feel; she was not trying to pretend to be something she was not.

Reaching out, Stephenie accepted the fact that she would have to endure the unpleasantness of having to connect herself with others while she acted as a healer. Ryia resisted at first, but the girl's mind was jumping from thought to thought and Stephenie easily broke through her defenses. A wave of self-conscious uncertainty poured out of Ryia's head, washing over Stephenie. It woke her own early childhood memories and the pain that had accompanied them. Turning away from emotional turmoil that was Ryia, Stephenie focused on the cut and healing the wound.

As Farfelee had said, the wound was painful and stood out easily in Ryia's subconscious. Not waiting for direction, Stephenie pushed energy into Ryia and directed her body to heal itself. The cry of pain that came from Ryia broke the connection Stephenie had formed.

"Do you hate me that much?"

Stephenie opened her eyes and looked at Ryia's hurt face. "I was only trying to heal you."

"Healing doesn't hurt that much!"

Farfelee grabbed Ryia's hand and examined it. "The wound is closed, but your spell, which I assume you cast silently, was too strong. A small wound does not need that much effort. You tried to force her body instead of allowing it to do its own work."

Stephenie nodded her head. "I am bad at regulating the power when healing." She looked at Ryia. "I am sorry; I did not mean to hurt you. I am not very good at healing."

Farfelee shook her head. "The healing was fine, but a body cannot handle too strong of a spell. You must learn to ease the power." Farfelee held out her hand to Stephenie. "Ryia's turn, give me your hand."

Stephenie did not flinch as the dagger cut deep into the back of her hand. It stung and burned, but the pain was far less than many of the other wounds she had received over the years.

Breathing slowly, she resisted the urge to heal her hand herself. It was now such a natural activity, she almost healed it the moment the blade finished cutting. Closing her eyes, she listened to Farfelee explain the healing to Ryia. However, when Ryia took her hand and tried to reach into her mind, Stephenie could not bring herself to lower the barriers around who she was. The idea someone else would have a chance to look into her thoughts was too frightening. *I have too many secrets.*

Realizing Ryia had let go of her hand, Stephenie opened her eyes.

"Are you trying to make me look like a fool?" A stream of tears was leaking from the girl's eyes. "You think I'm that useless that you want me kicked from the castle?"

"Quiet." Farfelee gave Stephenie a careful appraisal. "You resisted her."

Stephenie nodded her head. "I am sorry, I tried to relax, but...I just...I don't like anyone in my head. I couldn't do it."

Farfelee looked back at Ryia. "Quit your moaning, it is not a reflection on you. Her mind was quiet enough that not even I would have broken through. It is a challenge to heal another witch and not always possible. We tend to be protective of ourselves and there is always a risk in doing it. Most of our healing will be of common soldiers. We will find another person for you to practice on." Glancing to Stephenie, she added, "You will have to heal the cut yourself."

Stephenie nodded her head, having already closed the wound before Farfelee had finished speaking.

"We are done for today. Go eat the evening meal and return to your room."

Henton rubbed his hands together for warmth, but the cold wind was still biting though his gloves and coat. He envied Stephenie's ability to keep warm in the cold and knew that would be the one power he would most like to have.

Bending down, he picked up the large wooden bucket from the frozen ground and headed back into the stables under the inn. Argat had managed to get himself out of his stall and had eaten far more than his share of grain. Fortunately, he had shown no signs of colic and so far Arabella and her stable hand had not come to investigate Henton's activities.

After getting Stephenie's wayward horse back into his stall, Henton had tried to spread the grain in the barrel in the hopes it would not look like someone had stolen any. He also tied a length of twine around the edge of Argat's stall door and the post. That change would be obvious to the owner, but Henton had no choice and he could only hope Argat had not been working out how to untie the knot as he studied Henton tying it.

"Look, you pain in the rear, we only have so much money and we can't afford to pay for you to eat everyone's share." Argat tilted his large head, but did not take his attention from the food at the end of the barn isle. Henton waved a finger at the horse, "I mean it." Shaking his own head, Henton put the muck bucket back in the corner and put away the pitchfork he had used to clean the stall. He did not want to admit it, but the horses were growing on him.

"Sir Henton," Douglas said coming in from the outside door. "I saw you emptying the muck bucket. If you need ideas for work, I—"

"Lay off the Sir crap, Douglas. I mean it."

"But it is your title."

Henton turned to face his Corporal. "The title was never meant to be an honor. The King wasn't praising me over the rest of you."

"The land and money and title is not praise? Stephenie has been paying my small salary out of her own funds; you have a living when you choose to retire."

"Douglas, I was given the title in the hopes that she would see me as a viable marriage candidate and then once she was my wife, the King expected me to keep her in line and under control."

Douglas narrowed his eyes and it took him a moment to reply. "I knew Josh could be an ass, but that is bad even for him. Does Steph know?"

Henton shook his head and then changed it to a shrug. "I really don't know how much she knows. I was not in favor of it. I tried to talk him out of it once he let on that he expected me to curb her behavior. He expected to be able to control me and her through me."

"I'm sorry. I simply thought the rest of us had been slighted."

Henton nodded his head. "I didn't say anything because I didn't want Steph to find out. She loves her brother."

"But I think she sees the trouble as much as the rest of us."

Henton coughed into his elbow. "Be careful you don't start talking treason. He's our King."

Douglas shook his head. "No, I've sworn allegiance to Steph. I've given up Cothel as my home. Where Stephenie goes I go." He rubbed his own hands. "Come on; let's go get something warm to eat. I'll buy."

Stephenie looked up before the door had opened and reminded herself once again that she should not allow herself to get used to being around people who accepted magic. Behavior that could be construed as premonitory normally unnerved people who did not understand how things worked.

Farfelee also looked up from her work on the other side of the table, but her expression was one of concern and so Stephenie opened herself up just a little to get a better feel for what was happening. She sensed the anger and distress as the door banged against the wall.

Nilia, an advanced student who acted as an assistant to Farfelee, pushed her way into the room. She had a heavy wooden crate awkwardly held in her arms.

"Madam, they attacked Atia!"

Stephenie's senses narrowed in on the crate and the angry feline inside. It cried in distress as the crate shifted in Nilia's arms. Moving forward, she helped Farfelee's assistant put the crate on the floor.

Farfelee said something in a language Stephenie had not heard before, but she was certain it was a curse. The older woman carefully lifted the cover from the crate and looked inside. The cat started hissing and growling. Stephenie heard it trying to claw its way up the side of the large wooden box.

"I had to put her into the crate. She bit my hand too many times. The Captain made sure I saw her and Isa attack Atia."

Stephenie looked over Farfelee's shoulder and her jaw tightened. The cat's back appeared to be broken just in front of its hind legs. Most of its fur was burned away and one eye was oozing despite being welded shut. It was in incredible pain and distress and did not want Farfelee any closer.

When Atia's left eye met Stephenie's, the cat quieted and stared. Her ragged breathing calmed slightly, but she still wheezed from her burned nose. "Shh," Stephenie said, coming a little closer to the cat.

"Steph?" Farfelee said, standing up to move herself away from the cat. "Do you know what you are doing?"

Stephenie looked at the older woman and shook her head. "Ka— I've observed once before that I somehow managed to calm a horse that should have been frightened." She watched as Farfelee stared at her. She hoped the Senzar mage was not planning to invade her thoughts."

"Then try to heal the cat."

"What?" Stephenie shook her head. "I don't know how."

Farfelee only drew Stephenie's attention back to the pitiful creature who was slowly dying in the box. Nodding her head, Stephenie slowly lowered her hand to touch Atia's blackened head. The cat simply continued to stare back with her one green eye, anguish and distress evident.

Slowly, Stephenie opened herself to the cat, trying to make the mental connection to the small animal. She almost fell to her knees with the sudden ease in which the cat let her into its mind and the overwhelming distress and pain the animal radiated. However, Stephenie also felt a sense of anger and confusion, a sense of curiosity and affection, as well as the concept of loyalty and loneliness. She understood those emotions, but there were subtle differences that kept the concepts from being truly human. These were feline emotions with a feline sense of morals.

Breathing slowly, she allowed the bond between her and the cat to strengthen. The urge to run, jump, and pounce filled her body and she was sure if she had fur, it would be bristling all over her body. The longer and deeper the bond, the more she felt the instinctual beast in her rise up in her mind. However, instead of railing against the cat, it relished in the thought of wind whipping her hair about her face. It wanted to soar and run free.

Feeling the pain of the cat fill her body, she slowly released the energy she had pulled into herself and directed it to heal the cat. Stephenie was no longer seeing with her eyes and there was only a vague acknowledgment that she still had her own body. However, using her hands and magic, she straightened the cat's body and repaired the poor creature's broken back.

After some time, she realized there was purring coming from her own throat as well as the cat's. Opening her eyes, she noted Farfelee and Nilia staring at her. Looking down, Atia looked up with her pair of green eyes and tilted her head slowly. Most of her hair was still burned away, but a thin coat of grey and tan hairs had started to grow from her healed skin.

"You healed the cat," Nilia said with a bit of disbelief in her voice. "What spell did you use?"

"Nilia, go and check if there are any other of the castle's cats abused by Captain Nerida."

"Yes, Ma'am," she said, bowing her head. Leaving the room, she closed the door behind her.

"Steph, have you ever done that before?"

Stephenie shook her head, but did not stand up, as the cat was smelling her hand. "No, Ma'am. I just seemed to bond with the cat."

"In a way you had not done with any person."

Stephenie nodded her head again and put her other hand on the crate, feeling a bit unbalanced without a tail. "I can't explain it."

Madam Farfelee looked down at the cat, but did not approach any closer. "It is not unheard of, but it is rare. Your mind must respond better to the minds of animals than people. It is not something to worry about, but it will make your healing of people harder." Farfelee paused to consider Stephenie for a moment. "You do not believe in casting spells, do you? No fear of Elrin."

Biting her lip, Stephenie started to rise and the cat almost climbed into her hand as she did. Scooping up the tired animal, she cradled it in her arms before meeting Farfelee's eyes. "I would say you do not either."

Farfelee returned her gaze for a moment and then turned away. "The cat will need something to regain its strength. We cannot give it the same things we would give a person." She pulled a pouch from a drawer and poured out some coins. "I will send you into town. There is an old woman with a shop near the northern edge. She has lots of herbs and spices. See if you can get some leaves of the burnet plant. It should help rebuild the cat's strength."

Stephenie slowly disentangled herself from the cat, placing it on the table. "It is such a small animal. I can't understand the cruelty of some people."

Farfelee put the money in Stephenie's hand. "It was a message to me. I've looked after the animals in the keep and so they were telling me that I will not be able to protect those I look out for. Likely the next one will be dead." She sighed and then reached out to the cat. Atia pulled back some, but did not hiss and growl. "Go on. The sooner you're away the better."

Stephenie nodded her head and quickly ran back to get her coat from her bedchamber. She was thankful for the chance to finally have an opportunity to speak with Kas. She exited the keep and managed to get out of the main gate without being stopped, but the guards took definite note of her departure. Fearing she would not have much time before someone started to follow her, she headed into the town, hoping Kas was watching and would notice her. Cooped up in the keep under Farfelee's tutelage for three days, she had not felt his presence for too long and feared what he and the others might have done.

Stephenie!

She almost stumbled as relief filled her. Kas' approach had been like a lightning strike slamming into her. He had crossed from somewhere out of her range to partially enveloping her in an instant. *Kas*, she nearly moaned, feeling all her pent up emotions ready to burst free. On mutual understanding, they quickly shared the memories and emotions of the last few days as more of a dump of thoughts then of words. It took each of them a few moments to sort through what the other had shared, and in the end, Stephenie spoke first.

I screwed up, Kas. I really made a mess of things. I would have been in the dungeon by now. I might have had to wait for a while until things were right, but I would have at least had a chance to start making a plan. Now I have to find a way to sneak down there with what could be a dozen guards, who now all hate me. Tears started to fall from her eyes as she walked generally to the north through the frozen streets. *How am I going to get to Islet?*

Stephenie, you are at least in the keep now. She felt his confidence in her. *You will find a way.*

She dried her eyes with her sleeve. *I'll probably only get there as a prisoner myself.* She shook her head. *I've missed you so much. I wanted to do this on my own, to show everyone I could, but I'm so tired now. I saved a girl who'd rather be dead than a healer and lost my best chance to get to my sister.*

She felt him draw himself further around her, but he did not draw any energy from her body. *If what your memory shows is what happened, then I do not see how you could have done otherwise and remained who you are. Stephenie, you have compassion and that is one of the things I love about you. Even if it takes longer to rescue your sister, then it simply takes longer. I only wish you would come out of the keep more often so that I could see you are still safe. I...I was quite worried.*

She closed her eyes to keep the tears held back. She did not stop walking, since she could easily feel the world around her. *I am sorry, I will try, but they are very regimented and dictate what we do the whole day.* She glanced down a side street and looked at the signs, but she still could not read the language. On a hunch, she turned back toward the harbor. *I have a feeling it may be a while before I can get out again. Farfelee has me studying herbs and minerals and making other concoctions. It doesn't involve any time on the practice field, which would likely draw trouble from Captain Nerida.*

Stopping in front of an old storefront that had a faded image of dried plants painted on the door, she stepped off the street and onto the small porch. After knocking on the door, she heard a call from inside, which she assumed meant enter.

When Stephenie opened the door, her senses were assaulted with an overwhelming flood of odors that conflicted with good sense. She had thought the workroom in the castle had a powerful combination of smells; this small shop was far worse as many of the containers were open and dozens of different plants hung from the ceiling. To add further insult, incense burned on a stone plate sitting on a table in the middle of the room.

"Hello," Stephenie called in Pandar, hoping the woman inside spoke the trade language.

"Yes, enter, and close door. Outside cold."

Stephenie hurried inside and carefully moved across the old and worn planks that made up the floor. "I am in need of burnet...I don't know if it is leaves or the flower," she added, realizing Farfelee had not indicated. The woman moved out from behind a counter. A thick shawl covered her upper body and she wore frayed mittens on her hands.

"You have come from keep?" Shuffling her wraps to offer more protection from the cold, Stephenie noted how painfully thin the woman was. "Burnet is common enough. Use whole plant." She walked over to a large box sitting against the wall and pulled out a large handful of dried stems of buds. "How much?"

"It's for a cat that was nearly killed and badly hurt. It almost died."

The woman frowned. "Not need much."

"How much for that handful?" Stephenie asked, feeling like a fresh recruit that failed to ask a dozen important questions.

"It only cat, I give you tiverit...room...mushroom," she said, trying several words. "That will take care of cat peaceful. Sleep forever. It have no more pain."

Stephenie shook her head as she conveyed her dismay to Kas, *she just offered to give me mushrooms to kill the cat!* Aloud she remained more cordial, "No, we want to keep the cat. Not kill it."

The woman shrugged. "Not know how bad it was hurt." Looking down at the dried plants in her hand, she carried the handful over to the table and wrapped it in a piece of cloth. "Two marks," she said holding out the bundle.

Stephenie pulled the coins she had been given from her coat pocket and quickly realized Farfelee had given her a large sum of money. Trying to be discrete, she pulled three small coins from her hand and dropped the rest back into the pocket. "Thank you."

The woman nodded her head and pulled her shawl tighter in preparation for Stephenie opening the door. Stephenie paused a moment. *Kas, there are some people from the keep out there watching. I can feel them off to the right.*

Do you want me to do something to them?

Stephenie gave a mental shake of her head. *No, I need to get back to the keep. But you should remain here or head out a different way.* She frowned, *I miss you. I love you.*

As do I. I will keep watch for you later.

Stephenie pulled open the door and headed out into the cold wind. She held on to Kas' presence for as long as she could, but it was only a few moments before she was too far away. The two people from the keep she felt fall in behind her, far enough that they remained on the periphery of her ability to identify them.

Moving with purpose now that Kas was not near her, she reached the keep quickly. Elvira challenged her as she approached the gate. "I am just coming back from an errand for Madam Farfelee." Stephenie held up the bundle to offer proof.

Elvira nodded her head and glanced behind her, checking across the yard to see who might be watching. Speaking lowly, she said, "I just wanted to let you know that not everyone agrees with the Captain. There are many of us who think you were right, it's just...."

"You cannot risk being thrown out."

"Or worse." She glanced back across the yard, "Be careful. They are angry with you."

Stephenie wanted to hug Elvira, but she knew better. "Thank you. Be safe yourself." No longer feeling everyone was against her, she allowed herself a small grin as she moved quickly across the yard and into the keep.

When she reached the workroom, Farfelee stood in the middle of it with her hands on her hips and a scowl on her face. "What do you think you are doing? You stupid girl." The short woman shook her head. "Get in here and close the door."

Uncertain of where she had gone wrong, Stephenie complied, coming to stand before the older woman and looking at the floor. "I am sorry, Ma'am. I thought to bring the herb here."

Farfelee snatched the bundle from Stephenie's hand and tossed it on the counter. Pointing to another box on the table, she waited until Stephenie followed her hand. "And what do you think that is? We were working with burnet this morning." She lowered her voice to a growl, "do you not know your plants yet?"

Stephenie could not still her tongue before her response slipped out, "I've only been working in here for a few days, how should I know?" Knowing she had already committed herself to the angry retort, she went on, "I can learn this, but you've shown me a hundred different things today alone. I assumed you wouldn't send me out for a pointless errand."

Farfelee licked her lips and exhaled slowly. "Girl, I gave you a lot of money so that you would take the hint that you should leave. I told you the cat was a warning." She shook her head. "If Nerida would do that openly, she is telling me I cannot protect you."

Stephenie realized Farfelee's irritation was really fear for her safety. "But Ma'am, I can't simply run away. It's not who am."

Looking more worried than angry, Farfelee took Stephenie over to the cat, currently curled up in a blanket. "You are a foolish girl. Some fights are better to avoid, but it is too late. They will be watching for you to leave again and will either stop you or perhaps attack you in the city."

Stephenie quickly tried to estimate who and how many might try to attack her. She was not sure if the Captain would dirty her hands directly or if she would want to avoid the appearance that Stephenie's disobedience was so significant that she was compelled to act.

"We will keep you in the keep. Nerida may be bold, but she is not likely that bold. You'll have to spend more time in these workrooms with one or more of us."

"And Ryia," Stephenie added, worried that the girl would again be attacked to prove a point.

"Yes, and the girl." Farfelee paused and looked Stephenie up and down. "I would offer to teach you some combat skills, but I suspect you are more capable than you have demonstrated. The others might not have been at the angle to notice, but you stopped yourself short of the wall. That is wise. I think Nerida will underestimate you, but do not overestimate your skills. They have numbers and are not incapable."

"Yes, Ma'am."

Farfelee shook her head again. "Give me back the extra coin; it will be no good if they find it on you. Okay, now let's make a syrup the cat will like and you will be responsible for caring for the animal."

Chapter 16

The next two days had been long with lots of memorization and practice healing, this time on those without powers. Stephenie did not like the fact that the people were getting cut simply as a means to teach her and a dozen other students, but the people were not complaining. She sensed a level of obligation these people felt, but also a feeling of resolution to a defined fate.

She was slowly getting better at not causing pain, but the euphoric feeling many of them received from the other healers was not something they received from her. It was a frustration, but it was not something she could easily see in the fields that people generated. She began to wonder if it was some subconscious mental state the healer put the patient into during the process. Of course, with the worthless spell casting, she was not getting a good sense of the actual mechanics.

Tired and drained, she fell into bed each night. Her only solace was Atia keeping her company with a loud purr. Sometime late on that second night, Stephenie woke automatically as a man opened the door to her room. She could feel the old man and Ryia still sleeping. The approaching men had not woken them, but she sensed a change in the mental activity of the two men, which meant they likely knew she was awake.

"Can I help you?" she said caustically in Pandar.

The men paused slightly and she took the opportunity to slip from her bed to the floor, keeping a dagger in her right hand hidden behind her back.

"You are to come with us. We need a healer."

Stephenie looked at the men. Her senses opened, allowing her eyes to cut through the shadows obscuring their faces. She noted their hard expression. These were soldiers who had seen combat and emerged on the other side, but would never again be whom they once were. "You should see Madam Farfelee."

"She is indisposed. Come with us now. If the man dies, you will be held accountable. Otherwise, we'll take the girl and she'll be responsible."

She could feel the old man and Ryia start to wake, not wanting them to be used against her; she decided to go with the men. "Fine, where is the person who needs to be healed?"

The man nodded his head to indicate the hall outside the room. Still uncertain if this was going to be an attempt on her life, she slid the dagger between her belt and the small of her back. Then she made a point of straightening her wrinkled shirt she had been sleeping in and concealing the dagger in the progress. Walking past the first man, she followed the second into the hall and then deeper into the keep. She sensed a small draw of power from both of them, but that was nothing compared to what she was holding in herself.

It was not long before she realized they were leading her toward the dungeons. Her concern for her safety was growing, but she knew there would be no point in trying to sense anything from these men. Deciding to play ignorant of the potential danger, she hoped that if needed, she would be able to catch them by surprise.

On the other side of the reinforced door into the dungeon were three men, all sitting lazily in chairs around a small table set in an alcove barely big enough to accommodate them. A casual nodding of heads occurred in acknowledgment of their passing, but there was no indication of trouble.

Past the guards, the passage turned and emptied into a steep set of stairs descending into a dimly lit room thirty feet down. Stephenie followed the man in front of her and had to stop at the bottom where iron bars ran from the floor into the stone ceiling, which was barely seven feet high. A guard dressed in heavy leather armor rose from a chair at the base of the stairs and used a thick key to open a large cast iron lock set into a reinforced door.

As she passed, the guard said something to her in a language that she did not understand. He did not appear hostile, so she nodded her head and smiled. The sound of the door shutting and locking behind them set her further on edge, but she did her best to conceal her emotions.

Around her, she carefully let in just enough information to feel a warren of small rooms and narrow passages that connected them. At least six separate passages led away from the open room where she was currently standing. The room was damp and dirty with five men sitting in chairs around a table. They were sharing a cold meal while enjoying a game of cards. The level of attention they paid her and the men escorting her was minimal, which gave her hope the errand was legitimate.

"This way," the leading man said, heading toward an open door on the far wall. Beyond the door, the stone tunnel was rough-cut with an uneven floor and Stephenie could tell it headed deeper into the ground. After fifty yards, the passage opened into a room heavy with the iron smell of blood mingling with feces, urine, and the sweat from pain and death. While the stench burned her nose, it was the emotional energy of those in the room that made her gag.

"I knew she'd not be able to handle this," came the Captain's acidic voice from the other side of the room. "I'll have to report her failure to Lord Favian."

Stephenie straitened her spine and schooled her expression. On the other side of this smoky room a man was strapped to a table with blood scattered across his naked body. Captain Nerida stood beside three other men, one of which could have passed for a butcher, his leather apron covered in thick blood and gore.

"Why have you summoned me?" Stephenie asked, the defiance coming back into her voice.

The Captain smiled, "because my dear, this man needs a healer. He's no warlock and can't heal himself. He's also a personal pet of Lord Favian and is not allowed to die until our Lord wishes that to happen." She stepped to the side, making room for Stephenie next to the tortured prisoner. "If you don't want to displease our Lord, you better get started healing this man."

Stephenie tried to puzzle out what Captain Nerida was trying to prove. The only thought was that the Captain wanted to make sure she got to heal the most damaged people in an effort to frighten and torment her. Determined not to be intimidated, she crossed the room, her boots sticking to the gore that had accumulated on the straw covered floor. She passed machines designed to cause pain and kill slowly. Saws, blades, and hammers of various sizes lay next to blood-covered straps on a multitude of tables. Many of the devices she had never personally seen their type before and was growing thankful that her father had never used such punishments.

When she reached the man, she could see fresh cuts over most of his body. The wounds crossed over a multitude of scars that spoke of possible years of torture. The man's eyes were closed and his mind was so quiet she wondered if he was even still alive. However, the continued leaking of blood as well as the slow rise and fall of his chest told her that he still lived.

"If he dies, it will go badly for you."

Stephenie did not bother to acknowledge Nerida, who obviously was hoping that she would fail. Reaching out, she carefully set her hand on the man's thick arm; he was not exactly fat, but he was definitely not being starved.

I hate this, she thought to herself as she reached out with her mind to form a mental contact with the man. She started to chant a pointless spell, but before she could speak the first word the man had already forced his way into her head. She tried to shut him out, but it was too late and she could feel the man's snarled hatred.

Mine, you little cur.

She could feel energy being sucked through her and knew the man was simply using her mind and body as he wished, which appeared to be to heal himself. Rage and anger flooded her thoughts as a growl escaped her lips. *No!* It was not a word, but a certainty. Pushing back against the man's mind, she wrestled enough influence of her body that she regained control of the flow of energy, if not how it was being used. Instead of trying to stop it, which she doubted she would be able to do completely, she dumped a massive amount of energy into his body.

Almost immediately, she felt his mental assault falter. Not giving him a chance to recover, she put back up her mental barriers. *I'm trying to help you, damn it!*

She was not expecting to hear his reply, but it seemed he still had partial control of their link. *You are aiding them and facilitating their torture. You can die like the rest.* The words were not quite in a language she understood, but the meaning he affixed to the mental broadcast was clear. Along with the message came memories of pain and anguish. Stephenie did all she could to prevent them overwhelming her again.

No stranger to hurt, she bore the memories. Growling once more, she pushed through his assault and slammed more energy into him. His own scream echoed in her ears and she could tell the link to his mind was broken. Opening her eyes, she looked down and noticed her fingers were buried up to the fist knuckle into his forearm. Extracting her blood soaked nails; she noticed the remainder of his wounds had closed.

Free of the man, her sense of the room returned and she immediately was aware that the soldiers behind her had their swords drawn and pointed at her back. She gorged on the energy in the stone around her as she turned to face them before they could strike. A hardness in her eyes held them in check. "What is the meaning of that?"

The Captain raised her voice, "Kill her now, I said! She's been compromised!"

Stephenie pulled as much energy as she could, ready to deflect the physical attacks of the men while crushing the Captain under a wave of gravity.

"Hold yourselves!"

Stephenie barely kept herself in check, grimacing slightly under the pain of all the energy she was holding within her body. Despite the slight burning, she waited, not wanting to be the first to strike, but determined not to be the first to fall.

"She is showing no signs of possession and Orlan is unconscious. Lord Favian will be intrigued with this development." The butcher, as Stephenie thought of him, had moved between her and the men.

"But we saw her lose control initially!" Nerida swore. "His healing was too complete and too quick for a novice to have done so well."

Stephenie watched the blood covered man shake his head. "I'm guessing you did not even warn her of what Orlan would do. Your petty dispute is not my concern. I am master of this dungeon and the girl drove him back and taught him a decent lesson in the process. I suspect His Lordship will be quite interested."

The Captain's upper lip twitched, but she said nothing. A moment later, Nerida turned on her heels and retreated from the dungeon. The two men who had escorted Stephenie looked at each other, but their swords were lowered.

"Go on, you can go back to your duties. Your little plan has backfired." The butcher turned to face her. "I will inform His Lordship of your abilities personally. For now, go back to your room and sleep."

Stephenie bowed her head and started toward the tunnel that would lead her out of the dungeon. The thought of trying to take a look around before she left disappeared as soon as she sensed Madam Farfelee coming down the tunnel. She was obviously looking for Stephenie, "What do you think you were doing coming to the dungeon without orders from me?"

Stephenie bowed her head, "Ma'am, they said I had no choice and you were not available."

"The Captain had arranged it in the hopes I would not hear about it." The older woman looked around. "However, you are not dead, so Ryia's warning was not too late."

"She drove Sir Orlan from her head," the butcher said from behind her. "His Lordship will be intrigued."

Farfelee looked at Stephenie with fresh eyes. "Full of surprises." With a smile, she added just loud enough for Stephenie to hear, "That will make Nerida quite unhappy."

Stephenie looked back to the man who was still strapped to the table. The butcher had turned away and was tending to his blood stained tools. "I don't understand, he's not a mag—warlock."

Madam Farfelee nodded her head. "Come, I will take you back to your room and explain this to you just the once." Turning on her own heels, the older healer marched back into the passage that would lead them from the dungeon.

Stephenie used the last of the energy she had been holding in reserve to fling Sir Orlan's blood from her hand as she hastened to catch up.

Madam Farfelee spoke quietly over her shoulder as they made their way out of the dungeon. "That man is withholding secrets that Lord Favian wants. However, the old soldier was always exceedingly disciplined mentally. Even without power, he easily invades the minds of most of those who even accidentally brush against his thoughts. It is an uncommon gift, but not unheard of."

"But what is the point of him doing that?"

Farfelee turned her head to Stephenie. "If he had successfully taken over your mind, he'd be able to control you and use your powers to help him escape. He has tried it many times before. The last five people sent to heal him ended up dead on the end of Nerida's swords. We now only use the most weakly skilled people so the threat is minimal. He did some real damage initially with a few who had significant power. Even if you should lack power, which I doubt, you have mental discipline and that will be a blessing and a curse."

Stephenie now understood her summons; the Captain had intended her to die, a victim of Orlan's control. If she had not driven the soldier from her mind quickly enough, she would have had a pair of swords in her back.

"Sir Orlan was not scheduled for a session today. Unfortunately for you, since you survived, you will have garnered additional attention from our Lord. I fear you will now be expected to heal him after subsequent sessions, if not try to extract information from him. Of course, if you should at some point succumb to Orlan, we will be obligated to kill you. The man is too dangerous to be allowed control of a witch's powers."

Chapter 17

Henton sat down at the nearly empty bar, only two other men were at the bar's far end and another four patrons were at the table in the corner. He nodded his head to the older man standing behind the counter and a moment later a mug of warm ale was sitting before him. Douglas' ale followed shortly thereafter. "I'm worn out," Henton mumbled, rolling his head to get the kinks out of his neck. He had given in and also took work on the docks when Kas had informed him of Stephenie's situation.

"Well, it's been a while since you've done any real work."

Henton shook his head at Douglas. They had run into each other on the way back from the docks, but he had not seen Douglas since they parted ways that morning. He suspected Douglas was as sore as he was, but the younger man was hiding it better. "Don't make me hurt you," he said with a grin. The sore muscles were a good thing; the work at the dock kept his mind off the fact that Kas had not seen Stephenie in the three days since she had come out for herbs. Kas had pretended to not be worried, but Henton knew better. They were all worried and were feeling frustrated, but none of them really wanted to talk about it.

"That carrack you're unloading looks a bit worn," Douglas remarked as he sipped the warm drink.

"Cothel scum," growled one of the men at the far end of the bar. "Get yourself back to the piss trench you climbed out of."

Henton turned his head to look at the thin man who was dressed in fine clothing. His cheekbones and accent, while slurred with excessive drink, marked him from Kynto. "My Lord," Henton responded in Pandar, "have we done something to offend you?" Henton did not look to the table of four people he knew were now watching them; he counted on Douglas to keep an eye on them as well as the man behind the bar.

"You're the bloody reason I'm here. You rotten cur. Your damn country is what made a mess of everything."

Henton noted the man's companion, who was sitting against the wall, had a more athletic build, was in his early twenties, and was far less drunk. However, the companion simply shook his head and focused his attention back on his drink, as if this scenario had played out before. Allowing himself to relax a bit, Henton turned fully to face the drunk man. "If you have issue with Cothel, you won't get any complaint from me. I had no reason to stay and am happy not to be there."

The drunk man turned to Henton, lifting his face into the lamp light. Henton could see the man was as young as his more sober companion. It took a moment, but the man slid from his stool and weaved his way over to Henton. "Then you understand," he said once he was close enough that Henton could feel the fumes coming from his mouth. The man's head bobbing up and down with a wildly exaggerated motion. "My name is Lord Evrin. I am messenger and adviser for my mistress."

The man took a deep breath, slid himself on the stool next to Henton and turned back to the man behind the bar. Pointing into the mug, he demanded something in what Henton believed was the local tongue. The old man took his mug and Evrin turned back to Henton. "Have you seen her?"

Henton glanced to the old man behind the bar, but the man had already replaced the mug and was walking away. "I'm sorry, who do you mean?"

"The princess! Have you seen her?"

Henton failed to remove all the shock from his expression, but the drunk did not appear to notice. "No. I'm just a commoner. I don't mix with people that far above my station."

Evrin nodded his head. "I've seen her. I've seen her red hair and hateful blue eyes."

Henton more felt than saw Douglas tense. He had to move his own mug quickly to his lips to cover his reaction.

"She's evil. These Elrin worshiping bastards," Evrin said, raising his voice, then after a moment lowered it. "These bastards don't burn witches, but I think they'd burn her after what she did to them...evil blue eyes." Evrin sighed. "She's why I'm here instead of with the Princess."

Henton swallowed, not quite following Evrin's statement. The other people in the public house appeared to have all gone back to their own business, but Henton could not be certain someone was not listening. "You've seen Princess Stephenie recently?"

Evrin shook his head. "No, stupid. It was just after her father and brother left to start the bloody war. My mistress is Princess Elsia. She sent me here to get something to make the bitch come back." Evrin looked up and around the public house, "But these bastards won't let me have it! Won't even talk with me!" He sighed and slumped his shoulders before bringing the mug back to his lips. "Twenty days. I've been here twenty days and they refuse." He shook his head and stared into his drink.

Henton glanced quickly to Douglas; his Corporal was definitely unnerved by the conversation, but was keeping his head. Turning back to Evrin, Henton quietly prodded. "So, Princess Elsia sent you here to get something, but the Senzar won't let you have it?"

"Won't even talk with me. Bastards!" He sighed. "Ever since he died, this group will no longer work with us. Sure, we've had others, but this group has her hand."

"Who died?"

Evrin turned to Henton and poked him in the chest. "You're from Cothel. Why do they make it hard? Her Highness was treated foul. She deserves better. You treated her wrong!"

Henton slid his mug toward Evrin. "I left, remember? I don't know Her Highness."

Evrin nodded his head and took Henton's mug. "You're a good man. Good man."

"Who died?"

"Oh, it was Lord Yvima Orthas Corha."

Henton waited, keeping eye contact with Evrin, though the drunk man's eyes had almost no focus. Henton moved his head slightly closer and Evrin seemed to waken suddenly.

"Advisor to the King and the High Priest." Evrin shook his head as if Henton was an idiot. Then he lowered his voice and moved closer. "It was the work of that evil witch. The country's been in chaos. It's like His Majesty has lost his focus and direction. Even the High Priest is having a hard time without their adviser." Evrin sighed. "He scared me when I saw him. A powerful priest that could read your soul. But My Mistress trusted him. He told her how to break the curse." Evrin glanced around to make sure no one was close enough to listen. "Most people think it was My Mistress who brought on the curse, but it wasn't. It was that evil witch, but My Mistress is too smart. She's got a way. She's going to eat that witch's heart and rid herself, and all of us, of Elrin's spawn. She'll be free when it's done."

Henton kept his jaw relaxed, but it was not easy. The drunk confidence this younger man exuded made him want to break Evrin's nose. However, that would not help anyone. Putting all the pieces together in his mind, Henton nodded his head. "So, these Senzar here, they knew your Lord Yvi..."

"Yvima," Evrin almost snarled. "Yvima! How many times do I have to say it?"

"These Senzar here, they knew Yvima and now that he's dead, they won't work with you?"

Evrin, staring into Henton's broad shoulder, nodded his head. "That's right." After a moment he looked up to meet Henton's face and smiled. "But I won't leave until they talk with me. They will give in eventually." His grin growing wider, "Then that bitch will see. My Mistress is so smart. That redheaded tramp will see what it means to mess with a real princess."

Henton nodded his head in unison with Evrin. "So you hope to get the Senzar to help bring her back to her mother?"

Evrin shook his head with disappointment and turned away, "Don't be stupid." Looking back to glare at Henton, he continued to shake his head.

Fearful that Evrin would go back to his companion, Henton put his hand on Evrin's arm. "Okay, how is your Kyntian Mistress going to defeat that Cothel bitch?"

Evrin chuckled. "It's a secret."

Forcing down his rising irritation, Henton, nodded his head. "Probably a good thing. While the three of us would like nothing more than to see Cothel collapse, there might be others that support that failed country."

Evrin turned back and nodded his head. "They declared the witch cleansed," he said quietly. "Can you believe that?"

"It's one of the reasons we left."

Evrin nodded. "Well, they'll not see it coming. My Mistress wanted her daughter back, but the Senzar won't give her up. However, I don't see why they won't give me her right hand."

Henton raised his eyebrows. "Her right hand?"

Evrin glared again and then shook his head. "Her daughter, Islet, Queen of Ipith...well, former Queen." Evrin snickered as he held up his right hand and pointed to the back of it. "Well, Islet has a birthmark on her right hand. We cut it off, pickle it in a cask of spirits, and ship it to Cothel. Tell them if the bitch doesn't cooperate and do as she's told, we cut up the rest of her sister and send her one piece at a time until she does come."

Henton leaned a little closer. "But if they won't hand her over, then all you'd have is her right hand." .

Evrin smiled. "The bitch won't know that and she's so hung up on her family that she would come. I know it." Evrin swayed a bit. "Her Highness came up with a good plan. I can't fail her. I can't. They have to talk to me at some point." He sighed and slowly laid his head on the bar.

Henton watched the man's companion come over and poked Lord Evrin in the side. When the drunk man did not respond, his companion bent down and pulled the unconscious man onto his shoulders. Grunting with the effort, the young man stood and then glared at Henton. Without a word, he carried the young Lord out the front door.

Henton noticed the old man behind the bar come over to retrieve the mugs. "He do this often?" Henton asked in Pandar.

The old man looked at Henton for a moment, and then nodded his head after processing what had been said. "He's here most nights," the man said in heavily accented Pandar. "Big fight half week and one more back."

Henton nodded his head, then taking several coins from his pouch he paid for his and Douglas' drinks as he stood. "Come on Douglas, we've got a long day of moving cargo tomorrow."

Once they were outside and on their way back to the inn, he continued quietly in Cothish, "This is a problem. If he sees Steph in the keep, either when he's at the gate or if they finally do let him in, then she's in real trouble."

"And he's planning to cut off her sister's hand." Douglas shook his head. "Do we find where they are staying and quietly arrange for something to happen?"

Henton swallowed as his fist clenched. "I don't like the idea of murdering someone. That's not something I approve of and neither would Stephenie."

"But her life is in danger. Kas won't hesitate when he finds out."

Henton turned down a narrow lane and pulled his coat tighter as the cold wind whipped between the buildings. "Then we hold off in telling him. At least until we have a solution."

"Hold off telling Kas what?" came a disembodied voice.

"Kas," Henton stammered, "we ran into a problem. However, we don't want to draw suspicion and neither we nor Stephenie really condone murder."

It was several moments before Kas responded in Cothish. "I had never killed someone until after I had died. I was not a violent person. However, I have learned to do what is necessary."

Douglas shook his head. "He's not going to give up. Not if he's been here twenty days already. We have to do something."

Henton bit his lip, but continued walking. "I've never killed someone in cold blood and don't want to start now." They came out of the lane and headed for their inn that was across from the open park. "Perhaps we can tie them up and hold them somewhere until this is over."

Douglas snorted. "Just the two—three of us and for what, possibly a few weeks. We have no report from Stephenie and we don't have anywhere to hold someone, nor the man power." He stopped walking and looked in the direction of the harbor. "We've got jobs because most of the ships that come to port are pirates and more than half the crews are conscripted. I can quietly ask around if anyone knows of a ship that would be willing to take on a couple more crew members."

"Sell them into slavery?" Henton frowned.

"It's better than death and they treat the crews reasonably. Heck, the guy who hired me was once recruited. They put you to sea for ten years, and then you earn your freedom and can either stay on board for a share or disembark. They just watch everyone real carefully when they are in port, locking them in their quarters to prevent someone from running off early."

Henton was surprised at Douglas; none of them had ever sympathized with pirates or countries that force men to be sailors. "I never thought you would condone slavery."

Douglas held up his hands. "I don't, but what are we to do? We want to make sure Steph is safe and honestly I don't like the idea of killing them any more than you do."

"What about a forced passage? Have them taken somewhere a fair distance away, then leave them in port. They won't be stuck on the ship for ten years at least."

Douglas nodded his head. "Can't guarantee the pirates wouldn't double cross us and force them to stay and it would cost us a fair bit of money I would think, but I'll see if it is possible. I've made a few friends on the dock and I know who I can ask. Though I'll have to wait for morning."

Henton rubbed his bearded face with his gloved hands. "And then we'll have to figure out a way to get them on a ship. Passed out drunk will help, but we don't know that they aren't holy warriors. If they are, we'd be in for it."

"I can keep a watch on them. What did they look like?"

Henton hesitated. "We don't want them dead."

Kas' tone grew cold. "I told you I will watch them. I will not kill them, but I have to know what to look for."

Giving in to the disembodied voice, Henton described the two men in as much detail as he could. "We'll see if we can get them on a boat and out of our hair." He waited for Kas' response, but none came.

Stephenie rose in the morning, but she was exhausted from a poor night's sleep brought on by the memories of that man in her head. It was not as bad as when her mind had been invaded by Gernvir; this Sir Orlan had not rummaged through her memories. *He didn't have the time,* she admitted to herself.

After a quick meal, she was again in Madam Farfelee's workroom and answering to the older healer's demands. After cleaning up a mess left by someone else the day before, Farfelee told Stephenie to take a seat near the back of the room.

"How old do you think I am?"

Stephenie looking into Madam Farfelee's face. She noted only a couple of wrinkles, but her eyes appeared to have age. "Forty perhaps?"

"I am seventy-three. I have been with Lord Favian since I was twenty-four."

Stephenie raised her eyebrows.

"You think that is too long to serve one master?"

"No, Ma'am. I just had not expected you to be as old as you were or to have been in our Lord's service for so long."

The older woman eyed Stephenie for a moment. "That is a very safe way to respond." After a pause, she continued, "You will meet with Lord Favian before the next shift change. He will want to know all about you, including the events of last night. I want to provide you with some guidance before you meet him."

Stephenie nodded her head, feeling a bit less confident about the meeting she had known would eventually occur.

"Please do not share these facts with the others, it would only cause trouble and help no one. By accepting Lord Favian's training and support, you have unknowingly agreed to a period of servitude. The more powerful you are, the longer the period. Many of those under Nerida will likely serve for ten years or fewer, but based upon your demonstration last night, you may be expected to serve for twenty years or more."

"I don't understand. No one said I was going to be here for that long."

Farfelee raised her hand. "Did you ask?"

Stephenie swallowed. "I had assumed it would be a reasonable period."

"And what is reasonable to Favian is all that matters. Look at me, I've lived most of my life looking like I was simply a little older than you. The last few years I have aged and it is quickening. Ten years to someone who will live forty is more than twenty to someone who might live to be one hundred." She shook her head. "What's done is done and I do not know what he thinks of your skill yet. But I want to warn you that if you are not careful, you could extend your commitment of service."

Stephenie wanted to bristle and argue. She wanted to demand to know who in their right mind would simply join such a scheme without demanding better treatment, but she already knew the answer. Those who were desperate enough and needed to avoid the turmoil and likely death in their home countries would easily do as she did, snatching up the first chance at freedom they got, even if it was simply trading one prison for another. *The trouble is, these Senzar are driving that exodus and not being upfront about the commitment.*

"I tell you this because I want you to react wisely with his Lordship. If you prove somewhat useful, he may offer you the chance to serve with him instead of having your obligation transferred to another master. If you prove very useful, you will not have a choice. I would recommend waiting to respond until you have a chance to think about the consequences if he should offer the choice."

Stephenie nodded her head. "Why are you telling me this?"

Farfelee sighed. "You remind me of myself. Though I knew more of what I was committing to than you do. I am not Senzar. Unless you are born to one, you cannot be. I am a conscript from a land they conquered a dozen years before I was born. I chose to join the Senzar so I would have a better life."

"Thank you for telling me. I will try to make a wise decision."

"I have a feeling once his Lordship sees you, you may not have as much of one as you would like. What you have going for you is the fact that you were able to keep Orlan out of your head. That will cause most others to avoid the danger of trying to access your mind. The danger to them would be too great." Farfelee rose. "Favian is not a bad man; don't let my warning sour your opinions. In fact, he could be much more reasonable than some of those to the south who are still wanting to wage war. Those to the south have lost their greater purpose and so now are trying to salvage as much as they can from this endeavor. They will value local soldiers while they are here, but those that decide to return home will be less inclined to treat you well. You'll be a cost to them at that point, not an asset."

Stephenie nodded her head, realizing there was a much greater complexity to the Senzar than she had imagined. Looking up to meet the healer's eyes, she asked, "Are you free to leave or does he still have a claim to your life?"

"I am free and have been for nearly thirty years. I simply have nowhere else to go." Turning away, she added, "Finish cleaning the other table, but be ready to go to Lord Favian when they summon you."

The summons came before she finished cleaning. Stephenie was led out of the lower level of the keep and up to the second floor. The upper level was decorated with many odd sculptures that were more shape than substance. She did not have enough time to examine what they were made of, but she suspected some of the highly colored ones were glass.

The door to Lord Favian's chamber was opened for her and she was allowed to enter the warmly heated office. Books, sculptures, and paintings where spread about the room. On the far side, next to a large window with many glass panes, was a heavy oak desk with a young man who appeared no more than twenty years old sitting behind it.

"Please have a seat," the man said, his voice was strong, but not deep or rich in tone. He sounded like a youth not much older than she was. "You are surprised by my appearance?" he continued in Pandar, his accent similar to Madam Farfelee's.

Stephenie recovered and quickly crossed the room to the chair. She bowed her head as she sat. "No My Lord, well, perhaps a little. I did not know what you looked like."

He grinned. "Trust me, I am master of this keep and these lands. I am as young and virile as I seem, but I am also quite experienced." He sat back in his chair, appraising her for a moment. "You are quite attractive," he said after a few moments. "And you have a disciplined mind I am told."

"You mean the healing of Sir Orlan?"

She noted his jaw tighten slightly. "Yes. Orlan was once a distinguished warrior of mine. He fell from grace and betrayed me. Unfortunately, he's kept the extent of his betrayal secret. Until I learn how much damage he has done, I cannot let him die."

Stephenie nodded her head. She kept a careful check on what she allowed her mind to sense, not wanting to potentially offend someone who was at least in his seventies, if not significantly older, and yet appeared untouched by time.

"I understand Captain Nerida and you do not get along well."

"No, My Lord. I never intended to cause offense, but I felt the need to defend another trainee."

"And attacked a man when his back was turned to you, knocking him to the ground and injuring his hand. She also complained about sloppy spell use and not being careful to avoid the influence of Elrin."

Stephenie could not tell if he was serious in that statement or simply repeating Nerida's complaint. Taking a risk, she hoped he admired strength and not subservience. "My Lord, the man I attacked had been taunting me and would have killed someone if nothing was done. If he was not prepared to defend himself, perhaps he needs more training."

Favian grinned, but there was a slight bit of malice behind his eyes. "Indeed. A man trying to prove himself attacking the weak and caught unprepared to back up his taunts is not ready to fight for me. However, he is one of Captain Nerida's favorites and is promising. More to the point, you disrespected the Captain quite publicly. If you wish to redeem yourself, I want you to work on finding the extent of Orlan's betrayal. If you are able to find his secrets, then there will definitely be a place in my household for you. Perhaps even for your friend Ryia."

Stephenie nodded her understanding at the implied threat. "Is there something I should be looking for in his mind?"

This time Favian smiled widely. "That, young woman, is part of your test. Now go back to Farfelee. You are dismissed."

Stephenie rose and curtsied before leaving the office. Even keeping her senses dulled, she felt his power and the energy threads flying about the room. She never sensed him use any magic to examine her, but it was quite obvious he was used to wielding significant power.

Chapter 18

Henton had a hard time concentrating on moving the cargo off the carrack. He kept hoping Kas would appear and tell him that Lord Evrin had decided to leave Vinerxan and was no longer a concern. It was a silly hope he knew, but one that would make his life easier.

Around mid-day, Douglas took a break from his work further down the docks and pulled Henton aside. "Tomorrow or the next day, there is a ship coming in that will likely accommodate our needs. However, it will cost us quite a bit for the two of them and they will both have to be knocked out. There are commandments against taking anyone on board from here, but they will likely make an exception, for the right price."

Henton nodded his head, having expected there would be reluctance. "Any idea on the expected cost?"

"Probably the equivalent of a hundred marks each."

Henton's heart fell. "Assuming they value Kyntian crowns highly and we get a good exchange; that would take just about everything we have left. We'd need to cut back on dinners and use almost all of our wages to pay for our room."

Douglas nodded his head in agreement. "We might be able to negotiate a little and there are those special coins that Stephenie found on that one man. Not sure how valuable those would be."

"Or the risk in using them." Henton shook his head. "Only if we absolutely have to." He glanced over Douglas' right shoulder, indicating someone was coming up on their left. "I'll let you muck out the stalls later and I'll try to get an extra shift this afternoon."

Douglas nodded his head and went back to his job. The man who had been approaching passed without comment. Henton pulled a small ball of cloth from his pouch and opened it to reveal a handful of dried berries and nuts. Tossing all of the food into his mouth, he stuffed the cloth back into his pouch and went back to carrying cargo off the carrack and into the warehouse.

By mid-afternoon, Kas had reached out to him mentally and Henton relayed the conversation he had with Douglas to the ghost. *I hate to admit it, but doing the right thing might not be possible.*

Kas, still invisible, gave a mental chuckle. *When was doing the right thing ever simple. We humans are lazy and generally take the easiest path to any solution, correct or otherwise.*

Henton continued the process of opening the crates and sorting the goods, albeit a bit slower with his attention on Kas. *We have to find a way to knock them out, without too much damage, get enough money to pay for the ship, and not get caught doing it.*

Well, for funds, these men appear to be fairly well situated, they buy enough expensive food and drink. Though they are arguing significantly, over what I cannot say, but the one who is your Lord Evrin has rank. After they ate a large breakfast, they went to the gates of the keep and argued with the people there for a while and after quite some time; they went to a different public house for a midday meal, which is where I left them. I have seen them each day I have been watching for Stephenie, but I had not realized who they were at the time.

Henton wiped his brow despite the cold. *Well, what they have on them we can take, but I don't want to go to their room and remove anything. It would be too much of a risk. We can't be tied to their disappearance.*

Kas' mental tone took on his sometimes-annoying air of superiority. *I will simply remove it from the room and no one will ever see me. But, I also have an idea for your problem with making them unconscious. There is a woman with many herbs and spices in town. Stephenie was sent there to get some medicine for a cat—*

So you've told me.

And the woman offered to give her something to kill the cat to put it out of its misery. I would guess that you could buy something that would make these men unconscious for a period of time.

Henton nodded his head. *I'll check into it.*

Good, now I will go back to watching for Stephenie and to see what this Kyntian fool does next. By the way, neither of the two appears to be mages.

Henton tried to respond to Kas and ask if he was certain there were only two of them, but the ghost had either gone or was ignoring him. He would plan based on the idea there were only two, since while Kas could be difficult, he would not do anything to risk Stephenie and by stating there were two, he would assume that was sufficient confirmation of the number. *His damn obsessive need to be precise all the time and assume everyone else was as well.*

Henton had to search several streets in the dark for the shop that Kas mentioned. His arms and back ached from the extra work on the docks, but his pouch was a little heavier, having earned nearly another quarter mark for the day. It was something, though even with Douglas' earnings, at that rate, they would barely keep the room and stables at the inn if they were forced to use all of their reserves to pay to ship out two people who would kill Stephenie or any of them if they knew who they were.

Knocking on the door a second time, he heard a woman say something in the local language. He responded in Pandar, "Sorry for the late call, Ma'am, I just finished working and would like to purchase some supplies."

After a short while, a woman wrapped in blankets opened the door. "What you need?"

"Ma'am, may I come in out of the cold?"

She eyed him for a moment, then stepped back to make room. Stepping into the shop, he closed the door behind himself. The room was warmer than the outside, but not what he considered warm. "Ma'am, I am in the need of something to help a friend sleep. He... has not been able to sleep well for some time."

He watched the woman assessing him. Her eyes narrowed and she shook her head. "No, you lie. You want rob or kill. But you hurt me, you won't get what you want."

Henton held up his hands, "No, Ma'am, I won't hurt you. I just want to help a friend." Henton could tell the woman did not believe him. Kas had not mentioned the woman having magic, but he knew it did not require magic to read a person's body language. Taking a chance on his own impression of the woman, he continued slowly. "Okay, it is not for a friend, but I am trying to protect a woman I care about from a couple of people who would do her harm. I don't want to kill them, but I want to make sure they can't hurt her. I just want to give them something so that they will sleep for several turns of the glass. Perhaps a night."

The woman's posture relaxed slightly, but she was still hesitant. "I not need trouble. My shop respected."

"I promise, nothing will come back to you."

After further consideration, the woman nodded her head. "It cost you, but I can put together thing...powder, that cause sleep. But you use too much, it kill."

Henton relaxed slightly. "Tell me how much and I will be careful not to give too much. Can I slip it into a drink?"

The woman nodded her head. "Might slight taste, but mix strong drink, hide taste. Cost four marks."

Henton took a deep breath, he feared it would cost him a lot, but that was more than he expected. He considered trying to negotiate, but what he was planning could put him on the end of a rope if she decided to double cross him. In addition, the state of the shop showed a lack of repair and with her tattered clothing, he wondered how much business she did receive. Pulling out his coin pouch, he counted out the equivalent of four marks.

Stephenie was summoned to the dungeon that evening and escorted to the same torture room where Sir Orlan was already strapped naked to the table. She wanted to reach out and find her sister, but based on the threat that Sir Orlan was able to easily enter minds that touch his, she feared searching could be dangerous.

"You familiar with a man?" the Butcher asked her as she was ushered closer.

Orlan glared at her, anger and hatred in his expression. Stephenie noted the three guards with long daggers drawn, but the Captain was not present. She knew those blades would be for her if they felt she became compromised. Determined to show no fear, she stepped forward. Without blood and sweat covering his body, she could see the multitude of scars. Drawn to his crotch, partially out of curiosity, but also because the Butcher just hit him with a leather mallet, she wondered how Orlan showed so little reaction.

"Our Lordship made my job harder by removing Orlan's balls when he was first captured. That did nothing to make the bastard talk."

Stephenie was repulsed by the abuse, but she was not in a position to do anything about it. "What did he do?" she asked, hoping the torturer would tell her instead of inflicting pain on the man.

The Butcher put a rock on the back of Orlan's hand, which was strapped down so tightly he could not shift the stone. Stephenie noted the draw of energy and opened herself enough to see the torturer dumping energy into the stone, causing it to heat. She held her breath as the rock quickly stared to glow and Orlan's skin started to sizzle under the rock. Orlan glared at them, but refused to cry out, though his body shook from the pain.

"While I hurt him, you try to pry out his secrets."

Stephenie glanced at the Butcher, but he was not looking at her. The idea of trying to invade the man's thoughts while he was being tortured made her stomach clench. The men with their daggers drawn waited and so she stepped closer, placing her hand on Orlan's arm. She tentatively reached out with her mind, then raised her defenses in the equivalent of opening a door just a crack to peek through before slamming it shut.

She felt Orlan smash into her mental defenses, trying to break down the door into her mind. Struggling to hold her ground, she projected her thoughts to him. *I only want to heal you.*

Liar, she heard him project. Everyone in the room who could perform magic would have heard it. *You may have pushed me out, but I learned things about you the first time. You can't protect those you love.*

Fearing he had stolen some memories and might broadcast them to everyone present, she opened her mind ever so slightly and Orlan charged into her thoughts. She struggled to contain him initially and through the exercises she had performed with Kas, barely held him in check, leaving her slightly in his mind and him slightly in hers.

I know who you are, Stephenie Marn. This time the thoughts were transmitted through the physical contact and would not have been heard by anyone else.

What do you want? Stephenie felt his contempt at what he felt to be a question with such an obvious answer. *Look, I can't free you. I don't know what you've done, but I am one person and they are watching you closely.*

You plan to free your sister. When you do that, free me as well. If you don't I will turn you over to them and you can enjoy the fun they have put me through.

Stephenie felt her anger rising, but this man knew too much about her and she could not risk him revealing her plans. *Please,* she pleaded to herself, *I just want to save Islet.* She felt Orlan trying to work his way deeper into her thoughts and firmed her resolve and mental defenses. *Orlan, you are a murdering bastard who's caused the deaths of many innocent people trying to heal you, what makes you deserve to be freed?*

She felt his mental snort. *They were not any more innocent than you. They were healing me so I could suffer more pain. You enable them. You are as evil as Rilan who's burning my hand.*

Stephenie did not have time to reply; pain burst through the mental link and she felt the searing of his hand as if it were her own. A scream escaped her mouth as instinct responded and the rock flew across the room. She channeled healing to the wound and watched as Orlan used her distraction to worm his way further into her thoughts.

Help me, or you will die! he demanded.

Feeling the beast in her subconscious bubbling up, she mimicked Orlan's technique, grabbing a stronger foothold in his mind and pulled up the most painful memory she had: the burning of her body in the Grey Mountains. It was something she always tried to forget, the moment her very bones felt like they exploded from within as energy raged through her body.

The screaming of Orlan drew open her eyes. His body shook and sweat beaded on his skin as splotchy patches of redness emerged over his torso. Orlan was out of her head and he had completely blocked her from his mind.

"Interesting," the Butcher said as he waved aside the men with daggers. "It would appear you know something of causing pain."

"He thought he could make something of conveying the burning of his hand to mine. He's not the only one to suffer the pain of flames."

The balding man nodded his head. "And what did you get from his mind?"

Stephenie shook her head as Orlan opened his eyes and glared at her. "What did he do?"

"He betrayed our Lord."

Stephenie wanted to ball her hands into fists. Knowing something about the man could potentially help in bargaining with him or if she felt herself up to the task, extract the secrets Lord Favian wanted.

"Continue trying to do your job. I'll do mine."

Stephenie felt her stomach tighten. "He's blocked me out."

"That is your problem. The master wants results and he's given you the chance to please him or to fail him. I suggest you try to succeed."

Stephenie could see the hardness in the Butcher's eyes and knew he would cut on her or anyone else as readily as he tortured Orlan. If she failed or Orlan revealed her secrets, Islet would likely suffer as much as Ryia and herself. *And Henton and Douglas as well.*

Closing her eyes, she put her hand back on Orlan's arm as the man at her side brought over a dull knife. She felt the muscles in Orlan's arm tighten as the blade bit into his skin. But despite Stephenie's attempts to force and beg her way into Orlan's mind, he refused to allow her into his head. Time passed and the glass could have turned a dozen times for all Stephenie knew. It was not until Orlan finally passed out from blood loss that his mental defenses weakened sufficiently for her to get enough of a foothold to heal him. Even then, he regained enough consciousness to block her from his memories.

What is your answer, Witch? He demanded as she was about to give up.

Give me something, anything; if I cannot show I am making progress, I'll not be in any position to help you.

You'll have to rip it from my mind. I won't give anyone anything. She could feel him hesitate for a moment. *I don't know when you experienced that much pain or how you survived to be sane enough to be here today, but it will not change my resolve.*

Stephenie opened her eyes, but held the narrow link to Orlan. She had not gained any insight into the man through his words, but she picked up a sense of his character in the subtleties she had felt of his mind. *You are here because you are protecting someone.* She had not intended to broadcast the thought to him, but the mental flinch told her it was true. *You help me and I will help you as best I can.* As she said it, she realized she meant it. Despite what Kas said about being able to lie mentally, she did not have the capacity to do that yet.

Her name was Elrysa, but—

Is Elrysa, Stephenie corrected.

Was! Her name was Elrysa!

Stephenie gave a mental nod of her head. *For her sake, was.*

Sir Orlan bristled and then calmed. *That is all I will say until you have a plan that gets me out of here. I can tell you have not figured one out, so you will have to continue to work on me until you do.* With that, he forced her from his mind.

Stephenie took a step back; she was exhausted. Her back hurt and her stomach was growling. She desperately needed to use the chamberpot and she felt dirtier than she had ever felt before. Her clothing and hands were literally and figuratively splattered with blood. She knew standing by as a man was tortured in front of her was a new low in her life, but Orlan was right, as of yet, she did not even have a plan to free Islet.

The Butcher beside her nodded his head. "Did you get anything?"

"I'm not sure. Just a name, Elrysa."

The man smiled. "We've been working on him for months. You show amazing progress as well as the ability to put fear into Orlan. I am not sure what pain you gave him earlier, but it was quite effective.

I could have you detailed down here to truly learn the art of interrogation."

Stephenie's skin crawled and she shuddered at the thought. "I don't think so. I couldn't do this on a regular basis."

The balding man chuckled. "You say that now, but wait until someone has something you really need. Your morals will find room for me. They always do." He dismissed her with a wave of his hand. "Go back to Farfelee for now. We'll summon you in a day or two after he's had a chance to rest and rebuild his strength."

Stephenie walked away and quickly left the torture room. She briefly cast her mind out in the hopes of sensing Islet, but unlike Joshua, she had not spent as much time with Islet growing up and really did not know the feel of her mind. Without a more focused search of the cells, she knew she would have a hard time finding her sister. Too tired and with too many people in the outer room watching her passage, she simply kept going and headed back to her bedroom to wash the filth from her and contemplate what she had learned.

It was early afternoon before she woke and went to join the others in the training room. Nearly a dozen people were present, including Ryia, but Madam Farfelee was absent. No one said anything about her late arrival. Word had spread about her surviving Sir Orlan and that she would be tasked with his continued healing. Those who had spent time in the dungeon did not envy her and were thankful the risk to their own lives would be minimized as long as Stephenie was able to survive.

The afternoon training session again involved a number of people without magic being subjected to different injuries while the students healed them. A couple of advanced students were working on a person from the town who had a wasting disease, but they were near the back of the room and the office the instructors used. The bulk of the students were not involved with the complex healing.

The spells Stephenie was asked to cast still seemed pointless, but Stephenie repeated the words and gestures. Thinking back to what Orlan had done when he used her body, she tried to adjust her healing approach to be more symbiotic. The result was an improvement, but not a complete success. The patients she healed were no longer suffering pain as she tried to help their bodies to mend, but they still lacked the sensation that other healers seemed to produce.

Throughout the day, seeing people cut or burned so she could learn to heal, brought back more memories of Orlan and the torture she had witnessed. Worse, they made her think about the offer to work in the dungeons. While the task of facilitating the suffering of others was repulsive, the Butcher was right, the desperate need to find out more about where they were keeping her sister made her doubt the resolve she had with regard to refusing him. *Someone will heal them, what is the difference if it is me? And I would have a much better chance to find Islet.*

She shuddered, the very idea that she might compromise herself further, putting her and her sister's needs over other people who were prisoners of the Senzar, left her drained and tired. She had no intention of doing it, but the longer she was in the keep, the longer she would have to face the temptation. *I will not be like them*, she swore to herself, hoping it would remain true.

The following day was again training with the larger group of students. The morning was spent learning how to craft healing ointments and treat wounds without magic. The afternoon involved repairing broken bones. The cries of pain the volunteers let escape their lips when legs and arms where snapped and crushed was too much like war against the helpless.

The only thing that kept Stephenie going had been a glimpse into the office and a small library of books locked in a cabinet. Although she was no closer to breaking anyone out of the keep, she allowed herself to hope that perhaps she might find something to help rebuild Kas' body.

When evening set in and the students were dismissed to return to their rooms, Stephenie hung back with the excuse of wanting to clean up the bowls she had used earlier in the day. While partially true, she had only left one dirty bowl and she was able to clean that quickly.

Once that was done, she went to the back room and examined the door more closely. While the walls were made of stone, the doorjamb was wooden and floated against the stone due to differences in expansion of the materials.

Using her magic, she pushed on the jamb and was able to pull the door open without unlocking the simple bolt that held it shut. Knowing she was alone, she quickly went into the backroom and used a similar technique to open the cabinet. Inside, two rows of books sat tightly packed on their shelves. Scanning the spines, she stopped at the first book with recognizable characters. It was written in a form of Denarian or what her people called the Old Tongue. Setting it on the desk, she used her powers to light the candle inside the lamp next to her without even looking at it. She read through the top of several pages, finding various details about magical healing, none of which involved spells.

Becoming quickly lost in a detailed explanation of how a blood disease worked, she flipped several pages and continued her search for something that might recreate a limb or body parts. Slowly realizing the book was just about issues with blood, she returned it to the shelf and pulled out the next one. That one was in a language that she did not recognize and she put it back. Pulling the next three books, she went back to the desk and started flipping through the pages.

She just finished with the second book when she felt the door to the outer room open. It took a moment more to realize Farfelee was coming in her direction. Knowing her movement would be noted, even though the older healer could not physically see her, Stephenie remained at the desk with the books stacked to the side. She pulled a pen from the ink well and started writing on a piece of paper that was sitting loose on the table.

"What are you doing in here?"

Stephenie rose and bowed her head. "Ma'am, I stayed after to clean up from our lessons. Then I wanted to make some notes about what I learned today, so thought to borrow some paper."

Farfelee took note of the cabinet and the books on the desk, before glancing to the shelves on the back wall. "Do you think I am that unobservant?"

Stephenie opened her mouth, but had no immediate response.

"The bolt on door is set, so the door would not have been open. You forced it as you did the cabinet. When I felt you back here, I thought perhaps you had decided to try out the items on the shelf. Though, it seems you are interested in something else."

"Ma'am," Stephenie said, bowing her head again. "I'm not sure what you mean by the items on the shelves?" She glanced to the sealed jars, hoping Farfelee might get distracted from the books.

"Do not think to change the subject, what are you doing with the books?"

Stephenie nodded her head. "Ma'am, I am trying to learn how to help a friend. I want to learn how to regrow an arm and a leg. I want to make someone whole. I had hoped I'd find a drawing or pictures that would show how it was done."

Farfelee glanced at the paper Stephenie had started to write upon. "Your words were written in haste, but it is obvious you know how to read and write. Another surprise to add to your running list."

"Ma'am, I couldn't make sense of these books, but please, can you teach me how to do that kind of healing?"

Farfelee indicated Stephenie should again sit as she sat in the other chair present. "That is not a skill you will find available. Perhaps if the person was a witch or warlock, their body would slowly regrow a limb over many years, but creating something out of nothing is something only the very powerful could ever dream of doing. Perhaps Lord Favian could, though I have never seen him do so."

"How old is our Lord?"

Farfelee shook her head. "Do not voice that question to others. It is rude to ask that of someone of his rank and position. They guard their personal information closely and few will discuss such things, even in private. For common people, whose lives are short, it is more acceptable to discuss as everyone already knows or can guess their age."

Stephenie nodded her head, compiling more details of the Senzar culture for future consideration.

"This person who needs an arm regrown, they are not in Vinerxan are they?"

Stephenie looked up to meet Farfelee's eyes, "No," she lied automatically.

"Then do not worry yourself over their condition, they will likely be old and have lived what life they have by the time you are able to see them again."

Stephenie did not like the tone, but decided to ignore it. "What is so special about the items on these shelves?"

Farfelee followed Stephenie's gaze. "There are things that impact a person's mind. They are used to help those in severe pain, but can also cause delusions and make a person incoherent. Too much of some of them will kill. You do not want to start using those substances to feel good. That can destroy you and impact your ability to perform spells."

Stephenie looked away from them. "Poisons then."

"Some, but when used correctly, they can be very beneficial." Standing, Farfelee glanced to the books. "Put them back and then follow me. You have work to do with Orlan."

Stephenie shuddered despite herself. "Who was Elrysa? I know Lord Favian wants me to prove I can get the information out of Orlan, but if I know something more, that will help give me leverage. The only thing I know so far is a name."

"Elrysa was one of Lord Favian's mistresses. Orlan was to protect her and several others on a journey in the south. He betrayed them and Elrysa and the others were killed. Orlan was captured trying to escape. His Lordship wants to know what other betrayals Orlan committed and make him suffer for Elrysa's death. Now enough questions, you are late for the dungeon."

Chapter 19

Henton wiped his nose with the back of his glove. He hoped he was not catching a cold, but knew he would simply muddle through it if he was. He had allowed Douglas to handle all the negotiations for the passage, his presence would not have helped and could even have hurt. Kas was watching his friend and that would be far more effective.

Despite his confidence, Henton was relieved when he saw Douglas coming toward him. "Well?" he asked when Douglas was within a couple of feet.

"It's damn cold," Douglas said, rubbing his gloved hands together. "Kas went to find our friends. We have to get them on board tonight with no one seeing us. If we're seen, they'll turn us in."

Henton nodded his head. "How much?"

Douglas shook his head and started walking back toward town. "Pretty much everything and the captain will still put them to work for a year."

Henton's shoulders fell as he moved to catch up. "I had hoped to avoid that."

"Well, doing this is a big deal. If they are caught, it'll be a lot of trouble for them."

"And you're sure they won't turn us in?"

Douglas shrugged as he continued walking. "As sure as I can be. The Senzar want this town to be as safe as possible from what I was told, so they won't think too highly of what we are doing. But these men are pirates and have honor among themselves and pirates bristle under the rule of any master."

"Well, let's get to the pub and hope they are there."

Kas greeted Henton the moment they walked into the public house. *They have just left their room at the inn and are heading in this direction.*

Acknowledging the ghost's report, he walked over to a table that would sit six people and sat down. The public house had one other group of sailors sitting in the far corner.

Douglas went over to the bar and ordered two mugs of ale and some dinner. He returned with the ale, giving one to Henton as he sat. The two of them sipped their drinks while they waited. They did not wait long before Lord Evrin walked in, sending a blast of cold air through the main room from the open door. His friend, or guard, Henton was not sure exactly which it was, followed closely.

Evrin did not seem to notice Henton as he walked past, but his companion did and the look was not one of fondness. Ignoring the hateful looks, Henton raised his hand. "My Lord," he said in Pandar, drawing Evrin's attention. "Might I offer you a table and a drink?"

Evrin's eyes narrowed, but he stopped walking. "What is it you are after?"

The man was not yet drunk and Henton knew immediately he was one of those people who were mean when they were sober. "My Lord, I wanted to discuss a business proposition with you."

Evrin pursed his lips, but then sat down across from Henton, with his back to the bar. "We'll see how well you treat me for drinks and if it is sufficient, I'll give you enough condescension to listen to your proposal."

"Of course, My Lord. What would you like?"

"Some of their finest wine."

Henton could tell he did not expect to be humored with the request. Douglas nodded his head and rose from his seat. "I'll go get it."

The man's companion simply stood and stared, to which Lord Evrin said something curt in Kyntian. His companion turned on his heels and headed to the bar.

"I am assuming you also plan to feed me."

"Of course, My Lord."

When Douglas came back with the wine, he sent him back to the bar with Evrin's demand for some fish dinner Henton assumed would be incredibly expensive.

Once their food arrived and Evrin was finishing his third glass of wine, Henton decided to try and broach his subject. "My Lord, Douglas and I have been here waiting for a friend."

"You've hardly been waiting long. I've been waiting here for weeks."

"I know. And I am hopeful your wait will not be much longer, but for Douglas and myself, I fear the friend we have been waiting for has missed his ship; something has delayed him far too long. Which means there is little point to us remaining here."

"And what is your point in telling me this?"

"Would you like some ale?" Henton asked, noticing Evrin glance at Douglas when he took a drink to wash down the salted fish the two of them had for dinner.

"Sure."

Henton waited as Douglas put down his mug and went to the bar. "Well, you were telling me the other day about how you plan to return to Kynto with the means to make Cothel suffer. I was assuming you would not be trying to make a trip through the snow packed mountains, but would likely take a ship—"

"To Tusr and then a coach to Gren Haven to take another ship to West Port—the West Port in Kynto, not Epish," he added with contempt. "My lady awaits in Rativyr Keep near the grand Rativyr Peak."

Henton had no idea where Rativyr was, but he remembered enough of Stephenie's maps to know where West Port was. "Well, there are mostly pirates sailing between here and Tusr. I don't know what the port of Gren Haven looks like, but, I thought that perhaps we could help protect you on your journey and if we do a good enough job, you might put in a good word with your Mistress and find us a place in Kynto."

"So you are looking for my assistance in getting a position in Kynto."

Douglas placed a large mug of ale in front of Evrin.

"My Lord, we are solid sailors and good with a sword. We'll have to leave Vinerxan at some point and I'd rather sail or carry a sword for Kynto than a place that supports witchery."

Evrin wrinkled his nose slightly at the taste of the ale, but Henton could see him considering the request. "Well, what can you bring that Mitchel does not give me?"

He guessed Evrin was calculating how much free drink and food he could get before leaving Henton and Douglas behind when they did leave. "More lively conversation over dinner?"

Evrin grinned and took another drink of the ale, swallowing more than half of it in a single tip of the mug. "There is that. Mitchel is always complaining it is futile to remain and waste money. However, I will not fail My Lady, she deserves better than that."

"And we are not asking for much. If we do a good job on your journey back to Kynto, then simply provide a recommendation for us. If we do not, we won't bother you further."

"Another drink?" Douglas asked.

Evrin nodded his head, but the movement was stilted. "Yes to both," he said slowly.

"I'll get one for Mitchel as well."

Evrin's head hit the table as Douglas stood, briefly drawing the attention of the room. Henton immediately worried that Douglas had overdosed Evrin.

Mitchel appeared to swear in Kyntian. He downed the last of his drink and came over to the table. "Cothel scum," he said in Pandar, "you helped him into his drink."

"We just wanted to help and perhaps find a place in Kynto." Henton stood and held his hands out, "Here have a seat and some dinner. Lord Evrin doesn't seem to be polite to you. Let us buy you some dinner and we'll help you carry him back to your inn."

Mitchel sneered, "You won't get anything from Evrin. He's not likely to go back in honor, so get out of my sight." The young man pulled Lord Evrin to his shoulders and headed for the door.

Let them go, Henton heard Kas whisper in his head. *No one should see you follow them out. I will take care of it.*

Henton shrugged for the benefit of those in the room and then sat down. "So much for trying to be a friend."

Douglas covered any confusion he had and sat down as well. "So, we wait?"

Henton nodded his head and downed the rest of the ale in his mug. He hoped whatever Kas was planning would not result in a dead man. That was not something they wanted to deal with. *And hopefully, Evrin won't die either. He went down fast.*

It was an agonizingly long time before Kas returned to whisper into Henton's mind. *They are in a nearby alley and should hold for a little time. I hit the conscious one over the head. Hopefully he will remain unconscious until you get to him.*

Henton wiped his mouth with his sleeve and stood up. "Let's go back to our room Douglas. Tonight might have been a waste of money."

Douglas followed him out the door, and they both followed Kas' directions to a side alley a couple buildings away. The two men were on the ground and covered with a few pieces of debris to hide them. In the darkness and the biting cold, it was unlikely anyone would notice them.

With no one visible nearby, Henton went into the alley and checked on their condition. Evrin was still breathing and unconscious. Mitchel had a little blood on the back of his head, but was also breathing. Taking some of the powder back from Douglas, he forced open Mitchel's mouth and poured in a healthy dose.

"Will it work like that?"

Henton shrugged. "I am hoping so. I don't want either of them waking before morning, but I don't want them dead either."

"Yeah, we kill one, and the captain will expect more money for the loss of a year's service."

"Great," he mumbled as he emptied Evrin's pouch into his hand. There was a pile of small coins and a few other odds and ends.

Slipping everything into his own pouch, Henton quickly felt over the man's clothing for other valuables. Douglas did the same for Mitchel.

The search was quick and while they took the coin, they left the men with their jewelry, token holy symbols, and weapons. The coins were mostly Kyntian, but enough other people were spending those. The jewelry and weapons would be far too easy for someone to recognize as belonging to these men.

"Kas, are we clear to carry these men from the alley?"

The ghost's voice came softly to their ears. "Yes, I will scout the way and make sure you go unseen."

Nodding his head, Henton lifted Evrin to his shoulders.

"You got the lighter one," Douglas remarked, grunting slightly under Mitchel's heavier build.

"I'm the old, washed up one, remember."

Being careful to keep his balance on the slick ground, Henton emerged from the alley followed closely by Douglas. They had to cross half the city to get to the docks and neither man was exactly light. A slip could cause injury and neither of them could afford that.

Staying mainly to the alleys and side streets, Henton and Douglas carried the two men toward the docks. Kas had them stop several times to avoid people. Once they took a detour around a group of soldiers from the castle whom they assumed were mages. By the time they got to the docks, Henton was sweating and felt an ache in his shoulders and back.

Fortunately, an icy breeze was blowing off the water and most people were below deck. They managed to reach the ship that would take the men away from Vinerxan and Stephenie without drawing notice. A quick transfer of the men to a half dozen sailors went without comments or conversation.

Their transaction complete, Henton and Douglas retreated quietly away from the docks and back toward their inn. With the appearance of safety, Kas broke off and went to Lord Evrin's rooms to gather further money and search for anything else of use.

Stephenie entered the dungeon with her stomach growling, but by the time she reached the torture room, she had lost her appetite.

Again Orlan was strapped to the far table, but this time another person was present and locked into a chair with nails sticking up from the seat. Several large stones were in the man's lap. Sweat was dripping from his brow and blood from his legs and rear. A glazed look covered his face, but the pain was evident under the distant expression. Stephenie recognized him as one of the mages Nerida had been training.

"He displeased the Captain," the Butcher said. "We gave him a healthy dose of dream juice to keep his magic under control. The problem is it also deadens the pain."

Stephenie decided not to comment. The torturer was likely trying to goad her into a response, either of amusement or outrage. Amusement and approval she would never be able to successfully fake and outrage would gain her nothing. "I understand I am to work on Orlan," she said coming over to the table. She ignored the three soldiers with swords. That threat was losing its impact on her.

Stephenie grabbed Orlan's arm. With a deep breath, she reached out to his mind. He immediately pressed his attack and found a weakness Stephenie had left open for him. She felt satisfaction from him and an opening in his mind. She charged forth, burrowing into his thoughts and gaining a deeper foothold than she ever had before. Panic filled her, but it came from Orlan and not herself. Her own sense of success was short lived and Orlan reasserted himself and worked to keep her from his deeper memories.

That was cleaver, girl. Where'd you learn such a tactic? You really working for Favian after all?

Stephenie shook her head mentally. *When you become good enough with a sword, you learn to feint, draw your opponent in on a weakness that isn't there.* She steadied herself slightly. She still had a strong foothold in his mind and he had no hold in hers. *I am not your enemy, so stop trying to get me killed, okay.*

You really are a stupid girl. If I don't resist, they will suspect something.

She felt him grimace and with her connection, the burning pain of a hot blade cutting across his arm transferred to her as well. *Give me something useless so they can see I am making progress. I will not betray your protection. We both have knowledge the other wants hidden.*

She waited for Orlan to respond and after several moments of agonizing pain, he finally did. *You value knowledge and learning, if you want it, learn to do it yourself. I will not give in.*

Orlan, I will do everything I can to free you. You have my word, and you know I am not good enough at this to lie.

Then you just told your first one. He grimaced. *You are good enough.* With a wave of pain, he pushed her from his mind.

Stephenie stepped back, slightly dizzy. Free of the focus on Orlan, she realized additional people had come into the room at some point.

"See, she is compromised. Orlan must be using a new tactic of letting us think she has held him off!"

Stephenie turned to face Nerida and Lord Favian. "My Lord," she said with a curtsy.

Lord Favian looked at her for several moments. "Rilan, your opinion."

"My Lord, she has appeared to keep Orlan out of her head and has inflicted a fair amount of pain upon him. I would say she has the potential to be of use to me."

"My Lord," Nerida pleaded, "she is a common witch. There is no way she could do this."

Stephenie never sensed the field form; Favian's attack was just too quick. She cried out as her right arm twisted behind her back, threatening to break and pull from her shoulder. She managed to strengthen the bone and joint more out of instinct than skill.

"What is your name and who are your parents?"

Stephenie pulled power into her body, adding strength to her own fields that were keeping her arm from snapping.

"Tell me girl, or I'll break you into pieces."

"Steph. My name is Steph," she swore through the pain in her shoulder. Favian had formed a second field that was pressing hard against her chest and while she was managing to counter it, he was varying the field so quickly she barely was keeping up. "I don't know my parents. My mother didn't want me and I grew up on my own!"

"And Orlan, does he control you?"

Stephenie felt an explosion rip outward from her left leg and she fell onto her right knee as her shoulder popped and her forearm broke. She never sensed the fields form and change as it happened too fast. "No, damn you." She gritted her teeth, feeling the anger and rage bubbling up from within her. She was sucking in power and just barely keeping her mind focused enough not to try an attack of her own. She knew this man would beat her, so she was looking for options to avoid the direct fight.

She felt Nerida forming a gravity field of significant strength and the beast within her would not allow Nerida to kill her. Despite the pain, Stephenie disrupted and blocked Nerida's field before it slammed into her. The man behind her, who had moved to stick her with a sword, she flung against the far wall. She gorged on the energy in the stone beneath her, ready to start crushing everyone in the room.

"Enough!"

Stephenie took a deep breath, sucking in air as the pressure against her chest disappeared. Struggling to her feet, she felt her shoulder pop back into place as her body mended itself with all the energy in her.

"Nerida, you are valuable to me and you serve me well, but you will leave this one alone."

"My Lord, she—"

"I have spoken. I did not sense anything to make me believe Orlan has control of her."

"But she's casting spells without protection from Elrin. You saw that."

"Enough! Go back to training the soldiers, Nerida. I will deal with her." He turned to the Butcher who had taken a step away from Stephenie during the altercation. "You can continue Orlan's sessions tomorrow. She needs time to heal tonight." Without further comment, he turned and left the room with Nerida following behind him.

Stephenie glanced to the man she had flung into the wall. He was rubbing his shoulder and had blood on his head. However, she felt no pity for him. She had managed to keep her inner rage under some control, but mostly because it seemed to her that she realized Favian would not be defeated that easily. For this man who had thought to kill her, that inner anger was not so reserved. "Try to harm me again," she growled, "and I won't just throw you across the room."

"Easy girl," the Butcher said, "go back to Farfelee and get yourself healed."

Stephenie looked at her blood stained pants; *at least they had not burst open*. She felt chunks of flesh as well as cooling blood inside her pants and would have to clean them. Her left leg was already healed, as was the break in her forearm, though her shoulder was still sore.

Without taking her leave of the men, she turned and walked from the room. She was angry and frightened. Worse yet, she had drawn even more attention from Lord Favian. She needed to get out of the castle soon. The longer she stayed, the greater the risk.

The following morning she arrived in the class a little late, having slept longer than she had intended. Farfelee was not present, but Nilia was and she was acting as the instructor. All the students were staring at her. It was obvious that someone had spoken of the events of the prior night.

"Ma'am," Stephenie said, feeling contentious, "can you cover how some of the powders and syrups can be used to impact a person's mind?" She sat on the stool in front of the workbench reserved for her and petted Atia, who had seemed to know she needed some comfort.

"Steph, those are advanced topics. You could do more harm than good using them. If used wrong, at best, inhaling them could knock you out. At worst, it could kill you."

"Ma'am, I understand. However, considering my evening activities, I was hoping to find a way to be more effective. If you do not feel we are ready, can you perhaps tell us what not to do, then we'll at least know what to avoid if we should run into them when trying to heal someone?"

The rest of the students were staring at her. Stephenie had so far avoided trying to stand out too much, but was now feeling entitled.

"Very well," Nilia said, going into the backroom and returning with a jar of powder. "This first item will ease pain, but it will make people see things that are not there and make it difficult or impossible to cast spells."

Stephenie listened to the explanations as Nilia went through several powders, ointments, and fluids. They all had significant side effects and it was those side effects she was committing to memory. The basis of a plan was forming in her mind as to how to get past the guards in the dungeon and these items were key.

During the first break, Ryia came over and Stephenie eyed her cautiously. "May I say I am sorry?" she asked quietly. "I should not have acted so badly to you."

Stephenie softened her expression. "It's okay, Ryia. I know you were angry. And I should thank you as well for warning Farfelee on that first night they came to get me."

"Yeah, but I shouldn't have been angry at you. You saved my life. It's just that I so much wanted to be a warrior and fight for our freedom. I still do, but I guess I should be content to be a healer."

Stephenie nodded her head. "Ryia, let me tell you something a friend of mine once said. Not everyone can be good at everything. Don't try to be something you can't, find what you are good at doing and do that." She smiled. "Of course, he was a bit more sarcastic in the way he said it."

"But I really want to be a warrior."

"If wanting was all it took, then we'd all be somewhere else. Some things some people are not good at and will never master. They will be happier finding something they can be good at doing instead of struggling their whole life."

"But I'm not even any good at healing either. I can't seem to get the spells right, no matter how hard I try and everything they are telling us about potions is going right out of my head the moment I hear it. I have no idea what I would be good at."

Stephenie patted her on the arm. "Perhaps I can help you find something. But, don't worry so much about the spells. What we do is more mental than anything else. If you focus too much on the spell and not enough on what you want your power to do, you won't succeed."

"But without the proper spell, Elrin's evil will infect you."

Stephenie felt her limbs get heavy. "You have natural protections from Elrin's evil. Don't let fear rule you."

Ryia nodded her head. "Thanks. I wish I had a bigger sister to look out for me when I was growing up. Do you have any brothers or sisters?"

Stephenie sensed a slight discomfort in Ryia. "I have no family and my friends have left me or have been killed or maimed. I wanted to look after you because it was the right thing to do."

Ryia nodded her head, but she looked even more nervous. "You really are better at all this then you let on, aren't you?"

Stephenie forced a smile for the girl. "Ryia, I really don't know what I am doing most of the time. I've simply learned to survive by trial and error. So far nothing's killed me. Whenever I can learn something, I try to pay close attention, since you never know when it might become useful."

Ryia nodded her head, and with .Nilia calling everyone back to their stools, she walked away. Stephenie took a deep breath and wondered just what promises had been made to Ryia so that the girl would try and coax information from her. She just hoped they would not disappoint Ryia by lying to her.

Chapter 20

Henton squinted his eyes as he nodded his head to a tall woman in a thin tunic who was leading three men dressed in heavy leather armor. She glanced around and then approached him. She said something in the local language and he shook his head. "I speak Pandar," he offered.

She frowned. "What is your name?"

"Henton, Ma'am." He was not familiar with the insignia the Senzar used, but she appeared to consider herself important.

"I am looking for two men from Kynto. I am told you dined with them a couple of times."

"Ma'am, there was one man from Kynto, a Lord Evrin, whom I asked if he was interested in hiring me to help him get back to Kynto. He had said at some point he would be going home in glory. Going back to his mistress. He was often drunk, but he talked like a lord and I was interested in finding work back on the sea again. He seemed willing, but he passed out from drink and his companion, I never caught his name, carried him off. I believe it was a regular occurrence. He said he'd been in town for a few weeks."

"And have you seen him since?"

Henton had a feeling not unlike when Kas pressed against his mind to talk with him. A slight detachment, but he did his best to keep his thoughts on the woman's firm physique. "No, Ma'am, I have not. Not for a couple of days. I've been working the docks to pay the bills. I was waiting for a friend to come in by ship, but he's overdue and I suspect he might not be coming."

"Check his pouches."

Henton took a step back, but did not resist when the soldiers with the woman emptied his coins and possessions onto a nearby create.

"Looks to be just a few local marks a couple odd pieces from different places and one quarter crown from Kynto. Nothing much, just like his room."

"How do you come by four horses?"

Henton bowed his head. "Ma'am, my brother has a sizable farm and raises them. I rode into Vinerxan through the mountain pass and if my friend had arrived on the ship as he said he would, I would have rode out of Vinerxan with him. I'm working at the docks to make ends meet until he arrives, which as I said now seem unlikely. So I've been looking to find a better job offer."

"Captain, do you want us to take him in for further questioning?"

The woman narrowed her eyes and then shook her head. "No, the horses were not bought here and he's not carrying enough Kyntian coins or other valuables to have been responsible."

"Ma'am, did something happen to Lord Evrin?"

"He's missing. You did not see anyone follow him out of the public house, did you?"

"No."

"And have you heard of any ships recruiting from this port? We do not take kindly to ships kidnapping people here."

"I have not."

She nodded her head and then turned away. "Come, we'll send some others out to continue pursuing the issue."

Henton went back to work, but kept his mind open for Kas in case the ghost was near. However, he suspected Kas would be watching the keep for any sign of Stephenie. Having not seen her for several days was making all of them uneasy.

The next four days were exhausting for Stephenie. Farfelee had been assigned to a difficult task by Favian and Nilia continued to teach healing during the day. During the breaks, Stephenie often convinced the younger assistant to allow her in the backroom so she could learn more details on the special chemicals. By the second day of this, Stephenie already knew how to construct a dust she could administer into people's noses or lungs that would incapacitate them in just a few moments. She hoped that with compressing someone's chest and flinging dust in their face, when she released the pressure they would inhale the dust and quickly be out of her way.

For the bulk of the guards in the outer room, she planned to slip a liquid she learned to make into their food or drink and have them simply fall asleep at their posts. That would take work, but the more frequent her trips to the dungeon, the less attention they were paying her and one evening she had even been offered a spot at their table when she had finished a particularly rough session with Orlan. She had accepted that offer, which had come from Elvira. Even the other guards seemed to be slowly warming to her despite Nerida's hate of her.

Each evening she had a session with Orlan, but she resisted revealing her plan to him. When she could do so unobserved, Stephenie resumed her investigation of the books in the backroom. Taking the chance that no one would notice her in the middle of the night after her sessions with Orlan, she continued to break into the training room. She would review the books well into the morning. But unfortunately, many of the books were in languages Stephenie did not recognize and she again wished Kas was with her to see what he might be able to translate.

In one of the books she could understand, she found detailed drawings of a person's internal organs. At first the images repulsed her, as they were drawn with colored inks and reminded her too much of cutting up people in the dungeon. However, she knew if she needed to recreate a body for Kas, understanding all the parts of the body might be useful.

Ryia continued to try to be her friend and probe for information. Stephenie did not avoid the conversations, but offered nothing more than imagined extensions to the story she had already told everyone. She knew Ryia was acting as a spy, but the girl was undoubtedly being used and would suffer if Stephenie revealed her as such. The last thing Stephenie wanted to see was Ryia in the dungeon.

Her work with Orlan had not changed, and it was weighing heavily on her mind that she was delaying her attempt at escape. The

Butcher continued to torture the man, and Orlan continued to fight her. However, Stephenie felt she was improving her skills because she was forcing Orlan to adapt his defenses. Each day, she was figuring out more about how he did what he did. And while she continued to hold him out of her head, it was always just barely. By the end of the session on the fourth day, she lost some of her confidence. Orlan had pressed her defenses and her physical fatigue left her vulnerable. Surprisingly, he did not exploit the weakness.

Knowing she should have done it sooner, she finally decided to confide in him when she sensed Rilan was winding down his torture for the evening. *So, I have a plan.*

It has taken you a long time to come up with it. I was beginning to think you started to enjoy this too much.

Stephenie closed his wounds as he lay in more of his blood on the table. *How do you survive all that they do to you?* It was not so much a question for him and Orlan did not bother responding. *I have access to chemicals that will put the guards to sleep and render them senseless. I don't know when exactly, but as soon as the opportunity presents itself, I will get you and my sister out.* She opened her eyes, but maintained her connection to Orlan. *May I ask how you got to be so good at what you do?*

After several moments of silence, where Stephenie thought he decided to ignore her, Orlan opened up, *I learned to bridge multiple witches, taking control of them and combining their powers to make a more effective weapon. It started with one who loved me, then others were added. I learned my skill working for the Senzar in their war against the Marsa. It is a war that is still going on, but I grew tired of the fighting and decided to come with Favian to the north.* Orlan swallowed a memory and then continued, *The battles were so closely matched and fought that I had to burn up people. People I knew intimately from being in their minds. Most could never sacrifice themselves that way, but protected from the effects of the energy, I could drive their bodies and minds past the point of breaking, leaving nothing but a burnt out corpse.* He seemed to turn inward. *I am the evil bastard you think of me, but you better not leave me here. And if you are smart, you will bridge me into another warlock's mind when we leave. I am likely far more effective than you.*

Stephenie felt herself grow cold. *I promised you I would not leave you and I will keep that promise.* She said nothing more, but his request for control of someone else she would not do. With that he pushed her easily from his head and she hoped desperately he would not try to take over her mind when the time came.

"Learn anything useful yet? You've been going at this long enough. Or perhaps you're just starting to enjoy it."

Stephenie gave Rilan, her Butcher, the same hateful stare she always did. He laughed as usual and she simply headed toward the exit. She paused a moment and turned back. "Is Orlan the only one down here you work on like this?"

"The only one that needs someone expendable to heal. Though most of those down here are too valuable to waste on the table, and then there is nothing we need from them. However, sometimes I give them a session for the fun of it."

Stephenie expected that answer and turned back to the hall.

"If you ever want a tour of the fallen nobles of your lands, just wander down the passages and look."

She could not help but falter in her steps. Though he could not see it, her eyes lit up. "That actually sounds interesting." Quickening her pace, she was soon in the open guardroom at the top of the passage. Glancing about, she recognized Larence from her first and only shift on the curtain wall. "Hey, would you take me on a tour of the nobility? Lord Rilan recommended I see our countries' high and mighty brought down a level or two."

Larence glanced at the others who shrugged and then he rose to his feet. "If we're quick about it. I can't be away from my post for long."

Stephenie accepted his reluctance, knowing many still saw her as trouble and likely feared what Nerida would do to them if they were friendly to her. He led her down the first of the six side passages, mentioning names and countries quickly as they walked past doors with small barred windows. Stephenie did not recognize most of the names he mentioned, a few she knew he was mispronouncing, and a couple she actually knew from a book of paintings her father had of foreign dignitaries. She peeked through a couple of the barred windows, but skipped most of them.

When she did finally pass close to her sister's cell, she could not help but look inside. She could sense Islet and was surprised that she immediately knew her mind. She had never truly felt her sister mentally after her abilities had been awakened by Kas and it was like looking at an image one had only seen in a dream.

Islet was asleep on a mat spread over the stone floor. She knew the room was cold; there was less potential energy in the stone floor than she would see of stone sitting in the sun or next to a fire. It was dark enough that Islet would not be able to see her, but her sight expanded as she took in her sister's frail form. Feeling herself tense with anger, she turned away before Larence might take note of her emotions. She continued to follow him to the end of the block of cells where they stopped.

"Those are the nobles. The other blocks contain a few lesser people and people who have committed crimes in Vinerxan." He looked at her, "You good? Can we go back now?"

Stephenie nodded her head. "Yes, thank you."

It was late when Stephenie returned to her room, deciding to skip the training room because her exhaustion had caused her to make mistakes with Orlan. Stephenie frowned when she noticed Atia was away. After the first couple of days, the cat had become fickle and would only come to her when it wanted food or attention. She noted Ryia was also not in her bunk, but the old man, whose name she still did not know, was sound asleep.

She readied herself for bed and was about to extinguish the light when Ryia came into the room. The girl radiated distress and her clothing looked to be in disarray. *Damn it,* Stephenie swore silently. "Ryia, are you okay?"

The girl sniffed back some tears and nodded her head. "I'm fine."

Stephenie stepped closer. The smell of sex was heavy on the girl. "What happened? Who did this to you? Who hurt you?"

She shook her head. "Steph, don't get involved."

"I offered my protection for you, I am involved." Her fists were already tight and images of ripping Isa's head from his body filled her mind.

Ryia closed her eyes and sat on her bunk. "I knew he wouldn't love me, but I thought he at least cared about me. I've been a fool, and I've been used."

"Ryia, tell me what's happened," Stephenie said, sitting next to the girl.

"It's Lord Favian. He said if I pleased him, he'd make me a warrior. He said he could give me the ability to be a powerful witch. He just wanted to know some things about you, what you knew and where you came from. He said you were a gem to protect and take care of, but you were too afraid to share your story with him and he didn't blame you for that."

Stephenie could see how Ryia might believe such a story, but she had seen Favian's cruelty, and anyone who employed someone like Nerida in a position of power was not looking out for anyone but himself. Ryia was young enough and did not know enough about magic or the world to see Favian's lies for what they were. Her mental image changed to Favian's head on the ground, but the memory of the speed of his attacks kept her seated. She could not hope to face him in battle.

"He got into my head. Tonight he took me to his bed and then when he was done...." Tears leaked from her eyes. "He raped my mind, looking at everything in my head. I couldn't stop him. He just...now he's done with me and I am nothing."

"It's okay Ryia. I'll take care of you. I'll do what I can to protect you."

"How?" the girl demanded, staring into Stephenie's eyes. "Lord Favian is our master and he's not going to let either of us go. He told me so. Until he knows who your parents are, he will keep you here." She swallowed. "Who are you that you are so important to him?"

Stephenie pulled Ryia close and put her arm around the girl's shoulders. "Just a girl like you, alone and on my own. I have no idea why anyone would be interested in me." With the physical contact to Ryia, she became aware of a tiny thread of energy between the girl and something or someone in a room above them. Opening her senses slightly, Stephenie sensed a person who was mostly concealed to her mental awareness just above them. To be safe, she pulled back her senses. While she could not be certain, she was fairly sure it was Lord Favian. *So you still have your claws in this girl, do you?*

The morning after Ryia confided in her, she tried to convince Nilia to let her go into town and buy some more shepherd's purse. Stephenie had intentionally destroyed the supply they had on hand and they were low on other supplies to stop bleeding and treat infected cuts. However, Nilia said she was not permitted to send any of the students into town. Someone else would be sent for the supplies.

Frustrated, she almost considered writing a coded message for someone to try to deliver to Henton. However, she knew she was being watched closely and could not take the risk someone would discover her friends.

That night she was summoned to Lord Favian's chambers before she was supposed to report to the dungeon. She arrived at his office and was told to enter despite the fact that she sensed Captain Nerida was present. Fearing a confrontation with the two of them, Stephenie steadied herself in case she needed to fight.

Upon entering, it was obvious the Captain was making a report, "—nothing related to Lord Evrin's disappearance. There are a handful of suspicious foreigners, especially two working at the docks, but they do not appear to be involved, and we've had them watched since we talked to them."

"I was enjoying the fool wasting his money in our town. He was not about to leave without his prize, and he definitely would not leave most of his possessions. Find the ship that took him and ensure they suffer for it. I will not be known for allowing people to be kidnapped, even people who annoy me."

"Of course, My Lord," she said rising to her feet.

"Steph, please take a seat."

Stephenie bowed her head to Lord Favian and also to Captain Nerida as the woman passed her. The icy glare the Captain gave her said nothing had been forgiven.

"My Lord, you asked to see me."

"Yes. What have you learned from Orlan?"

Stephenie nodded her head. She had a hard time seeing him as an old man; he barely looked a day older than herself, but she would not let herself be taken in by his youthful appearance. "I have not learned enough yet to satisfy you, My Lord. The only additional piece of information I have not reported to Lord Rilan is that I understand Orlan at one time was helping you fight against a people known as the Marsa. I believe that was the name."

He raised his eyebrows. "Interesting. You pull some very random bits of information from Orlan. Have you learned nothing more about Elrysa?"

Stephenie shook her head. "I have not."

"What if I said the words iptys voltu morcan? Do they mean anything to you?"

Stephenie shook her head. The words sounded similar to Dalish, but she did not think anyone alive knew that language aside from her, Kas, and a few thousand ghosts living in a trance under Antar.

"Have you seen this mark before?" He turned over a piece of paper that had the accent mark she found on the coins: the three lines joined by a triangle and a solid dot.

She looked at the marks more closely, but shook her head. "Should I have?"

Favian narrowed his eyes. "I believe you are lying to me. Who are you working for and what is your purpose in being here?"

She felt her blood run cold, but did not sense him actually in her head, at least not through a means she had experienced so far. However, she had lied and he somehow could tell. "My Lord, I have no reason to lie. I am here for myself, to learn how to use my powers and free those I care about from tyranny."

He watched her for a moment and then licked his lips. "Perhaps another means of persuasion is necessary."

Stephenie did not have to look over her shoulder, she sensed Ryia enter the room and walk over to stand next to her. The girl was staring straight ahead and could have been a statue for all the life that shown in her eyes. "What have you done to her?"

"She is mine to do with as I please. As are you. You came to me looking for protection and training, which means you have sworn your life to my service until I release you. However, someone with your potential and skill does not act as a supplicant. You are here for a purpose. It is interesting to see you compromise yourself for this girl. I have been through her thoughts and found no knowledge of you before you arrived here." He glanced in her direction and Ryia stiffened as her breathing stopped. "I have complete control of her body. If you want her to live, you will tell me the truth."

Stephenie felt the rage deep within her building. She had grown close to freeing Islet; at least she had thought she had. The man before her was powerful and fast and was going to stop her from reaching her goal, if not outright kill her.

"I really thought having Ryia confess my abuse of her would have triggered a confession from you, but you are cold inside."

"Release her," Stephenie demanded, her own back straighter and more regal. "The families will not stand for your abuse any longer." She hoped some vague threat of a higher class of people would give him pause.

Stephenie just barely sensed the field that struck her across the face, but she definitely felt the pain of the blow.

"You are no match for me girl! Do not threaten me with what you do not know. If you do not properly claim allegiance, you can claim no rank or protection."

She felt Ryia's panic building as her body cried out for air. Reaching deep within herself, she let out a mental scream across the whole spectrum of fields she had ever seen. The effort physically hurt her and she felt blood drain from her nose, but the disruption had the effect she had hoped. Ryia was on the floor and gasping for air. Favian had fallen forward, his hands supporting him on his desk.

As quickly as she could, Stephenie grabbed Ryia's hand and smashed her way into the girl's mind. Frightened and panicked, Ryia barely noticed her and Stephenie worked to keep it that way, hiding her connection behind the girl's confusion.

"Bitch," Favian swore.

She felt Favian reach out to regain control of Ryia's mind and the instant he did, Stephenie unleashed a gravitational attack of her own against the man, distracting him enough that she used one of Orlan's techniques and plowed her way into Favian's mind through the connection he had established with Ryia.

He struggled, but Stephenie dumped enough gravity under his feet to collapse his chair and force him to defend himself against her physical attack, preventing him from defending his mind against her mental one. Firmly into his head, she felt his pain as his counter to her field started to fail. Dizzy with the confusion of being in three places at once, she ceased the flow of energy directed at crushing the man and told her own body to continue breathing.

What have you done? He screamed. *How is this possible?*

Taking a moment to center her thoughts, Stephenie took a deep breath. She knew with certainty that she had him locked away in his own head. However, she had broken free of what Gernvir had done to her, so she also knew her certainty was misplaced. Watching Favian closely for that sense of rage that lived within herself, she assessed what she could and should do now.

Tell me, I demand to know!

"I have never been in three heads at once," Stephenie said aloud and hearing her voice across all three sets of ears. The effect was dizzying. *I am sorry to have done that to you Ryia, but it seemed the only solution at the time.*

Stephenie could tell the girl was terrified, but there was nothing to be done about that at the moment. Turning her attention more fully on Favian, she acknowledged him mentally. *'Seventh generation' I sense you repeating to yourself. Yvima Orthas Corha claimed to be sixth generation.*

Who are you?

I am Stephenie Marn, Princess of Cothel. I'm the one that brought a mountain peak down on you bastards. You have my sister in your dungeon, but that will change. She took a breath and calmed the rage. She took a moment more before standing up. Once on her feet, she commanded Ryia to do the same, giving the girl back some control of her body.

She looked at Favian who was on the floor, still whole, but laying on the ruins of his chair. Using all of her concentration, she slowly took control of his body and tried to bring him to a standing position. After two spectacularly failed attempts, she managed to keep him on his feet.

This will never work. You will not keep control of me. His contempt for her coming through so strongly it almost overwhelmed her and caused her to lose control of his mind.

Silence! She screamed at him mentally. *Do not speak again unless I ask you a question!* Feeling Favian quiet his mental presence, she undertook the task of walking him about the room. Without his constant screaming in her head, she managed to move his body without him falling down. Adding the complexity of moving her own body at the same time gave her a headache and she could see through his eyes the blood that was leaking from her nose.

She had her hand wipe it clean and Ryia and Favian repeated the motion with their own hands. *Damn, this is hard.* Taking a deep breath, she steadied herself as Nerida opened the door.

"My Lord, I felt something happen up here, are you okay?"

Concentrating, she forced Favian's mouth to speak. "Do not interrupt me without my leave to do so. I am in the middle of something, Captain Nerida. You are dismissed."

His voice did not quite have the proper inflection, but Nerida bowed her head and retreated from the room.

Well Ryia, this might work. However, I am going to need you to do some of the work yourself. Just follow us and say nothing to anyone.

Stephenie sensed an acknowledgment from the girl and gave her a little more control over her own body. Turning her focus back to Favian, she had him walk forward while her own body followed behind his. It was easier that way, where she could think one action and have both bodies respond.

As they descended the stairs to the first floor, she considered going after the chemicals to put the guards to sleep, but decided the effort to do that might be more challenging than she could achieve in the current situation. Instead, she would rely on using Favian's presence to control those in the castle.

When she entered the dungeon's upper room, the guards jumped to attention and immediately opened the doors for them. Trying to avoid drawing suspicions with his voice, she simply glared at them in response to any comment or question and continued deeper into the dungeon. In the open area where the bulk of the guards sat, she used

Favian to bark two commands. "Bring Orlan here now as well as that Queen of Ipith, Islet."

The guards jumped to action, a pair running into the block that contained the noble prisoners and another pair back to the torture room. After a short time, Islet's thin form emerged from the passage, the guards pushing her forward.

"Stephenie?" she asked, blinking her eyes against the light and disbelief.

"Silence girl. Your freedom has been purchased; do not make me change my mind."

Islet straightened at the harsh tone that came from Favian's mouth.

To a different pair of guards, Stephenie turned Favian's attention. "Fetch boots and warm clothing for her. Immediately!" The guards leaped to action.

A few moments later, a bruised but conscious and walking Orlan was ushered into the main chamber without any clothing. The Butcher standing behind him. "My Lord, what is happening?"

"Rilan, I am releasing this woman and based on what Steph has provided to me, I find Orlan to be guilty of many crimes. I will take him outside and personally deliver my punishment."

"Bitch," Orlan growled. "I trusted you!"

"And through it, she bought the freedom of this woman." To another set of guards, Favian turned. "Bring boots and warm clothing for Orlan as well. I don't want him to succumb to the cold too quickly."

The guards quickly returned with clothing. Islet slowly started to dress, her eyes not moving from Stephenie. Orlan took a couple blows to the gut before he started to dress.

"My Lord, may I have a word with you in private?"

"What is it Rilan?"

"Please, My Lord, just a private word."

Stephenie would have bit her lip if she did not fear that Favian's body would respond in the same fashion. Ryia's panic was growing and if she did not settle down, Stephenie would have to reassert control of the girl. But for now, she settled on moving Favian down the passage holding the nobles. "What do you want to ask me, Rilan?"

"My Lord, are you certain about this. Queen Islet is valuable for use against Cothel. And Orlan? I sense there is something wrong here."

"Rilan, you are aware of who I am and the connections I have, yes?"

"I know you are part of some greater class of people, but I do not know the details, My Lord."

"As it should be. So do not question my actions." Stephenie turned Favian around and marched his body back into the main room. She saw her own legs move, but fortunately, she kept herself in one place.

Once the others were dressed, she turned Favian to the stairs. "Bring them."

Going back up the stairs was actually easier than going down. The trip down the stairs had required Stephenie to use a gravity field to keep herself and Favian from tumbling forward. The ascent was much easier and before long, she was on the first floor of the castle. Making a quick detour to her room, she sent Ryia inside to get their coats and limited possessions.

Dressed warmly, she now spared a moment to hope that Kas had felt her mental blast and readied the others. If not, she was not sure how easy getting out of Vinerxan was going to be. She took a deep breath. She had hoped to sneak out without anyone knowing, now the whole castle was likely to know and unless she somehow disabled Favian, she would either have to take him with her or kill him.

She sensed Favian increase his struggle against her and the Lord of the Keep's steps faltered just before they reached the door to the bailey. *What is it you want to say?*

I am two hundred and five years old, you can't just kill me! You want to leave, I will allow it, just don't kill me.

Stephenie considered his words and tried to determine if he was speaking truthfully or not. She wanted to believe him, but she sensed the words contained an overtone of commandment and her instincts rejected that. *Do not lie to me, Favian. You are a piece of overindulged garbage and should have been drowned as a baby.*

I would have looked after you and made you great. All you would have had to do was tell me who you were. Your power is great, that I can see, and with me, I would have made you greater. The Senzar would have taken you in, and you'd never have to worry about being burned for being a witch.

Stephenie gave a mental shake of her head. *Your mistake is thinking I want to see Cothel or any of these countries fall. Just because there are people who are my enemy in those places, does not mean I am your friend. The enemy of my enemy is not always my friend. Now silence!*

She forced his body to move forward, open the door, and cut across the yard toward the gates. Several people came to attention and she sensed Nerida exiting the keep behind the group that had formed around them.

Stephenie felt her stomach tightening. She did not want to kill him at this time, though she knew a single thought from her could end the life of his body. If that happened, the castle would mobilize against her. She also could not bring him with her; that would draw even more suspicion than the nighttime release of valuable prisoners to a couple of witches.

To Favian she turned her focus. She could feel his shivering, for she had blocked his body's natural urge to draw power and generate warmth. *Interesting how easy it is to dominate another person. The very thought makes me sick.* She took a deep breath. Generating as much command in her tone as possible, she pushed against Favian's mind with all the force she could muster. *You will remain here! You will not follow us! You will not send others to follow us! You will not speak a word of this to anyone! You will not convey any knowledge of us at all to anyone ever!*

She took a deep breath. Favian had retreated deeper into his own mind. He was no longer actively fighting her and his memories were now completely open to her. However, several dozen people gathered around and she had no time to waste.

"Be it known that Steph has provided a service to me and in doing so, as I promised her, I am releasing Islet of Ipith into her custody. Ryia will accompany them."

The crowd alternated from staring at Favian to meeting her eyes and this tri-location was wearing her mind way too thin. "Sir Orlan, step forward." Stephenie quickly used the magic in Favian's body to pull a small stone to his hand, hopefully without anyone noticing. Using his magic, she forced open Orlan's mouth and shoved in the rock. She forced his mouth shut and then drove the stone down his throat. "You, I have poisoned and cursed. I have placed a durnit into your body," she quickly invented. "It will grow and consume you from the inside. It will sustain you for days before you finally succumb. Unfortunately, your body will become quite toxic. There is a cure which you already know of from your battles against the Marsa, but by my best estimates, you will not be able to reach that cure until five days after your death. However, I give you the futile chance to try."

Stephenie could see the slight confusion on Orlan's face, but he chose to say nothing. Turning Favian's body back toward the gate, she gave him one final command to remain there. She pulled back all but the thinnest of threads of control and quickly walked out of the gates with Ryia, Islet, and Orlan behind her. When she was too far to maintain the link, she released Favian and Ryia, and then hurried her pace away from the keep.

"What is happening, Stephenie," Islet asked in Cothish as they rushed through the city streets.

"We're not safe yet, I will explain when I can."

Searching around, she almost cried out in relief when she felt Kas coming toward her. *My Love, never let me go off alone again!*

What has happened? I sensed a weird field that felt like an explosion. You have blood all over your face. Who are these people?

Kas, we have to move, I don't know how long we have. I'll explain as we go.

Follow me. Henton and Douglas are readying the horses just in case it was a signal from you.

Chapter 21

Stephenie drove the others through the biting wind. She could tell Islet was not used to the exertion and she grabbed her sister's arm to help her along. When they finally reached the inn where Henton and Douglas had taken lodging, she let out a cry of relief and hurried forward to give each of them a hug. Then she turned to Argat and patted his neck, "Good boy, you took care of them."

"Steph, who are these people? We're short two horses by my count."

"Henton, Douglas, this is Islet, my sister, Ryia, a friend, and Orlan, who was a captive of the Senzar that I promised to free."

"Everyone, these are my friends, Henton and Douglas."

Henton nodded his head. "You were supposed to give us warning, and I really appreciate the fact that we are doing this in the middle of a cold night."

Stephenie smiled at his grin; he was glad to see her and the complaints were just bluster to cover that fact. She reached up and gave him another hug before pulling back and beckoning Islet over to them.

Henton spoke quietly before Islet arrived, "Kas has already retrieved our money and extra supplies from the eaves of the inn. I suggest we get moving if you think there will be pursuit."

Stephenie nodded her head. "Islet, let me help you on Argat so you can ride. Ryia, you've also had a rough night, get on Douglas' bay, he'll take care of you." The girl nodded her head slowly and Stephenie hoped there would not be any lasting effects from what

Favian and she had done. Turning back to Islet, she lifted her sister's small form easily into the saddle and tossed up her own cloak to cover Islets legs. "Keep warm sister, we've got a long night ahead of us."

Turning back to the men, she continued, "Orlan, you look to be in good enough shape to lead a horse, take the spare, the rest of us will lead the others." Without waiting for anyone to complain, she started toward the mountains and the pass that would take them away from the coast.

"Steph," Douglas said, leading his horse and Ryia forward to match her pace. "Kas scouted a few side valleys. We might be able to hide out and let any pursuit go into the pass."

Stephenie shook her head. "Not with the fresh powder on the ground and there are too many mages that could follow. I'd rather they can only come at us from one direction. We'll be running with minimal sleep until we get free of them. I've managed to escape from a castle without killing anyone and I want to keep it that way."

"We also didn't kill a couple of people as well," Douglas offered.

Stephenie, if what you have relayed about this Lord Favian is correct, you may not have succeeded in avoiding causing death. If your command was as strong as you recalled for me, it is likely he will not be able to move from that spot. His mind may be so damaged and changed it will never recover.

Kas, don't ruin my mood, he was alive when I left and that is what I will count. She turned to where he floated invisibly next to her and smiled at him. *I've missed you.*

They were well on their way up the switchbacks before Stephenie noticed the light of lamps moving across the valley floor. She had hoped they would have more time, but she feared Kas was right. Favian was likely standing unmoving in front of the gate. There would be no doubt that their release was not an act of his will. *Perhaps someone will take him inside so he doesn't freeze?* She wanted to say she did not care, but that would be a lie. Killing was something she hated, but sometimes she had no choice.

"Henton, take Argat as well. I'll try to make it harder on those that are following." Pausing to let everyone pass, she looked up the slope and instead of seeing with her eyes, she examined the potential energies of the snow, trees, and rocks. Finding an area that looked fragmented enough, she reached down and pulled energy from the mountain. Carefully, she drove her force deep into the rock, looking for fractures and natural breaks in the frozen ground. Groaning from the effort to control the complex fields, she pulled at the mountainside and carefully shifted a large mass of boulders, snow, and trees, causing it to slide down the slope with a low rumble. Being careful to control the landslide, she stopped it on top of the path behind them. It would cause trouble for travelers, but she did not want to face an army of mages.

She took a moment to steady herself. Already taxed from the effort of controlling Ryia and Favian, her head throbbed with the pulsing of blood that again started to leak from her nose. She could taste it running down the back of her throat and knew it was going to be a cold night. Her fingers trembled slightly and she could not afford to use more energy to protect everyone from the wind and cold.

Turning back to the trail, she worked to catch up to the others. It was hard going to manually trudge through the couple feet of snow, but once the mages were past the delay she had caused, she would need to have the strength to fight.

They reached the top of the ridge as the sun started to brighten the sky ahead of them. A thin film of ice crystals covered all of their clothing and gear. The horses' lashes and whiskers sparkled from frozen breath in the growing light. Everyone was exhausted, but without the darkness, there were no longer lamps to mark the progress of their pursuers.

"Stephenie," Islet called from behind her. "I am freezing and need to find a place of privacy."

"We're a number of miles from that inn we stayed at on the way here," Henton offered.

"I'm not going to risk the lady of that inn or any of the other people there." She came around the side of Argat and reached up to help Islet down. In the process, she pushed energy into Islet, warming her arms and legs."

"What are you doing?" Islet screamed in Cothish.

"Warming you. Don't panic. I can't keep it up; I've done too much already."

Once on the ground Islet took a step away from Stephenie, but she faltered in the snow. "I don't want any of Elrin's evil touching me!"

"Well, don't worry about that. I'm the Prophet of Catheri, not Elrin's spawn. The High Priest of Felis declared me cleansed. The proclamations were passed around to many countries."

"What? Who is Catheri?"

Stephenie grabbed Islet's hand and led her off the path, clearing the snow with a gravitation field that caused a cloud of white powder to swirl around them. She was thankful Islet's outburst had been in Cothish and hoped Ryia and Orlan did not understand what she had just claimed. The juggling of her association with gods versus witchcraft versus magic would be tricky. She wanted to fully explain the truth to everyone, but that had to wait for the proper time.

Helping the reluctant Islet to a somewhat secluded place behind a copse of evergreens white with snow, she cleared a spot so her sister could relieve herself in private. For a moment, she wondered if Islet would raise an objection, but it appeared nature offered enough motivation that the Queen of Ipith made do without a chamber pot, perhaps for the first time in her life.

By the time they got back to the path, Henton had dispersed some of the dried fruit and salted meat to the others as well as put feedbags on all of the horses. "Here you go," he said, offering food to Islet and Stephenie.

"Soldier of Cothel, I am a queen, do you feel yourself so superior that you would address me so informally?"

Henton's mouth dropped and slowly closed, but before he could respond, Stephenie turned Islet to face her. "Don't ever talk to my friends in that manner. They are equal to any, including yourself." To Henton she added, "Thank you for the food."

"Of course." He turned to Islet. "No insult was intended, Your Majesty. We are just informal on the trail."

Stephenie shook her head. "The break's over, Islet, get back on the horse. It took us thirteen days to go west through the mountains, we'll have to do it faster going east, we've almost doubled the number of mouths to feed and we'll run out of food if we don't."

By mid-afternoon even Stephenie had to admit defeat. The horses were stumbling and the snow had grown deeper as it continued to fall and blow sideways with a bitter wind. Everyone had been up for more than a day and the effort to continue marching was too much.

In a level area that offered a minimum of shelter just off the trail, she tended to the horses, putting on their heavy blankets and melting snow for them to drink. Henton and Douglas, along with help from Orlan, assembled the small tent that would barely fit four people, assuming they were willing to squeeze in close. With six of them, they would either need to take turns in the shelter or sleep on top of each other. Once it was assembled, Islet and Ryia climbed inside.

"Steph, you should get in and out of the cold," Henton said, trying to guide her to the tent. "I've seen you wiping blood from your face. You need to rest."

"Of everyone here, I'm the best able to handle this weather. You and Douglas should rest first."

"What?" Douglas asked, "and then we get a guard shift when the sun goes down and it gets colder?" He shook his head, "No, you rest now and get to deal with the night's cold."

She looked at him and smiled. "I can't argue with that logic."

Inside the tent, the temperature was already several degrees warmer from Islet and Ryia's body heat. Islet had fallen asleep immediately and Stephenie knew that more than a year of imprisonment left her sister, who had never been athletic, in even worse shape.

Ryia was sitting up and staring. "I thought you to be a coward, but you are a god. You defeated the Senzar by yourself. Brought down a mountain. I...I...."

"Ryia, I knew Favian had his hooks in you, so I didn't tell you who I was because I knew he would find out. My mission was to rescue my sister and that's what I did. I am not a god, just a person."

"She's a queen...you're a princess...."

"I'm Stephenie, or Steph, if you want. She's my completely normal sister who's lived a life of privilege and will likely be a pain on our journey. I will help you learn to be what you are good at, but not right now. Right now I need to sleep."

"Yes, Ma'am."

"Yes, Steph. Don't start adding titles to either of our names unless we have a reason to do so. We are just travelers and don't need the attention." With a sigh, she patted the girl on the leg and crawled in between Ryia and her sister. She hated having to feel like an adult and police people.

You have a very commanding personality when you want.

Yeah, and your point is? She shook her head. *Tell me everything that's happened to you. What's with 'not killing a couple of people'?*

I have resumed the grand life of a thief, Kas sent smugly, *picked up a very large bag of Kyntian coins.*

Stephenie was not sure how long she had slept, but she could feel the sun going down and so she slipped from the tent. Islet and Ryia woke in the process and she motioned for Islet to stay and Ryia to follow her.

"It's cold out there," Ryia complained.

"Yeah, and the guys need a chance to rest and get warm. You've got magic and can warm yourself."

Islet sat up. "Are you telling me those men will be sharing the tent with me?"

"Unless you want to stand out in the cold, yes. Henton and Douglas are completely honorable. I'd suggest sleeping next to one or both of them."

"And the other one?"

Stephenie shrugged, "He's a bastard, but won't hurt you either. Be happy that they will help keep the tent warm."

Stephenie pulled Ryia out and signaled the men to come over. "You let me sleep too long. Get in there and out of the cold."

Douglas stepped forward and bent down to enter the tent. "Make sure you have a warm meal for us when the sun comes up."

She smiled at him and held the tent flap for Henton and Orlan. Once they were in, she took Ryia over to the horses to check them. Argat interrogated her for treats, but she could only push his nose away. "Not now, Big Guy," she said with a pat on his neck. Slipping off her glove, she checked the temperature of his ears and frowned. He was cold, but she would not be able to keep them warm all night and making them hot and cold would be worse than leaving them huddled together with a chill.

"Are those men your lovers?"

Stephenie turned back to Ryia and sighed with exasperation. "Why is it everyone always assumes that? No Ryia they are not. They are my friends and they've saved my life more times than I can count."

The girl nodded her head, but seemed to doubt what Stephenie had said.

"All right, throw away that stupid stone the Senzar gave you and put all those stupid phrases and jumping about waving your hands out of your head. Magic is a mental discipline, not something you chant."

"Magic?"

"The proper word for witchcraft. Most people will look at you like you just did me if you use it, but I've grown to hate the word witchcraft, so don't use it when we are alone."

"But if we don't use the spells, Elrin's—"

"Elrin doesn't exist and you can take that as fact. Which is another thing that you should not share with people outside of Henton and Douglas, since people will not believe you. If you want to come back to Antar with me, I will mentor you. Perhaps if we teach you the proper way to use magic you won't have so much trouble with it. If you would rather go elsewhere, we can still give you the basics and find what you are good at."

"You want me to come with you? After everything I did and said?"

Stephenie smiled. "I was not easy to get along with at your age either. But, you have to understand that in Cothel, people believe I am the Prophet of Catheri. They assume I have been cleansed of Elrin and are getting my powers from a god. A god whose priests died off a hundred years ago. I am working to change the opinions of Cothel, but it will take years, and to avoid the conflicts, I am allowing people to believe a lie for now. So, if you decide to come to Cothel with me, I will make you a priestess of Catheri and I will need your word that you will help conceal the truth until the people are ready to hear it."

"I don't even know what the truth is."

Stephenie smiled. "You'll learn it. Now, we—"

Stephenie, she heard Kas as he was approaching from the southwest, *there is a group of people moving this way.*

And I hoped we'd get away without killing anyone. To Ryia she said, "Quietly tell the others to get armed, we have people coming." She grabbed Ryia's arm before she could turn away. "And don't touch Orlan or try to reach out to his mind. He'll take you over like Favian did and that will make me have to kill him." Stephenie ignored the fear Ryia was suddenly broadcasting and turned away from the camp and headed back to the trail. Her head was still throbbing and she was not in the mood to fight. If she could, she would try to prevent the conflict.

The trail was easy to reach, their earlier activities having compressed an area of snow enough to keep her from having to work through the drifts. Behind her, she sensed Henton and the others mobilizing. Ahead of her, she was just able to sense a group of people, at least twenty in number.

I'm glad to have you at my side, she told Kas, who was partially enveloping her to hide his presence. *If there are Senzar in that group, I'm not sure we'll survive the night.*

Now you are damaging my mood. His tone was light, but with a layer of fear.

As the group came closer, she sensed Nerida was leading two and a half lines of mages. They had no horses and in the current terrain, with fit people, it was likely the faster mode to travel. "Nerida," Stephenie called out. "I left in a manner that meant I didn't need to kill anyone. Don't change that now."

Stephenie heard Nerida bark a quick order to kill Orlan since he was likely controlling her. None of the mages slowed their advance.

"Please, I am trying to offer you a chance to go home alive. We don't need this conflict."

"You destroyed our home, bitch! Lord Favian is completely unresponsive and Madam Farfelee said his mind is damaged beyond repair. For your crimes, you will die as the traitor you are!"

"I never supported your cause. I came for my sister. You were fool enough to believe that just because I have powers I would side with the Senzar. I am no traitor, so turn around and leave." Stephenie recognized all the people before her, none of them were Senzar mages and she began to hope they would make it out alive.

"Our lives are lost. You destroyed what we had; there is nothing to return to. The Senzar are planning to abandon Vinerxan."

"Nerida, you are a fool for believing the Senzar actually have your best interests in mind. They are using you, and you are letting them."

"Lord Favian protected us and offered safety. You've thrown us back to the mercy of the priests and their fires. You've killed our hopes!" In a lower voice, Nerida ordered the front line to advance and kill everyone.

Stephenie felt Henton and Douglas take positions behind her. Islet and Ryia were still close to the tent with Orlan somewhere in between. His mind was quiet enough that Stephenie could only sense his movement, not that she had any intention of touching his thoughts.

"You," she heard Nerida swear.

"Ma'am," Henton responded, "pleasure to meet you again."

Stephenie did not bother to glance behind her. She took a deep breath and gorged herself on the massive energy reserve deep in the mountain. Forming a long gravity line between her and Nerida's soldiers, the ground eripted with a rumbling explosion, sending snow, rocks, and trees into the air. Feeling her rage simmering just under the surface, she flung the debris around, circling it a dozen feet overhead and surrounding everyone present. The winds whipped through the trees that were still standing. A torrent of flying snow pelting everyone, save for Stephenie, Henton, and Douglas, who were standing in the eye of the storm.

With a growl that rumbled through the ground, she flung the maelstrom outward in all directions and into the dark of the night. The sounds and crashing boulders and trees filled the stillness that settled in the wake of her display. "Before any of you decide to continue, know this, I am Her Royal Highness, Princess Stephenie of Cothel, Defender of the Realm, and the very person who brought a mountain peak down on the Senzar in the Greys. If you want war with me, by all means keep coming forward." She heard the undertones of the growl in her voice and it sounded strange to her ears.

Seven people in the back of the group turned and ran into the darkness. Nerida, Isa, and several others on the front line held their place and resolve. All the others were standing with fear and uncertainty.

"You all have a choice. I am trying to change things in our countries. I am working to build a world where those of us with power can live peacefully with those who do not have it."

"And you'll stop the priests from burning us?" Nerida's contempt was thick in her voice.

"On my way to free my sister from Senzar captivity, we found it was not our people, but Senzar pretending to be priests, who were putting people to flame. They were burning our families and friends to put fear into those of us with power, driving us to false promises. They have no cure for Elrin because none is needed. Elrin is a lie and they know it. But they are using your fear and superstition against you. They were not even teaching you how to really use your powers. They were filling your heads with lies and giving you just enough knowledge to go and fight the people of our homelands. Most of you would die and that is fine with them. Any that might survive will essentially be a slave caste, always subservient."

"That is a lie!"

"Is it? Look at Farfelee. She's not Senzar born. While she has some freedom, it took her years to get what she has and her powers are not shackled by ignorance. They are driving you away from your lands to prevent you from challenging them when they come back again with more forces. Once they have what they need, they will toss you aside or kill you because it becomes too expensive to keep you around. That's what Favian does; he sells you to others in the south. It makes him rich, and you are little more than property." Stephenie nodded her head. "I see it in your eyes Nerida; you know that's the truth."

"We get protection and training in exchange for service. That is the way you nobles work. It is what you do to peasants, so what if the Senzar do it too?"

Stephenie shook her head. "My father never lied to get someone's service. Both sides know what is expected and what is exchanged." Stephenie could see the threat dissolving as the ranks lost faith in their ability to succeed. "I am not saying things are good or even fair in Cothel or any other country we used to call our homes, but I am working to change that. Yes, we still have to hide our powers. But I have been declared cleansed of Elrin by the High Priest of Felis and I am regarded as the Prophet of Catheri. Instead of working for invaders, those who want to go to Cothel can potentially take a role in the church of Catheri. While you will have to be labeled as priests or priestesses, with time, we can change the hearts of people and put an end to witch burnings forever."

"I will never follow you!"

Stephenie shook her head. "Nerida, your cruelty is not wanted in my land. You want to join your Senzar; do so. But know this, I will defend my home and these lands from any invader and if your masters send you to war with me, I will crush you as I crushed the last Senzar army." She looked to the others. "Those of you who still have human decency, the invitation is extended."

Nerida looked behind her. Another five of her soldiers had abandoned their positions. "You have ruined the lives of many."

Stephenie nodded her head. "Indeed, thousands have died at my hands. Leave this place and never pursue me or I'll add you to those numbers."

"Coward," Isa said, "won't even fight. She just threatens."

Stephenie took a step forward and Isa tried to hit her, Henton, and Douglas with a strong gravity field. She disrupted the field before it fully formed and exploded the rock in his hand sending fingers and flesh across the snow. He screamed in pain and fell to his knees in the red stained snow. "Never attack anyone I care about. It was not Orlan that destroyed Favian's mind that was me. If I can reduce your Lord to an empty shell and he was as powerful as you knew him to be, consider what I will do to you if I get angry. Now get that worthless boy who picks on young girls out of my sight and never return."

The man next to Isa bent down and lifted the young mage by his armpits. The others had already retreated. Nerida glared once more, and then turned away. Stephenie watched them go until they were no longer within her ability to sense them.

I will watch to make sure they do not come back.

Thank you. I love you Kas.

As I you.

She turned around and everyone was staring at her. To Henton and Douglas she whispered, "It is getting harder and harder to convince people not to get themselves killed."

"I'm proud of you," Henton said, "but was it wise to reveal so much?"

She shrugged. "I'll deny it if someone comes to Cothel making accusations. There are people who still think I am a witch, what's a few more making the accusation."

Islet stepped closer, "But I heard what you said. I could speak out against you." Stephenie turned to her sister, but Islet stood defiant. "I learned you were a witch when one of the Senzar came asking questions of me. They invaded my mind and rummaged through every thought. They wanted to know what I know about you and how you became so powerful. Of course I knew nothing, but now I understand Mother's hate of you."

"Mother hated me because she thought I was a punishment from the gods for something she had done. Then she betrayed father and Josh, leaving father dead and Josh a captive. She wants to cut out my heart and eat it. If she had gotten her way, even Josh would be dead and they'd have no use for you either."

Islet stood silently.

"It is true, Your Highness," Henton offered. "Your mother had me imprison Stephenie as a punishment to her brother's soldiers that failed her. Stephenie escaped just before your mother robbed the treasury and took all of Cothel's wealth north into Kynto."

"I wasn't aware of that, but I do know mother tried to free me."

Stephenie shook her head, "At the expense of all of Cothel and the rest of the family. I grieved for you and Kara, but Father had a responsibility to the thousands of people in Cothel. He could not turn aside and let the Senzar have what they wanted. I would have done anything I could for you, but not at the expense of all the people."

"But Mother was the only one to even try to save me."

Stephenie's jaw tightened. "This Mother of yours, she never showed me love. Every day of my life I had to endure her hate. And Regina relished tormenting me as well. You tried to be nice, sometimes, but when you were with Regina, the two of you could be so hateful. I am appealing to the sister who was not full of hate. If Josh or I had been in your place, there would still have been nothing anyone could have done for us. Leaving you was not because we didn't care, but that we had no idea where you were. As soon I as found out, I came to get you."

"Why? Why risk yourself?"

"Because you are family and...and I still love you. Because when you were by yourself, you tried to be kind and even stood up for me once against mother."

Islet looked to the ground. "You remember that?"

"I felt badly for you, wishing you had not gotten into so much trouble on my behalf."

Islet looked up, tears in her eyes. "What happened to make our family fall apart so much? I was not old enough to remember a time before you were there, but Kara told me there was a time everyone was so happy. She didn't know why, but when you came along, things got so cold in our family."

"You'd have to ask mother. She's been trying to kill me ever since someone told her there is a way to break this stupid, non-existent curse. I fear she might try to harm Josh as a means to get to me. And now, possibly even you, if she finds out you've been rescued."

Douglas cleared his throat.

"She doesn't need to know," Henton said softly.

Stephenie turned to them. "Who doesn't need to know what?"

"She should know," Douglas insisted.

Kas, what didn't you tell me?

Henton cleared his throat. "Steph, we were going to tell you once we were on the other side of these mountains and let you decide if your sister should be told." He nodded his head in acknowledgment of Stephenie's look. "Your mother dispatched some people to retrieve

Islet's right hand. She wanted it cut off and placed in a barrel of spirits. She planned to have it shipped to you with the threat the rest of Islet would be sent piece by piece until you came to her."

Islet raised her hand to look at the birthmark on the back of it. "Mother would not do that," Islet said, shaking her head.

"We know where she is," Henton offered. "In a place called Rativyr."

Stephenie turned and started back to the campsite.

"She wouldn't ask to have my hand cut off," Islet repeated.

"Henton, Douglas, Orlan," Stephenie said, switching to Pandar, "the three of you need some rest. I think Nerida and the others will stay away, but I'll keep watch with Ryia for a while. We'll try to travel by day starting tomorrow, but we'll likely need to get a bit cozier in the tent at night."

"Steph, what are you going to do?" Islet asked, but Stephenie did not respond.

Chapter 22

Stephenie spent the initial part of the night working with Ryia to help the girl allow her body to automatically regulate its temperature. After some progress, she let the girl get some food and it was not long before Ryia grew tired enough that she squeezed her way into the tent with the others. Stephenie noted the girl had slid in next to Henton and not Orlan, which was a wise choice. Surprisingly, it did not bother her the way Ryia had draped herself over her friend. *Am I getting better?*

By the time the sun started to brighten the mountain peaks, Stephenie was barely keeping her eyes open and was again bleeding from her nose. The effort to stay warm had taxed her exhausted body and she was thankful that there had been no sign of Nerida or the her solider.

When Henton roused the others, he put her back into the tent to rest while everyone else readied the camp and fixed a quick morning meal. The sleep was not long, but it helped her recover to the point that when they were ready to pack away the tent, she was coherent enough to speak with the others.

"Steph," Islet pleaded, "what are you going to do? You didn't answer me last night."

"I was planning to take you home."

"I am not sure I can go back to Reol Cove. I know my husband is dead and I never gave him a child to succeed him. The throne will fall to others of his family."

Stephenie shook her head. "I am sorry, but we understand that all of his family is dead and the Senzar have placed another family on the throne, one that supports them. I had meant Antar, but before I can take you home to Josh, I need to pay a visit to Mother. I can't have her hurting anyone else."

"You're going to kill her. I don't care what your men heard from someone claiming to work for Mother, you can't kill her. It would be murder."

Stephenie shook her head. "I'm too tired to discuss this with you. If you want to go your own way, I won't stop you, but for now there is only one way out of these mountains and I suggest you get on my horse so we can get going."

Islet looked at her with contempt, but then marched over to Argat. The chestnut looked at Stephenie and then to Islet. Henton patted his neck and slipped him a handful of grain before helping Islet into the saddle.

Not in the mood for more discussion, Stephenie led them northeast along the trail. She kept a steady pace during the warmest part of the day and allowed them to make an early camp as the temperature started to drop in the evening. However, while everyone else tended to tasks in the campsite, Islet stood around complaining about the wind and her cold feet. When Henton provided her dinner, she complained about the taste and the quality of the food.

"Islet, you seem to have the mistaken opinion that any of us care you were ever a queen. Get over it or you can freeze and starve."

"Well, at least you are talking to me again. But I will make this trip as miserable as I can until you agree not to kill the only parent I have left. You've just told me Father is dead and now you plan to kill Mother. I won't let you be so callous. You claim to be cleansed by the god of justice, but then say there is nothing to be cleansed of. How do I know you are not lying about Mother as well?"

Stephenie took a deep breath, exhaling a cloud of vapor into the cold air. In Pandar, so Ryia and Orlan could understand, she said, "How about I fill you in on everything that's happened since you were captured, then you can tell me what you've been doing and," she looked over at Henton and Douglas, "the two of you can fill me in on your recent adventures, then we can have a reasonably even ground to argue from."

Islet swallowed and then nodded her head.

Stephenie looked around, but no one said anything. She quickly filled in Kas as to what they were planning, since his understanding of the trade tongue was limited. "Very well, let me start back at the beginning of the war. Kara was killed by the first Senzar ships that landed, she was our oldest sister," Stephenie added for Ryia and Orlan. "Then you and your husband reacted, sending people to Esland. Durland and Selith sent troops while Father mobilized Cothel to arms. The Senzar had expected to walk through the lands hardly challenged, but with all of our countries having ties of some kind, they did not anticipate the response. Somehow the Senzar learned you were Father's daughter and tried to get Cothel's troops out of the fight by taking you." Stephenie swallowed. "When we heard, it broke our hearts, but Father knew he could not surrender all of the countries to the Senzar for you, or Josh, or any of us. And none of us knew where you were, so there was little we could do."

She glanced at Henton and Douglas, then back to Islet. "Mother, likely through a priest who was actually running Kynto behind the scenes—"

"Lord Yvima Orthas Corha," Henton offered.

Orlan cleared his throat. "Yvima was a friend of Favian, they were not related, but I had journeyed with Favian more than once to visit Yvima. Yvima, I understood left Senzar many years ago and came here to conquer some lands for himself."

"This bastard who was responsible for much of the death and hate in Kynto, convinced Mother to abandon Father, Josh, Cothel, and everyone else in exchange for you." Stephenie turned back to Orlan, "I'm assuming the robbing of the treasury was one of the conditions."

Orlan shrugged, "I was not privy to what was discussed. However, Yvima was a coldhearted bastard who amassed a lot of wealth and tools."

"And concocted a lie that has made my mother think that if she cuts out my heart and eats it, she'll be rid of this stupid curse that doesn't exist because that's not how magic works."

Orlan nodded his head. "The Senzar lied to those who came looking for their aid. They do not believe in any of these gods you have. They don't know how the augmentation devices came to be associated with gods and priests, but it does suit their needs. This whole concept of Elrin is an easy means of control."

Ryia shook her head. "I heard what Steph said, but I really didn't want to believe it."

Orlan shrugged, "Believe as you will, truth does not conform to belief, but to reality."

Truth and its perception seldom converge, Kas whispered in Stephenie's mind as she relayed the conversation to him.

"Well, let me tell you about how the war went and how Henton, Douglas, and I ended up here." After a deep breath, Stephenie started talking about all the things that led up to Henton capturing her and then, with his and Douglas' help, they went into detail about their journeys since, leaving out any mention of the passages to Arkani, the library, Kas, or the other ghosts. Stephenie suspected Orlan noted some odd gaps in the story, but neither Ryia nor Islet questioned any details.

The sun had fully set by the time the whole set of events were relayed. Henton and Douglas then detailed their time in Vinerxan with Kas filling in the omissions privately to Stephenie.

"My story is pretty boring in comparison," Ryia said. "I was a homeless girl making a living on the streets and hoping to avoid the priests. I heard word of Vinerxan and managed to come across the mountain pass before winter fully hit. But I didn't respond well to Nerida's teaching, so I got stuck there instead of going south with the others that came around the time I did." She looked over to Orlan, "What's your story? I know they were torturing you."

Orlan shook his head. "I have no story. I am simply a bastard who burns up witches and warlocks, so don't piss me off."

Stephenie could hear the pain in Orlan's voice, though probably no one else could. "Orlan doesn't have powers, but can effectively get into someone's mind, just like Gernvir did to me outside of Antar."

"I still don't understand how you defeated him," Orlan remarked. "We both were wise enough—or fearful enough—of each other that he refused to try to read my mind. Favian, I suspect, never pressed the issue for fear of me gaining control of a full Senzar warlock."

"No longer so confident you could have taken me at any point?"

Orlan shook his head, "No, I could have taken you any time I wanted, but you were of more use to me with everyone thinking you were protected."

Stephenie nodded her head. "You are probably right, but I don't think you would have liked what you found if you had."

Islet crossed her arms. "Very nice displays of ego, but, Steph, even if everything you say is true about Elrin, this magic as you call it, the gods," she raised her eyebrows and rolled her eyes, "and even Mother, you still can't just go and kill her."

Stephenie kept herself calm. "Islet, she is responsible for the deaths of thousands and is a traitor to Cothel. For those things she deserves death. On a personal level, she killed Father and sent people to take Will and cut him to pieces as well as sent people to cut off your hand."

"Please, Steph, if you go to her, let's try talking with her and see if we can reason with her. Father is dead, I don't want to lose the only other parent I have and have the reason be that you killed her."

Stephenie clenched her fists and then stretched her fingers. "Fine, we can talk with her, but that doesn't mean she gets to live."

Orlan cleared his throat, "This is all touching, but I plan to head south and I don't want to be in the middle of your family troubles."

Stephenie nodded her head, "I didn't expect you would come with us. You are welcome to leave at any point, but I would recommend you go as far northeast as Oakval, that is the first place you will find a major road south around this mountain range."

Orlan smiled. "My friend, I will take your advice and go that far. You know these lands better than I." He rose to his feet. "I will turn in for the night. I am now more accustomed to having people cut into my body than trudging through snow."

Once Orlan had disappeared into the tent, Henton quietly asked in the Old Tongue, "Do you actually trust him?"

Stephenie shrugged. "He's a soldier and I think he has a sense of honor, though months of being on the Butcher's table will wear at a person, no matter how strong willed."

Islet hesitated, and then spoke up, having learned the Old Tongue as a head of state. "If he was a prisoner of the Senzar, wouldn't that make him our friend?"

Stephenie stood up and helped her sister to her feet. "That, Islet, is the mistake the Senzar made when they brought me into their castle. While our goals don't conflict, I expect we can trust him. If that should change, he is as deadly as Henton and even more dangerous to someone with magic."

Islet, having won a concession from Stephenie, became less difficult and even started helping around the camp with small duties. She did not have skills in cooking or taking care of the animals, but she was willing to follow direction and over the next eight days, managed to become reasonably useful.

The weather had started to warm, even in the mountains, and that actually made the traveling worse. Now instead of being just cold, the ground turned into a layer of slick mud on top of frozen rock and clay. Their feet were always wet and cold and more than one ankle was sprained. With the exception of Orlan, whom she did not trust, Stephenie took the time to demonstrate her improved skills, healing a multitude of injuries and scrapes on the people as well as the horses.

Ryia had also changed, the sullen girl Stephenie had seen in Vinerxan became energized and actively sought work from Henton and Douglas. While she worked with Stephenie to learn magic, she deferred to Henton for help learning combat skills. Stephenie did not mind, since that gave her a chance to talk with Kas, who was feeling left out of their lives. *I promise, when Orlan is gone, I will introduce you to Islet and Ryia,* she had said one night.

They ran out of food before they reached the secluded valley community and Stephenie resorted to hunting with her magic. She brought back a mountain sheep, which she used as a means to teach Ryia how to selectively heat things.

Early on the eleventh day out of Vinerxan, they finally arrived at the valley community. After arranging lodging for the night and getting a warm meal, Henton and Orlan took responsibility for purchasing more supplies while Douglas guarded Islet, who was taking the chance to freshen up in one of the two rooms they had rented for the night. By the late afternoon, Stephenie, anxious for some time away from her sister, took Ryia into the stables to tend the horses.

"So, you really only met Henton earlier this year?" Ryia asked, her head resting on the top of the stall door. "The two of you seem so familiar with each other."

Stephenie laughed, "I didn't do it justice when I told you how we first met. It's hard to imagine, but he tackled me, straddled me, and slammed my head into the ground." Stephenie used the pitchfork to pick out more of Argat's manure. "He did some serous manhandling."

"The two of you definitely make a good couple."

Stephenie stopped and pushed the pitchfork into the ground so it would stand on its own. "We're just friends. Good friends, but just friends."

"Douglas was talking about how the two of you pretended to be husband and wife. Taking a room together and dressing alike," Ryia was grinning. "I think even Islet wonders about the two of you, squeezing so close at night in the tent."

"Yeah, but nothing happened and we are all squished together in the tent." She sighed, "Look, I trust all of them enough to sleep next to them, even though I normally don't like people getting too close. It's just different on the trail. If it wasn't for the cost here, I'd have gotten another room so I would have a little time alone, but some things you just have to accept when traveling."

Ryia got a mischievous look in her eyes. "You ever see him naked?"

Stephenie shook her head, "No."

"He see you?"

Stephenie did not like the direction of the conversation, but it had been work to get Ryia to open up with her. "Several times. And he's had plenty of chances to take liberties," she added to prevent the next question. "You'll eventually hear enough stories about how I keep burning off all my clothes. Typically, he'll end up carrying me someplace safe after I do that."

"Well, that's hardly fair!" She said standing up, "He's seen you; you should get to see him."

Stephenie shook her head. "That's okay. I don't need to see Henton without his clothes."

"Why not?"

Stephenie pulled the pitchfork from the ground. She picked it up and looked at the metal tines. "That could lead to things, and I don't want it to."

Ryia's eyebrows rose. "Because he's a commoner?"

Stephenie turned back to the girl. "That has nothing to do with it. I love someone else."

"Who?"

Stephenie shook her head. "Just leave it, okay."

Ryia nodded her head and went back to cleaning the next stall.

You are being harsh with the young girl.

And just how should I explain you.. I'm having a hard enough time convincing them there is no Elrin, even with Orlan supporting me. Stephenie could feel Kas drift closer and brush against her, which was his way of expressing his support and affection. *Sorry, I am just feeling bad. I drew out my time there in the hopes of finding something to help you. It meant Orlan and Islet were locked up and tortured longer than they needed to be and I came away with nothing.*

You got nothing from Favian?

She shook her head. *Not really, he was fighting me and I was having to control his body and Ryia's as well as keep my own from tripping over its feet.* She patted Argat's head. The chestnut had decided that if she was done working, perhaps she had some treats to share. *There is one thing, if I said 'iptys voltu morcan', would that mean anything to you?*

The words are not exactly Dalish, but perhaps derivatives. If I was to speculate the meaning, I would say 'voltuc iptysdu alti mo morcan'. He drifted around to effectively be in front of her. *Which would roughly translate to 'in the line of the origin'.*

Line, as in family descendants?

Yes, perhaps another way to say it would be 'descended from the source.'

The source of what? She hefted the pitchfork and left the stall, closing the door and retying the door shut with a bit of twine based on Henton's recommendation. *It relates to the three lines joined by the circle and triangle. They are basically that secret society. Favian thought I was one of them, perhaps sent by another faction to infiltrate his house and undermine him. He kept asking if I knew those things. I think he wanted to make sure he wasn't committing a crime by attacking me.*

Because of the strength of your power, he wanted to make sure you were not part of his caste?

She nodded her head. *He was seventh generation and older than Yvima, who claimed to be sixth generation.*

So children of different family lines. Orlan said they were not related.

Stephenie gave a mental shrug, *Or different sources. If source is the correct translation.*

In the morning, they left the valley. Orlan, Ryia, and Islet were dressed in some new wool clothing to help keep them warm. They purchased enough supplies that they expected to be able to reach West Port with a few days' worth to spare. The money Kas took from Lord Evrin's room was more than enough to cover the costs.

As they continued down the mountain the rains started, making things even more treacherous and no matter how hard Ryia tried to help shield them from the rain, she just did not have the skill and the task fell to Stephenie. Because of the rain falling on and off for three days, it ended up taking five days to make it out of the mountain range and another five to get to West Port. However, once they were out of the higher elevations of the mountains, it became obvious that spring had arrived. The lower lands had started to turn green and farmers were already in the fields.

When they reached West Port, they were able to confirm the New Year had begun just before they cleared the last of the mountain ranges. However, there was no time for celebrations and after quickly purchasing supplies, they resumed their journey the following morning.

They managed to travel the nearly one hundred miles to Oakval in three and a half long days. Orlan had grown more jovial with everyone, but still provided no additional information on his background. With some coaxing, he agreed to stay one more night and then part in the morning.

Nearing the end of a quiet dinner in a pub, Douglas again shifted the conversation to probe Orlan's past. "You going back to your home?"

Orlan glanced at Douglas and then back to his drink. "I've heard you say to Islet that you have no home, save for where Stephenie is located. I have no home as well."

Sensing the unspoken pain in Orlan's demeanor, Stephenie offered her own well wishes, "When you get back to Elrysa, make a home with her."

"She's dead," he almost snarled.

Stephenie shook her head, "No, she was carrying your child, which was why you had to get her away from Favian."

Orlan remained very still and then took a deep breath. "Though we are on opposite sides of the war, I think in another life we would have been good friends. Perhaps one day we might meet when there is no conflict."

"I would like that," she said, sensing that Orlan was getting ready to leave them instead of remaining for the night. "Remember one thing, which since you've been in my head should be quite clear, no one hurts the ones I protect and gets away with it."

He smiled as he stood. "Indeed. Good luck with your endeavors." He nodded to everyone in turn and then quietly left the pub.

"We could have used another sword," Douglas remarked.

"He was quiet, but I liked him," Islet offered, knocking Douglas' mug with her own.

"He also burned up and killed the people he was closest to and got a number of other people killed who were trying to do what they could for him," Stephenie said, "but I can't claim innocence with regard to what happened to him, so I hope he finds the peace he needs." Looking up from her own drink she glanced around the table. "Tomorrow we'll make a quick stop at a bookseller and then be on our way."

"Before we leave," Henton said, "I was thinking to buy some things, not unlike what I picked up from that shop with all the dried flowers."

"To what aim?"

"Primarily to put someone to sleep. I don't like the permanent solution, too easy to accidentally get some into the wrong person."

Stephenie nodded. "I have some ideas for things to mix up. We can pick up some of it tonight and more on the way."

"One question," Douglas asked as they all stood up, "we going there overland or on ship?"

"We're going overland. I won't sell Argat."

Chapter 23

In the morning they visited the bookseller and while he believed he had been able to place some sounds to the characters of the unknown language, he had not gained much additional insight from the document. Stephenie took a copy of what he developed for a pronunciation guide and thanked him for his efforts.

After that, they left Oakval and headed back toward Iron Heart. This time, the weather was pleasant and the roads were mostly dry, allowing them to make the journey in only four days instead of the seven it had taken them going in the other direction.

At Iron Heart, they turned north along a well-maintained road through a small break in the mountain range and headed for Bilwid, the last city in Epish before they would reach Midland. Stephenie estimated it would be about two hundred miles further to get to Rativyr.

On the first night in the mountains, they camped along the side of the road in an isolated area normally used by merchants. Being the only people in the secluded campsite, Stephenie built up her courage and decided to reveal Kas to her sister and Ryia.

"Islet, Ryia, I need to confess something I have not shared with either of you." Stephenie waited until both of them had turned their attention to her. "For reasons that will become very clear, we decided to keep the knowledge of another member of our party from you. Orlan, while I could trust him not to attack any of us, I really did not trust him enough to share this secret."

"What, or who is it?" Islet asked. "Does your horse talk to you? We see you talking to him enough that it wouldn't surprise me."

"Argat is not the secret, though he does beg for treats enough. The other member of our group is named Kas. He's a very dear friend. He saved my life countless times and I can say that I love him. However, his body was destroyed a long time ago." Stephenie looked at Kas who was sitting invisibly beside her and nodded her head. When he did not luminescence, she frowned. "Kas, you are not helping by playing games."

Ryia and Islet glanced at each other and then back to Stephenie. "Are you saying your friend is dead? Are you the only one that can see him?"

Kas, don't be an ass, this is hard enough as it is, they will think I am crazy.

"He can be a bit of a pain sometimes," Henton offered.

Shared delusions perhaps, Kas thought to her with a chuckle

Stephenie rolled her eyes, "Please."

"Very well," Kas said in Cothish, slowly illuminating his form and turning it opaque.

Islet fell back off the log she was sitting on while Ryia's eyes widened. "That's what I've been feeling all this time," she said. "I thought I was crazy or it was just something you were generating, Steph."

"What...what...how?" Islet stammered, picking herself up from the ground. "Is he a demon?"

Stephenie shook her head. "He can be a jerk sometimes, but he's truly kind. I met Kas shortly after I escaped Mother."

Henton smiled as he stood to pull some twigs from Islet's hair. "He took a while to warm to, but half of what we've done wouldn't have happened without him."

Islet kept turning about, looking at everyone. "But he's a ghost!"

"I am, but that doesn't mean I am some twisted monster. I am mostly as I was when I died. Though, my thoughts tend to wander a little more now."

"And you've been invisible all this time, watching us, even when..."

"Kas is mostly with me, but he helps keep guard and scout. We can speak mentally. The way he talks right now is by using what powers he has left to vibrate the air to make sound. Kind of like an artificial throat crafted from gravity."

"Learning that skill required a great deal of practice and study. Initially, my attempts yielded some very painful sounds."

Stephenie watched as Ryia stared with awe and Islet with apprehension. "Look, it will take time to get used to, but Kas won't hurt either of you. However, it is very important that neither of you talk about Kas to anyone else. You are now part of a very small circle of people who know Kas exists. If other people became generally aware of him, then one of our very significant advantages would be lost and I fear the hysteria that some people might feel realizing he exists."

"Does everyone become a ghost when they die?" Ryia asked, far more intrigued than frightened.

Stephenie shook her head. "Almost no one. Some very special conditions led to Kas existing. I promise to answer your questions, through the night if it takes, but do I have your word? Please, promise me you will speak of Kas to no one."

Ryia nodded her head immediately and Islet after a short pause. Stephenie smiled, hoping they would remain true to the promise.

Over the next ten days, Stephenie started working to acclimate Ryia and Islet with her tactics and some of the plans she had for gaining access to their mother. The initial phase was to show them flight; Ryia took to the feeling immediately, but Islet's first flight resulted in her vomiting. After that, the once Queen of Ipith cried during every flight. Stephenie tried several things to make the flight more enjoyable for Islet, but the best she was able to achieve was a quiet panic.

During the evenings, she worked with Henton, Douglas, and Ryia on fabricating powders and pastes that could disable a person, assuming they were able to get them ingested. She also helped them make a pair of liquids that when combined formed a very noxious gas. An unfavorable wind during a test left Douglas coughing for most of one night.

Henton stored the liquids into a number of separate ceramic jars that he sealed with wax to keep them from leaking. "My hope is to throw them at something hard and break the jars, allowing the liquids to mix," he explained to Islet and Ryia, neither of whom appeared overly impressed.

The journey through Midland was pleasant. Just as the last time they traveled through the country, the people were generally friendly and willing to talk about anything. Most of the time they traveled along the coast and had daily views of spectacular sunsets out over the Endless Sea.

As they left the last major city in Midland, a port town named Dunkin, they crossed over the Pumar River and followed a road with far less maintenance through what quickly became lowlands that had large areas that could be fully described as a swamp. With the warming weather and new spring growth sprouting up all around them, they found the bugs far more annoying than the smell of decaying vegetation.

Stephenie adapted her technique of generating wind to try and drive the bugs away, but the effort was taxing and she could not do it while sleeping. The day after they crossed into Kynto, the ground started to rise and dry out as they headed quickly for a lone mountain peak surrounded by a scattering of smaller hills and ridges. It was a relief to be away from the bugs, but for Islet, it drove her anxiety higher and she resumed her pleading with Stephenie to not kill their mother out-of-hand.

Chapter 24

Rativyr Keep was located on the east side of a small mountain peak bearing the same name; a name that originally belonged to the man who conquered the area over three hundred years earlier. While people had lived near the mountain for many hundreds of years, often considering the pinkish slopes to be sacred, the keep itself was less than two hundred years old. Its massive granite walls, towering high above what was now the town of Rativyr, were originally constructed by the priests of a god who died out shortly after the construction was finished.

The current town was large, but lacked any defensive walls and was mostly a way station for passing merchants. As they found in traveling it, the road from Midland was not a primary trade route and so the keep and town, aside from glorifying the egos of the Huten family, offered little more protection than the area's difficult and unpleasant terrain.

Stephenie sat with Henton and Kas high above the keep on a small ledge formed from a fracture in the middle of an exposed granite rock face. The part of the mountain where they sat was only accessible because she had flown them up there. The approach on foot would have been treacherous due to the loose boulder fields that covered much of the mountain's slopes. Furthermore, even if someone reached the base of the rock face, they would have to climb almost four-hundred feet straight up.

Stephenie nodded her head toward the keep, which was a couple of miles down slope. "I'd guess there are at least seven hundred to a thousand people living in the city and what, a hundred in the keep."

Henton nodded his head, but kept his back against the stone behind him. "Douglas did see quite a few priests walking about town when he scouted it. What do you think Kas?"

"There are likely many of them around because of Stephenie's mother. I have doubts that we will see any Senzar here. Your mother, while she may deal with them, does not appear to like them. However, it is always possible that another one of the Senzar is masquerading as a priest."

Stephenie stared at the keep, "Let's hope not."

"What of the demand your sister continues to put forth that she see your mother. You still plan to allow it?"

Stephenie looked toward Kas, "I am going to kill the bitch, but Islet does deserve a chance to confront her. If I don't let her, Islet will despise me for the rest of her life."

"And what if that makes things worse?" Henton asked. "What if she continues her demands to spare her? Will you still kill her in front of Islet?"

Stephenie took a deep breath and tried to push the thought from her mind. It was hard enough to deal with death when it came in the heat of battle, but to take the time to travel here and plot out the execution was already eating at her. If Islet continued to intervene, actually performing the deed would take all of her will, *but I will do it.* "I have hopes that my mother will convince Islet that I am right all on her own. The woman is evil and deserves a long slow death. A quick execution is a mercy."

Neither Henton nor Kas responded, but she did not expect them to. They were opposed to Islet complicating the situation, but she owed her sister at least that much. *It will not change the fact my mother needs to be stopped,* she said to herself. *I owe the people of Cothel for the deaths she caused. For Father, and the soldiers, and the commoners, and nobles, all of whom suffered because she despises me. It can be tracked back to me. The family turned unhappy when I was born, Islet has said as much.* Changing the subject, she asked, "Have you seen enough, Henton?"

He shrugged, "It is a large square keep with an inner courtyard and a couple of towers. Douglas said there are bars over every window he could see. I am guessing they made note of how we got into Wyntac Castle." He rubbed his gloved hands together; the breeze at their elevation was cool. "How do you plan to get inside?"

"Fly us into the inner courtyard and open a door from there. Kas, do you think you can scout without detection?"

"I can try. Some people are more sensitive than others, but these 'priests'," he said with contempt, "tend to be limited in ability and skill. If they are not expecting trouble and do not station lines of watchers on the walls, which due to their lazy nature I would not expect them to do, I should be able to go unnoticed."

"Good. I want to limit who gets hurt and knowing where to go will help with that. If possible, I'd like to confront my mother without anyone else in the castle being aware we are there."

Henton nodded his head. "That would make it much easier to leave again. Let's, get back to the camp. If we are to do it tonight, we need to get ready."

They waited until full dark before Stephenie led Henton, Islet, and Kas along the lower slopes of the mountain. Douglas and Ryia did not want to remain behind, but someone needed to stay with the horses and make sure everything was ready for a quick departure. The killing of a Royal Princess of Kynto would not go unpursued. They just needed as much time as possible to put distance between them and Rativyr.

"Steph, it's too dark for me to see," Islet complained. "I'll break a leg climbing over this ground."

Stephenie looked further up the slope. She had not explicitly timed it so the Mother Moon would be little more than a waning sliver, but it had helped to cover their approach. Looking back at Islet, she could tell her sister was sweating and though she was improving, she was not really fit enough to make the climb. Stephenie's plan had been to start from a high vantage point so she could use minimal effort and more glide than fly into the keep, which could help reduce the effect of the motion on Islet. Unfortunately, they did not have much choice. "Okay, I'll take us in from here."

"I do not like this," Islet's voice broke.

"You don't have to, but you do have to keep quiet." Turning to Henton she acknowledged the glance he gave her indicating he was ready. *You good, Kas?*

I believe you want to enter the southern section of the keep, but I will go ahead and locate her again.

Stephenie stepped closer to Islet and wrapped her arm around her sister's waist and grabbed her sister's hands. "I won't drop you. You'll be perfectly safe, but don't cry out. We don't want to draw attention."

"You agreed to talk with her first!"

"And we will, which is why you are coming. However, I think the discussion will go better if we are not being forced to kill other people at the same time, so no sounds."

Islet swallowed and nodded her head. Stephenie had grown to love the feeling of flying from the first time she had done it and even Henton had warmed to it, though she doubted he would admit that aloud. She had trouble understanding why Islet feared it so much. She suspected it was likely a matter of trust and Islet did not truly trust her.

With a smile to try and calm her sister, Stephenie pulled in energy and formed a field around the three of them. Henton's was as normal, just around his legs and back. For Islet, Stephenie was much more careful, working to ensure she did not assert too much pressure, but also making sure to support her sister in ways that would minimize her feeling of falling.

When Islet closed her eyes, Stephenie slowly launched the three of them high into the air. The wind was cool, but she shielded them from the worst of it and even pushed a little heat into Islet's body to keep her warm.

Unfortunately, the physical contact made her sister's terror so much more pronounced to Stephenie's senses. Without the fear, Stephenie would have loved jumping off the side of the mountain, flinging herself more than two miles through the night, to glide just a couple feet over the top of the keep, and slide silently down the wall into the inner courtyard. As it was, the journey was uncomfortable and she was happy when it ended.

By the time they touched down, Islet was trembling and tears were leaking from her still closed eyes. Stephenie gave her a hug and rubbed her back. "You're back on solid ground. All is well," she whispered. She wished she could make Islet see her as something other than a disturbed relative potentially filled with evil. Her insistence on killing their mother was not helping that, but Stephenie would risk Islet's hate in order to rid the world of a monster.

Islet nodded her head, but could not bring herself to say anything. Henton came up behind Islet and put his hand on her shoulder to steady her while Stephenie turned back to the south wall of the keep and the door that was a couple feet away.

She is on the second floor and still in the chapel. There is another man with her, likely a priest. Otherwise, she is alone.

Lead the way, she replied to Kas as she approached the reinforced door. It was locked, but after reaching out with her mind, she could tell there were no bars on the inside, just a sophisticated key lock. Drawing in energy, she put her hand on the metal plate of the lock. Just as in Wyntac, she forced her attention to narrow in on the fields that held the minute particles of steel together. It was a subtle field that was hard to see and visualize, often getting lost in the noise from the potential energy of the material she was focusing on.

As her focus narrowed even further, she carefully created her own field, varying its form until it started to interfere with the natural one holding the tiny bits of metal in a solid form. It took several moments, but once she had disrupted the bonds holding the lock components together, the steel inside the lock simply turned to liquid and slumped into a solid mass at the bottom of the lock cavity. Unlike when she poured energy into something to make it melt from heat, the steel never grew warm and so it would not set the wooden door on fire.

Stepping back, she felt a little dizzy as her focus moved from the very narrow back to the larger world. Glad she had not eaten anything recently, she felt Henton's hand on her own back to lend her stability.

"You're getting better at that," he remarked.

She smiled at him and after a deep breath, felt her head clear. "It still gives me a headache," she said, shouldering the door open and breaking a thin film of steel that had leaked between the frame and the door when the bolt liquefied.

Entering the keep, she stretched out her mind even further and felt a couple people a few rooms away as well as someone moving on the floor beneath them. Fortunately, there was still no one close. Once Henton and Islet were inside, she pushed the door shut and followed after Kas, who led them down a couple of halls to a narrow set of servant stairs that took them to the second floor.

On the second floor, they ducked into a bedroom to avoid a pair of servants who walked past while discussing a dance they were hoping to attend. Then they diverted around a series of rooms where a potential priest was awake, but no one went close enough to investigate his activities.

When they finally reached the chapel's door, Islet was trembling and sweating. Stephenie noted the color had drained from her face and Stephenie wished she had some sweetmeats to put some strength back into Islet's limbs. "It's okay, Sis," Stephenie said, patting her arm. "I'll let you talk with her, then we'll get out of here and no one will know we've even been here."

Stephenie could see the doubt in her sister's eyes and so she turned back to the chapel's outer doors. Intricately carved reliefs depicting various stories of the god Ravim's many deeds covered the doors. If the hate and murder of innocent beings were not associated with the people who created the work, Stephenie would have greatly appreciated the artistry.

"Two people inside, mother and a man," she whispered as she cracked open the doors and slid inside. Stephenie entered with Kas practically on top of her to minimize the chance he would be sensed. Henton followed immediately behind her, breaking to the left so he could shield Islet, who he led behind him. Stephenie shared a quick thought of thankfulness with Kas, letting him know that she was glad that she had people with her that cared for her.

Inside the chapel, Stephenie noted the many rows of richly upholstered pews lined up before a dais at the far end. A large metal statue of a man stood ten feet tall in the center of the raised area; the back wall was rounded and curved to make a large alcove that tied into the vaulted ceiling twenty feet above their heads.

The priest, who was sitting in a chair along the curved wall of the alcove, lifted his head at their entrance. However, Stephenie's focus narrowed on her mother, who was kneeling before the statue.

The priest stood quickly and was about to call-out a warning when her mother slowly turned her head at the noise of the door closing. "What is the meaning of this dist—", she started in Kyntian. "You!"

"And I am here, Mother," Islet said in Cothish, stepping around Henton.

Their mother's face went from rage to disbelief and then hope, "Islet, my darling girl, it is you! How are you here?"

Islet stepped closer, leaving Henton behind. "Steph came to free me. She rescued me from the Senzar." ·

Their mother came to the edge of the dais and held open her arms, tears streaming from her eyes, "Islet, I tried so hard to free you. I begged and pleaded ever since you were taken."

Stephenie mentally watched the priest, who was still standing quietly to the right of the statue, but did not completely remove her attention from her mother. She would not allow herself to feel anything at the moment. She had no empathy for the woman who had done everything possible to ruin her life, *and kill·thousands of people, including Father.*

Islet embraced her mother and they hugged for several moments. "My darling girl, I was so worried about you."

Islet pulled away slightly. "Mother, did you send some people to Vinerxan?" Islet's eyes narrowed. "What is around your neck?"

Her mother smiled. "I sent many people to the Senzar to have you brought back to me. I needed to have you close. Everyone else is dead to me, you are the last one."

"I was told you wanted to have my right hand cut off."

Her mother straightened as she held Islet's right hand in her left one, lifting it slightly to look at the mark. "That demon would never come here for Regina; she hated your sister too much. But for you, she would come." Her mother moved without warning, grabbing Islet's hair and pulling her head close so that she could get her arm around her daughter's neck. Drawing a dagger from her belt, she placed the blade against Islet's throat.

Stephenie focused on her mother and sister, strengthening the fields she had already created around Islet when her sister went to her mother. If her mother tried to use the dagger, Stephenie would sense it and intervene instantly.

Kas had moved closer, but the priest appeared to sense something amiss. Now the ghost was hovering in the middle of the room.

Islet's initial cry of surprise quieted and she ceased her struggling, realizing it was a dagger at her neck. Tears were flowing freely down her face. "I told Steph you would not have done such a thing. I cannot believe it."

The once Queen of Cothel met Stephenie's eyes, but left the dagger against her daughter's neck. "I wanted you to come here. I feared I would have to capture Joshua and have him dragged here. The Senzar had utterly refused to release Islet and I had no word for far too long from Evrin. I am—"

"Release her now, Mother."

Her mother shook her head. "I've protected myself against your evil witchcraft. You can't do anything to me. Unless you surrender yourself, I will remove Islet's head!"

Stephenie forced herself to relax and her senses opened wider. "Whose fingers are you wearing around your neck?"

"The sacrifice had to be made. I am now safe from you." Her mother adjusted her grip on Islet, whose hands were pulling at their mother's arm. "Don't make me kill Islet as well."

"You killed Regina and put her fingers around your neck," it was a statement. She felt Henton move behind her and to her right. To Kas she said, *Cover the priest and keep Henton safe.*

"I had to protect myself!"

"Mother, how could you?" Islet demanded with tears pouring down her face.

"Silence Islet or I'll cut out your tongue. I will not take the curse from Stephenie."

"From me?" Stephenie shook her head. "You are a fool and a monster. While I despised Regina, not even she deserved to be cut up and worn as ornaments. And for nothing. You've been fed lies all your life. There is no Elrin and there is no curse. You could have killed me at any point and nothing would have happened to you. I've hated you for as long as I can remember. You tried to inflict pain on me every day of my life. Too many times I had wished you really would just kill me to put me out of my misery. My life was torture—"

"You lie! Elrin is real!"

Stephenie sensed her mother pull back the blade at Islet's throat in preparation to strike. Hardening the fields around her sister and mother, she yanked the blade away while pushing Islet to the side. Both women screamed at the sudden force that hit them.

Henton threw a blade at the priest, but the priest blocked it with a gravitational field, sending the blade past him and into the curved wall behind the statue.

Stephenie stepped toward her mother, pulling out her sword. "In the name of justice, I sentence you to death."

Henton charged forward, but slammed into an invisible wall and flew back when the priest used his powers against him. The priest's attack was short lived as Kas drove his hand into the man's forehead.

"I do not acknowledge you!" her mother screamed, throwing the necklace of fingers she ripped from her throat at Stephenie.

Stephenie batted the repulsive object to the floor. "For your crimes, Mother, I will kill you."

Her mother straightened and sneered at Stephenie just as Stephenie felt a field form under her. The gravity wave that hit her was so intense that a cry of pain escaped her mouth. She immediately tried to compensate, but the field only grew stronger, pulling her off her feet and onto her hands and knees. She whimpered from the pain as the field continued to pull her down, matching her every attempt to counter it. Gorging on energy, she tried to disrupt the field pulling on her, but her own fields collapsed and her energy seemed to pour into the device, giving it more strength.

Feeling her shoulder joints straining, she increased her counter field, barely resisting the crushing force. Whatever her mother had done, it was responding immediately to her actions and keeping her pinned to the floor.

Henton, having picked himself up from the ground rushed forward.

"Harm me and the cage will crush her!" came her mother's shrill screech.

Henton paused as he shouted in the Old Tongue, "Kas, wait! She said, hurting her will kill Steph!"

Stephenie tried to focus again on the gravity field as she drew more energy into herself. She dumped energy into fighting the force pulling her down, but the energy drained off as fast as she released it. Whatever was affecting her was behaving much like one of the augmentation devices and she spared a brief thought that perhaps that was what she was fighting.

She tried to open her eyes, but the field felt as if it would rip her eyes from her face if she did. Her back ached from trying to stay on her hands and knees. As the draw of energy through her body increased, she tasted the blood that suddenly ran from her nose. It was sucked out of her body and pooled on the floor. She cried out as the power she drew burned her insides. No matter how much she tried to push against the field, its strength just intensified.

"Release her!" Henton shouted, coming another step closer.

"Leave here or it will kill her!" Elsia Durman demanded, brandishing a second dagger she had pulled from behind her back. "Knocking me out will not save her."

"Mother, please, don't do this!" Islet pleaded as Stephenie continued to wail in pain as more blood fell from her face.

"She will submit or die! Leave now or I will kill her!"

Henton shook his head, "We leave and you kill her just the same. If she dies, so do you."

Stephenie tried reducing the energy she was using to fight the gravity, hoping the device would reduce its pull, but the strength did not fade, instead her left wrist snapped and she fell onto her elbow. Growling from frustration, she cried out to Kas, *I don't know what to do. Help me!*

If he responded, she was not certain. Pain laced her mind as more blood drained from her nose and mouth. Unwilling to give in, she continued drawing power, hoping that she could still overcome the device, but her body was trembling from exhaustion.

Henton pulled Islet back, preventing the girl from going to her sister. "I can feel the pull from here, you'll be crushed." To Stephenie he shouted, "We can't get close, can you move the necklace!"

Tears, or perhaps blood, she was not sure which, leaked from her eyes. She reached out with her mind, searching for the hideous necklace, hoping she would be able to fling it aside. But she could not physically move her hands. Worse, she could tell the necklace had crushed the stone below it, the immense gravity embedding it into the floor. *I can't*, she swore.

"Submit to me!"

Henton turned after the chapel doors flew open and a man dressed in robes ran inside shouting something in Kyntian. "Kas, the door, take my pack!" Henton ripped the backpack from his shoulder and tossed it into the air.

Kas invisibly grabbed the bag and flew toward the man. He felt gravity grab at the bag, trying to fling it to the side. He even felt the force slightly on his subatomic particles, but the man was moving the bag to the side and not trying to stop it. As he flew past the priest, Kas drew energy into himself, and dragging a hand through the man's face, he sucked all the energy he could from the priest's flesh, freezing his brain and killing him instantly.

The priest fell backwards and Kas dragged the body into the hall, allowing the doors to swing shut. Sensing more people approaching, Kas pulled open Henton's bag. Invisibly ripping off the wax-seals, he quickly dumped all of the two part chemical solutions on the floor, generating a cloud of noxious fumes that filled the hallway. The first man to come close started choking and coughing. He stumbled to the ground. Kas did not wait to see if someone would rescue the man, instead he floated back through the door with the hopes of protecting Stephenie or at least killing her mother.

Stephenie felt her right shoulder giving out and knew it was about to break from the strain. Trembling from the pain and exhaustion, she collapsed onto her other elbow; her head smacking the floor. Running out of time, she opened her mind to the device, reaching out to it. Surprisingly, it let her make contact, but the device was alien in its thought processes. Its mind did not make sense to her, spitting back incoherent thoughts and words. Roaring with frustration, she screamed at it mentally, dumping what energy she could into the device over her mental link as her hips collapsed and she toppled onto her side. She tried using Orlan's technique of sharing pain, hoping it would respond to some base emotion.

Still screaming mentally at the device, she felt the gravity fluctuate and then the device sparked and ignited in blue flames. Suddenly she was in the air, rushing at the ceiling. Instinct saved her, but only barely. She still hit the vaulted ceiling, but did not smash through it. Having cut off her own flow of energy, she fell back to the floor, landing hard, but managed to slow herself enough to protect her left wrist and avoided breaking anything else.

"How? That's not possible! He swore it would hold you!"

Stephenie spat blood from her mouth and took a deep breath. Her insides were raw and her very bones ached, but not as badly as when she had been in the Grey Mountains. She knew she would hurt for a long time after this, but this damage would heal.

"No, Kas," she said, forcing herself to her feet. She raised her eyes, wiped away the blood that covered her face and was still running from her nose. Meeting her mother's eyes, she felt nothing but contempt for the woman before her. "Your priest Yvima lied to you. He lied about there being a cure. He lied about there being a curse. You killed Father, Regina,—"

"The King was not your father!"

Stephenie stood staring at her mother, watching the woman's eyes and face. At the door, she could hear Henton sliding the heavy pews to barricade the entrance shut. Islet was helping him. Her mother's lips began to tighten into a smirk as she raised her dagger.

Stephenie steadied herself and then swallowed a mass of blood that was running down her throat. "What do you think to achieve by telling me that? Do you think I will fall into a fit and allow you to escape? Or allow you to kill me?" She watched her mother's expression dim and could tell Henton and Islet were watching them both closely. She wanted to shrug, but her shoulders ached too much. "He was a father to me and nothing you say will change that. Do you think I didn't realize he might not have sired me?" She lifted a loose lock of her red hair that had been torn free by the gravity. "If not my red hair, then my magic makes it obvious. My powers meant one of my ancestors was a mage, and since it wasn't in your family or Father's, it had to be someone else. But that doesn't change the fact that the king loved me. He cared for me. He raised me, and he called me daughter."

"He knew you were not his, that's why he didn't marry you off. He didn't want you tainting his line!"

"No, he knew exactly what I was and still loved me. He was protecting me. Unlike you. You are the evil one, spewing hate and pain. He was a father when he didn't have to be, but you were no mother."

"You stupid little bitch, your father is Elrin! Every time I see your hair, I see his. His dead eyes stare back at me from your face! They said he was a messenger from the north, come to offer a trade agreement." She shuddered while looking at the floor. Then turned her hate filled gaze back to Stephenie. "He came to my rooms," she swore. "He took my mind and then my body! I could do nothing; he made me enjoy it. He foretold I would give birth to his daughter, the spawn of Elrin, and if I did anything to kill you, the curse would fall on me! The demon told me who he was and what you are, not Lord Yvima! You are the daughter of the Demon! The spawn of evil!"

Stephenie wiped away more blood and swallowed what was in her mouth again. "The man was a bastard and a coward, but he lied to you. There is no Elrin. He should pay for what he did, but every day after he released you, you had a choice. You were raped and abused, but you didn't have to spread the hate. You destroyed thousands of people, ruined a country, killed my father, and gave no thought to your son, murdered one daughter, and threatened another, all so you could try and kill me. I'd rather you had drowned me at birth than make so many people suffer. You could have chosen not to do those things at any time, but instead you only thought about yourself."

"I didn't want the curse! I would not rot in Elrin's power for eternity!"

"A curse that doesn't exist!" Stephenie shook her head. "Damn you, woman. You are damaged and in the name of all those that suffered, I condemn you to death." Reaching down, she picked up her sword from the floor.

"You're not murdering me for them, but because you hate me."

Drawing power through her tired body, Stephenie forced herself forward. "One does not preclude the other."

"Wait, a child should never—"

Ignoring Kas, she took her mother's raised hand and head with a single swing. She watched her mother's head bounce and roll, falling off the dais and under a pew. Breathing with a little difficulty, Stephenie looked back to Henton and Islet who had pushed four pews against the doors. She sensed Kas next to her. In Dalish, she said, "If you were going to say 'kill a parent', that thing was never a parent."

Henton, wiping his brow, looked back at her. "I didn't see any other exits from this room and you don't look to be in any shape to deal with the soldiers that are coming."

"The gas cloud was holding, but it will not last," Kas said, materializing next to Stephenie. "I can take care of them."

"No. Don't kill them if there is a choice." She continued to breathe heavily, her sword tip scraping the floor. "Wait, are there any other ways out of here? Concealed doors?" She had tried to look herself, but she could not draw any more energy. The heat in her blood that had allowed her to kill her mother was draining away and now all she felt was physical pain.

Kas frowned, but faded slightly as he looked around. After a moment, he nodded his head at the alcove. "The back wall is lath and plaster. There is what appears to be an old servant's passage on the other side of the wall." He looked to Henton, "You may be able to break a hole in it."

"Steph, sit for a moment. Islet, stay with her." Putting Stephenie onto a pew, he ran to where his knife was stuck in the wall, he pulled out the blade and used the pommel to tap against the wall.

"Go two feet to your left," Kas said, "there is a gap between the studs." Kas moved quickly to Stephenie, "Let me go invisible, I will try to frighten them." She nodded her head and he disappeared from sight.

Stephenie looked up as Henton ran to the front of the statue and grabbed the bench Stephenie's mother had been kneeling on. Picking it up, he ran back to the wall and started smashing it with the wooden bench. Initially, the only result was a few cracks in the wall, but as his strikes got stronger, large pieces of plaster fell free.

Stephenie glanced at the door as screams erupted from down the hall. She spit out more blood and leaned her head back as she pinched her nose. Islet had pulled her close and she allowed herself to relax into her sister's side. A few moments later, Kas reappeared.

"We do not have long; I believe they are getting priests."

Stephenie pushed herself to her feet and with Islet's help, quickly made it to Henton's side. His pounding had broken a hole large enough for them to slip through. Tossing aside the bench, he helped Stephenie through the opening and into the dark and dusty passage behind the chapel.

"How are we getting out?" Islet almost moaned as she followed behind Henton, "They'll kill us if they catch us."

Stephenie turned her head to look back at her sister, "We are good at running away. You'll get used to it."

The old servants' passage led them along the outer wall of the keep. With Kas' help, they took another set of stairs to the first floor and into the east side of the keep.

Islet took over helping Stephenie so that Henton could be free to fight if needed. Fortunately, with the attention on the chapel doors, few people were in this part of the complex and they came across an empty barracks room. Henton paused for a moment to consider the time and then had everyone quickly pull on local tunics and don the helmets that were on hand.

While they were dressing, Kas scouted the passages near them and found that a short distance from the barracks was a concealed door out of the side of the keep. There were only two guards. Using Kas to generate a noise as a distraction, Henton was able to quickly overcome the guards. After binding and gagging them, he hid the men in a small closet and then they slipped out the side door into the night.

Once they were out of sight of the keep, Henton lifted Stephenie into his arms and carried her away from Rativyr. It was nearly dawn when they reached the camp with Douglas and Ryia. Not wanting to remain too close to the city, they mounted their horses and headed north with the intention of going the long way around the city. Islet rode behind Stephenie, holding her in the saddle until they found a secluded place to stop late in the afternoon.

It was not until the following morning that Stephenie was fully coherent and conscious. Kas, being the first to notice the change in her mental activity, reached out to her. *You did not tell me you knew the King was not your father.*

What would have been the point? He was my father, just not my sire.

You are not mad at me for not bringing up my suspicions are you?

Stephenie sighed mentally, *Of course not, Kas, how does one ever bring up such a subject with one they care about?* Stephenie felt him relax.

What are you going to do now?

Rest for a few weeks I think. I hurt everywhere. Then, go find my sire. She sensed Kas grow hesitant. *I tried to find something in Vinerxan to help me rebuild a body for you. Farfelee said that someone as powerful as Favian might be able to rebuild a limb, but I didn't get the chance to dig through his head or ask him.* She sat up, but continued looking in his direction. *I have the feeling that I have more capacity than either the sixth or seventh generation mage. That would mean my sire is likely very powerful. If anyone can help us, it would be him.*

Stephenie, after what he did, how could you want to meet him?

Stephenie swallowed, *I don't have a choice. My mother was a horrible person, perhaps she could not free herself from what happened, but that does not excuse all the suffering, pain, and death she chose to commit.* She glanced to Henton and Douglas who were coming in her direction. *My sire deserves to die as well, no man should do what she said he did, but if I can make him give you a body or tell me how....*

"You doing okay, Steph?"

She smiled up at Henton and flexed her left wrist. It hurt, but the bones were no longer broken. "I'll live."

"I meant about what happened?" He knelt beside her. "How long have you known?"

Stephenie had known the questions would come, so she simply addressed them. "Ever since Kas started talking about breeding and magic being passed down from generation to generation." She looked away for a moment. "The trouble is, my mother was a twisted bitch and my sire hardly seems better." She looked back at him, "One has to wonder what that makes me."

Henton shook his head as quickly as Kas. "Do not think yourself a reflection of them. I have seen you come through terrible adversity and you are still a kind and generous person."

With a dark interior, she thought to herself. "I know that and I don't consider myself a monster, but I can see how easily a person could drift into becoming twisted. Look how long I kept helping the Senzar torture Orlan."

"Which was partially by his design," Kas offered. "You risked yourself to free him and kept your word."

Stephenie forced herself up. Ryia and Islet had come over to join in the conversation. "Look guys, I'm not any more messed up than I was before. And really, I've damaged by body far worse in the past. I do want to figure out how my mother crafted such a device, but right now, all I want to do is go home. It's a long enough journey from here as it is."

Kas drifted to the left slightly, "I would speculate the device was something that mage who ruled Kynto gave her. The fingers were likely pointless things he did because he enjoyed destroying people."

"You are probably right and it's been destroyed and my mother is dead."

"Sis, you don't have to worry about me telling anyone. You were right about Mother and we should just let all that die with her. No one needs to know anything else about you."

Stephenie smiled at Islet, who had wrapped her arms around herself for warmth, despite the temperature not being very cold. "I've never desired the throne and won't take it if it is offered. However, Will is trying to help protect mages and my image is a big part of that. If the truth got out, it could hurt that."

Ryia stood quietly waiting; not speaking Cothish, she was being excluded from the conversation. "All right, let's get moving," Stephenie said in Pandar. "Ryia, if you are still coming to Antar, we'll start teaching you Cothish."

"Yes, please," she said with a smile. "I want to get out of Kynto and someplace safe before anyone from Rativyr catches up with us."

And when will you tell everyone that you plan to go after your father?

I have to figure out where to look. All we know is he had red hair and dead eyes. But I have some ideas. If I can find some leads, then I'll break the news to the others. We'll get you a body yet. I love you too much to give up.

I love you too, Stephenie.

She smiled. It felt good to be surrounded by her family and friends with an open road ahead of her, though she knew her journey would only get worse by digging into her past. "Never fear to explore," she said, just loud enough only those who had been paying attention would have heard, but it had not been meant for them.

26944082R00187

Made in the USA
Charleston, SC
25 February 2014